ut
ew
ningh
ingh

ingha

THE STONECUTTER

By the same author

THE ICE PRINCESS
THE PREACHER

CAMILLA LÄCKBERG

The Stonecutter

Translated by Steven T. Murray

HarperCollins*Publishers*

HarperCollins*Publishers*
77–85 Fulham Palace Road, Hammersmith, London W6 8JB

www.harpercollins.co.uk

Published by HarperCollins*Publishers* 2010

1

A catalogue record for this book
is available from the British Library

ISBN-13 978 0 00 730593 3 (hardback)
ISBN-13 978 0 00 725398 2 (trade paperback)

Set in Meridien by Palimpsest Book Production Limited,
Grangemouth, Stirlingshire

Printed and bound in Great Britain by
Clays Ltd, St Ives plc

Mixed Sources
Product group from well-managed
forests and other controlled sources
www.fsc.org Cert no. SW-COC-1806
© 1996 Forest Stewardship Council
FSC

FSC is a non-profit international organisation established to promote the
responsible management of the world's forests. Products carrying the FSC
label are independently certified to assure consumers that they come
from forests that are managed to meet the social, economic and
ecological needs of present and future generations.

Find out more about HarperCollins and the environment at
www.harpercollins.co.uk/green

To Ulle
All possible happiness

The lobster fishery was not what it once was. Back then hard-working professional lobstermen trapped the black crustaceans. Now summertime visitors spent a week fishing for lobsters purely for their own enjoyment. And they didn't obey the regulations either. He had seen plenty of it over the years. Brushes discreetly used to remove the visible roe from the females to make the lobsters look legal, poaching from other people's pots. Some people even dived into the water and plucked the lobsters right out of the pots. Sometimes he wondered where it would all end and whether there was any honour left among lobstermen. On one occasion there had even been a bottle of cognac in the pot he pulled up, instead of an unknown number of lobsters that had been stolen from it. At least that thief had some honour, or a sense of humour.

Frans Bengtsson sighed deeply as he stood hauling up his lobster-pots, but his face brightened when he saw two marvellous lobsters in the first pot. He had a good eye for where lobsters tended to congregate, as well as a number of favourite spots where the pots could be placed with the same luck from one year to the next.

Three pots later and he had accumulated a passable heap of the valuable creatures. He didn't really understand why they commanded such scandalous prices. Not that they were unappetizing in any way, but if he had to choose he'd rather have herring for dinner. They were tastier and a better buy. But the income from the lobster fishery was a more than welcome addition to his pension at this time of the year.

The last pot seemed to be stuck, and he stood with his foot on the rail of the boat for a bit more support as he tried to wrench it loose. He felt the pot slowly begin to give, and he hoped it wasn't damaged. He peered over the rail of his old wooden *snipa* to see what sort of shape it was in. But it wasn't the pot that came up first. A white hand broke the heaving surface of the water, looking for a moment like it was pointing at the sky.

His first instinct was to release the line and let whatever was floating beneath the surface vanish into the depths again along with the lobster-pot. But then his expertise took over, and he resumed pulling on the line that was attached to the pot. He still had a good deal of strength in his body, and he needed it. He had to haul with all his might to manoeuvre his macabre find over the rail. He didn't lose his composure until the pale, lifeless body fell to the deck with a thud. It was a child he'd pulled up from the sea. A girl, with her long hair plastered round her face, and lips just as blue as her eyes, which now stared unseeing at the sky.

Bengtsson threw himself against the rail and vomited.

Patrik was more exhausted than he'd ever thought possible. All his illusions that babies slept a lot had been thoroughly crushed in the past two months. He ran his hands through his short brown hair but managed only to make it look even more tousled. And if he thought *he* was tired, he couldn't even imagine how Erica must feel. At least he didn't have to keep getting up at night to nurse. Besides, he was really worried about her. He couldn't recall seeing her laugh since she came home from the maternity ward, and she had dark circles under her eyes. When he saw Erica's look of despair in the morning, it was hard for him to leave her and Maja. And yet he had to admit that he felt a great relief at being able to drive off to his familiar adult world. He loved Maja more than anything, but bringing home a baby was like stepping into a foreign, unfamiliar world, with all sorts of new worries lurking behind every corner. Why won't she sleep? Why is she shrieking? Is she too hot? Too cold? What are those strange spots on her skin?

Grown-up hooligans were at least something he knew about, something he knew how to handle.

He stared vacantly at the papers in front of him and tried to clean the cobwebs out of his brain enough to keep working. When the telephone rang he almost jumped out of his seat, and it rang three times before he collected himself enough to pick up the receiver.

'Patrik Hedström.'

Ten minutes later he grabbed his jacket from a hook by the door, dashed over to Martin Molin's office and said, 'Martin, some old guy out pulling up lobster pots, a Frans Bengtsson, has brought up a body.'

'Whereabouts?' Martin said, looking confused. The dramatic news had broken the listless Monday morning at the Tanumshede police station.

'Outside Fjällbacka. He's moored at the wharf by Ingrid Bergman Square. We have to get moving. The ambulance is on the way.'

Martin didn't have to be told twice. He too grabbed his jacket to face the bitter October weather and then followed Patrik out to the car. The trip to Fjällbacka went quickly, and Martin had to hold on anxiously to the handle above the door when the car careened onto the verge around the sharp curves.

'Is it a drowning accident?' Martin asked.

'How the hell should I know?' said Patrik, instantly regretting snapping at Martin. 'Sorry – not enough sleep.'

'That's okay,' said Martin. Thinking about how worn-out Patrik had looked the past few weeks, he was more than willing to forgive him.

'All we know is that she was found about an hour ago. According to the old man, it didn't look like she'd been in the water very long. But we'll see about that soon,' Patrik said as they drove down Galärbacken towards the wharf, where a wooden *snipa* was moored.

'Did you say "she"?'

'Yes, it's a girl, a kid.'

'Oh, shit,' said Martin, wishing he'd followed his first instinct and stayed in bed with Pia instead of coming in to work this morning.

They parked at Café Bryggan and hurried over to the boat. Incredibly enough, no one had yet noticed what had happened, so there was no need to ward off the usual gawkers.

'The girl's lying there in the boat,' said the old man who came to meet them on the wharf. 'I didn't want to touch her more than necessary.'

Patrik had no trouble recognizing the pallor on the old man's face. It was the same on his own face whenever he had to look at a dead body.

'Where was it you pulled her up?' asked Patrik, using the question to postpone having to confront the dead girl for another few seconds. He hadn't even seen her yet, and already his stomach was turning over uneasily.

'Out by Porsholmen. The south side of the island. She got tangled in the line of the fifth pot I pulled up. Otherwise it would have been a long time before we found her. Maybe never, if the currents had swept her out to sea.'

It didn't surprise Patrik that Bengtsson knew how a dead body would react to the effect of the sea. All the old-timers knew that a body first sank, then slowly came up to the surface after it was filled with gases, until finally, after more time passed, it sank back into the deep. In the old days drowning had been a real risk for a fisherman, and Bengtsson had surely been out searching for unfortunate victims before.

As if to confirm this the lobsterman said, 'She couldn't have been down there long. She hadn't begun to float yet.'

Patrik nodded. 'You said that when you called in the report. Well, I suppose we'd better have a look.'

Martin and Patrik walked very slowly out to the end of the wharf where the boat was moored. Not until they were almost there did they have enough of a view over the rail to discern what was lying on the deck. The girl had landed on her back when the old man pulled her into the boat, and her wet, tangled hair covered most of her face.

'The ambulance is here,' said Patrik.

Martin nodded feebly. His freckles and reddish-blond hair seemed several shades redder against his white face, and he was fighting to keep his nausea in check.

4

The greyness of the weather and the wind that had begun to gust created a ghastly backdrop. Patrik waved to the ambulance team, who seemed in no hurry to unload a gurney from the vehicle and roll it towards them.

'Drowning accident?' The first of the two EMTs nodded inquiringly towards the boat.

'Looks like it,' replied Patrik. 'But the Medical Examiner will have to make that call. There's nothing you can do for her, in any case, besides transporting her.'

'No, we heard that,' said the man. 'We'll start by getting her up on the gurney.'

Patrik nodded. He had always thought that situations in which children had fallen victim to misfortune were the worst things a police officer could encounter on the job. Ever since Maja was born the discomfort he felt seemed multiplied a thousandfold. Now his heart ached at the thought of the task that lay before them. As soon as the girl had been identified they would have to destroy her parents' lives.

The medics had hopped down into the boat. They carefully picked the girl up and lifted her onto the wharf. Her wet red hair fell on the planking like a fan around her pale face, and her glazed eyes seemed to be watching the scudding grey clouds.

At first Patrik had turned away, but now he reluctantly looked down at the girl. Then a cold hand gripped his heart.

'Oh no, oh no, Jesus God.'

Martin looked at him in dismay. Then it dawned on him what Patrik meant. 'You know who she is?'

Patrik nodded mutely.

STRÖMSTAD 1923

Agnes never would have dared to say it out loud, but sometimes she thought it was lucky that her mother had died when she was born. That way she'd had her father all to herself, and considering what she'd heard about her mother, she wouldn't have been able to wrap her round her little finger so easily. But her father didn't have the heart to deny his motherless daughter anything. Agnes was well aware of this fact and exploited it to the utmost. Certain well-meaning relatives and friends had tried to point this out to her father, but even if he made half-hearted attempts to say no to his darling, sooner or later her lovely face won out. Those big eyes of hers could so easily well up with heavy tears that would run down her cheeks. When things reached that point, his heart would relent, and she usually got what she wanted.

As a result she was now, at the age of nineteen, an exceptionally spoiled girl. Many of the people who had known her over the years would probably venture to say that she had quite a nasty side to her. It was mostly girls who dared say that. The boys, Agnes had discovered, seldom looked further than at her beautiful face, big eyes, and long, thick hair, all of which had made her father give her anything she wanted.

Their villa in Strömstad was one of the grandest in town. It stood high up on the hill, with a view over the water. It had been paid for partly with her mother's inherited fortune and partly with the money her father had made in the granite business. He had been close to losing everything once, during the strike of 1914, when to a man the stonecutters rose up against the big companies. But order was eventually restored; after the war, business had begun flourishing anew. The quarry in Krokstrand outside Strömstad, in particular, began pulling in big profits with deliveries primarily to France.

Agnes didn't care much about where the money came from. She was born rich and had always lived as rich people do. It made no difference whether the money was inherited or earned, as long as she could buy jewellery and fine clothes. She knew that not everyone viewed things this way. Her mother's parents had been horrified when their daughter married Agnes's father. His wealth was newly acquired, and his parents had been poor folk. They didn't fit in at big dinner parties; they were only invited when no one outside the immediate family was present. Even these gatherings were embarrassing. The poor things had no idea how to behave in the finer salons, and their contributions to the conversation were hopelessly meagre. Agnes's maternal grandparents had never understood what their daughter could see in August Stjernkvist, or rather Persson, which was his surname at birth. His attempt to move up the social ladder by simply changing his last name was nothing that could fool them. But they were enchanted with their granddaughter, and they competed with her father in spoiling Agnes after her mother died so suddenly after giving birth.

'Sweetheart, I'm driving down to the office.'

Agnes turned round when her father came into the room. She had been playing the grand piano that stood facing the window, mostly because she knew how lovely she looked sitting there. Musicality was not her strong point. Despite the expensive piano lessons she had taken since she was little, she could only struggle passably through the sheet music on the stand in front of her.

'Father, have you thought about that dress I showed you the other day?' She gave him an entreating look and saw how he was torn, as usual, between his desire to say no and his inability to do so.

'My dear, I just bought you a new dress in Oslo . . .'

'But it had a quilted lining, Father. You can't expect me to wear a dress with a quilted lining to the party on Saturday, when it's so warm outside, can you?'

She gave him a vexed frown and waited for his reaction. If contrary to habit he put up more resistance, she would have to make her lip quiver, and if that didn't help, well, a few tears usually did the trick. But today he looked tired, and she didn't think it would take any more effort on her part. As usual she was correct.

'Yes, all right, run down to the shop tomorrow and order it, then. But you're going to give your old father grey hair one day.' He shook his head but couldn't help smiling when she bounded over to him and kissed him on the cheek.

'Now look,' he said, 'you'd better sit down and practice your scales. It's possible that they might ask you to play a little on Saturday, so you'd better be prepared.'

Satisfied, Agnes sat back down on the piano bench and obediently began practising. She could already picture the scene. Everyone's eyes would be fixed on her as she sat at the piano in the flickering candlelight, wearing her new red dress.

The migraine was finally beginning to subside. The iron band across her forehead was gradually releasing its grip, and she could cautiously open her eyes. It was quiet upstairs. Good. Charlotte turned over in bed and closed her eyes again, enjoying feeling the pain fade. Slowly it was replaced by a relaxed feeling in her limbs.

After resting for a while she gingerly sat up on the edge of the bed and massaged her temples. They were still a bit tender after the attack, and she knew from experience that the soreness would linger for a couple of hours.

Albin must be taking a nap upstairs. That meant that in good conscience she could wait a bit before going up to him. God knows she needed all the rest she could get. The increased stress in recent months had made the migraines come on more often, sapping her of every last ounce of energy.

She decided to give her fellow sufferer a ring and hear how she was doing. Even though Charlotte was stressed out at the moment, she couldn't help worrying about Erica's state of mind. The two women hadn't known each other long. They'd started talking because they kept running into each other when they were out walking with the baby prams. Erica with Maja, and Charlotte with her eight-month-old son Albin. After they had discovered that they only lived a stone's throw from each other, they began meeting almost every day. But Charlotte soon began to worry about her new-found friend. Of course, she had never met Erica before Maja arrived, but her intuition told her that it was unusual for her friend to be as apathetic and depressed as she most often was these days. Charlotte had even carefully brought up the subject of post-natal depression with Patrik. But he had dismissed the idea, saying that having a new baby was a big adjustment and that everything would be fine as soon as they got into a routine.

She reached for the phone on the nightstand and punched in Erica's number.

'Hi, it's Charlotte.'

Erica sounded groggy and subdued when she replied, and Charlotte felt even more uneasy. Something wasn't right. Not right at all.

But after a while Erica perked up a bit. Even Charlotte thought it felt good to be able to chat for a few minutes and postpone the inevitable a little longer. But soon she would have to go upstairs to the reality that awaited her there.

As if sensing what Charlotte was thinking, Erica asked how the house-hunting was going.

'Slow. Much too slow. Niclas is working all the time, it seems. He never has time to drive around and look at houses. And there isn't much to choose from right now anyway, so I suppose we're stuck here for a while longer.' She gave a deep sigh.

'It'll all work out, you'll see.' Erica's voice was comforting, but unfortunately Charlotte didn't put much faith in her reassurance. She, Niclas and the children had already been living with her mother and Stig for six months. The way things looked now, they were going to have to stay for another half a year. That might be all right for Niclas, who was at the clinic from morning to night, but for Charlotte being cooped up with the kids was unbearable.

In theory it had sounded so good when Niclas suggested the idea. A position for a district physician had opened up in Fjällbacka, and after five years in Uddevalla they had felt ready for a change of scene. Besides, Albin was on the way, conceived as a last attempt to save their marriage. So why not start their life over completely? The more he had talked about the plan, the better it had sounded. And the thought of having close access to babysitting, now that they were going to have two kids, had also sounded tempting. But reality was an entirely different story. It took no more than a few days before Charlotte remembered exactly why she had been so eager to leave her parents' house. On the other hand, a few things had definitely changed the way they had hoped. But this wasn't a topic she could discuss with Erica, no matter how much she would have liked to. It had to remain a secret, otherwise it might destroy their whole family.

Erica's voice interrupted her reverie. 'So how's it going with your mum? Is she driving you nuts?'

'To say the least. Everything I do is wrong. I'm too strict with the kids, I'm too lenient with the kids, I make them wear too many clothes, I make them wear too few clothes, they don't get enough to eat, I stuff them with too much food, I'm too fat, I'm too sloppy . . . The list never ends, and I've had it up to here,' she said, holding her hand at chin level.

'What about Niclas?'

'Oh no, Niclas is perfect in Mamma's eyes. She coos and fawns all over him and feels sorry that he has such a worthless wife. He can do no wrong as far as she's concerned.'

'But doesn't he see how she treats you?'

'Like I said, he's almost never at home. And she's on her best behaviour whenever he's around. You know what he said yesterday when I had the audacity to complain? "But Charlotte, dear, why can't you just give in a little?" Give in a little? If I gave in any more I'd be completely obliterated. It made me so mad that I haven't said a word to him since. So now he's probably sitting there at work feeling sorry for himself because he has such an unreasonable wife. No wonder I came down with the world's worst migraine this morning.'

A sound from upstairs made Charlotte get up reluctantly.

'Erica, I've got to run upstairs and see to Albin. Otherwise Mamma will be doing the whole martyr bit before I get there . . . But remember, I'm coming by this afternoon with some pastries. Here I've been going on about myself, and I haven't even asked how you're doing. But I'll be over later.'

She hung up and combed her fingers quickly through her hair before she took a deep breath and went upstairs.

It wasn't supposed to be like this. It wasn't supposed to be like this at all. She had ploughed through lots of books about having

13

a child and what life would be like as a parent, but nothing she'd read had prepared her for the reality of the situation. Instead, she felt that everything that had been written was part of a huge plot. The authors raved about happy hormones and floating on a pink cloud as you held your baby, feeling a totally overwhelming natural love-at-first-sight towards the little bundle of joy. Of course it was mentioned, in passing, that you would probably be more exhausted than you'd ever been in your life. But even that fact was surrounded by a romantic halo and deemed to be part of the wondrous motherhood package.

Bullshit! was Erica's honest assessment after two months as a mother. Lies, propaganda, utter crap! She had never in her entire life felt so miserable, tired, angry, frustrated and worn out as she had since Maja arrived. And she hadn't experienced any all-consuming love when the red, shrieking, and yes, ugly bundle was placed on her breast. Even though her maternal feelings had crept in ever so slowly, it still felt as though a stranger had invaded their home. Sometimes she almost regretted she and Patrik had decided to have a child. They'd been getting along so well, just the two of them. Then the selfishness they shared with the rest of humanity had combined with their desire to see their own excellent genes reproduced. In one stroke they had changed their lives and reduced her to a round-the-clock milking machine.

How such a little baby could be so ravenous was beyond her comprehension. Maja was constantly clinging to Erica's breasts, swollen with milk, which had also exploded in size so that she felt that she was just two huge walking breasts. Nor was her physique in general anything to cheer about. When she came home from the maternity hospital she still looked very pregnant, and the kilos had not dropped away as fast as she wanted. Her only consolation was that Patrik had also gained weight when she was pregnant, eating like a horse. Now he too carried a few extra kilos around the middle.

Thank goodness the pain was almost gone by now, but she still felt sweaty, bloated, and generally lousy. Her legs had not seen a razor in several months, and she was in desperate need of a haircut and maybe some highlights to get rid of the mousy-brown colour of her normally blonde, shoulder-length hair. Erica got a dreamy

14

look in her eye, but then reality took over. How the hell could she get out of the house to do that? Oh, how she envied Patrik. For at least eight of the hours in the day he could be in the real world, the world of grown-ups. Nowadays her only company was Ricki Lake and Oprah Winfrey, as she listlessly zapped the remote while Maja sucked and sucked.

Patrik assured Erica that he would rather stay home with her and Maja than go to work, but she could see in his eyes that what he really felt was relief at being able to escape their little world for a while. And she sympathized. At the same time she could feel bitterness growing inside her. Why did she have to bear such a heavy load when it had been a mutual decision and should have been a mutual project? Shouldn't he carry an equal share of the burden?

So every day she kept close tabs on the time he had promised to come home. If he was only five minutes late she would be consumed by annoyance, and if he lingered even longer he could expect a real onslaught of fury. As soon as he came in the door she would dump Maja into his arms, if his arrival coincided with one of the rare breaks in her breastfeeding schedule. Then Erica would fall into bed wearing earplugs, just to get away from the shrieks of the baby for a while.

Erica sighed as she sat holding the phone in her hand. Everything seemed so hopeless. But her chats with her friend were a welcome break in the gloom. As the mother of two kids Charlotte was a steady rock to lean on, and full of calm assurances. Erica was ashamed to admit that it was also rather nice to listen to her hardships instead of always focusing merely on her own.

Of course, there was one other source of concern in Erica's life – her sister Anna. She had only talked to her a few times since Maja was born, and she felt that something was not as it should be. Anna sounded subdued and distant when they talked on the phone, but claimed that everything was fine. And Erica was so wrapped up in her own misery that she didn't feel like pressing her sister for more information. But something was wrong, she was sure of that.

She pushed aside the troubling thoughts and shifted Maja from one breast to the other, which made the baby fuss a bit. Listlessly she picked up the remote and changed the channel. 'Glamour' was about to start. The only thing she had to look forward to was this afternoon's coffee break with Charlotte.

Lilian stirred the soup with brisk strokes. She had to do everything in this house. Cook, clean, and take care of the kids. At least Albin had finally gone to sleep. Her expression softened at the thought of her grandson. He was a little angel. Hardly made a peep. Not at all like the other one. She frowned and stirred even faster, making little drops of soup splash over the edge to sizzle and stick to the surface of the stove.

She had already prepared a tray on the worktop with glasses, soup plates, and spoons. Now she carefully took the pot from the stove and poured the hot soup into the bowl. She inhaled the aroma rising up with the steam and smiled contentedly. Chicken soup, that was Stig's favourite. She hoped that he would eat it with a good appetite.

She cautiously picked up the tray and, using her elbow, pushed open the door to the stairs. Always this dashing up and down stairs, she thought peevishly. Some day she'd end up lying at the bottom with a broken leg, and then they'd see how hard it was to get along without her. She did everything for them, like a house slave. At this very moment, for instance, Charlotte was downstairs in the basement loafing in bed, with some lame excuse about a migraine. What bloody rubbish. If there was anyone with a migraine around here it was Lilian herself. She couldn't imagine how Niclas could stand it. All day long he worked hard at the clinic, doing his best to support the family, and then came home to a basement where it looked like a bomb had gone off. Just because they were living there only temporarily didn't mean they couldn't clean up and keep the place tidy. And Charlotte had the nerve to insist that her husband help her take care of the kids when he came home in the evening. What she ought to do instead was let him rest after a hard day's work, sit in peace in front of the TV and keep the kids away as best she could. No wonder the older girl was so impossible. No doubt she could see how little respect her mother showed her father. It could lead to only one thing.

16

With determined steps Lilian ascended the last steps to the top floor, taking the tray to the guest room. That was where she installed Stig when he was sick. It wouldn't do to have him moaning and groaning in the bedroom. If she was to take care of him properly, she had to get a good night's sleep.

'Dear?' She cautiously pushed open the door. 'Wake up now, I'm bringing you a little something. It's your favourite: chicken soup.'

Stig wanly returned her smile. 'I'm not hungry, maybe later,' he said weakly.

'Nonsense, you'll never get well if you don't eat properly. Come on, sit up a little and I'll feed you.'

She helped him up to a half-sitting position and then sank down on the edge of the bed. As if he were a child, she fed him soup wiping off any dribbles at the corners of his mouth.

'See, that wasn't so bad, was it? I know exactly what my darling needs, and if you just eat properly you'll be back on your feet in no time, you'll see.'

Once again the same weak smile in reply. Lilian helped him lie back down and pulled the blanket over his legs.

'The doctor?'

'But sweetie, have you entirely forgotten? It's Niclas who's the doctor now, so we have our very own doctor right here in the house. I'm sure he'll look in on you this evening. He just had to go over his diagnosis again, he said, and consult with a colleague in Uddevalla. It will all work out very soon, you'll see.'

Lilian fussily tucked in her patient one last time and took the tray with the empty soup bowl. She headed for the stairs, shaking her head. Now she had to be a nurse as well, on top of everything else that needed her attention.

She heard a knock at the front door and hurried downstairs.

Patrik's hand struck the door with a sharp rap. Around them the wind had come up quickly to gale force. Droplets of rain were landing on them, not from above but from behind, as the stormy gusts whipped up a fine mist from the ground. The sky had turned dark, its light-grey hue streaked with darker grey clouds, and the dirty brown of the sea was far from its summery blue sparkle, with whitecaps now scudding along. There were white geese on the sea, as Patrik's mother used to say.

The door opened and both Patrik and Martin took deep breaths in order to summon extra reserves of strength. The woman standing before them was a head shorter than Patrik and very, very thin. She had short hair curled in a permanent wave and tinted to an indeterminate brown shade. Her eyebrows were a bit too severely plucked and had been replaced by a couple of lines drawn with a kohl pencil, which gave her a slightly comical look. But there was nothing funny about the situation they were now facing.

'Hello, we're from the police. We're looking for Charlotte Klinga.'

'She's my daughter. What is this regarding?'

Her voice was a bit too shrill to be pleasant. Patrik had heard enough about Charlotte's mother from Erica to know how trying it must be to listen to her all day long. But such trivial matters were about to lose any importance.

'We'd appreciate it if you could tell her that we'd like to talk to her.'

'Of course, but what's this all about?'

Patrik insisted. 'We would like to speak with your daughter first. If you wouldn't mind –' He was interrupted by footsteps on the stairs, and a second later he saw Charlotte's familiar face appear in the doorway.

'Well, hi, Patrik! How nice to see you! What are you doing here?'

All at once an expression of concern settled on her face. 'Has something happened to Erica? I spoke to her recently and she sounded all right, I thought . . .'

Patrik held up his hand. Martin stood silently at his side with his eyes fixed on a knothole on the floor. He usually loved his job, but at the moment he was cursing the day he'd decided to become a cop.

'May we come in?'

'Now you're making me nervous, Patrik. What's happened?' A thought struck her. 'Is it Niclas, did he have an accident in the car, or something?'

'Let's go inside first.'

Since neither Charlotte nor her mother seemed capable of

budging from the spot, Patrik took charge and led them into the kitchen with Martin bringing up the rear. He noted absently that they hadn't taken off their shoes and were surely leaving wet footprints behind. But a little mud wouldn't make much difference now.

He motioned to Charlotte and Lilian to take a seat across from them at the kitchen table, and they silently obeyed. Patrik and Martin sat down across from them.

'I'm sorry, Charlotte, but I have . . .' he hesitated, 'terrible news for you.' The words lurched stiffly out of his mouth. His choice of words already felt wrong, but was there any right way to say what he had to say?

'An hour ago a lobsterman found a little girl drowned. I'm so, so sorry, Charlotte . . .' Then he found himself incapable of going on. Even though the words were in his mind, they were so horrific that they refused to come out. But he didn't need to say any more.

Charlotte gasped for breath with a wheezing, guttural sound. She grabbed the tabletop with both hands, as if to hold herself upright, and stared with empty eyes at Patrik. In the silence of the kitchen that single wheezing gasp seemed louder than a scream. Patrik swallowed to hold back the tears and keep his voice steady.

'It must be a mistake. It couldn't be Sara!' Lilian looked wildly back and forth between Patrik and Martin, but Patrik only shook his head.

'I'm sorry,' he said again, 'but I just saw the girl and there's no doubt that it's Sara.'

'But she said she was just going over to Frida's to play. I saw her heading that way. There must be some mistake. I'm sure she's over there playing.' As if in a trance Lilian got up and went over to the telephone on the wall. She checked the address book hanging next to it and briskly punched in the numbers.

'Hello, Veronika, it's Lilian. Listen, is Sara over there?' She listened for a second and then dropped the receiver so it hung from the cord, swaying back and forth.

'She hasn't been there.' She sat down heavily at the table and stared helplessly at the police officers facing her.

The shriek came out of nowhere, and both Patrik and Martin

19

jumped. Charlotte was screaming, motionless, with eyes that didn't seem to see. It was a loud, primitive, piercing sound. The raw pain that pitilessly forced out the scream gave both officers gooseflesh.

Lilian threw herself at her daughter, trying to put her arms round her, but Charlotte brusquely batted her away.

Patrik tried to talk over the scream. 'We've tried to get hold of Niclas, but he wasn't at the clinic. We left him a message to come home as soon as he can. And the pastor is on his way.' He directed his words more to Lilian than to Charlotte, who was now beyond their reach. Patrik knew that he'd handled the situation terribly. He should have made sure that a doctor was present to administer a sedative if needed. Unfortunately the only doctor in Fjällbacka was the girl's father, and they hadn't been able to get hold of him. He turned to Martin.

'Ring the clinic on your mobile and see if you can get the nurse over here at once. And ask her to bring a sedative.'

Martin did as he asked, relieved to have an excuse to leave the kitchen for a moment. Ten minutes later Aina Lundby came in without knocking. She gave Charlotte a pill to calm her down, and then with Patrik's help led her into the living room, so she could lie down on the sofa.

'Shouldn't I be given a sedative too?' asked Lilian. 'I've always had bad nerves, and something like this . . .'

The district nurse, who looked to be about the same age as Lilian, merely snorted and continued tucking a blanket round Charlotte with maternal care as she lay there, teeth chattering as if she were freezing.

'You'll survive without it,' she said, gathering up her things.

Patrik turned to Lilian and said softly, 'We'll probably have to talk to the mother of the friend Sara was going to visit. Which house is it?'

'The blue one just up the street,' said Lilian without looking him in the eyes.

By the time the pastor knocked on the door a few minutes later, Patrik felt that he and Martin had done all they could. They left the house which had been plunged into grief with their news and got into their car in the driveway. But Patrik didn't start the engine.

'Bloody hell,' said Martin.

'Bloody hell indeed,' said Patrik.

Kaj Wiberg peered out of the kitchen window facing the Florins' driveway.

'I wonder what the old cow's up to now?' he muttered petulantly.

'What?' his wife Monica called from the living room.

He turned halfway in her direction and shouted back, 'There's a police car parked outside the Florins'. I bloody well bet there's some mischief going on. I've been saddled with that old woman as a neighbour to pay for my sins.'

Monica came into the kitchen with a worried look. 'You really think it's about us? We haven't done anything.' She was combing her smooth, blonde page-boy but stopped with the comb in mid-air to peer out of the window.

Kaj snorted. 'Try to tell her that. No, just wait till the small claims court agrees with me about the balcony. Then she'll be standing there with egg on her face. I hope it'll cost her a bundle to tear it down.'

'Yes, but do you think we're really doing the right thing, Kaj? I mean, it only sticks over a few centimetres into our property, and it's not really bothering us. And now poor Stig is sick in bed and everything.'

'Sick, oh yeah, thanks a lot. I'd be sick too if I had to live with that damn bitch. What's right is right. If they build a balcony that infringes on our property, they're either going to have to pay or tear the bleeding thing down. They forced us to cut down our tree, didn't they? Our fine old birch tree, reduced to firewood, just because Lilian Florin thought it was blocking her view of the sea. Or am I wrong? Did I miss something here?' He turned spitefully towards his wife, incensed by the memory of all the injustices that had been done to them in the ten years they had been the Florins' neighbours.

'No, Kaj, you're quite right.' Monica looked down, well aware that retreat was the best defence when her husband got in this mood. For him Lilian Florin was like a red flag to a bull, and it was no use talking to him about common sense and reason when her name came up. Though Monica had to admit that it wasn't only Kaj's fault there had been so much trouble. Lilian wasn't easy to take, and if she'd only left them in peace it never would have come to this. Instead she had dragged them through one court appearance after another, for everything from incorrectly drawn property lines, a path that went through the lot behind her house, a garden shed that she claimed stood too close to her property, and not least the fine old birch tree they'd been forced to cut down a couple of years ago. And it had all started when they began building the house they lived in now. Kaj had just sold his office supply business for several million kronor, and they had decided to take early retirement, sell the house in Göteborg, and settle down in Fjällbacka where they had always spent their summers. But they certainly hadn't found much peace. Lilian had voiced a thousand objections to the new construction. She had organized petitions and collected complaints to try and put obstacles in their way. When she failed to stop them, she'd begun to quarrel with them about everything imaginable. Exacerbated by Kaj's volatile temperament, the feud between the neighbours had escalated beyond all common sense. The balcony that the Florins had built was only the latest bone of contention in the battle. The fact that it looked as though the Wibergs would win had given Kaj the high ground, and he was happy to exploit it.

Kaj whispered excitedly as he stood peering out behind the curtain. 'Now two guys are coming out of the house and getting in the police car. Just you wait, now they're going to come knock on our door any minute. Well, whatever it's about, I'm going to tell them the facts. And Lilian Florin isn't the only one who can file a police report. Didn't she stand there screaming insults over the hedge a couple of days ago, saying she'd make sure I got what I deserved? Illegal intimidation, I think that's what it's called. She could go to jail for that . . .' Kaj licked his lips in anticipation and prepared for the coming battle.

Monica sighed and went back to the easy chair in the living room. She picked up a women's magazine and began to read. She no longer had the energy to care.

* * *

'We might as well drive over and talk to the friend and her mother, don't you think? As long as we're here.'

'All right,' said Patrik with a sigh, backing out the driveway. They didn't really need to take the car since it was only a few houses up the street to the right, but he didn't want to block the Florins' drive with Sara's father on his way home.

Looking solemn, they knocked on the door of the blue house, which was only three houses away. A girl about the same age as Sara opened the door.

'Hello, are you Frida?' asked Martin in a friendly voice. She nodded in reply and stepped aside to let them in. They stood awkwardly in the hall for a moment as Frida observed them from under her fringe. Ill at ease, Patrik finally said, 'Is your mother at home?'

The girl still didn't say a word but ran a little way down the hall and turned left into a room that Patrik guessed was the kitchen. He heard a low murmur and then a dark-haired woman in her thirties came out to meet them. Her eyes flitted nervously and she gave the two men standing in her hall an inquisitive look. Patrik saw that she didn't know who they were.

'Good afternoon, Mrs Karlgren. We're from the police,' said Martin, apparently thinking the same thing. 'May we have a word with you? In private?' He gave Frida a meaningful glance. Her mother blanched, drawing her own conclusions about why they didn't think what they had to say was suitable for her daughter's ears.

'Frida, go up and play in your room.'

'But Mamma –' the girl protested.

'No arguments. Go up to your room and stay there until I call you.'

The girl looked as if she had a mind to object again, but a hint of steel in her mother's voice told her that this was one of those battles she was not going to win. Sullenly Frida dragged herself up the stairs, casting a few hopeful glances back at the adults to see whether they might relent. No one moved until she reached the top of the stairs and the door to her room slammed behind her.

'We can sit in the kitchen.'

Veronika Karlgren led them into a big, cosy kitchen, where apparently she'd been making lunch.

They shook hands politely and introduced themselves, then sat

23

down at the kitchen table. Frida's mother took some cups out of the cupboard, poured coffee, and put some biscuits on a plate. Patrik saw that her hands were shaking as she did so, and he realized that she was trying to postpone the inevitable, what they had come to tell her. But finally there was no putting it off any longer, and she sat down heavily on a chair across from them.

'Something has happened to Sara, hasn't it? Why else would Lilian ring and then hang up like that?'

Patrik and Martin sat in silence a few seconds too long, since both hoped the other would start. Their silence was a form of confirmation that made tears well up in Veronika's eyes.

Patrik cleared his throat. 'Yes, unfortunately we have to inform you that Sara was found drowned this morning.'

Veronika gasped but said nothing.

Patrik went on, 'It seems to have been an accident, but we're making inquiries to see whether we can determine exactly how it happened.' He looked at Martin, who sat ready with his pen and notebook.

'According to Lilian Florin, Sara was supposed to come over here and play with your daughter Frida today. Was that something the girls had planned? It is Monday, after all, so why weren't they in school?'

Veronika was staring at the tabletop. 'They were both ill this weekend, so Charlotte and I decided to keep them home from school, but we thought it was okay if they played together. Sara was supposed to come over sometime before noon.'

'But she never arrived?'

'No, she never did.' Veronika said no more, and Patrik had to keep asking questions to get more information.

'Didn't you wonder why she never showed up? Why didn't you ring and ask where she was?'

Veronika hesitated. 'Sara was a little . . . what should I say? . . . different. She more or less did whatever she liked. Quite often she wouldn't come over as agreed because she suddenly decided she felt like doing something else. The girls sometimes quarrelled because of that, I think, but I didn't want to get involved. From what I've heard, Sara suffered from one of those problems with all the initials, so it wouldn't be good to make matters worse . . .'

She sat there shredding a paper napkin to bits. A little pile of white paper was growing on the table before her.

Martin looked up from his notebook with a frown. 'A problem with all the initials? What do you mean by that?'

'You know, one of those things that every other child seems to have these days: ADHD, DAMP, MBD, and whatever else they're called.'

'Why do you think something was wrong with Sara?'

She shrugged. 'People talked. And I thought it fit quite well. Sara could be utterly impossible to deal with, so either she was suffering from some problem or else she hadn't been brought up right.' She cringed as she heard herself talking about a dead girl that way, and quickly looked down. With even greater frenzy she resumed tearing up the napkin, and soon there was nothing left of it.

'So you never saw Sara at all this morning? And never heard from her by phone either?'

Veronika shook her head.

'And you're sure the same is true for Frida?'

'Yes, she's been at home with me the whole time, so if she had talked to Sara I would have known. And she was a bit peeved that Sara never showed up, so I'm quite sure they didn't talk to each other.'

'Well then, I don't suppose we have much more to ask you.'

With a voice that quavered a bit Veronika asked, 'How is Charlotte doing?'

'As can be expected under the circumstances,' was the only answer Patrik could give her.

In Veronika's eyes he saw the abyss open that all mothers must experience when for an instant they picture their own child a victim of an accident. And he also saw the relief that this time it was someone else's child and not her own. He couldn't reproach her for feeling that way. His own thoughts had all too often shifted to Maja in the past hour. Visions of her limp and lifeless body had forced their way in and made his heart skip a few beats. He too was grateful that it was someone else's child and not his own. The feeling may not have been honourable, but it was human.

STRÖMSTAD 1923

He made a practised judgement of where the stone would be easiest to cleave and then brought the hammer down on the chisel. Quite rightly, the granite split precisely where he had calculated it would. Experience had taught him well over the years, but natural talent was also a large part of it. You either had it or you didn't.

Anders Andersson had loved the stone since he had first come to work at the quarry as a small boy, and the stone loved him. But it was a profession that took its toll on a man. The granite dust bothered his lungs more and more with each passing year, and the chips that flew from the stone could ruin a man's eyesight in a day, or cloud his vision over time. In the cold of winter it was impossible to do a proper job wearing gloves, so his fingers would freeze until they felt like they would fall off. In the summer he would sweat profusely in the broiling heat. And yet there was nothing else he would rather do. Whether he was cutting the four-inch cubic paving stones called 'two-örings' used to construct roads, or had the privilege of working on something more advanced, he loved every laborious and painful minute. He knew this was the work he was born to do. His back already ached at the age of twenty-eight, and he coughed interminably at the least dampness, but when he focused all his energy on the task before him, his ailments were forgotten and he would feel only the angular hardness of the stone beneath his fingers.

Granite was the most beautiful stone he knew. He had come to the province of Bohuslän from Blekinge, as so many stonecutters had done over the years. The granite in Blekinge was considerably more difficult to work with than in the regions near the Norwegian border. Consequently the cutters from Blekinge enjoyed great respect thanks to the skill they had acquired by working with less tractable material. Three years he had been here, attracted by the granite right from the start. There was something about the pink colour against the grey, and the ingenuity it took to cleave the stone correctly, that appealed to him. Sometimes he talked to the stone as he worked, cajoling it if it was an unusually difficult piece, or caressing it lovingly if it was easy to work and soft like a woman.

Not that he lacked offers from the genuine article. Like the other unmarried cutters he'd had his amusements when the occasion presented itself, but no woman had attracted him so that his heart leapt in his breast. He'd learned to accept that. He got along fine on his own. He was also well-liked by the other lads in his crew, so he was often invited home for a meal prepared by a woman's hand. And he had the stone. It was both more beautiful and more faithful than most of the women he had encountered. He and the stone had a good partnership.

'Hey Andersson, can you come over here for a moment?'

Anders interrupted his work on the big block and turned round. It was the foreman calling him, and as always he felt a mixture of anticipation and alarm. If the foreman wanted something from you, it was either good news or bad. Either an offer of more work, or notification that you could go home from the quarry with your cap in hand. In fact, Anders believed more in the former alternative. He knew that he was skilled at his profession, and there were probably others who would get the boot before him if the workforce were cut back. On the other hand, logic did not always win out. Politics and power struggles had sent home many a good stonecutter, so nothing was ever guaranteed. His strong involvement in the trade-union movement also made him vulnerable when the boss had to get rid of people. Politically active cutters were not appreciated.

He cast a final glance at the stone block before he went to see the foreman. It was piecework, and every interruption in his work

28

meant lost income. For this particular job he was getting two öre per paving stone, hence the name 'two-örings'. He would have to work hard to make up for lost time if the foreman was long-winded.

'Good day, Larsson,' said Anders, bowing with his cap in hand. The foreman was a stern believer in protocol. Failing to show him the respect he felt he deserved had proven to be reason enough for dismissal.

'Good day, Andersson,' muttered the rotund man, tugging on his moustache.

Anders waited tensely for what would come.

'Well, it's like this. We've got an order for a big memorial stone from France. It's going to be a statue, so we thought we'd have you cut the stone.'

His heart hammered with joy, but he also felt a stab of fright. It was a great opportunity to be given the responsibility to cut the raw material for a statue. It could pay a great deal more than the usual work, and it was both more fun and more challenging. But at the same time it was an enormous risk. He would be responsible until the statue was shipped off, and if anything went wrong he wouldn't be paid a single öre for all the work he had done. There was a legend about a cutter who had been given two statues to cut, and just as he was in the final stages of the work he made a wrong cut and ruined them both. It was said that he'd been so despondent that he took his own life, leaving behind a widow and seven children. But those were the conditions. There was nothing he could do about it, and the opportunity was too good to pass up.

Anders spat in his hand and held it out to the foreman, who did the same so that their hands were united in a firm handshake. It was a deal. Anders would be in charge of the work on the memorial stone. It worried him a bit what the others at the quarry would say. There were many men who had considerably more years on the job than he did. Some would undoubtedly complain that the commission should have gone to one of them, especially since unlike him they had families to support. They would have viewed the extra money as a welcome windfall with winter coming on. At the same time they all knew that Anders was the most skilled stonecutter of them all, even as young as he was. That consensus would dampen most of the backbiting. Besides, Anders would choose some of them to work with him, and he had previously shown that he could wisely weigh the pros and cons of who was most skilled and who was in greatest need of extra income.

'Come down to the office tomorrow and we'll discuss the details,' said the foreman, twirling his moustache. 'The architect won't be coming until sometime towards spring, but we've received the plans and can begin the rough cut.'

Anders pulled a face. It would probably take a couple of hours to go over the drawings, and that meant even more time away from the job he was currently working on. He was going to need every öre now, because the terms stated that the work on the memorial stone would be paid for at the end, when everything was completed. That meant that he would have to get used to longer work-days, since he would have to try and make time to cut paving stones on the side. But the involuntary interruption of his work wasn't the only reason that he was displeased about going down to the office. Somehow that place always made him feel uncomfortable. The people who worked there had such soft white hands, and they moved so gingerly in their elegant office attire, while he felt like a crude oaf. And even though he always did a thorough job of washing up, he couldn't help the fact that the dirt worked its way into his skin. But what had to be done had to be done. He would have to drag himself down there and look over the drawings; then he could go back to the quarry, where he felt at home.

'I'll see you tomorrow then,' said the foreman, rocking back and forth on the balls of his feet. 'At seven. Don't be late,' he admonished, and Anders merely nodded. There was no risk of that. He didn't often get a chance like this.

With a new spring in his step he went back to the stone he was working on. The happiness he was feeling made him cleave the stone like butter. Life was good.

She was spinning through space. Free falling among the planets and other heavenly bodies that spread a soft glow all around as she sped past them. Dream scenes were mixed with small glimpses of reality. In her dreams she saw Sara. She was smiling. Her little baby body had been so perfect. Alabaster white with long, sensitive fingers on the tiny hands. Already in the first minutes of life she had grabbed hold of Charlotte's index finger and held on as if it were her only anchor in this frightening new world. And maybe it was. For her daughter's firm grip on her index finger would become an even harder grip around her heart in the days to come. A grip that even then she had known would last a lifetime.

Now she passed the sun on her path across the heavens, and its dazzling light reminded her of the colour of Sara's hair. Red like fire. Red like the Devil himself, someone had said in jest, and she remembered in her dream that she hadn't appreciated that joke. There was nothing devilish about the child lying in her arms. Nothing devilish about the red hair that had at first stood straight up like a punk-rocker's, but with the years had grown long and thick till it tumbled down her shoulders.

But now the nightmare pushed away both the feeling of the child's fingers round her heart and the sight of the red hair that bounced on Sara's narrow shoulders when she hopped about, full of life. Instead she saw her hair dark with water, the strands floating round Sara's head like a misshapen halo. It was waving to and fro, and below she saw long green arms of seaweed reaching out for it. Even the sea had found pleasure in her daughter's red hair, claiming it for its own. In her nightmare she saw the alabaster white darken to blue and purple, and Sara's eyes were closed and dead. Ever so slowly the girl began to turn in the water, with her toes pointed to the sky and her hands clasped over her stomach. Then the speed increased, and when she was spinning so fast that a small backwash was formed on the grey water, and the green arms withdrew. The girl opened her eyes. They were completely, utterly white.

The shriek that woke her seemed to come from a deep abyss. Not until she felt Niclas's hands on her shoulders, shaking her hard, did she realize that it was her own voice. For an instant relief washed over her. All that evil had been a dream. Sara was alive and well; it was only a nightmare playing a nasty trick on her. But then she looked into Niclas's eyes, and what she saw made a new scream build up in her breast. He forestalled this by pulling her close to him, so that the scream metamorphosed into deep sobs. His shirt was wet in front and she tasted the unfamiliar salt of his tears.

'Sara, Sara,' she moaned. Even though she was now awake she was still in freefall through space. The only thing holding her back was the pressure of Niclas's arms round her body.

'I know, I know.' He rocked her, his voice thick.

'Where have you been?' she sobbed quietly, but he just kept rocking her and stroking her hair with a trembling hand.

'Shh, I'm here now. Go back to sleep . . .'

'I can't!'

'Yes, you can. Shh . . .' And he rocked her rhythmically until the darkness and the dreams again descended upon her.

The news had spread through the police station while they were out. Dead children were a rarity, the victims of the occasional rare car accident, perhaps. Nothing else could cast such a pall of sadness over the whole building.

Annika gave Patrik a questioning look when he and Martin passed the reception desk, but he didn't feel like talking to anyone. He just wanted to go to his office and close the door. They ran into Ernst Lundgren in the corridor but he didn't say anything either, so Patrik quickly slipped into the silence of his little den and Martin did the same. There was nothing in their professional training that prepared any of them for situations like this. Informing someone of a death was one of the most odious tasks of their profession. Informing parents of the death of a child in an accident was worse than anything else. It defied all sense and all decency. No one should have to be forced to deliver such news.

Patrik sat down at his desk, rested his head in his hands, and closed his eyes. Soon he opened his eyes again, because all he could see in the dark behind his eyelids was Sara's bluish, pale skin and her eyes that stared unseeing at the sky. Instead he picked up the picture frame that stood before him and brought the glass as close to his face as possible. The first picture of Maja. Exhausted and bruised, resting in Erica's arms in the maternity ward. Ugly yet beautiful, in that unique way that only those who have seen their child for the first time can understand. And Erica, worn out and smiling feebly, but with a new sense of resolve and pride over having accomplished something that could only be described as a miracle.

Patrik knew that he was being sentimental and maudlin. But it was only now, this morning, that he had understood the scope of the responsibility that had been placed in his hands with his daughter's birth. Only now did he realize the extent of both his love and his fear. When he saw the drowned girl lying like a statue on the deck of the boat, for a moment he wished that Maja had never been born. Because how could he live with the risk of losing her?

He carefully put the photograph back on his desk and leaned back in his chair with his hands clasped behind his head. It suddenly felt utterly meaningless to continue with the tasks he'd been working on before they got the call from Fjällbacka. Most of all he wanted to drive home, crawl into bed and pull the covers over his head for the rest of the day. A knock on the door interrupted his dismal ruminations. 'Come in,' he assented and Annika cautiously pushed open the door.

'Hi, Patrik, excuse me for disturbing you. But I just wanted to tell you that Forensic Medicine rang and said they'd received the body. We'll have the autopsy report the day after tomorrow.'

Patrik gave a weary nod. 'Thanks, Annika.'

She hesitated. 'Did you know her?'

'Yes, I've met the girl, Sara, and her mother quite a few times lately. Charlotte and Erica have been spending a good deal of time together since Maja was born.'

'How do you think it happened?'

He sighed and fidgeted absently with the papers before him without looking up. 'She drowned, as I'm sure you heard. Apparently she went down to the wharf to play, fell in the water, and then couldn't get out. The water is so cold that she probably got hypothermia very quickly. But driving out to tell Charlotte, that was the most terrible . . .' His voice broke and he turned away so that Annika wouldn't see how the tears threatened to spill out of his eyes.

She tactfully closed the door to his office and left him in peace. She wasn't going to get much done on a day like this, either.

Erica looked at the clock again. Charlotte should have been here half an hour ago. She carefully shifted Maja, who was snoozing at her breast, and reached for the telephone. It rang many times at Charlotte's house, but no one answered. How odd. She must have gone out and forgotten that they were supposed to get together that afternoon. Although that really wasn't like her.

Erica felt that they had become close friends in a very short time. Maybe because they both were in a fragile time of their lives, maybe because they were simply very similar to each other. It was funny, really. She and Charlotte seemed more like sisters than she and Anna ever had. She knew that Charlotte worried about her, and that gave her a secure feeling in the midst of all the chaos. Her whole life Erica had worried about other people, especially Anna. To be viewed for once as the person who was little and scared felt strangely liberating.

At the same time she knew that Charlotte had her own problems. It wasn't only that she and her family were forced to live at home with her parents, Lilian and Stig. Lilian especially didn't seem easy to live with. But something unsure and tense came over Charlotte's face each time she talked about her husband Niclas. Erica had only met him briefly on a few occasions, but her spontaneous impression was that there was something unreliable about the man. Or perhaps unreliable was too strong a word. Maybe it was more a feeling that Niclas was one of those people who has good intentions but in the end will always allow his own needs and desires to take precedence over everyone else's. Charlotte had told her a few things that had confirmed this impression, even though she mostly had to read between the lines, since her friend usually spoke of her husband in adoring terms. Charlotte looked up to Niclas and on several occasions had said straight out that she couldn't understand how she had been so lucky. It seemed inconceivable to her that she was married to someone like him.

Erica could see, of course, that from a purely objective point of view he rated higher on the looks scale than Charlotte. Tall, blond, and handsome was the ladies' assessment of the new doctor. And he had certainly had an extensive academic background, unlike his wife. But if one looked at their inner qualities, Erica realized that the situation was just the opposite. Niclas ought to be thanking his lucky stars. Charlotte was a loving, wise, gentle human being and as soon as Erica managed to pull herself out of this listless state, she was going to do everything she could to make Charlotte realize her own strong points. Unfortunately at the moment Erica had no energy to do more than ponder her friend's situation.

A couple of hours later darkness had fallen, and the storm had reached full force outside her window. Erica saw by the clock that she must have dozed off for an hour or two with Maja, who was using her breast as a dummy. She was just about to reach for the phone to ring Charlotte when she heard the front door open.

'Hello?' she called. Patrik wasn't due home for an hour or two, so perhaps it was Charlotte finally showing up.

'It's me.' Patrik's voice had an empty sound to it, and Erica was instantly uneasy.

When he entered the living room she was even more concerned. His face was grey, and his eyes had a dead expression that didn't vanish until he caught sight of Maja, still asleep in Erica's arms. With two long strides he came over to them, and before Erica could react he had swept up the sleeping baby, pressing her hard to his chest. He didn't even stop when Maja woke up from the shock of being picked up so abruptly and started shrieking as loud as she could.

'What are you doing? You're scaring Maja!'

Erica tried to take the screaming baby from Patrik to calm her down, but he fended off her attempt and just hugged the infant even harder. Maja was now screaming hysterically, and for lack of any better idea Erica slapped him on the arm and said, 'Stop that! What's wrong with you? Can't you see that she's terrified?'

Then Patrik seemed to snap out of it. He cast a confused look at his daughter, who was bright red in the face from anger and fright.

'Sorry.' He handed Maja over to Erica, who did her best to soothe the baby. After a few minutes she succeeded, and Maja's screams gave way to low sobbing. Erica looked at Patrik, who had sat down on the sofa and was staring out at the storm.

'What's happened, Patrik?' said Erica, now in a kinder tone. She couldn't prevent a hint of uneasiness from creeping into her voice.

'We got a report of a drowned child today. From here in Fjällbacka. Martin and I took the call.' He paused, unable to go on.

'Oh my God, what happened? Who was it?'

Then her thoughts began whirling until they all fell into place at once, like tiny puzzle pieces.

'Oh my God,' she repeated. 'It's Sara, isn't it? Charlotte was supposed to come over for coffee this afternoon, but she never showed up and there was no answer when I rang her at home. That's it, isn't it? It was Sara you found, right?'

Patrik could only nod. Erica sank into the easy chair to prevent her legs from buckling under her. Before her she could see Sara jumping on their living room sofa as recently as two days ago. With her long red hair flying about her head and laughter bubbling up inside her like an unstoppable primal force.

'Oh my God,' Erica said again, putting her hand to her mouth as she felt her heart sink like a stone to her stomach. Patrik just stared out of the window, and she saw in profile his jaws clenching tight.

'It was so horrible, Erica. I haven't seen Sara that many times, but seeing her lying there in that boat, totally lifeless . . . I kept picturing Maja in my mind. Since then my thoughts have been churning round in my head. I can't stop imagining if something like that happened to Maja. And then having to tell Charlotte what happened . . .'

Erica uttered a whimpering, tormented sound. She had no words to describe the depth of the sympathy she felt for Charlotte, and Niclas too. She understood at once Patrik's reaction, and found herself holding Maja even closer. She was never going to let her go. She would sit here holding her tight, keeping her safe, for ever. But Maja squirmed restlessly, intuiting as most children can that things were not as they should be.

Outside the storm continued to rage. Patrik and Erica just sat there for a long time, watching the wild play of nature. Neither of them could stop thinking about the child who was taken by the sea.

Medical examiner Tord Pedersen began the task with an unusually resolute expression on his face. After many years in his profession he had developed a hardened attitude – either desirable or loathsome, depending on how one wanted to view it – which meant that most of the ghastly things he observed in his work left little trace at the end of the day. But there was something about cutting open a child that conflicted with a primal instinct and disrupted all routine, undermining the objective professionalism that his years as a medical examiner had given him. The defencelessness of a child tore down all the defensive walls that his psyche could put up, so his hand shook a bit as he moved it towards the girl's chest.

When she was brought in he had been told that drowning was the presumed cause of death. Now it was up to him to confirm or reject that hypothesis. But so far there was nothing he could see with the naked eye to contradict it.

The mercilessly bright glare in the post-mortem room emphasized her blue pallor so that it looked like she was freezing. The cold aluminium table beneath her seemed to reflect the cold, and Pedersen shivered in his green scrubs. She was naked as she lay there, and he felt as though he were violating her as he prized open and cut into the defenceless body. But he forced himself to shake off that feeling. He knew that the task he was performing was important, both for the girl and her parents, even if they didn't realize it themselves. It was necessary for the grieving process to have a final determination of the cause of death. Even though there didn't seem to be any ambiguities in this case, the rules were in place for a reason. He knew this on a professional level, but as a human being and father with two boys at home, he sometimes wondered in cases like this how much humanity there was in the work he was doing.

STRÖMSTAD 1923

'Agnes, I have nothing but tedious meetings today. It's not a good idea for you to come along.'

'But I want to go with you today. I'm so bored. There's nothing to do.'

'What about your girlfriends?'

'They're all busy,' Agnes replied, sulking. 'Britta's getting ready for her wedding, Laila's going to Halden with her parents to visit her brother, and Sonja has to help her mother.' In a sad voice she added, 'Imagine having a mother to help . . .' She peered at her father from under her fringe. Yes, the ploy had worked, as usual.

He sighed. 'Well then, come along if you like. But you have to promise to sit still and be quiet, and not run about like a whirl-wind talking to the staff. The last time you completely confused those poor old men; it took them several days to get over it.' He couldn't help smiling at his daughter. She was unruly, certainly, but a more dazzling girl could not be found on this side of the Norwegian border.

Agnes gave a happy laugh, having once again emerged victori-ous, and she rewarded her father with a hug and a pat on his big belly.

'Nobody has a father like mine,' she cooed, and August Stjernkvist chuckled with pleasure.

'What would I do without you?' he said half in earnest, half in jest, pulling her close.

'Oh, you don't have to worry about that. I'm not going anywhere.'

39

'No, not at the moment, anyway,' he said sombrely, caressing her dark hair. 'But it won't be long before some man is going to come and steal you away from me. If you can find one who's good enough, that is,' he laughed. 'Up until now it's been slim pickings, I must say.'

'Well, I can't just take any man who comes along,' Agnes laughed in reply. 'Not with the example I've had. So it's no wonder I'm particular.'

'Look here, my girl, enough flattery,' August preened. 'Get a move on if you're coming with me to the office. It wouldn't do for the boss to arrive late.'

Despite his admonishing words it took almost an hour before they were on their way. First there was the whole business of tending to her hair and clothes, but by the time Agnes was ready, her father had to admit that the result was worth it.

'I'm sorry I'm late,' said August as he swept into the room where three men were sat waiting. 'But I hope you'll forgive me when you see the reason for my tardiness.' He gestured towards Agnes, who was close behind him. She was wearing a red dress that clung to her body, accentuating her slim waist. Although many girls had let their hair fall to the scissors in a bob, as was the fashion in the Twenties, Agnes had been smart enough to resist the temptation. Her thick black hair was done up in a simple chignon at her neck. She was well aware of the impression she made, thanks to the mirror at home. Now she exploited it fully as she paused in front of the men, slowly removing her gloves, and then letting them shake her hand, one by one.

With great satisfaction she could tell she was having an effect. Two of them sat there gaping like fish, as they held on to her hand a trifle too long. But the third man was different. To her astonishment Agnes felt her heart give a leap. The big, burly man hardly looked up at her and only took her hand briefly. The hands of the other two men had felt soft and almost feminine against hers, but this man's hand was different. She could feel the calluses scraping against her palm, and his fingers were long and strong. For a moment she considered not letting go of his hand, but she caught herself and merely nodded to him demurely. His eyes, which only looked into hers fleetingly, were brown, and she guessed there was Walloon blood in his family.

After the introductions she hurried to sit down on a chair in the corner and clasped her hands in her lap. She could see that her father hesitated for a moment. He probably would rather have sent her out of the room, but she put on her most angelic expression and gave him an entreating look. As usual he did as she wished. Wordlessly he nodded that she could stay. She decided for a change to sit as quiet as a little churchmouse so as not to risk being sent out of the room like a child. She didn't want to be subjected to that sort of treatment in front of this man.

Normally after an hour of silent participation she would have been almost in tears from boredom, but not this time. The hour flew past, and by the time the meeting was over, Agnes was sure of her cause. She wanted this man, more than she had ever wanted anything else.

And what she wanted, she usually got.

'Shouldn't we visit Niclas?' Asta implored her husband. But she saw no sign of sympathy in his stony expression.

'I told you his name must never be mentioned in my house again!' Arne stared hard out of the kitchen window, and there was nothing but granite in his gaze.

'But after what happened to the girl . . .'

'God's punishment. Didn't I tell you that would happen someday? No, this is all his own fault. If he'd listened to me it never would have happened. Nothing bad happens to God-fearing people. And now we shall speak no more of this!' His fist slammed the table.

Asta sighed to herself. Of course she respected her husband, and he did usually know best, but in this case she wondered if he might not be wrong. Something in her heart told her that this couldn't be consistent with God's wishes. Surely they should rush to their son's side when such a terrible blow had struck him. True, she had never got to know the girl, but she was still their own flesh and blood, and children did belong to the kingdom of God, that's what it said in the Bible. But these were only the thoughts of a lowly woman. Arne was a man, after all, and he knew best. It had always been that way. Like so many times before, she kept her thoughts to herself and got up to clear the table.

Too many years had passed since she had seen her son. They did run into each other occasionally, of course; that was unavoidable now that he had moved back to Fjällbacka, but she knew better than to stop and talk to him. He had tried to speak to her a few times, but she always looked away and just walked off briskly, as she had been instructed to do. But she hadn't cast down her eyes quickly enough to avoid seeing the hurt in her son's eyes.

Yet the Bible said that one should honour one's father and mother, and what had happened on that day so long ago was, as far as she could see, a breach of God's word. That's why she couldn't let him back into her heart.

She gazed at Arne as he sat at the table. His back was still as straight as a fir tree, and his dark hair had not thinned, in spite of a few flecks of grey. But they were both over seventy. She remembered how all the girls had run after him when they were young, but Arne had never seemed the least bit interested. He had married her when she was just eighteen, and as far as she knew he had never even looked at another woman. Not that he had been particularly keen on carnal matters at home either. Asta's mother had always said it was a woman's duty to endure that aspect of marriage. It was not something to enjoy, so Asta had considered herself fortunate since she had no great expectations.

Nevertheless, they did have a son. A big, splendid, blond boy, who was the spitting image of his mother but had few traits from his father. Maybe that was why things had gone so wrong. If he'd been more like his father, then Arne might have had more of a connection with his son. But that was not to be. The boy had been hers from the start, and she had loved him as much as she could. But it wasn't enough. Because when the decisive day arrived and she was forced to choose between the boy and his father, she had let her son down. How could she have done otherwise? A wife must stand by her husband, she had been taught that since childhood. But sometimes, in bleak moments, when the lamp was off and she lay in bed looking up at the ceiling, then the thoughts would come. She would wonder how something she had learned to be right could feel so wrong. That was why it was such a relief that Arne always knew exactly how things should be. Many times he had told her that a woman's judgement was not to be trusted; it was the man's job to lead the woman. There was security in that. Since her father had been like Arne in many ways, a world in which the man decided was the only world she knew. And he was so smart, her Arne. Everyone agreed about that.

Even the new pastor had praised Arne recently. He had said that Arne was the most reliable sexton he had ever had the privilege to work with, and God could be grateful to have such loyal servants. Arne had told her this, swelling with pride, when he had come home. But it was not for nothing that Arne had been the sexton in Fjällbacka for twenty years. Not counting the unfortunate years when that woman was the pastor here, of course. Asta would not want those years back for anything in the world. Thank goodness the woman finally understood that she wasn't wanted, and stepped aside to make way for a real pastor. How poor Arne had suffered during that woman's tenure. For the first time in more than fifty years of marriage Asta had seen her husband get tears in his eyes. The thought of a woman in the pulpit of his beloved church had almost destroyed him. But he'd also said that he trusted that God would finally cast the moneylenders out of the temple. And this time, too, Arne was right.

Her only wish was that he could somehow find room in his heart to forgive his son for what had happened. Until then she would never again have a day of happiness. But she also realized that if Arne could not forgive Niclas now, after this terrible incident, there was no hope of reconciliation.

If only she had gotten to know the girl. Now it was too late.

Two days had passed since Sara was found. The prevailing gloom of that day had inexorably dispersed as they were forced to go back to their daily responsibilities which hadn't disappeared because a child had died.

Patrik was writing up the last lines of a report on an assault case, when the telephone rang. He saw from the display who was calling and picked up the receiver with a sigh. Just as well to get it over with. He heard the familiar voice of Medical Examiner Tord Pedersen on the other end. They exchanged polite greetings before they broached the actual reason for the call. The first indication that Patrik was not hearing what he had expected was that a furrow formed between his eyebrows. After another minute it had deepened, and when he had heard everything the M.E. had to

45

report he slammed down the receiver with a bang. He tried to collect himself for a minute as the thoughts swirled in his head. Then he got up, grabbed the notebook he'd been writing in as they talked, and went into Martin's office. Actually he should have gone to Bertil Mellberg first, being the chief of police, but he felt that he needed to discuss the information he had received with someone he trusted. Unfortunately his boss was not in that category. Martin was the only one of his colleagues who qualified.

'Martin?'

He was on the phone when Patrik came in, but he motioned towards a chair. The conversation sounded like it was winding down, and Martin concluded it cryptically with a quiet 'hmm . . . sure . . . me too . . . hmm . . . likewise,' as he flushed from his scalp downwards.

Despite his own concerns, Patrik couldn't resist teasing his young colleague a little. 'So who were you talking to?'

He got an inaudible mumble in reply from Martin, whose face flushed even more.

'Someone calling to report a crime? One of our colleagues in Strömstad? Or Uddevalla? Or maybe Leif G. W. Persson, interested in writing your biography?'

Martin squirmed in his chair but then muttered a bit more audibly, 'Pia.'

'Oh, I see, *Pia*. I never would have guessed. Let's see, what's it been – three months, right? That must be a record for you, don't you think?' Patrik teased him. Up until this past summer Martin had been known as something of a specialist in short, unhappy love affairs, usually because of his unfailing ability to get mixed up with women who were already taken and were mostly out for a little adventure on the side. But Pia was not only available, she was also an extremely attractive and serious young woman.

'We're celebrating three months on Saturday.' Martin's eyes sparkled. 'And we're moving in together. She just rang to say that she'd found a perfect flat in Grebbestad. We're going out to look at it this evening.' His colouring had returned to normal, but he couldn't hide how obviously head over heels in love he was.

Patrik remembered how he and Erica had been at the start of their relationship. P.B. Pre-baby. He loved her fiercely, but that

46

stormy infatuation all of a sudden felt as distant as a woolly dream. Dirty nappies and sleepless nights were no doubt having their effect.

'But what about you – when are you going to make an honest woman of Erica? And don't you want to be recognized as Maja's legal father?'

'That's for me to know and you to find out . . .' said Patrik with a grin.

'So, did you come here to root around in my private life, or did you have something you wanted to tell me?' By now Martin had regained his composure.

All at once Patrik's face turned serious. He reminded himself that they were facing something that was as far from a joke as one could get.

'Pedersen just rang. He's sending the report from Sara's post-mortem by fax, but he summarized the contents for me. What he told me means that her drowning was no accident. She was murdered.'

'What the hell are you saying?' Martin threw out his hands in dismay, knocking over his pen-holder, but he ignored the pens that had spilled onto his desk. Instead he focused his undivided attention on Patrik.

'At first he assumed as we did that it was an accident. No visible marks on the body, and she was fully dressed, in clothing appropriate to the season, except that she had no jacket, but it could have floated away. But most important of all: when he examined her lungs he found water in them.' He fell silent.

Martin threw out his hands again and raised his eyebrows. 'So what did he find that didn't gibe with an accident?'

'Bathwater.'

'Bathwater?'

'Yes, she didn't have seawater in her lungs as you might expect if she had drowned in the sea. It was bathwater. Or rather *presumably* bathwater, I should say. Pedersen found residue of both soap and shampoo in the water, which suggests that it's bathwater.'

'So she was drowned in a bathtub?' said Martin, sounding sceptical. They had been so convinced that it was a tragic yet normal drowning accident that he was having a hard time adjusting to this new theory.

'Yes, that's what it looks like. It also explains the bruises that Pedersen found on the body.'

'I thought you said there were no injuries to the body?'

'Well, not at first glance. But when they lifted the hair on the back of her neck and checked more thoroughly, they could clearly see bruises that match the imprint of a hand. The hand of someone who held her head under the surface by force.'

'Jesus Christ.' Martin looked like he was going to be sick. Patrik had felt the same way when he first heard the news. 'So we're dealing with a homicide,' said Martin, as if trying to make himself face the fact.

'Yes, and we've already lost two days. We have to start knocking on doors, interviewing the family and friends, and finding out all we can about the girl and those who knew her.'

Martin grimaced, and Patrik understood his reaction. This wasn't going to be fun. The family was already devastated, and now the police would have to go in and stir everything up again. All too often, children were murdered by someone who ought to grieve the most over the death. So Patrik and Martin couldn't display the sympathy that would normally be expected when meeting with a family that had lost a child.

'Have you been in to see Mellberg yet?'

'No,' Patrik sighed. 'But I'm going there now. Since we were the ones who took the call the other day, I thought I'd ask you to join me in conducting the investigation. Do you have any objections?' He knew that the question was merely rhetorical. Neither of them wanted to see their colleagues Ernst Lundgren or Gösta Flygare be put in charge of anything more challenging than bicycle thefts.

Martin nodded curtly in reply.

'Okay,' said Patrik, 'then we might as well get it over with.'

Superintendent Mellberg looked at the letter before him as if it were a poisonous snake. This was one of the worst things that could have happened to him. Even that mortifying incident with Irina last summer paled in comparison.

Tiny beads of sweat had formed on his brow, although the temperature in his office was rather on the cool side. Mellberg wiped off the sweat absentmindedly and at the same time managed to dislodge the few strands left of his hair, which he had carefully wound in a nest atop his bald head. Annoyed, he was trying to put everything back in place when there was a knock on the door. He gave his hair one last pat and called out a surly, 'Come in!'

Hedström seemed unperturbed by Mellberg's tone of voice, but he had an uncommonly serious look on his face. Normally the superintendent thought that Patrik too often displayed a distasteful lack of decorum. He preferred working with men like Ernst Lundgren, who always treated their superiors with the respect they deserved. When it came to Hedström he always had the feeling that the man might stick his tongue out as soon as he turned his back. But time would separate the wheat from the chaff, Mellberg thought sternly. With his long experience in police work, he knew that the guys who were too soft and the ones who joked around always broke first.

For a second he had managed to forget the contents of the letter, but when Hedström sat down in the chair across his desk Mellberg remembered that it was lying there in full view. He quickly slipped the letter into his top drawer. He would have to deal with that matter soon enough.

'So, what's going on?' Mellberg could hear his voice quavering a bit from the shock of the letter, and he forced himself to bring it under control. Never show weakness – that was his motto. If he exposed his throat to his subordinates they would soon sink their teeth into it.

'A homicide,' Patrik said tensely.

'What now?' Mellberg sighed. 'Has one of our old iron-fisted acquaintances managed to hit his wife in the head a little too hard?'

Hedström's face was still unusually resolute. 'No,' he said, 'it's about the drowning accident the other day. Or rather it wasn't an accident after all. The girl was murdered.'

Mellberg gave a low whistle. 'You don't say, you don't say,' he murmured as confused thoughts ran through his head. For one thing, he was always upset by crimes perpetrated against children, and for another he tried to do a rapid evaluation of how this unexpected development would affect him in his capacity as police

49

chief of Tanumshede. There were two ways to look at it: either as a damned lot of extra work and administration, or as a means of advancing his career that might get him back to the excitement of the big city, Göteborg. Although he had to admit that the successful conclusion of the two homicide investigations he had been involved with up to now had not yielded the desired effect. But sooner or later something would convince his superiors that he belonged back at the main station. Perhaps this was just the ticket.

He realized that Hedström was waiting for some other type of response from him and hastily added, 'You mean someone murdered a child? Well, that pervert isn't going to get away with it.' Mellberg clenched his fist to stress the gravity of his words, but that only managed to induce a worried expression in Patrik's eyes.

'Don't you want to know the cause of death?' Hedström asked, as if wanting to lend him a helping hand. Mellberg found his tone of voice extremely irritating.

'Of course, I was just getting to that. So, what did the M.E. say about the case?'

'She drowned, but not in the sea. They found only fresh water in her lungs, and since they also found residue of soap and such things, Pedersen assumed it was probably bathwater. So the girl, Sara, was drowned indoors in a bathtub and then carried down to the sea and thrown in. It was an attempt to make it look like an accident.'

The image that Hedström's account conjured up in Mellberg's mind made the chief shiver, and for a moment he forgot all about his own chances of promotion. He assumed he'd seen just about everything during his years on the force. He was proud of being able to maintain a sense of objectivity, but there was something about the murder of children that made it impossible to remain unmoved. It crossed the boundaries of all decency to attack a little girl. The feeling of indignation that the murder awoke inside him was unfamiliar but, he actually had to admit, quite pleasant.

'No obvious perpetrator?' he asked.

Hedström shook his head. 'No, we don't know of any problems in the family, and there have been no other reported attacks on children in Fjällbacka. Nothing like this. So we should probably start by interviewing the family, don't you agree?' asked Patrik tentatively.

Mellberg understood at once what he was getting at. He had no objections. It had worked fine in the past to let Hedström do the legwork, and then he could step into the spotlight when the case was resolved. Not that it was anything to be ashamed of. After all, knowing how to delegate responsibilities was the key to successful leadership.

'It sounds as though you'd like to head up this investigation.'

'Well, I'm actually already on the case. Martin and I responded to the call when it came in, and we've met with the girl's family.'

'Well, that sounds like a good idea, then,' Mellberg said, nodding in agreement. 'Just see that you keep me informed.'

'All right,' said Hedström with a nod, 'then Martin and I will get going on it.'

'Martin?' said Mellberg in an ominous tone. He was still irritated at the lack of respect in Patrik's voice and now saw a chance to put him in his place. Sometimes Hedström acted as if he was the chief of this station. This would be an excellent opportunity to show him who made the decisions around here.

'No, I don't think I can spare Martin at the moment. I assigned him to investigate a series of car thefts yesterday, possibly a Baltic gang operating in the area, so he's got plenty to do. But . . .' he paused for dramatic effect, enjoying the distressed look on Hedström's face. 'Ernst doesn't have that much work right now, so it would probably be good if you two worked on this case together.'

Now Patrik had started squirming as if in agony, and Mellberg knew that he'd figuratively put his thumb on the most vulnerable spot, right in the middle of the officer's eye. He decided to assuage Hedström's agony a bit. 'But I'm putting you in charge of the investigation, so Lundgren will report directly to you.'

Even though Ernst Lundgren was a more pleasant colleague to deal with than Hedström, Mellberg was smart enough to realize that the guy had certain limitations. It would be stupid to shoot himself in the foot . . .

As soon as the door closed behind Hedström, Mellberg took out the letter again and read it for at least the tenth time.

* * *

51

Morgan did a few stretching exercises with his fingers and shoulders before he sat down in front of the computer. He knew that sometimes he could disappear so deeply into the world before him that he would sit in the same position for hours. He checked carefully that he had everything he needed in front of him so that he wouldn't have to get up unless it was absolutely necessary. Yes, everything was there. A large bottle of Coke, a big Heath bar and a King-size Snickers. That would keep him going for a while.

The binder he'd received from Fredrik felt heavy lying on his lap. It contained everything he needed to know. The whole fantasy world he himself was unable to create was gathered there inside the binder's stiff covers and would soon be converted into ones and zeros. That was something he had mastered. While emotions, imagination, dreams and fairy tales had, by a caprice of nature, never found space in his brain, he was a wizard at the logical, the elegantly predictable in ones and zeros, the tiny electrical impulses in the computer that were converted into something legible on the screen.

Sometimes he wondered how it would feel to do what Fredrik was able to do. Plucking other worlds out of his brain, summoning up other people's feelings and entering into their lives. Most often these speculations led Morgan to shrug his shoulders and dismiss them as unimportant. But during the periods of deep depression that sometimes struck him he occasionally felt the full weight of his handicap and despaired that he had been made so different from everyone else.

At the same time it was a consolation to know that he was not alone. He often visited the websites of people who were like him, and he had exchanged emails with some of the others. On one occasion he had even gone to meet one of them in Göteborg, but he wouldn't be doing that again. The fact that they were so essentially different from other people made it hard for them to relate even to each other, and the meeting had been a failure from beginning to end.

But it had still been great to find out that there were others. That knowledge was enough. He actually felt no longing for the sense of community that seemed to be so important for ordinary people. He did best when he was all alone in the little cabin with only his computers to keep him company. Sometimes he tolerated his parents' company, but they were the only ones. It was safe to spend time with them. He'd had many years to learn to read them, to interpret all the complex non-verbal communications in the form of facial expressions and body language and thousands of other tiny signals that his brain simply didn't seem designed to handle. They had also learned to adapt themselves to him, to speak in a way that he could understand, at least adequately.

The screen before him was blank and waiting. This was the moment he liked best. Ordinary people might say that they 'loved' such a moment, but he wasn't really sure what 'loving' involved. But maybe it was what he felt right now. That inner feeling of satisfaction, of belonging, of being normal.

Morgan began to type, making his fingers race over the keyboard. Once in a while he glanced down at the binder on his lap, but most often his gaze was fixed on the screen. He never ceased to be amazed that the problems he had co-ordinating the movements of his body and his fingers miraculously disappeared whenever he was working. Suddenly he was just as dextrous as he always should have been. They called it 'deficient motor skills', the problems he had with getting his fingers to move as they should when he had to tie his shoes or button his shirt. He knew that was part of the diagnosis. He understood precisely what made him different from the others, but he couldn't do anything to change the situation. For that matter, he thought it was wrong to call the others 'normal' while people like him were dubbed 'abnormal'. Actually it was only societal preconceptions that landed him in the wrong group. He was simply different. His thought processes simply moved in other directions. They weren't necessarily worse, just not the same.

He paused to take a swig of Coca Cola straight out of the bottle, then his fingers moved rapidly over the keys again.

Morgan was content.

STRÖMSTAD 1923

Anders lay on the bed with his hands clasped behind his head, staring up at the ceiling. It was already late, and as always he felt the weight of a long day's work in his limbs. But this evening he couldn't really seem to relax. So many thoughts were buzzing round in his head that it was like trying to sleep in the midst of a swarm of flies.

The meeting about the memorial stone had gone well, and that was one of the reasons for his ruminations. He knew that the job would be a challenge, and he ran through the different approaches, trying to decide on the best way to proceed. He already knew where he wanted to cut the big stone out of the mountain. In the south-west corner of the quarry there was a sizeable cliff that was as yet untouched. That was where he thought he could cut out a large, fine piece of granite. With a little luck the stone would be free of any defects or weaknesses that might cause it to crack.

The other reason for his musing was the girl with the dark hair and blue eyes. He knew that these were forbidden thoughts. Girls like that were not for someone like him; he shouldn't even give them a thought. But he couldn't help it. When he held her little hand in his he'd had to force himself to release it at once. With each second that her skin touched his, he felt it more difficult to let go, and he had never been fond of playing with fire. The whole meeting had been a trial. The hands on the clock on the wall had crept along, and the whole time he'd had to restrain himself from turning round and looking at her as she sat so quietly in the corner.

He'd never seen anything so beautiful. None of the girls, or women for that matter, who had been a fleeting part of his life could even be mentioned in the same breath. She belonged to a whole other world. He sighed and turned on his side, attempting once again to get to sleep. The new day would begin at five o'clock, just like every other day, and took no account of whether he had lain awake all night mulling over his thoughts.

There was a sharp noise. It sounded like a pebble hitting the windowpane, but the sound came and went so quickly that he wondered whether he'd just imagined it. In any case it was quiet now, so he closed his eyes again. But then the sound was back. There was no doubt about it. Someone was throwing pebbles at his window. Anders sat bolt upright. It must be one of the friends he sometimes joined for a beer. He thought indignantly that if his widowed landlady woke up, someone would have to answer for it. His lodging arrangement had functioned well for the past three years, and he didn't need any trouble.

Cautiously he unlatched the window and opened it. He lived on the ground floor, but a big lilac bush partially blocked his view. He squinted to see who was standing in the faint moonlight.

And he couldn't believe the testimony of his own eyes.

She hesitated for a long time. She even put on her jacket and then took it off again, twice. But finally Erica made up her mind. There could be nothing wrong with offering her support; then she could see whether Charlotte wanted to have a visitor or not. It felt impossible just to sit at home when she knew that her friend was mired in her own private hell.

As she walked she saw evidence of the storm from two days earlier still scattered along her route. Trees that had toppled, branches and debris lay strewn about, mixed with small piles of red and yellow leaves. But the wind also seemed to have blown away a dirty autumn layer that had settled over the town. Now the air smelled fresh, and it was as clear as a washed pane of glass.

Maja was shrieking at the top of her lungs in the pram, and Erica walked faster. For some reason the baby seemed to have decided that it was utterly meaningless to lie in the pram if she was awake, and she was again protesting loudly. Her screams made Erica's heart beat faster, and tiny panicked beads of sweat appeared on her brow. A primitive instinct was telling her that she had to stop the pram at once and pick up Maja to save her from the wolves, but she steeled herself. It was such a short way to Charlotte's mother's house, and she would be there soon.

It was odd that a single event could alter so completely the way she looked at the world. Erica had always thought that the houses along the cove below the Sälvik campground stood like a peaceful string of pearls along the road, with a view over the sea and the islands. Now a gloomy mood seemed to have descended on the rooftops and especially onto the house of the Florin family. She hesitated once again, but now she was so close that it seemed foolish to turn round. They could just ask her to leave if they thought she was coming at an inopportune time. Friendships were tested in times of crisis, and she didn't want to be one of those people who out of exaggerated caution and perhaps even cowardice avoided friends who were having a hard time.

Puffing, she pushed the pram up the hill. The Florins' house was partway up the slope, and she paused for a second at their driveway to catch her breath. Maja's yells had reached a decibel level that would have been classified as unlawful in a workplace, so she hurried to park the pram and picked her up in her arms.

For several long seconds she stood at the front door with her hand raised and her heart pounding. Finally she gave the wood a sharp rap. There was a doorbell, but sending that shrill sound into the house seemed somehow too intrusive. A long moment passed in silence, and Erica was just about to turn and go when she heard footsteps inside the house. It was Niclas who opened the door.

'Hi,' she said softly.

'Hi,' said Niclas, grief evident in his red-rimmed eyes, glistening with tears in his pale face. Erica thought that he looked like someone who had died but was still condemned to walk the earth.

'Pardon me for bothering you, it's not what I intended, I just thought . . .' She sought for words but found none. A heavy silence settled between them. Niclas fixed his gaze on his feet, and for the second time since she knocked on the door Erica was about to turn on her heel and flee back home.

'Would you like to come in?' he asked.

'Do you think it would be all right?' Erica asked. 'I mean, do you think it would be any . . .' she searched for the right word, 'help?'

'She's been given a sedative and isn't really . . .' He didn't finish the sentence. 'But she said several times that she should have rung you, so it would be good if you could reassure her on that point.'

The fact that Charlotte had worried about not ringing to cancel, after what had happened, told Erica something about how confused her friend must be. But when she followed Niclas into the living room she still couldn't help uttering a startled cry. If Niclas looked like the walking dead, Charlotte looked like someone who'd been buried long ago. Nothing of the energetic, warm, lively Charlotte was left. It was as though an empty shell were lying on the sofa. Her dark hair, which usually formed a frame of curls around her face, now hung in lank wisps. The extra weight that her mother had always criticized had seemed becoming in Erica's eyes, making Charlotte look like one of Zorn's voluptuous Dalecarlian women. Yet as she now lay huddled up under the blanket her complexion and body had taken on a doughy, unhealthy look.

She wasn't asleep. Rather, her eyes stared lifelessly into empty space, and under the blanket she was shivering a little as if from the cold. Without taking off her jacket, Erica instinctively rushed over to Charlotte and knelt down on the floor by the sofa. She put Maja down on the floor beside her, and the baby seemed to sense the mood and lay perfectly still for a change.

'Oh, Charlotte, I'm so sorry.' Erica was crying and took Charlotte's face in her hands, but there was no sign of life in her empty gaze.

'Has she been like this the whole time?' Erica asked, turning to Niclas. He was still standing in the middle of the room, swaying a little. Finally he nodded and wearily rubbed his hand over his eyes. 'It's the medication. But as soon as we stop the pills she starts screaming. She sounds like a wounded animal. I just can't stand that sound.'

Erica turned back to Charlotte and stroked her hair tenderly. She didn't seem to have bathed or changed her clothes in days, and her body gave off a faint odour of sweat and fear. Her mouth moved as if she wanted to say something, but at first it was impossible to make out anything from the mumbling. After trying for a moment, Charlotte said in a hoarse voice, 'Couldn't make it. Should have called.'

Erica shook her head vigorously and continued stroking her friend's hair.

'That doesn't matter. Don't worry about it.'

'Sara, gone,' said Charlotte, focussing her gaze on Erica for the first time. Her eyes seemed to burn right through her, they were so full of sorrow.

'Yes, Charlotte. Sara is gone. But Albin is here, and Niclas. You're going to have to help each other now.' She could hear for herself that it sounded like she was simply mouthing platitudes, but maybe the simplicity of a cliché could reach Charlotte. Yet the only result was that Charlotte gave a wry smile and said in a dull, bitter voice: 'Help each other.' The smile looked more like a grimace, and there seemed to be some sort of underlying message in her bitter voice when she repeated those words. But maybe Erica was imagining things. Strong sedatives could produce strange effects.

A sound behind them made her turn round. Lilian was standing in the doorway, and she seemed to be choking with rage. She directed her flashing gaze at Niclas.

'Didn't we say that Charlotte wasn't to have any visitors?'

The situation felt incredibly uncomfortable for Erica, but Niclas apparently took no notice of his mother-in-law's tone of voice. Getting no answer from him, Lilian turned to look at Erica, who was still sitting on the floor.

'Charlotte is feeling much too frail to have people running in and out. I should think everyone would know better!' She made a gesture as if wanting to go over and shoo Erica away from her daughter like a fly, but for the first time Charlotte's eyes showed some sign of life. She raised her head from the pillow and looked her mother straight in the eye. 'I want Erica here.'

Her daughter's protest merely increased Lilian's rage, but with an obvious show of will she swallowed what she was about to say and stormed out to the kitchen. The commotion roused Maja from her temporary silence, and her shrill cries sliced through the room. Laboriously Charlotte sat up on the sofa. Niclas snapped out of his lethargy and took a quick step forward to help her. She brusquely waved him away and instead reached out to Erica.

'Are you sure you're all right sitting up? Shouldn't you lie down and rest some more?' Erica said anxiously, but Charlotte merely shook her head. Her speech was a bit slurred, but with obvious effort she managed to say '. . . lain here long enough.' Then her eyes filled with tears and she whispered, 'Not a dream?'

'No, it was not a dream,' said Erica. Then she didn't know what

60

else to say. She sat down on the sofa next to Charlotte, took Maja on her lap, and put one arm around her friend's shoulders. Her T-shirt felt damp against her skin, and Erica wondered whether she dared suggest to Niclas that he help Charlotte take a shower and change her clothes.

'Would you like another pill?' said Niclas, not daring even to look at his wife after being so roundly dismissed.

'No more pills,' Charlotte said, again shaking her head vigorously. 'Have to keep a clear head.'

'Would you like to take a shower?' asked Erica. 'I'm sure Niclas or your mother would be happy to help you.'

'Couldn't you help me?' said Charlotte, whose voice was now sounding stronger with each sentence she uttered.

Erica hesitated for a moment, then she said, 'Of course.'

With Maja on one arm she helped Charlotte up from the sofa and led her out of the living room.

'Where's the bathroom?' Erica asked. Niclas pointed mutely to a door at the end of the hall.

The walk to that door felt endless. When they passed the kitchen, Lilian caught sight of them. She was just about to open her mouth and fire off a salvo when Niclas stepped in and silenced her with a look. Erica could hear an agitated muttering issuing from the kitchen, but she didn't pay it much attention. The main thing was for Charlotte to feel better, and she was a firm believer in the restorative properties of a shower and a fresh change of clothes.

STRÖMSTAD 1923

It wasn't the first time Agnes had sneaked out of the house. It was so easy. She just opened the window, climbed out on the roof and down the tree, whose thick crown was right next to the house. It was a piece of cake. But after careful consideration she'd decided not to wear a dress, which could make tree-climbing difficult. Instead she chose a pair of trousers with narrow legs that hugged her thighs.

She felt as if driven by an enormous wave, which she neither wanted to nor could resist. It was both frightening and pleasant to feel such strong feelings for someone, and she realized that the fleeting infatuations she had previously taken seriously had been nothing but child's play. What she felt now were the emotions of a grown woman, and they were more powerful than she could ever have imagined. During the many hours she'd spent pondering since that morning, she had occasionally been clear-sighted enough to understand that a longing for forbidden fruit was largely respon-sible for the heat in her breast. Nevertheless the feeling was real, and she was not in the habit of denying herself anything. She was not about to start now, even though she had no precise plan. Only an awareness of what she wanted, and she wanted it now. Consequences were not something she ever took into consideration, and after all, things had always tended to work out for her, so why wouldn't they now?

She did not even entertain the notion that Anders might not want her. To this day she had never met a man who was indifferent to her. Men were like apples on a tree, and she only needed to reach out her hand to pick them, though she was inclined to admit that this apple might present a slightly greater risk than most. She had kissed married men without her father's knowledge, and in some instances had even gone farther than that, but they were all safer than the man she was about to meet. At least they belonged to the same class as she did. Even though it might have initially caused a scandal if her relations with any of them had come out, such affairs would have been regarded with a certain indulgence. But a man from the working class. A stonecutter. No one even dared think such a thought. It simply would never occur to them.

But she was tired of men from her own class. Spineless, pale, with limp handshakes and shrill voices. None of them was a man in the same way as the man she was about to meet. She shivered when she remembered the feeling of his callused hand against hers.

It hadn't been easy to find out where he lived. Not without arousing suspicion. But a glance at the wage slips during an unguarded moment had provided his address, and then she had been able to work out which room was his by peering in the windows.

The first pebble produced no response, and she waited a moment, afraid of waking the old landlady. But no one moved inside the house. She paused to preen in the ethereal moonlight. She had chosen simple, dark clothing so as not to emphasize the difference in their social standing. For that reason she had also plaited her hair and wound it atop her head in one of the simple hairdos that were common among the working-class women. Pleased with the result, she picked up another pebble from the gravel walkway and tossed it against the window. Now she saw a shadow moving inside, and her heart skipped a beat. The euphoria of the chase pumped adrenaline into her body, and Agnes felt her cheeks flush. When he opened the window, puzzled, she sneaked behind the lilac bush that partly covered the window and took a deep breath. The hunt was on.

It was with a heaviness in both his heart and his step that Patrik
left Mellberg's office. What a damned old fool! That was the thought
that immediately popped into his mind. He understood quite well
that the superintendent had forced Ernst on him merely out of
spite. If it wasn't so bloody tragic it would almost be comical. How
stupid.

Patrik went into Martin's office, his body language signalling
that things hadn't gone the way they had imagined.

'What did he say?' asked Martin with dark foreboding in his
voice.

'Unfortunately he can't spare you. You have to keep working
on some car-theft mess. But he apparently has no problem getting
along without Ernst.'

'You're kidding,' Martin said in a low voice, since Patrik hadn't
closed the door behind him. 'You and Lundgren are going to work
together?'

Patrik nodded gloomily. 'Looks that way. If we knew who the
killer was we could send him a telegram and congratulate him.
This investigation is going to be hopelessly sunk if I can't keep
him out of it as much as possible.'

'Well, shit!' said Martin, and Patrik could do nothing but agree.
After a moment's silence he slapped his hands on his thighs and
stood up, trying to muster a little enthusiasm.

'I suppose there's nothing for it but to get to work.'

'Where did you intend to start?'

'Well, the first thing will be to inform the girl's parents about the recent developments and cautiously try to ask a few questions.'

'Are you taking Ernst along?' Martin asked sceptically.

'No, I think I'll try to slip off by myself. Hopefully I can wait to inform him about his change of assignment until a little later.'

But when he came out in the corridor he realized that Mellberg had foiled his plans.

'Hedström!' Ernst's voice, whiny and loud, grated on his ears.

For an instant Patrik considered running back into Martin's office to hide, but he resisted this childish impulse. At least one person on this newly formed police team would have to behave like a grownup.

'Over here!' He waved to Lundgren, who came steaming towards him. Tall and thin, and with a perpetually grumpy expression on his face, Ernst was not a pretty sight. What he was best at was kissing up and kicking down. He had neither the temperament nor the ability for regular police work. And after the incident of the past summer, Patrik considered his colleague downright dangerous because of his foolhardiness and desire to show off. And now he was forced to be partners with Lundgren. With a deep sigh he went to meet him.

'I just talked to Mellberg. He said the little girl was murdered and that we're going to lead the investigation together.'

Patrik looked nervous. He sincerely hoped that Mellberg hadn't decided to subvert his authority behind his back.

'What I think Mellberg said was that I'm going to lead the investigation and you're going to work with me. Isn't that right?' said Patrik in a voice soft as velvet.

Lundgren looked down, but not fast enough for Patrik to miss a quick glimpse of loathing in his eyes. He had taken a gamble, but apparently it had worked. 'Yes, I suppose that's right,' Ernst said crossly. 'Well, where do we start – boss?' He said the last word with deep contempt, and Patrik clenched his fists in frustration. After five minutes of this partnership he already wanted to throttle the fellow.

'Come on, let's go into my office.' He led the way and sat down behind the desk. Ernst sat down in the visitor's chair with his long legs stuck out in front of him.

Ten minutes later Ernst had been brought up to speed on all the information, and they grabbed their jackets to drive over to the house where Sara's parents lived.

The drive to Fjällbacka took place in total silence. Neither of them had anything to say to the other. When they turned up the hill and into the family's driveway Patrik recognized the pram standing outside. His first thought was: oh shit! But he quickly revised his reaction. It might be good for the family if Erica was there. At least for Charlotte. She was the one he was most worried about; he had no idea how she was going to take the news they were bringing. People responded so differently. He had actually met relatives who thought it was better that their loved one had been murdered than that the death was accidental. It gave them some-one to blame, and they were able to centre their grief on something specific. But he didn't know if that was how Sara's parents would react.

With Ernst at his heels Patrik went up to the front door and knocked cautiously. Charlotte's mother opened it, and he could see that she was upset. Her face was flushed, and her eyes had a glint of steel that made Patrik hope he never had to cross her.

When she recognized Patrik she made a visible effort to control herself and instead put on an inquiring expression.

'The police?' she said, stepping aside to let them in.

Patrik was just about to introduce his colleague when Ernst said: 'We've met.' He nodded to Lilian, who nodded back.

Well, well, Patrik thought. Of course with the number of police reports flying back and forth between Lilian and the next-door neighbour, most people at the station should have met her by now. But today they were here on a more serious errand than a petty dispute between neighbours.

'May we come in for a moment?' Patrik asked. Lilian nodded and led them into the kitchen, where Niclas was sitting at the table. He too had the flush of anger on his cheeks. Patrik looked around for Charlotte and Erica. Niclas noticed and said, 'Erica is helping Charlotte take a shower.'

'How is Charlotte doing?' Patrik asked as Lilian poured coffee for him and Ernst and placed the cups in front of them on the kitchen table.

'She's been completely out of it. But it worked wonders for Erica to come over. It's the first time Charlotte's been able to get up and take a shower and change her clothes since . . .' he hesitated, 'it happened.'

Patrik was wrestling with himself. Should he speak to Niclas and Lilian in private and ask Erica to break the news to Charlotte, or was she strong enough to join them? He decided on the latter option. If she was on her feet now, and also had the support of the family, then it ought to go all right. And Niclas was a doctor, after all.

'Why exactly are you here?' said Niclas in confusion, giving first Ernst and then Patrik a puzzled look.

'I think we should wait until Charlotte can join us.'

Both Lilian and Niclas seemed content to wait but they exchanged a hasty, inscrutable glance. Five minutes passed in silence. Small talk would have felt out of place under the circumstances.

Patrik looked around the kitchen. It was pleasant enough but obviously the domain of a world-class obsessive-compulsive. Everything was sparkling clean and arranged in straight lines. A bit different than his and Erica's kitchen, he mused, where there was most often total chaos in the sink while the dustbin overflowed with packaging from frozen meals that could be heated in the microwave. Then he heard a door open, and there stood Erica holding Maja asleep in one arm. Beside her stood Charlotte, fresh from the shower. The astonished look on Erica's face quickly changed to concern, and she slipped her other hand under Charlotte's elbow to guide her friend to a kitchen chair. Patrik didn't know how Charlotte had looked before, but now she had a little colour in her face and her eyes were clear and alert.

'What are you doing here?' Charlotte asked in a voice that was still hoarse from several days spent alternating between shrieks and silence. She looked at Niclas, who shrugged his shoulders to indicate that he didn't know either.

'We wanted to wait for you before we . . .' Patrik's words failed him as he searched for a good way to present what he had to say. Thankfully Ernst kept his mouth shut and let Patrik handle the situation.

'We've received some new information about Sara's death.'

'You've found out something else about the accident? What is it?' said Lilian excitedly.

'It looks as though it wasn't an accident.'

'What do you mean? Why wouldn't it look like an accident?' said Niclas in obvious frustration.

'It wasn't an accident at all. Sara was murdered.'

'Murdered? What do you mean? She drowned, didn't she?' Charlotte look confused, and Erica grabbed her hand. Maja was still asleep in Erica's arms, unaware of what was playing out around her.

'She was drowned, but not in the sea. The medical examiner found no seawater in her lungs as he'd expected. It was fresh water, apparently from a bathtub.'

The silence around the table felt explosive. Patrik looked with concern at Charlotte, and Erica fixed her big eyes on her husband's face, obviously alarmed.

Patrik understood that the family was in shock, and he began cautiously asking questions to bring them back to reality. Right now he thought that was the best approach. Or at least he hoped it was. In any case, that was his job, and for the sake of both Sara and her family he had to get on with the interview.

'So now we need to go over in detail the chronology of everything Sara did that morning. Which of you saw her last?'

'I did,' said Lilian. 'I saw her last. Charlotte was lying down in the basement resting, and Niclas had driven off to work, so I was taking care of Sara for a while. Just after nine she said she was going over to Frida's house. She put on her coat and went out. She waved as she left,' said Lilian in an empty, mechanical tone of voice.

'Could you be more precise than just past nine o'clock? Was it twenty after? Five after? How close to nine was it? Every minute will have to be accounted for,' said Patrik.

Lilian thought it over. 'I suppose it was about ten after nine. But I can't say for sure.'

'Okay, we'll check and see if any of the neighbours saw anything, so maybe we can get the time corroborated.' He made a note in his book and went on: 'And after that no one saw her?'

They shook their heads.

Ernst asked brusquely, 'So what were the rest of you doing at that time?'

Patrik cringed inside and cursed his colleague's less than sensitive interviewing technique.

'What Ernst means is that procedural routine requires us to ask both you and Charlotte the same thing, Niclas. Purely routine, as I said, just to be able to rule you out as suspects as quickly as possible.'

His attempt to dilute the impact of his colleague's question seemed to work. Both Niclas and Charlotte replied without showing great emotional distress, and they seemed to accept Patrik's explanation for this uncomfortable question.

'I was at the clinic,' said Niclas. 'I start work at eight.'

'And you, Charlotte?' Patrik asked.

'As Mother said, I was lying down in the basement, resting. I had a migraine,' she replied in a surprised voice. As if she were shocked that a couple of days earlier she could have viewed that as a big problem in her life.

'Stig was at home too. He was upstairs resting. He's been bedridden for a couple of weeks,' Lilian explained. She seemed annoyed that Patrik and Ernst dared to ask about her family's activities.

'Ah yes, Stig, we'll need to talk to him too eventually, but that can wait a bit,' said Patrik, who had to admit that he had completely forgotten about Lilian's husband.

A long silence followed. There was the shriek of a child from another room, and Lilian got up to go and fetch Albin. Like Maja he had slept through all the commotion. He still looked half asleep and wore his usual serious expression as Lilian carried him into the kitchen. She sat down on her chair again and let her grandson play with the gold chain she wore round her neck.

Ernst took a breath and seemed about to ask some more questions, but a warning glance from Patrik made him stop. Patrik continued instead, cautiously. 'Can you think of anyone at all who you think might have wanted to harm Sara?'

Charlotte gave him an incredulous look and said in her hoarse voice, 'Who would want to hurt Sara? She was only seven years old.' Her voice broke, but she was making an obvious effort to control herself.

'So none of you can think of any motive? Nobody who wanted to hurt you, nothing like that?'

That last question prompted Lilian to speak. The red patches of anger she'd had on her face when they arrived flared up again.

'Somebody who wanted to hurt us? I should say so. There's only one person who fits that description, and that's our neighbour Kaj. He hates our family and has done everything to make our life a living hell for years!'

'Don't be stupid, Mamma,' said Charlotte. 'You and Kaj have been fighting with *each other* for years, and why would he want to hurt Sara?'

'That man is capable of anything. He's a psychopath, I have to tell you. And take a closer look at his son Morgan. He's not right in the head, and people like that are capable of anything. Just look at all those psychos that have been let back out on the streets and what they've done. He'd be locked up if anyone had any sense!'

Niclas put his hand on her arm to calm her down, but it had no effect. Albin whimpered when he heard the tone of their voices.

'Kaj hates me, simply because he's finally met somebody who dares to contradict him. He thinks he's a big shot just because he was the manager of a company and has plenty of money. That's why he and his wife can move here and everyone in town treats them like some sort of royalty. He's totally inconsiderate, so I wouldn't put anything past him.'

'Stop it, Mamma!' Charlotte's voice now had a new sharpness to it, and she glared at her mother. 'Don't go making a scene.'

Her daughter's outburst made Lilian stop talking. She clenched her jaws hard with anger, but she didn't dare contradict her daughter.

'So,' Patrik hesitated, a bit shocked by Lilian's vehement remarks, 'besides your neighbour you can't think of anyone who has anything against your family?'

They all shook their heads. He closed up his notebook.

'Well then, we have no more questions for the time being. Once again, I just want to say that I'm truly sorry for your loss.'

Niclas nodded and got up to show the policemen out. Patrik turned to Erica.

'Are you staying, or would you like a lift home?'

With her eyes fixed on Charlotte, Erica replied, 'I'll be here for a while yet.'

Outside the front door Patrik paused to take a deep breath.

Stig could hear voices rising and falling downstairs. He wondered who had come to visit. As usual nobody bothered to inform him about what was going on. But maybe that was just as well. To be honest he didn't know whether he could handle all the details about what had happened. In a way it was nicer to lie up here in bed, in his private cocoon, and let his mind process in peace and quiet all the feelings that Sara's death had provoked. His illness somehow made it strangely easier for him to deal with the grief. The physical pain was always assaulting his consciousness and pushing away some of the emotional torment.

With an effort Stig turned over in bed and stared blankly at the wall. He had loved the girl as if she were his own granddaughter. Naturally he saw that she could be difficult and moody, but never when she came up to see him. It was as if she instinctively sensed the full extent of the illness that was ravaging his body. She showed respect for both him and his illness. She was probably the only one who knew what a bad state he was in. With the others he made every effort not to show how great the pain was. Both his father and grandfather had died a miserable and humiliating death in a crowded hospital room, and that was a fate he intended to do everything to avoid. So to Lilian and Niclas he always managed to call up his last reserves of energy and put on a relatively controlled façade. And the illness seemed to be doing its part to help him stay out of the hospital. At intervals he would get better, perhaps feeling a little weaker and more tired than usual, but fully capable of functioning in everyday circumstances. But he always took sick again and ended up back in bed for a couple of weeks. Niclas had begun to look more and more concerned, but thank goodness Lilian had so far managed to convince him that it was best for Stig to be at home.

She was truly a gift from God. Of course they'd had their clashes during the more than six years they'd been married, and sometimes she could be a very hard woman, but the best and most tender side of her seemed to come out in caring for him. Since he'd taken ill they had lived in an exceedingly symbiotic relationship. She loved taking care of him, and he loved having her do it. Now he had a hard time imagining that they had been so close to going their separate ways. There was nothing so bad that it didn't bring some good with it, he always told himself. But that was before the worst of all possible evils had befallen them. And he couldn't find anything good in that.

The girl had understood the state he was in. Her soft hand on his cheek had left a warmth that he could feel even now. She would sit on the edge of his bed and tell him about everything that had happened that day, and he would nod and listen intently. He didn't treat her like a child, but as an equal. She had appreciated that.

That she was gone was inconceivable.

He closed his eyes and let a strong new wave of pain carry him away.

STRÖMSTAD 1923

It was a strange autumn. Anders had never before felt so exhausted, and yet so full of energy. Agnes seemed to infuse him with new strength, and sometimes he wondered how he'd been able to make his body function before she came into his life.

After that first evening, when she plucked up her courage and came to his window, his whole life had changed. Nowadays the sun didn't shine until Agnes arrived, and it went out when they parted. The first month they had approached each other cautiously. She was very shy and quiet, and he was still astonished that she had dared take that first step. It was unlike her to be so forward, and he felt a warmth come over him at the thought that she had made such a departure from her principles for his sake.

He would willingly admit that at first he had hesitated. He had sensed problems on the horizon and could see only how impossible the situation was. Yet the feeling inside him was so strong that he somehow managed to convince himself that everything would work out in the end. And she was brimming with confidence. When she leaned her head on his shoulder and rested her slender hand in his, he felt as though he could move mountains for her.

There weren't many hours when they could meet. He didn't get home from the quarry until late in the evening, and then he had to get up early in the morning to go to work again. But she always found a way, and he loved her for it. They took many long walks round the edge of town under cover of darkness, and despite the raw autumn cold they always found some dry spot where they could sit and kiss. By the time their hands began venturing under each other's clothes it was already far into November, and he knew they had reached a crossroads.

He cautiously brought up the subject of the future. He didn't want her to get in trouble, he loved her too much for that, but at the same time his body was urging him to choose the path that would lead them to a union. Yet his attempts to talk about his torment were silenced by a kiss from her.

'Let's not talk about that,' she said, kissing him again. 'Tomorrow when I come to your place, don't come outside to me. Instead let me come inside.'

'But what about the widow –' he said before she interrupted him again with a kiss.

'Shh,' she said. 'We'll be as quiet as two mice.' She caressed his cheek and went on, 'Two quiet mice who love each other.'

'But what about –' he continued, nervous but at the same time excited.

'Don't think so much,' she said with a smile. 'Let's just live in the present. Who knows, tomorrow we could be dead.'

'Oh no, don't talk like that,' he said, pulling her close. She was right. He thought too much.

'It's probably just as well we get this over with right away.' Patrik sighed.

'I don't see the point,' Ernst muttered. 'Lilian and Kaj have been fighting for years, but I have a hard time believing that was reason enough for him to kill the girl.'

Patrik was taken aback. 'It sounds as if you know them. I got the same impression when Lilian opened the door.'

'I only know Kaj,' said Ernst sullenly. 'Some of us old guys get together to play cards occasionally.'

Patrik frowned. 'Is that something I need to worry about? To be quite honest, I'm not sure you should even be taking part in the investigation under the circumstances.'

'Bullshit,' said Ernst sourly. 'If we couldn't work on a case because of some minor objection, we wouldn't be able to investigate shit. Everybody knows everybody else in this town, you know that as well as I do. And I'm quite capable of keeping my work and my private life separate.'

Patrik wasn't really satisfied with that answer, but he also knew that Ernst was right to some extent. The town was so small that everyone had some connection to everyone else, so it wouldn't be possible to use that as an excuse for removing an office from an investigation. If that did happen, it would be because of a considerably closer relationship. But it was a shame. For a second he had smelled the morning air and seen a chance for getting rid of Lundgren.

Walking side by side they approached the house next door. A curtain fluttered in the window next to the door but fell back into place so fast that they couldn't see who was standing behind it.

Patrik studied the house, the 'showplace,' as Lilian had called it. He'd seen it every day as he drove back and forth from his home but had never given it a closer look. He agreed that it wasn't very attractive. It was a modern design with lots of glass and artificial angles. It seemed that an architect had been given a free hand, and Patrik had to admit that to some extent Lilian had a point. The house was perfect for *Beautiful Homes* magazine, but it fitted in as poorly with the old neighbourhood as a teenager at a party for pensioners. Whoever said that money and taste went hand in hand? The town architect must have been blind the day he approved that building permit.

Patrik turned to his colleague. 'What sort of job does Kaj do? Since he's home on a weekday, I mean? Lilian said something about managing director.'

'He sold the company and took early retirement,' said Ernst, whose tone was still grouchy after having his professionalism questioned. 'But he also coaches the football team. He's very good at it, actually. He would have turned pro when he was young, but he had some kind of accident that made it impossible. And I say again, this is a waste of time. Kaj Wiberg is one of the really good guys, and anyone who says different is lying. All this is just ridiculous.'

Patrik ignored his comments and kept climbing the front steps.

They rang the doorbell and waited. Soon they heard footsteps and the door was opened by a man Patrik assumed was Kaj. He brightened up when he saw Ernst.

'Hi, Lundgren, how are things? There's no card game today, is there?'

His broad smile faded quickly when he saw that neither of them reacted. He rolled his eyes. 'So what's the old bitch come up with this time?' He showed them in to the big, open living room and sat down heavily in an easy chair, motioning them to have a seat on the sofa.

'Well, not that I don't feel sorry about what's happened to them; it's a real tragedy. But it's incredible that she has the stomach to keep quarrelling with us even under these circumstances. I think that says a good deal about what sort of person she is.'

Patrik ignored this comment and studied the man before him. He was thin, of average height, with the physique of a greyhound and silver hair cut short. Nevertheless there was actually something quite nondescript about him – he was the sort of man witnesses would never be able to describe if he decided to rob a bank.

'We're going round to all the neighbours who might have seen anything. It has nothing to do with your disputes.' Patrik had already decided before they came in not to say anything about Lilian having singled out her neighbour.

'I see,' said Kaj in a tone that had a slight hint of disappointment. A clear indication that the feud with his neighbour had become a constant and almost essential element in his life.

'But why the questions?' he went on. 'It's tragic that the little girl drowned, but there can't be anything for the police to investigate further. Surely there can't be much else for you to do,' he chuckled, but quickly altered his expression when he saw that Patrik did not find the situation the least bit amusing. Then something dawned on him.

'Am I wrong about that? People are saying that the girl drowned, but you know how people talk. If the police are going around asking questions, that can only mean that a different cause of death. Am I right or not?' he said excitedly.

Patrik gave him a look of distaste. What was the matter with people? How could they view the death of a little girl as something exciting? Didn't people have any basic common decency anymore? He forced himself to maintain a neutral expression when he answered Kaj.

'Well, that's partially right. I can't go into the details, but it turns out that Sara Klinga was murdered, so it's of the utmost importance that we find out everything she did that day.'

'Murdered,' said Kaj. 'Wow, that's horrible.' His expression was sympathetic, but Patrik could sense, rather than see, that the sympathy did not run very deep.

Patrik had to repress a desire to slap Kaj in the face. He found the man's phoney sympathy disgusting but he merely said, 'As I mentioned, I can't go into the details, but if you saw Sara on

Monday morning then it's important that we find out where and when. As precisely as you can remember.'

Kaj frowned and thought hard. 'Let me see now, Monday. Yes, I did see her sometime that morning, but I can't say exactly when. She came out of the house and scampered off. That kid could never walk like regular people, she always bounced up and down like a blasted rubber ball.'

'Did you see which direction she went?' said Ernst, speaking for the first time during their visit. Kaj looked at him in amusement; apparently he found it funny to see his card-playing buddy in his professional role.

'No, I just saw her go down the driveway. She turned and waved at someone before she bounded off, but I didn't see which way she went.'

'And you don't recall what time this was?' asked Patrik.

'Not really, but it must have been sometime around nine. I'm sorry I can't be more exact.'

Patrik hesitated a moment before he continued. 'I understand that you and Lilian Florin are not on a friendly footing.'

Kaj snorted out loud. 'No, you could certainly say that. There's probably nobody who could stay on a "friendly footing" with that hag.'

'Is there any special reason for this . . .' Patrik searched for the right word, 'antagonism?'

'Not that there needs to be any special reason to quarrel with Lilian Florin, but I do happen to have a very good excuse. The trouble began as soon as we bought the lot and were about to build a house here. She had objections to the design and did everything she could to try and stop construction. She stirred up a small storm of protest, I must say.' He chuckled. 'A storm of protest in Fjällbacka. Can you hear my knees shaking?' Kaj opened his eyes wide and pretended to look scared, and then burst out laughing. Then he collected himself and went on, 'Well, we managed of course to take the wind out of that little commotion, even though it cost us both time and money. But since then it's been one thing after another. And I'm sure you know the extremes she's willing to go to. It's simply been hell all these years.' He leaned back and crossed one leg over the other.

'Couldn't you have sold the house and moved somewhere else?' Patrik asked cautiously, but the question sparked a fire in Kaj's eyes.

'Move? Not on your life! I would never give her the satisfaction. If anyone should move, she should. Now I'm just waiting for word from the court of appeals.'

'The court of appeals?' Patrik asked.

'They built a balcony on their house without checking the building code first. And it sticks out two centimetres onto my property, so it's against the law. They're going to have to tear that balcony down as soon as the verdict comes in. It should be coming any day now, and I can't wait to see Lilian's face,' Kaj beamed.

'Don't you think that they have bigger concerns at the moment than the existence or non-existence of a balcony?' Patrik couldn't help interjecting.

Kaj's face darkened. 'Certainly I'm not insensitive to their tragedy, but fair's fair. And such things are of no concern to Lady Justice,' he added, looking to Ernst for support. Ernst nodded appreciatively, giving Patrik yet another reason to worry about the suitability of his participation in this investigation. There was enough cause for concern even before it turned out that Ernst was mates with one of the persons on their interview list.

They had split up to cover the houses in the vicinity. Ernst muttered as he trudged through the biting wind. His tall body seemed to catch the wind quite effectively, and his lankiness made him sway back and forth, fighting to keep his balance. He could taste the gall at the back of his mouth. Once again he had to take orders from a snot-nosed kid who was scarcely half his age. It was a mystery to Ernst. Why were his years of experience and skill constantly overlooked? A conspiracy was the only explanation he could come up with. He was a bit fuzzy as to the motive or the brains behind it all, but that didn't bother him. Apparently he was regarded as a threat precisely because of the qualities he knew he possessed.

Knocking on doors was deadly boring, and he wished he were inside where it was warm. People had nothing sensible to say, either. No one had seen the little girl that morning, and all they could say was how terrible it all was. And Ernst had to agree. It was lucky that he'd never been stupid enough to have kids. He'd managed to keep his distance from women too, he thought, effectively repressing the fact that it was the women who had never shown much interest in him.

He glanced over at Hedström, who was covering the houses to the right of the Florins. Sometimes his fingers itched to give his colleague a punch in the nose. He had seen the look in Hedström's eyes when he was forced to take him along this morning. That had actually given Ernst a brief moment of satisfaction. Otherwise Hedström and Molin were as thick as thieves, and they refused to listen to older colleagues like himself and Gösta. Well, Gösta was probably not the best example of a good cop, Ernst had to admit, but his many years on the force deserved respect. And it was no wonder that he'd lost interest in putting any energy into his job under the current conditions. When Ernst thought about it more closely, it was probably the fault of the younger officers that he often didn't feel like working and instead made a point of sneaking off on breaks whenever possible. It was a comforting thought. Naturally it wasn't his fault. Not that he hadn't had pangs of guilt about his lacklustre work performance, but it felt good that he'd finally put his finger on the source of the problem. The crux of the matter, so to speak. It was all because of those snot-nosed kids. All at once life felt much, much better. He knocked on the next door.

Frida was carefully combing the doll's hair. It was important for her to look good because she was going to a party. The table in front of her was already set with coffee and cakes. Tiny little plastic cups with fancy red plates. Naturally they were only pretend cakes, but dolls couldn't eat real ones, so that didn't matter.

Sara had always thought it was dumb to play with dolls. She said they were too old for that. Dolls were for babies, Sara had said, but Frida loved playing with dolls. Sara could be so tiresome sometimes. She always had to be the one to decide. Everything had to be the way she wanted it, or else she would sulk and break things. Mamma would get really mad at Sara when she broke Frida's things. Then Sara would have to go home, and Mamma would ring Sara's mamma and her voice sounded so angry. But when

Sara was nice then Frida liked her a lot, so she still wanted to play with her. Just hoping that she'd be nice.

She didn't understand what had happened to Sara. Mamma had explained that she was dead, that she drowned in the sea, but where was she then? In heaven, Mamma had said, but Frida had stood for a long, long time looking up at the sky, and she hadn't seen Sara. She was sure that if Sara had been in heaven she would have waved to her. Since she hadn't, that must mean she wasn't there. So the question was: where was she? She couldn't just disappear, could she? Imagine if Mamma disappeared like that. Frida felt scared all over. If Sara could disappear, could mammas disappear too? She hugged her doll tight to her chest, trying to push away that nasty idea.

There was something else she wondered about too. Mamma had said that the old men who came and rang the doorbell and told them about Sara were police officers. Frida knew that you were supposed to tell the police everything. You could never lie to them. But she had promised Sara not to tell anybody about the nasty old man. Did she have to keep her promise to someone who was gone? If Sara was gone, then she wouldn't find out that Frida had told about the old man. But what if she came back and heard that Frida had tattled? Then she'd be madder than she ever was before. She might even smash everything in Frida's room, including her doll. Frida decided that it was best not to say anything about the nasty old man.

'Flygare, have you got a minute?' Patrik had been careful to knock on Gösta's door, but he saw his colleague hastily shut down a golf game on his computer.

'Sure, I probably have a minute,' said Gösta sullenly, painfully aware that Patrik had glimpsed his less than noble pursuit during working hours. 'Is this about the girl?' he went on in a more pleasant tone. 'I heard from Annika that it wasn't an accident. Bloody awful,' he said, shaking his head.

'Yes, Ernst and I have just been out talking with the family,' Patrik said, taking a seat in the visitor's chair. 'We told them that now it's a murder investigation. We asked all the family members where they were at the time Sara disappeared, and whether they knew anyone who'd want to harm her.'

Gösta gave Patrik an inquisitive look. 'Do you think that someone in the family might have killed her?'

'Right now I don't think anything. But in any case, it's important to eliminate them from the investigation as soon as possible. At the same time we'll have to check whether there are any known sex offenders in the area.'

'But I thought the girl hadn't been violated, from what Annika told me,' said Gösta.

'Not according to what the M.E. could see, but a little girl who's been murdered . . .' Patrik didn't finish his sentence, but Gösta understood what he meant. There had been far too many stories in the media about the exploitation of children for them to ignore that possibility.

'On the other hand,' Patrik went on, 'to my surprise I got an immediate answer when I asked whether they knew anyone who might wish them harm.'

Gösta held up his hand. 'Let me guess: Lilian threw Kaj to the wolves.'

Patrik gave a little frown at the expression. 'Well, I suppose you could put it that way. In any event there doesn't seem to be any love lost between them. We canvassed the neighbourhood and had an informal interview with Kaj as well. You might say there are plenty of old grudges beneath the surface.'

Gösta snorted. 'Beneath the surface isn't the expression I'd use. It's a drama that's been going on in broad daylight for almost ten years. And personally I'm fed up with it.'

'Well, I gathered from Annika that you're the one who has taken the reports they've filed against each other over the years. Could you tell me a bit about them?'

Without answering at once, Gösta turned round and took a binder from the bookshelf behind his desk. He hastily paged through it and found what he was looking for.

'I only have stuff from the most recent years here; the rest is down in archives.'

Patrik nodded.

Gösta leafed through the binder, skimming over some of the pages he found.

'You might as well take this binder. There's a bunch of good details in here. Complaints from both sides about everything you could imagine.'

'About what, for example?'

'Trespassing – Kaj apparently cut across their property on one occasion, and his life was actually threatened – Lilian clearly said to Kaj that he should watch out if he valued his life.' Gösta kept paging through the binder. 'And then we have a number of complaints about Kaj's son, Morgan. Lilian claimed that he was spying on her, and I quote, " boys like that have an overdeveloped sex drive, I've heard, so he's surely planning to rape me," end quote. And this is just a small selection.'

Patrik shook his head in astonishment. 'Don't they have anything better to do?'

'Apparently not,' said Gösta dryly. 'And for some reason they always insist on coming to me with their woes. But I'll gladly let you take over for the time being,' he said, handing the binder to Patrik, who took it with some misgivings.

'But even if both Kaj and Lilian are quarrelsome devils, I find it hard to believe that Kaj would have gone so far as to kill the girl.'

'No doubt you're right,' said Patrik, getting up with the binder in his arms, 'but, as I said, now his name has been brought up, so I'm at least going to have to examine that possibility.'

Gösta hesitated. 'Let me know if you need any more help. Mellberg couldn't have been serious when he said that you and Ernst were supposed to take care of this by yourselves. It's a homicide investigation, after all. So if I can be of any assistance . . .'

'Thanks, I appreciate it. And I think you're right. Mellberg was probably just trying to rile me. Not even he could have meant that you and Martin wouldn't be allowed to help out. So I thought I'd call in everyone for a briefing, probably tomorrow. If Mellberg has anything against it, he'll have to speak up. But as I said, I don't think he will.'

He thanked Gösta with a nod before he left the office and turned left towards his own. Settled in his desk chair, he opened the binder and began to read. It turned out to be a journey through the pettiness of humankind.

STRÖMSTAD 1923

Her hand shook a bit as she cautiously knocked on his window pane. The window was opened at once, and she thought with satisfaction that he must have been sitting there waiting for her. It was warm in the room, and she didn't know whether his cheeks were flushed from the warmth or from the prospect of the hours they had before them. Probably the latter, she thought, because she felt the same heat in her own face.

Finally they had arrived at the moment she had been longing for ever since she threw that first pebble against his window. She had instinctively known that she needed to proceed cautiously with him. And if there was one thing she knew how to do, it was to read men. Read them and then give them the woman they wanted. In Anders's case that meant she would have to play the shrinking violet for a couple of interminable weeks, even though she wanted to creep into his room and slip into his bed that very first evening. But she knew he would have been scared off by such behaviour. If she wanted to win him she would have to play the game. Whore or madonna. She could give men both.

'Are you frightened?' he asked her as she sat next to him on his narrow bed.

She forced back a smile. If he knew how well-versed she was in what was now about to take place, he would be the one shaking with alarm. But she couldn't show her true self. Not now, when for the first time she wanted a man as much as he wanted her. So she looked down at the floor and just nodded feebly. When he tried to reassure her by putting his arms around her, she couldn't help smiling against his shoulder.

Then she sought out his mouth with her own. When the kiss deepened and got serious, she felt him carefully unbuttoning her blouse. He moved at a devastatingly slow pace. She wanted to grab hold of her blouse and tear it off. Yet she knew that would destroy the image that she had spent weeks creating. Soon enough she'd be able to slow the passionate side of her nature, but by then he'd be able to credit himself for having enticed her. Men were so simple.

When the last piece of clothing fell, she pulled the covers modestly over herself. Anders caressed her hair and looked into her eyes, silently asking her permission. Then he waited for her affirmative nod before he crept in beside her.

'Could you blow out the candle?' she asked, making her voice sound tiny and frightened.

'Yes, of course, absolutely,' he said, embarrassed that he hadn't realized she might prefer the cover of darkness. He reached towards the nightstand and pinched off the flame with his fingers. In the dark she felt him turn towards her and unbearably slowly begin to explore her body.

At precisely the right moment she let out a whimper of feigned pain, hoping that he wouldn't take the absence of blood as a telltale sign. But judging from his tender solicitude afterwards, he had no suspicions, and she felt satisfied with her performance. Since she'd had to stifle her natural instincts, it had been somewhat more boring than she'd expected, but the potential was there. Soon she'd be able to blossom in a way that would be a pleasant surprise for him.

Lying in the hollow of his arm, she thought about whether she might cautiously initiate a second round, but decided she'd better wait a while. For the time being she would have to be content at having played her part well. She had him right where she wanted him. Now it was merely a question of recouping the maximum dividend from all the time she'd invested in him. If she played her cards right, she could look forward to an entertaining pastime this winter.

Monica went round with her cart, replacing books on the shelves. She had loved books her whole life. Having almost died of boredom the first year at home after Kaj sold the business, she had seized the opportunity when she heard that the library needed someone to help out part-time. Kaj thought she was barmy, working when she didn't need to, and she suspected that he considered it a loss of prestige for him. But she was enjoying herself too much to care. There was a good atmosphere at work, and she needed some feeling of community to see any meaning in her life. Kaj had grown more and more short-tempered and grumpy with each passing year, and Morgan didn't need her anymore. There probably weren't going to be any grandchildren either; in any case she thought it highly unlikely. Even that joy had been denied her. She couldn't help feeling a consuming envy when the others at work talked about their grandchildren. The light in their eyes made Monica shrink inside with jealousy. Not that she didn't love Morgan. She did, even though he hadn't made it easy for them to love him. And she believed that he loved her too. He just didn't know how to show it. Maybe he didn't even know that what he felt was called love.

It had taken many years before they understood that there was something wrong with him. Or rather, they knew that something wasn't as it should be, but there was nothing in their experience that jibed with what they observed in Morgan. He wasn't mentally challenged, but instead extremely intelligent for his age. She didn't think that he was autistic, because he didn't withdraw inside his shell and had no aversion to being touched – all reactions that were often associated with autism, according to what she'd read. Morgan had gone to school long before ADHD and DAMP became household words, so such diagnoses had never even been considered. And yet Monica realized that something wasn't quite right. He behaved strangely and seemed resistant to any guidance. He simply didn't seem to comprehend the invisible communication between people, and the rules that governed social intercourse were like Hebrew to him. He kept doing and saying the wrong thing, and Monica knew that people whispered behind her back, assuming that her son's behaviour was due to lax discipline on her part. But she knew that it was more than that. Even his motor skills were erratic. He kept causing mishaps both big and small, because of his clumsiness. Sometimes the accidents weren't even accidents but something he did on purpose. That was what worried her most, that it seemed impossible to teach him the difference between right and wrong. They had tried everything: punishment, bribery, threats and promises, all the tools that parents use to instil a conscience in their children. But nothing had worked. Morgan could do the most awful things without showing any remorse when he was discovered.

But fifteen years earlier they'd had an improbable stroke of luck. One of the many teachers they had visited over the years had a real passion for his profession, and he read everything he could find about new research in the field. One day he told them that he'd discovered a diagnosis that fitted Morgan's condition: Asperger's syndrome. A form of autism, but with normal to high intelligence in the patient. The burden of all those years of hardship seemed to lift from Monica's shoulders the minute she heard the term for the first time. She had tasted it, rolled it around on her tongue with pleasure: Asperger's. It wasn't something they had simply imagined, nor were they at fault in failing to bring up their child properly. She had been right that it was difficult if not impossible for Morgan to comprehend what made daily life so much easier for everyone else: body language, facial expressions, and implicit meanings. None of this registered in Morgan's brain. For the first time they were finally able to offer him serious help.

Or rather *she* was. To be honest, Kaj hadn't been particularly involved with Morgan. Not since he coldly stated that his son would never live up to his expectations. After that, Morgan had become Monica's boy. So it was she who read everything she could find about Asperger's and developed some basic tools that would help her son get through the day. Little cards that described various scenarios and how one was supposed to behave, role-playing games in which they practised various situations, and conversations to try and get him to understand intellectually what his brain refused to assimilate intuitively. She also took great pains to speak clearly with Morgan. To clear away all the metaphors, exaggerations and figures of speech that people used in order to give colour and meaning to language. To a large degree, she had been successful. At least he had learned to function tolerably in the world, but he still kept mostly to himself. With his computers.

That was why Lilian Florin had managed to transform Monica's vague sense of irritation into hatred. She was able to put up with everything else. She didn't give a damn about building codes and infringements and threats about one thing and another. As far as she was concerned, Kaj was just as much to blame in the feud, and she even believed that he sometimes enjoyed it. But the fact that Lilian had gone after Morgan time after time had aroused the ferocity of a tigress in Monica. Just because her son was different it seemed to give Lilian, and many others for that matter, a free hand to mock him. God forbid that anyone should be the least bit different. The mere fact that he still lived, if not at home, then on the same lot as his parents, grated on many people. But none of them was as malicious as Lilian. Some of the accusations she concocted made Monica so angry that she could hardly see straight. Many times she regretted moving to Fjällbacka. She had even taken up the matter with Kaj a few times, but she knew that it was pointless. He was far too bull-headed.

She shelved the last books from the cart and made another round of the shelves to see whether there were any more to collect. But her hands shook with rage when she replayed in her mind all the malicious attacks on Morgan that Lilian had instigated over the years. Not only had she run to the police a few times, she had spread false rumours in town as well, and that kind of gossip was almost impossible to refute. Where there's smoke there's fire, as they say. Even though practically everybody knew that Lilian Florin was a regular gossipmonger, her words gradually became accepted as truth, through the sheer force of repetition.

Now she was also garnering a large amount of sympathy in town. Much of Lilian's nastiness had been forgiven in one blow. She had lost a grandchild, after all. But even that couldn't make Monica feel sorry for her. No, she was saving her sympathy for the daughter. How Charlotte could be Lilian's child was a mystery to her. It would be hard to find a nicer person, and Monica felt so sorry for Charlotte that she thought her heart would break.

But she didn't intend to waste a single tear on Lilian.

Aina looked surprised when the doctor showed up at the clinic at his usual time, eight in the morning.

'Hi, Niclas,' she said hesitantly. 'I thought you were going to come in late today.'

He just shook his head and went into his examination room. He didn't have the energy to explain. He simply couldn't stand to be at home for a minute longer, even though the guilt he felt at leaving was like a weight on his shoulders. Because it was a different and worse sort of guilt that made him leave Charlotte alone with her despair at home with Lilian and Stig. A guilt that made his throat tighten so he found it hard to breathe. If he had stayed there any longer he would have suffocated, he was sure of it. He couldn't even look at Charlotte's face, or meet her gaze. The pain in her eyes, together with his own guilt-ridden conscience, was more than he could bear. That's why he had fled to his job instead. It was cowardly, he knew that. But he had long since lost all illusions about himself. He was not a strong or courageous person.

But he hadn't intended for Sara to be affected. He hadn't intended for anyone to be affected. Niclas pressed his hand to his chest as he sat as if paralysed behind his big desk, cluttered with casebooks and other papers. The pain was so sharp that he could feel it racing up and down his veins and collecting in his heart. Suddenly he understood how a heart attack must feel. That pain surely couldn't be any worse than this.

Niclas ran his hands through his hair. What had happened, what needed to be resolved, lay before him like a baffling riddle. And yet he had to solve it. He was forced to do something. Somehow he had to get out of the bind he was in. Everything had always gone so well before. Charm, adroitness and an open and honest smile had saved him from most of the consequences of his actions over the years, but perhaps he had finally come to the end of the road.

The telephone began to ring in front of him. Consultation hours had begun. Although he felt so devastated, he had to go and heal the sick.

With Maja in a baby sling on her stomach, Erica made a desperate attempt to clean house. She had her mother-in-law's previous visit fresh in her mind, so she almost manically pushed the vacuum cleaner round the living room. Hopefully Kristina would have no reason to go upstairs, so if Erica managed to make the ground floor presentable before she arrived, everything would be fine.

The last time Kristina came over, Maja had been three weeks old, and Erica was still in a stunned fog. The dust bunnies had been as big as rats, and the dirty dishes were piled up in the sink. Of course Patrik had made some attempts to start cleaning up, but since Erica flung Maja into his arms as soon as he came home, he had got no further than to take the vacuum cleaner out of the broom cupboard.

As soon as Kristina came in the door her face took on a disgusted expression, which disappeared only when she caught sight of her granddaughter. For the next three days Erica listened through her fog as Kristina muttered that it was certainly good she had come, or else Maja would soon develop asthma in all this dust. She said that in her day nobody sat staring at the TV all day long. Women managed to take care of a baby and a number of siblings, clean house, and also see to it that a good meal was on the table when the husband came home. Fortunately Erica had been much too weak to be irritated by her mother-in-law's remarks. In fact, she had been grateful for the moments she had to herself when Kristina proudly went out with Maja in the pram or helped bathe and change the baby. But by now Erica had regained some of her strength, and combined with her constant melancholy it made her instinctively understand that it would be better to try as much as possible to avoid drawing any criticism from her mother-in-law.

Erica looked at the clock. An hour before Kristina was scheduled to come waltzing in, and she still hadn't done the dishes. She probably ought to dust as well. She glanced down at her daughter. Maja had gone to sleep contentedly in the sling to the sound of the vacuum cleaner, and Erica mused whether this might be something that would work in future when putting the baby to bed. So far all such attempts had been accompanied by loud protests, but she had read that babies liked to fall asleep to monotonous sounds, like the vacuum cleaner or a clothes dryer. It was worth a try, at least. For the time being the only way to get their daughter to sleep was to have her lie on Erica's stomach or at her breast, and that was beginning to be intolerable. Maybe she ought to test the methods she'd read about in *The Baby Book*, the excellent child care manual by nine-time mother Anna Wahlgren. She had read it before Maja arrived, and a stack of other books for that matter, but when a real baby appeared on the scene, all the theoretical knowledge she had assimilated flew out of the window. Instead she and Patrik practised a sort of ad hoc survival philosophy with Maja. Erica felt that it might be time to retake control. It didn't make sense that a baby two months old could control the whole house to such a large extent. If Erica could have handled such a situation, that would be one thing, but she could feel how she was gradually slipping further into the darkness.

A quick rap at the door interrupted her thoughts. Either an hour had passed in record time, or her mother-in-law had arrived early. The latter was more likely, and Erica looked around the room in dismay. Oh well, nothing to be done about it now. She just had to put on a smile and let her mother-in-law in. She opened the front door.

'But my dear, you're standing there with Maja in the draught! She'll catch a cold, you know.'

Erica closed her eyes and counted to ten.

Patrik hoped that things would go well when his mother came to visit. He knew that she could be a bit . . . overwhelming, one might say. Even though Erica usually had no problem dealing with her mother-in-law, she hadn't been herself since Maja was born. At the same time she badly needed a break, and since he couldn't provide it for her, they had to make use of the resources that were available. Once again he wondered whether he ought to try and find someone Erica could talk to, a professional. But where could he turn? No, it was probably best to let her work through things on her own. The depression would surely pass as soon as they got a routine established. At least that was what he tried to believe. But he couldn't prevent a little nagging suspicion from creeping in, a suspicion that maybe he was choosing to believe this because it required the smallest amount of effort on his part.

He forced himself to stop thinking about home and return to the notes he had before him. He had called a meeting in his office for nine o'clock, five minutes from now. As he suspected, Mellberg hadn't objected to involving additional personnel; he seemed to view it as inevitable. Anything else would have been idiotic, even by Mellberg's standards. How could they have conducted a homicide investigation with just two detectives, Ernst and himself?

First to arrive was Martin, who sat down in the only visitor's chair in the room. The others would have to bring their own chairs.

'How'd it go with the flat?' Patrik asked. 'Was it any good?'

'It was fantastic!' said Martin, his eyes shining. 'We took it on the spot. Weekend after next you can come and help carry cartons.'

'Oh, is that right?' Patrik laughed. 'How nice of you. I'll have to get back to you on that, after conferring with the boss at home. Erica's being a little stingy with my time right now, so I can't promise you anything.'

'I understand,' said Martin. 'I have a number of favours I can call in from people I've helped move, so we'll probably manage fine without you.'

'What's this I hear about moving?' Annika asked, sweeping in with a coffee cup in one hand and notebook in the other. 'Should I really believe my ears? Are you finally going to join the rest of us and settle down, Martin?'

He flushed, as he always did when Annika teased him, but he couldn't help smiling.

'Yeah, you heard right. Pia and I found a flat in Grebbestad. We're moving in two weeks from today.'

'Well, I'm certainly glad to hear it,' said Annika. 'It's about time too. I'd been worrying that you were going to end up gathering dust on the shelf. So . . . when are we going to hear the pitter-patter of little feet?'

'Oh, give me a break,' said Martin. 'I remember the way you badgered Patrik when he met Erica, and now look how things have turned out for him. That poor guy felt so much pressure to propagate with his woman, and now he sits here looking ten years older.' He winked at Patrik to show that he was joking.

'Well, let me know if you need any tips on how to do it,' Patrik offered cheerfully.

Martin was just about to come back with a witty rejoinder when Ernst and Gösta simultaneously tried to wedge through the doorway with their chairs. Grumbling, Gösta slipped past Ernst, who nonchalantly took a place in the middle of the room.

'It's going to be tight with the whole crowd in here,' said Gösta, glowering at Martin and Annika, who scooted their chairs over.

'There's always room for one more, as my mother used to say,' Annika commented a bit sarcastically.

Mellberg came sauntering in last of all; he was content to lean against the door jamb.

Patrik spread out his papers on his desk and took a deep breath. The full force of what it meant to head a homicide investigation suddenly struck him. This wasn't the first time, but still he was nervous. He didn't like being the centre of attention, and the gravity of the task caused his shoulders to slump. But the only other option was for Mellberg to take charge, and Patrik wanted to avoid that at all costs. So it was just a matter of getting started.

'As you know, we've now received confirmation that Sara Klinga's death was not an accident, but a murder. She did drown, but the water in her lungs was fresh, not saltwater, which indicates that she was drowned somewhere else and then dumped in the sea. I know this is nothing new, but all the details are in the report from Pedersen, the M.E. Annika has made copies for you.' He passed a stack of stapled reports around the table, and they each took one.

'Can anything be deduced based on the water in her lungs? For example, it says here that there were remnants of soap in the water. Could we find out what sort of soap it was?' asked Martin, pointing at an item in the autopsy report.

'Yes, hopefully we can,' replied Patrik. 'A water sample was sent off to the National Forensic Laboratory for analysis, and in a few days we'll know more about what they've been able to find.'

'What about the clothes?' Martin went on. 'Can we say whether she was dressed or not when she was drowned in the bathtub? Because we can almost certainly assume it was a bathtub she was drowned in, can't we?'

'I'm afraid the answer is the same. Her clothes were also sent off, and until we get the results back I don't know any more than the rest of you.'

Ernst rolled his eyes and Patrik gave him a sharp look. He knew precisely what was going on inside the man's head. He was jealous because it was Martin and not him who had thought of some intelligent questions to ask. Patrik wondered whether Ernst would ever understand that they worked together in a team in order to solve a task, and that it wasn't a matter of a contest between individuals.

'Are we dealing with a sex crime here?' Gösta asked, prompting Ernst to look more annoyed, if possible. Even his partner in lethargy had managed to come up with a relevant question.

'Impossible to say,' replied Patrik. 'But I'd like Martin to start checking whether there's anyone on our list who's been convicted of sex crimes against children.'

Martin nodded and made a note.

'Then we also have to look more closely at the family,' Patrik said. 'Ernst and I had a preliminary talk with them when we informed them that Sara had been murdered. We've also spoken with the individual that Sara's mother pointed out as a possible suspect.'

'Let me guess,' said Annika acidly. 'Could it possibly have been a certain Kaj Wiberg?'

'That's right,' said Gösta. 'I gave Patrik all the documents I have about their contacts with us over the years.'

'A waste of time and resources,' said Ernst. 'It's completely absurd to believe that Kaj had anything to do with the girl's death.'

'Oh, right, you two know each other,' said Gösta and gave Patrik a questioning look to see whether he was aware of this. Patrik confirmed with a nod that he knew.

'At any rate,' Patrik interrupted when Ernst again tried to say something, 'we'll continue to investigate Kaj to decide as soon as possible whether he was involved. And we need to keep all options open at this stage. First we have to find out more about the girl and her family. I thought Ernst and I would begin by talking to the girl's teachers to see whether they know of any problem concerning the family. Since we know so little, we might need to get some help from the local press as well. Would you be able to help with that, Bertil?'

He got no answer and repeated a bit louder: 'Bertil?' Still no answer. Mellberg looked to be far away in his own thoughts as he stood leaning on the door jamb. After raising his voice another notch Patrik finally got a reaction.

'Oh, sorry. What did you say?' asked Mellberg. Patrik once again had a hard time believing that he was the one playing the part of chief in this building.

'I just wondered whether you might consider talking to the local press. Tell them it was a murder and that anyone's information is of interest. I have a feeling we're going to need the public's help on this case.'

'Oh, uh, of course,' said Mellberg, who still had a dazed look on his face. 'Okay, I'll talk to the press.'

'All right. That's about all we can do for now,' said Patrik, slapping his hands on his desk. 'Any more questions?'

No one said a word, and after a few seconds of silence everyone began gathering up their things as if on command.

'Ernst?' Patrik stopped his colleague just as he was heading out the door. 'Will you be ready to go in half an hour?'

'Go where?' said Ernst with his usual grumpiness.

Patrik took a deep breath. Sometimes he wondered whether he just thought he was talking while really it was only his lips moving. 'To Sara's school. To talk to her teachers,' he said, carefully enunciating each word.

'Oh right, that. Sure, I can be ready in half an hour,' said Ernst, turning his back to Patrik.

Patrik gave him a dirty look. He would give this unwelcome partner of his a couple more days before he dared to defy Mellberg and discreetly take Molin along instead.

STRÖMSTAD 1924

The pleasure of novelty had truly begun to wear off. The whole winter had been filled with trysts, and at first Agnes had enjoyed every moment. But now that winter was in retreat and spring was quietly approaching, she felt indolence beginning to creep in. To be honest, she no longer saw what it was about him that she had found so attractive. Of course he was good-looking, she couldn't deny that, but his speech was crude and uneducated and there was a constant odour of sweat about him. It had also become harder and harder to sneak down to his place, now that the winter darkness was relinquishing its protective cover. No, she would have to put an end to this, she decided as she sat in front of the mirror in her room.

She attended to the last details of her dress and went down to have breakfast with her father. She had seen Anders yesterday, so her body was still overwhelmed by a great weariness. She sat down at the breakfast table after kissing her father on the cheek and began listlessly cracking open the shell of a soft-boiled egg. Her exhaustion made the smell of the egg turn her stomach.

'What is it, my heart?' August asked in concern, gazing at her across the large table.

'Just a little tired,' she replied miserably. 'I didn't sleep well last night.'

'You poor thing,' he said in sympathy. 'See that you eat something, then you can go back to bed for a while. Perhaps we should take you to see Dr Fern. You've been rather out of sorts all winter.'

Agnes couldn't help smiling, though she had to hide the smile hastily behind her serviette. With a downcast look she answered her father, 'Yes, I have been a bit worn out. But it was probably mostly because of the winter darkness. Just wait, once spring comes I'll be more lively again.'

'Hmm, well, we shall see. But think about it. Perhaps the doctor should have a look at you all the same.'

'Yes, Father,' she said, forcing herself to take a bite of egg.

She shouldn't have done that. The instant she put the boiled egg-white in her mouth she felt her stomach turn over and something rose up in her throat. She jumped up from the table and with her hand to her mouth she dashed to the toilet they had on the ground floor. She had scarcely raised the lid before a cascade of yesterday's dinner mixed with gall splashed into the toilet bowl. She felt her eyes fill with tears. Her stomach turned inside out several more times. She waited a while, and when there didn't seem to be any more coming, she wiped her mouth in disgust and left the little room on shaky legs. Outside stood her father, looking worried.

'Dear heart, how are you?'

She just shook her head and swallowed to get rid of the repulsive taste of vomit in her mouth.

August put his arm round her shoulders, led her into the parlour, and sat her down on one of the sofas. He put his hand on her forehead.

'Agnes, you're in a cold sweat. No, I'm going to ring Dr Fern at once and ask him to come over and have a look at you.'

She managed only a feeble nod and then lay down on the sofa and shut her eyes. The room was spinning behind her closed eyelids.

It was like living in a shadow world with no connection to reality. Anna hadn't really had a choice, and yet she was consumed by doubt that she had done the right thing. She knew that nobody else would understand. After she'd finally succeeded in breaking away from Lucas, why had she gone back to him? Especially when he'd done what he had to Emma. The answer was that she went back because she thought it was the only chance for her and her children to survive. Lucas had always been dangerous, yet he kept himself restrained. Now it was as though something had snapped inside him, and his self-control had yielded to a brooding insanity. That was the only way she could describe it: insanity. That had always been part of him; she'd sensed. Indeed, perhaps it was that underlying current of potential danger that had attracted her to him in the first place. Now it had risen to the surface and she feared for her life.

The fact that she had left him and taken the kids wasn't the only reason that his madness had come to light. Several factors had combined to flip that little circuit-breaker inside him. Even his job, which had always been his biggest arena of success, had now betrayed him. A few failed business deals and his career was over. Just before Anna went back to him she had run into one of his colleagues, who had told her that Lucas was starting to act more and more irrationally on the job when things didn't go well. He gave in to sudden outbursts of anger and aggressive attacks. Finally he had shoved an important client up against the wall and been fired on the spot. The client had pressed charges, so there would be an investigation as soon as the police had the time.

The reports of Lucas's mental condition had worried her, but it wasn't until she came home one day to a totally vandalized flat that she realized she no longer had a choice. He was going to harm her, or even worse, harm the kids, if she didn't humour him and come back. The only way to create a bit of security for Emma and Adrian was to stay as close to the enemy as possible.

Anna knew this, and yet it felt as though she were going from the frying pan into the fire. She was practically a prisoner in her own home, her jailer an aggressive and irrational Lucas. First, he forced her to quit her part-time job at Stockholm Auction House, a job she had loved and found deeply satisfying. He wouldn't allow her to leave the flat except to shop for food or take the kids to school. Meanwhile he hadn't been able to find another job, nor did he even try. He'd had to give up the big, elegant flat in Östermalm, and now they were squeezed into a little two-room flat outside the city. But as long as he didn't hit the children, she could put up with anything. She herself once again had bruises on her body, but in a way it felt like putting on an old, familiar dress. She had lived that way for so many years that her brief period of freedom now seemed unreal, a dream that just happened one time. Anna also did her best to hide what was going on from the children. She had managed to convince Lucas that they should keep going to day-care, and she tried to pretend that their daily life was the same as always. But she wasn't sure that she was fooling them. At least not Emma, who was now four years old. At first she'd been ecstatic that they were moving in with Pappa again, but Anna had begun to notice her daughter giving her puzzled looks.

Despite the fact that Anna kept trying to convince herself that she had made the right decision, she still realized that they couldn't live the rest of their lives this way. The more irrational Lucas got, the more frightened of him she became. She was sure that one day he would cross the line and actually kill her. The question was how she could make her escape. She had thought about ringing Erica and asking for help, but Lucas watched the telephone like a hawk. And there was something inside her that held her back. She had relied on Erica so many times before, and for once she felt that she had to tackle this problem herself, like an adult. Gradually she had worked out a plan. She needed to gather enough evidence against Lucas so that the abuse could no longer be denied. Then she and the children would be given safe haven and new identities. Sometimes she was overwhelmed by the desire to take the kids and simply flee to the nearest women's shelter, but she knew full well that without evidence against Lucas it would only be a temporary solution. Then they would be back in hell again.

So she had started to document everything she could. In one of the department stores on her way to the day-care centre, there was a photo booth. She would sneak in there and take pictures of her injuries. She wrote down the date and time when she received them and hid the notes and photos inside the frame of the wedding photo of her and Lucas. There was a symbolism in this that she appreciated. Soon she would have enough material to entrust her fate and that of her children to the authorities. Until then she simply had to put up with Lucas. And see about surviving.

It was recess when Patrik and Ernst turned into the car park at the school. Crowds of children were outside playing in the biting wind, bundled up and seemingly unconcerned with the cold. But Patrik shivered and hurried to get inside.

Their daughter would be going to this school in a few years. It was a pleasant thought, and he could picture Maja scampering about here in the hall with blonde pigtails and a gap between her front teeth, just the way Erica looked in the picture taken when she was a kid. He hoped that Maja would be like her mother. Erica had been incredibly cute as a little girl. She still was, in his eyes.

They took a chance and headed for the first classroom they saw, knocking on the door, which stood open. The room was bright and pleasant, with big windows and children's drawings on the walls. A young teacher sat at a desk immersed in the papers in front of her. She jumped when she heard the knock.

'Yes?' Despite her young age she had already managed to acquire that perfect teacher's tone of voice, which made Patrik repress a desire to stand at attention and bow.

'We're from the police. We're looking for Sara Klinga's teacher.'

A shadow crept over her face and she nodded. 'That's me.' She got up and came over to shake their hands. 'Beatrice Lind. I teach first through third grade.' She motioned for them to take a seat on one of the small chairs next to the school desks. Patrik felt like a giant as he cautiously sat down. The sight of Ernst trying to co-ordinate all parts of his gangly frame to fit in the tiny chair made him smirk. But as soon as Patrik turned his gaze to the teacher his expression turned sombre again and he focused on the task at hand.

'It's so terribly tragic,' said Beatrice, her voice quavering. 'That a child can be here one day and gone the next . . .' Now her lower lip was trembling too. 'And drowned . . .'

'Yes, especially since it turns out that her death was not an accident.' Patrik had thought the news would have spread to everyone in town, but Beatrice looked undeniably shocked.

'What? What do you mean? No accident? But she drowned, didn't she?'

'Sara was murdered,' said Patrik, hearing how brusque that sounded. In a gentler tone of voice he added, 'She didn't die from an accident, so we have to find out more about Sara. What she was like as a person, whether there were any problems in the family, that sort of thing.'

He could see that Beatrice was still upset at the news, but she seemed to be pondering what it might mean. After a while she had collected herself and said, 'Well, what is there to say about Sara? She was . . .' she searched for the right word, 'a very lively child. And that was both good and bad. There wasn't a quiet moment when Sara was around, and to be honest it could be difficult to maintain order in the classroom sometimes. She was something of a leader, pulling the others along, and if I didn't put a stop to it, utter chaos could result. At the same time . . .' Beatrice hesitated again and looked as though she were weighing each word very carefully, 'at the same time, it was precisely that energy that made her so creative. She was incredibly talented in drawing and every other artistic pursuit, and she had the most active imagination I've ever seen. She was quite simply a very creative child, whether she was pulling pranks or producing a work of art.'

Ernst squirmed in the little chair and said, 'We heard that she had one of those problems with initials, DAMP or whatever it's called.'

His disrespectful tone prompted Beatrice to give him a sharp look, and to Patrik's amusement his colleague actually cringed.

'Sara did have DAMP, that's correct. She was given special tutoring for it. We have a good deal of experience in this field, so we can give these children what they need to function optimally.' It sounded like a lecture, and Patrik understood that this was something of a pet topic for her.

'How did the problems manifest themselves for Sara?' Patrik asked.

'In the way I described. She had a very high energy level and could sometimes throw terrible tantrums. But as I said, she was also a very creative child. She wasn't mean or nasty or badly brought up, as many ignorant people might say of children like Sara. She simply had a hard time controlling her impulses.'

'How did the other children react to her behaviour?' Patrik was truly curious.

'It varied. Some couldn't get along with her at all and retreated. Others seemed to be able to handle her outbursts with equanimity and got along fine with her. I would say that her best friend was Frida Karlgren. They happen to live right near each other.'

'Yes, we've spoken with her,' said Patrik with a nod. He twisted on the chair once again. He had begun to get pins and needles in his legs, and he could feel a cramp forming in his right calf. He sincerely hoped that Ernst was feeling equally uncomfortable.

'What about her family?' Ernst interjected. 'Do you know if Sara had any problems at home?'

Patrik had to suppress a smile when he saw that his colleague was indeed massaging his calves.

'Unfortunately I can't help you there,' said Beatrice, pursing her lips. It was obvious that she wasn't in the habit of telling tales about the home life of her pupils. 'I've only met her parents and her grandmother once. They seemed to be stable, pleasant people. And I never had any indication from Sara that anything was wrong.'

A bell rang shrilly to signal that recess was over, and a lively commotion in the corridor revealed that the children had obediently responded to the call. Beatrice got up and held out her hand as a sign that the conversation was finished. Patrik managed to extricate himself from the chair and stand up. Out of the corner of his eye he saw Ernst massaging one leg, which had evidently gone to sleep. Like two old men they tottered out of the classroom after saying goodbye to the teacher.

'Damn, what uncomfortable chairs,' said Ernst as he limped out to the car.

'Well, I guess we're not that limber anymore,' said Patrik, sinking into the driver's seat of the car. All of a sudden the comfortable seat with plenty of leg room felt like an incredible luxury.

'Speak for yourself,' muttered Ernst. 'My physical condition is just as good as when I was a teenager, but nobody is built to sit on that bloody miniature furniture.'

Patrik changed the subject. 'We certainly didn't find out much of any use from that visit.'

'Sounds to me like the girl was a hell of a pest,' said Ernst. 'Nowadays it seems that any kid who doesn't know how to behave is excused with some damn variant of DAMP. In my day that sort of behaviour would get you a couple of raps with the ruler. But now the kids have to be medicated and soothed by psychologists and pampered. No wonder society is going to hell.' Ernst stared gloomily out of the window on the passenger side and shook his head.

Patrik didn't acknowledge his comment with an answer. There was really no point.

'Are you really going to feed her again? In my day we never nursed more often than every four hours,' said Kristina, giving Erica a critical look as she sat down in the easy chair to nurse Maja after a mere two and a half hours.

In this situation Erica knew better than to argue, so she simply ignored Kristina's remark. It was only one of many that had been hurled through the air that morning, and Erica felt that soon she would reach her limit. Her failed attempts to clean house adequately had been noticed, just as she had predicted. Now her mother-in-law was dashing about with the vacuum cleaner like a madwoman, muttering comments on her favourite topic: dust causing asthma in small children. Before this she had demonstratively gone into the kitchen and washed all the dishes in the sink and on the drain-board, all the while instructing Erica in the correct way to wash up. The dishes had to be rinsed off promptly so that remnants of food wouldn't stick, and it was just as well to do the washing up at once. Otherwise the dishes would just pile up. Clenching her teeth, Erica tried to focus on the long catnap she'd be able to take when Kristina went out with the pram. Although she was starting to wonder whether it was worth the trouble.

She made herself comfortable in the easy chair and tried to get Maja to nurse. But the baby sensed the tension in the air. She had fretted and fussed most of the morning, and now she stub-bornly resisted the little milk offered to soothe her. Erica was sweating as she fought this battle of wills with her infant daughter. Only when Maja finally gave in and began to nurse did Erica relax. Cautiously, so she wouldn't have struggled in vain, she switched on the TV. *The Bold and the Beautiful* was on, and Erica tried to immerse herself in Brooke and Ridge's complex relationship. Kristina glanced at the TV screen as she hurried by with the vacuum cleaner.

'Ugh, how can you stand to watch such trash? Why don't you read a book instead?'

Erica retaliated by turning up the volume on the TV. For a second she permitted herself to enjoy the satisfaction of such a spiteful response. But when she saw her mother-in-law's insulted look, she turned it back down. She knew she would pay a high price for any attempts at rebellion. She glanced at her watch. Good Lord, it was only a little before noon. It would be an eternity until Patrik came home. And then another day just like this one would follow, before Kristina packed her bags and went home, convinced that she had been of invaluable help to her son and daughter-in-law. Two more interminable days . . .

STRÖMSTAD 1924

The milder weather worked wonders for the mood of the stone-cutters. When Anders arrived at work he could hear how his comrades had already started on their rhythmic work songs that accompanied the sound of their hammers striking the crowbars. They were busy making holes for the gunpowder to blast out the larger blocks of granite. One man held the crowbar, and two took turns striking it until they had made a substantial hole straight into the stone. Then the black powder was poured in and ignited. Attempts had been made with dynamite, but it hadn't worked properly. The pressure of the detonation was too great and pulverized the granite, making it shatter in all directions.

The men nodded to Anders as he walked by, without interrupting the rhythm of their work.

With joy in his heart he went over to the place where he was working on carving out the statue. Progress had been painfully slow during the winter; on many days the cold had made it well-nigh impossible to work the stone. For long periods he had been forced to simply stop and wait for weather to improve, making it difficult to earn enough wages. But now he could get started in earnest on the huge piece of granite, and he wasn't complaining. The winter had brought other reasons to be happy.

Sometimes he could hardly believe it was true, that such an angel had come down to earth and crept into his bed. Every minute they had spent together was a precious memory that he stored in a special place in his heart. But at times, thoughts of the future could cloud his joy. He had tried to bring up the subject with her on several occasions, but she always silenced him with a kiss. They shouldn't speak of such things, she said, often adding that everything was bound to work out. He had interpreted this to mean that she, like him, still hoped for a future together. Sometimes he actually permitted himself to believe her words, that everything was going to work out. Deep inside he was a true romantic, and the belief that love could conquer all obstacles was firmly rooted in his soul. Of course they didn't belong to the same social class, but he was a skilled, hard-working man. He would undoubtedly be able to provide a good life for her if he only got the chance. And if she felt for him what he felt for her, then material things would not be so important to her. A life shared with him would be worth some sacrifices on her part. On a day like this, with the spring sunshine warming his fingers, he was convinced that everything would really turn out the way he hoped. Now he was merely waiting to receive her permission to speak with her father. Then he would set about preparing the speech of his life.

With a pounding heart he meticulously hammered out the statue from the stone. In his head the words kept spinning round. Along with images of Agnes.

Arne was studying carefully the obituary in the newspaper. He wrinkled his nose. He suspected as much. They had chosen a teddy bear as an illustration, and that was a custom that he really hated. An obituary should contain the symbols of the Christian church, nothing more. A teddy bear was simply ungodly. But he hadn't expected anything else. The boy had been a disappointment from beginning to end, and nothing he did surprised Arne anymore. It was really a crying shame that such a God-fearing person as himself should have progeny who had so stubbornly repudiated the right path. People who didn't know any better had tried to bring about a reconciliation between them. They had said that his son, from what they had heard, was a fine and intelligent man. He also had an honourable profession, since he was a doctor, after all. Mostly it was women who had come to their door spouting such nonsense. Men knew better than to comment on things they knew nothing about. Of course he had to agree that his son had taken on a proper profession and seemed to be doing well. But if he didn't have God in his heart it was all meaningless.

Arne's greatest dream had been to have a son who would follow his grandfather's footsteps and become a pastor. He himself had been forced to put aside such ambitions early on, since his father drank up all the money that was supposed to go for his seminary training. Instead he'd had to content himself with working as a verger in the church. At least that still allowed him to spend his days in God's house.

But the church was no longer what it had once been. Things used to be different. Back then everyone knew his place, and the pastor was shown the proper respect. People also followed the words of Pastor Schartus as best they could, and they did not occupy themselves with things that even pastors appeared to enjoy nowadays: dancing, music and living together out of wedlock, to name just a few vices. But the hardest thing for Arne to accept was that females now had the right to act as God's representatives. He just couldn't understand it. The Bible was perfectly clear on this point: 'Woman shall be silent in the congregation.' What was there to discuss? Women had no business being members of the clergy. They could offer good support as pastors' wives or even as deaconesses, but otherwise they should remain silent in the congregation. It had been a sorry time when that female had taken over Fjällbacka Church. Arne had been forced to drive to Kville on Sundays to attend worship service, and he had simply refused to show up for work. He had paid a high price, but it was worth it. Now the hideous creature was gone. Of course, the new pastor was a bit too modern for his taste, but at least he was a man. Now all that remained was to make sure that the female cantor became a temporary chapter in the history of Fjällbacka Church. A female cantor wasn't as bad as a female pastor, of course, but still.

Arne morosely turned the page in the regional paper, *Bohusläningen*. Asta was continuing to go about the house with a long face. He knew that it was for the little girl's sake. It bothered her that their son now lived so close by. But he had explained that she had to be strong in her faith and true to their conviction. He could agree that it was a shame about the girl, but that just proved his point. Their son had not kept to the straight and narrow, and sooner or later he was bound to be punished. He paged back to look again at the teddy bear in the obituary. It was a crying shame, it certainly was . . .

Mellberg didn't feel the same sense of satisfaction that he usually did when he was the focus of media attention. He hadn't even called a press conference, but had simply gathered some reporters from the local newspapers in his office. The memory of the letter he'd received overshadowed everything else right now, and he was having a hard time concentrating on anything else.

'Do you have any solid leads to follow up on?' A cub reporter was eagerly awaiting his reply.

'Nothing that we can comment on in the present situation,' the chief said.

'Is anyone in the family a suspect?' The question came from a reporter from the competing paper.

'We're keeping all our options open right now, but we have nothing concrete that points in a specific direction.'

'Was it a sex crime?' The same reporter again.

'I can't go into that,' Mellberg said vaguely.

'How did you confirm it was murder?' the third journalist interjected. 'Did she have external injuries that indicated it was homicide?'

'For investigative reasons I can't comment on that,' said Mellberg, seeing how the frustration was growing on the reporters' faces. It was always like walking a slack line where the press was concerned. Give them just enough so that they felt the police were doing their job, but not so much that it hurt the investigation. Usually he regarded himself as a master of this balancing act, but today he was having a hard time with it. He didn't know what to do about the information he had received in the letter. Could it really be true?

One of the reporters gave him a querulous look, and Mellberg realized he'd missed a question.

'Pardon me, could you please repeat the question?' he said in confusion, and the reporter's expression turned quizzical. They had met at several of these types of meetings, and the super-intendent usually acted grandiose and boastful, rather than low-key and absent-minded as he was today.

'All right. I asked whether there is any reason for parents in the area to worry about the safety of their children.'

'We always recommend that parents keep a close eye on their children, but I want to emphasize that this shouldn't lead to any sort of mass hysteria. I'm convinced that this is an isolated event and that we will soon have a suspect in custody.'

He stood up as a sign that the meeting was over. The reporters obediently put away their notebooks and pens and thanked him. They all felt that they might have questioned the superintendent a bit harder, but at the same time it was important for the regional press to maintain a good relationship with the local police. They would leave the hard-hitting questions to their colleagues in the big cities. Here in Bohuslän they were often neighbours of the subjects of their interviews. They had children in the same sports leagues and schools, so they had to forgo any desire to get the big scoop for the sake of harmony in the community.

Mellberg leaned back contentedly. Despite his lack of focus, the newspapers hadn't received more information than he intended to give, and tomorrow the news would be plastered on the front pages of all the papers in the area. Hopefully that would make the general public wake up and start calling in tips. If the police were lucky, there might even be something they could use among all the gossip that usually came in.

He pulled out the letter and began reading it again. He still couldn't believe his eyes.

STRÖMSTAD 1924

She lay in her room with a cold, damp washcloth on her forehead. The doctor had examined her carefully and then ordered bed rest. Now he was downstairs in the parlour talking with her father, and for a moment she worried that there might be something seriously wrong with her. An expression of alarm had appeared in his eyes, but it was gone the next instant. Then he patted her hand and told her that everything would be all right. She just needed to rest for a while.

She couldn't tell the good doctor the real reason for her malaise. All those late nights during the winter had affected her health. That was the diagnosis she had come up with herself, but she had to keep it a secret. Hopefully Dr Fern would write a prescription for some restorative drops for her. Since she had now decided to terminate her escapades with Anders, she should soon be her old self again. In the meantime it couldn't hurt to stay in bed and be waited on for a week or two. Agnes pondered what she should ask to have for lunch. Now that she had lost yesterday's dinner in the WC, she could feel her stomach growling and asking to be filled. Maybe pancakes, or those excellent meatballs the cook made, with boiled potatoes, cream gravy and lingonberries.

Footsteps on the stairs made her shrink a little farther under the covers and moan a bit. She would ask for meatballs, she decided, the second before the door to her room opened.

Anger had been growing inside him since the previous day. The nerve of her, that damned woman really had no scruples at all. Fingering him to the police. Kaj wasn't stupid; he knew full well that the rumours would soon start flying all over town, so it really didn't make any difference what he said. The only thing that would stick in people's minds was that the police had been to his house to ask questions about the girl's death. He clenched his fists until his knuckles turned white. After a moment of hesitation he put on his jacket and went outside, walking with determined steps. The plank fence he'd put up between the lots prevented him from cutting straight across, so he went out to the street and then up the drive toward the Florins' house. He had checked that both Niclas and Charlotte had left the house before he approached. He was going to give her a piece of his mind, that bitch. Since he assumed that she, like everyone else in town, seldom locked her front door, he walked right in without knocking and went straight to the kitchen. She jumped when he came in but quickly collected herself, and her face took on that snippy, holier-than-thou expression. She really thought she was somebody. As if she were a bloody queen and not just an ordinary old bag in a fucking small town.

'What the hell's the meaning of sending the police over to my house?' he yelled, slamming his fist on the kitchen table.

She gave him a cold stare. 'They asked if we knew of anyone who might wish our family harm, so I immediately thought of you. And if you don't hurry up and get out of my house, I'm going to call the police. Then they can see for themselves what you're capable of.'

He had to restrain himself from lunging at her and putting his hands around her throat. Her apparent calm only intensified his rage, and spots began to dance before his eyes.

'Just try it, you shitty fucking bitch!'

'Don't think I wouldn't. Because you can bet I will. You've continually harassed me and my family and threatened and badgered us.' She put her hand to her breast in a histrionic fashion and assumed the martyr expression that he'd learned to hate over the years.

Yet once again she succeeded in pulling off the same trick. To portray him as the villain and herself as the victim. When it was actually just the opposite. He had tried to be the better person, he really had. Tried to remain above the fray and refuse to sink to her level. But a couple of years ago he'd decided that if it was war she wanted, it was war she was going to get. Since then it had been no holds barred.

He again had to restrain himself and simply hissed through clenched teeth: 'You didn't succeed, at any rate. The police didn't seem very inclined to believe your lies about me.'

'Well, there are several other possibilities that the police can investigate,' Lilian said in a nasty tone of voice.

'What do you mean?' Kaj asked, but he answered his own question when he realized what she was getting at. 'You leave Morgan out of this, do you hear me?'

'I hardly need to say a thing.' Her tone was even more malevolent. 'The police will no doubt soon discover for themselves that there's someone living next door who isn't quite right in the head. And everyone knows what someone like that might do. If not, all they have to do is look at the reports on file.'

'Those complaints were pure bullshit, and you know it! Morgan has never even set foot on your property, much less run around looking in your windows.'

'Well, I know what I saw,' said Lilian. 'And the police will work it out as well, as soon as they look through the reports.'

He didn't answer her. There was no use trying.

Then the rage took over.

*   *   *

Deeply engrossed in the papers on his desk, Martin jumped when Patrik knocked on his office door.

'I didn't mean to give you a heart attack,' said Patrik with a smile. 'Are you busy?'

'No, come on in,' he said, waving Patrik in. 'So, how'd it go? Did you find out anything about the family from the teacher? Did he tell you anything?'

'She,' Patrik clarified. 'No, she didn't have much to say,' he said, drumming his hand impatiently on his leg. 'She didn't know of any problems in connection with Sara's family. But we did find out a bit more about Sara. The girl apparently had DAMP and could be quite trying.'

'In what way?' said Martin, who had only a vague understanding of a diagnosis that had become so common in recent years.

'She was excitable, restless and aggressive if she didn't get her way. She also had difficulty concentrating.'

'Sounds like she must have been rather hard to deal with,' said Martin.

Patrik nodded. 'Yes, that's how I interpret it too, even though the teacher didn't come right out and say it, naturally.'

'Did you notice anything like this when you saw Sara before?'

'Erica was the one who saw her more often. I just saw her a few times, and all I remember is that I thought she seemed lively. But nothing that I reacted to.'

'So what exactly is the difference between DAMP and ADHD?' Martin asked. 'It seems to me I've heard both used to describe pretty much the same conditions.'

'No idea,' said Patrik with a shrug. 'And I don't know whether her problem had anything to do with her murder, but we have to start somewhere, don't we?'

Martin nodded and then pointed at the papers in front of him. 'I've checked through the reports we've received about sex crimes in recent years, and there's nothing that really matches. A few reports of offences committed against children by a close family member, but we had to drop the charges because of lack of evidence. We do have one conviction in such a case. You probably recall the father who assaulted his daughter, don't you?'

Patrik nodded. There were few cases that left such a horrid taste in his mouth. 'Torbjörn Stiglund, yeah, but he's probably still in prison, isn't he?'

'Yes, I rang and checked. He hasn't even been out on any furloughs. So we can cross him off the list. As to the rest, they're mostly rapes, but against adults; and then there are a few cases of molestation, also against adults. By the way, a familiar name popped up there.' Martin pointed at the binder that Patrik had last seen on his own desk, but which now lay before his colleague. 'I hope you don't mind that I took the Florin family binder from your office.'

Patrik shook his head. 'No, of course, that's quite all right. And I presume you're alluding to Lilian's complaints against Morgan Wiberg?'

'Yes, she claims that he was sneaking about outside their house and tried to peep in on several occasions when she was changing her clothes.'

'Yeah, I read that,' Patrik said wearily. 'But I honestly don't know how to view all these reports. None of the claims seem to have any basis in reality. They're mostly accusations coming from both sides and a particularly effective way to waste police time and resources.'

'I'm inclined to agree with you. But we can't close our eyes to the fact that there's a potential Peeping Tom in the house next door. You know, sex crimes often start with just that sort of activity,' Martin said.

'I know, but it still seems pretty far-fetched. Suppose that what Lilian Florin says is true – which I strongly doubt. It *is* a grown woman that Morgan was trying to see naked, after all. There's nothing to suggest that he would have any sexual interest in children. Besides, we don't even know if Sara's murder began with a sexual offence. Nothing from the post-mortem indicates that. But it could be worthwhile to check out Morgan more closely. Have a talk with him, at least.'

'Do you think there's any chance I could come with you?' Martin said eagerly. 'Or are you starting to prefer Ernst?'

Patrik grimaced. 'No, that day will never come. As far as I'm concerned, you're welcome to come along. The question is what Mellberg will say about it.'

'Well, we can at least ask. I think he's been a bit calmer the past few days. Who knows, maybe he's mellowing out in his old age.'

'I doubt it,' Patrik said with a laugh. 'But I'll go find out if he'll agree to the plan. We could head over there this afternoon. I've got some paperwork to catch up on first.'

'Fine with me. Then I can finish up with this stuff too,' Martin said, pointing at the stack of reports. 'I hope to have a complete report ready by then. But as I said, don't expect too much; there doesn't seem to be anything that matches.'

Patrik nodded. 'Just do the best you can.'

Gösta had almost dozed off in front of his computer. Only the thud of his chin hitting his chest kept him awake enough that he hadn't completely floated off to dreamland. If only I could put up my feet for a while, he thought. If he could just take a little nap, he'd be ready to plunge into the work later. Like in Spain. People down there understood the value of taking a siesta. But not in Sweden, that's for sure. Here you had to plod through an eight-hour workday while keeping your enthusiasm high and your motivation to work at its peak. What a terrible country he lived in.

The shrill ring of the telephone gave him a start.

'Damn,' he said. His mood didn't improve when he recognized the phone number on the display. What did that old biddy want now? Then he reminded himself that he ought to have a bit more sympathy considering what had happened. So he vowed to be patient and then picked up the receiver.

'Gösta Flygare, Tanumshede police station.'

The voice on the other end was agitated, and he had to ask her to calm down so that he could hear what she wanted to say. It didn't seem to help, so he repeated: 'Lilian, you have to talk a little slower, I can barely understand what you're saying. Now take a deep breath and repeat what you just said.'

That finally seemed to work, and she started over from the beginning. Gösta raised his eyebrows as he listened. This was an unexpected turn of events. After reassuring her repeatedly he got her to hang up at last. He grabbed his jacket and went into Patrik's office.

'Hey, Hedström.' Gösta hadn't bothered to knock, but Patrik was working with his office door open, and in Gösta's opinion it was his own fault if people just walked right in.

'Yes?' Patrik asked.

'I just had a call from Lilian Florin.'

'You did?' Patrik repeated, his interest aroused.

'Something seems to be going on out there. She claims that Kaj assaulted her.'

'What the hell are you saying?' Patrik swivelled in his chair so that he was face to face with Gösta.

'Yeah, she claims that he came home a little while ago and started yelling and screaming, and when she tried to get him to leave, he started punching her.'

'That sounds totally crazy,' said Patrik incredulously.

Gösta shrugged. 'That's what she told me, anyway. I promised we'd come over right away.' He held up his jacket demonstratively.

'Yes, of course,' said Patrik, jumping up from his chair and grabbing his own jacket from the coat rack in the corner.

Twenty minutes later they were back at the Florins' house. Lilian opened the door as soon as they knocked and let them in. As soon as they stepped over the threshold she began wildly waving her arms about.

'Do you see what he did to me?!' She pointed at a slight flush on her cheek and then pulled up the sleeve of her blouse and showed them a red mark on her upper arm. 'If he doesn't go to jail for this, then . . .' She was working herself up even more, and she seemed to have a hard time talking from sheer outrage.

Patrik placed a soothing hand on her uninjured arm and said, 'We're going to take a closer look at this, I promise you. By the way, have you had a doctor examine you?'

She shook her head. 'No, do I have to? He hit me in the face and grabbed my arm hard, but I don't think there are any serious injuries,' she admitted reluctantly. 'Although maybe you need proof in the form of photographs?' Lilian's face lit up for a moment before Patrik was compelled to quash that hope.

'No, that won't be necessary now that we've had a chance to look at it ourselves. We'll go over and have a talk with Kaj. Then we'll decide how to proceed later. Is there anyone you can call to come over?'

Lilian nodded. 'Yes, I can ask my friend Eva.'

'Good. I think you ought to ring her. Then put on a pot of coffee and try to take it easy for a while. This is all going to work out, you'll see.' Patrik tried to sound reassuring, but to be honest there was something in her histrionic behaviour that bothered him. Something didn't feel right.

'Shouldn't I file a formal complaint? Fill out some forms?' asked Lilian hopefully.

'We'll deal with that later. First of all, Patrik and I will have a little talk with Kaj.' Gösta sounded unusually authoritative, but Lilian wouldn't settle for vague promises.

'Don't tell me that you intend to drop the matter, because you're too lazy to intervene when a defenceless woman is subjected to such a horrible attack. Because I don't plan to shut up, that's for sure. First I'll ring your chief, then I'll go to the newspapers if I have to and –'

Gösta interrupted her harangue and said with steel in his voice, 'No one is planning to drop the matter, Lilian, but right now this is what we're going to do: first we'll talk to Kaj, and then we'll take care of the formalities. If you have any objections, you're quite welcome to ring our chief, Bertil Mellberg, at the station and present your complaints. Otherwise we'll come back as soon as we've talked to the accused.'

After a brief internal struggle Lilian looked ready to accept that it was time to back off. 'Well, if that's how it has to be, then I guess I'll go and ring Eva. But I'm counting on you to come back in a little while,' she muttered sullenly. Then she couldn't resist one last demonstrative act: she slammed the door behind them so hard that it echoed through the whole neighbourhood.

'What do you think about all this?' said Patrik, who still couldn't believe that Gösta of all people had succeeded in exercising his authority.

'I don't know, but I . . .' said Gösta, mulling over his words. 'Something doesn't feel quite . . . right.'

'I agree, that's what I think too. Has Kaj ever resorted to violence during all these years of quarrelling?'

'No, and if he had, we would have had a talk about it at once, believe me. On the other hand, he's never had a blatant charge of murder flung in his face before.'

'You're right about that,' replied Patrik. 'But he just doesn't seem like the type that would resort to violence, if you know what I mean. He's more like someone who would try to trip her up if he had the chance.'

'Yeah, I'm inclined to agree with you. But first we'll have to see what he says.'

'I suppose we will,' said Patrik and knocked on the door.

STRÖMSTAD 1924

The minute her father walked in the door, a cold hand gripped Agnes's heart. Something was wrong. Something was seriously wrong. August looked as though he'd aged twenty years since she'd seen him last, and she instantly understood that she must be dying. That was the only thing that could have caused such deep furrows on her father's face in such a short time.

She clutched at her chest and steeled herself for what she was about to hear. But there was something that didn't really fit. The sorrow she expected to see in her father's eyes was conspicuous by its absence; instead they were black with rage. It was a strange response, to say the least. Why would he be angry that she was dying?

Despite his short stature he loomed with an air of menace by the side of the bed where she lay, and Agnes instinctively did her utmost to look as pitiful as possible. That had always worked best on the few occasions her father had been really angry at her. But it didn't seem to be working this time, and her sense of disquiet grew. Then a thought occurred to her. But it was so unbelievable and appalling that she instantly cast it aside.

But the thought returned, without mercy. Then she saw that her father's lips were moving in an attempt to speak, but he was so upset that his vocal cords were unable to produce a sound. That was when she realized in terror that what had been simply a wild speculation was now a distinct possibility.

Slowly she crept even further under the covers. When her

father's hand suddenly came down forcefully on her cheek and she felt the sting of unexpected pain, her misgivings changed to certainty.

'You, you . . .' stammered her father, desperately searching for the words that were trying to issue from his lips. 'You, you slut! Who . . . what?' he continued stammering. From her recumbent position she saw him swallow repeatedly, as if trying to help the words come out. She had never seen her stout, good-natured father like this before, and she found the sight terrifying.

Agnes also felt bewilderment grip her in the midst of her fear. How could this have happened? They had taken the necessary precautions and always stopped in time. In her worst fantasies she had never imagined that she would end up in trouble. Of course she had heard of other girls who got pregnant by accident, but she had always thought scornfully that they must not have been careful enough. They must have let the man go further than he should.

And now here she lay. Her thoughts wandered feverishly in search of a solution. Things had always worked out for her. Surely this situation could be resolved too. She had to make her father understand, as she had always been able to do whenever she had got herself into a mess. Of course it had never been anything this serious, but all her life he had come to her rescue and smoothed the way for her. He would have to do the same now. She felt herself growing calmer after the first shock subsided. Naturally the situation could be handled. Father would be angry for a while, she could stand that, but he would help her out of this predicament. There were places one could go to have something like this fixed, it was merely a matter of money, and at least in that respect she didn't have to worry.

Pleased at having worked out a plan, she opened her mouth to speak and begin cajoling her father. But her words were checked before she could even begin when August's hand again landed on her cheek with a smack. She gazed at him incredulously. She had never imagined that he would take his hand to her, and now he had slapped her twice in short order. The unfairness of his treatment ignited a rage inside her, and she sat up in bed and again opened her mouth to try and explain. Smack! A third slap struck

128

her already tender cheek, and Agnes felt angry tears filling her eyes. What was the meaning of treating her like this? In resignation she sank back on the pillows and stared in both confusion and anger at this father she thought she knew so well. But the man before her was a stranger.

Slowly it began to dawn on Agnes that her life might be about to take a nasty turn.

A cautious knock on the door made Niclas look up. He wasn't expecting a patient, and he was fully occupied going through all the papers that had piled up on his desk. He frowned in annoyance.

'Yes?' His tone was dismissive, and the person outside the door seemed to hesitate. But then the door handle was pressed down and the door slowly swung open.

'Am I interrupting?'

Her voice was just as timorous as he remembered it, and the annoyed frown disappeared at once.

'Mother?' Niclas jumped out of his chair and stared in wonderment at the little woman standing hesitantly in the doorway. She had always aroused his protective instincts, and right now he just wanted to rush over and throw his arms around her. But he knew that she had grown wary of such open displays of emotion over the years. It would only upset her, so he restrained himself and waited for her to take the initiative.

'May I come in? Or are you busy?' She glanced at the piles of papers in front of him and made a move to turn round.

'No, absolutely not, come in, come in.' He felt like a schoolboy and rushed round the desk to pull up a chair for her. She sat down carefully, on the very edge of the seat, and looked around nervously. She had never seen him in his professional role, so he understood that it must seem odd to find him in this environment. In fact, she had hardly seen him at all in years, so that

131

alone must feel strange. As if he had metamorphosed from a seventeen-year-old boy to a grown man in an instant. That thought made anger begin to swell in his chest. There was so much they had denied themselves, he and his mother, because of that nasty old man. Thank goodness Niclas had managed to escape from him, but when he studied his mother he realized that the years had not been kind to her. He saw the same weary, submissive expression on her face as when he'd left, but now made worse by all the new wrinkles she had acquired.

Niclas pulled up a chair next to hers, but not too close, and waited for her to begin. She didn't really seem to know what she had come there to say. After a moment's silence she said, 'I'm so, so sorry about the girl, Niclas.' That was all she said, and all he could do was nod.

'I didn't know her . . . but I wish I had.' Her voice quavered slightly, and he sensed the emotions that lay beneath the surface. It must have been very hard for her to come here. As far as he knew, she had never gone against his father's orders before.

'She was wonderful,' he said, and even though there was a lump in his throat behind the words, no tears came. There had been so many the past few days that he doubted he had any left. 'She had your eyes, but I don't know where she got the red hair.'

'My grandmother had the loveliest red hair you ever saw. It must have been from her' – she hesitated before saying the name but finally managed it – 'that Sara got her red hair.'

Asta looked down at her hands resting in her lap. 'I saw her now and then. Her and the boy. Also saw your wife when she was out walking with them. But I never said anything. We just looked at each other. Now I wish that I'd spoken with the girl at least once. Did she know that she had a grandmother here?'

Niclas nodded. 'I talked a lot about you. She knew your name and we showed her pictures of you as well. The few that I took with me when . . .' He let the words die out. Neither of them dared set foot on the minefield that had caused their estrangement.

'Is it true what I heard?' She raised her eyes and looked straight at him for the first time. 'Did someone harm the girl?'

He tried to answer, but the words lodged deep in his throat. There was so much he wanted to tell her, so many secrets that weighed like an enormous boulder on his chest. He wanted nothing more than to cast it off at her feet. But he could not. Too many years had passed.

Now the tears came which he thought were done. They spilled over and ran down his cheeks. He didn't dare look at his mother, but her instinct conquered all admonitions and prohibitions, and in the next second he felt her fragile arms around his neck. She was so tiny and he was so big, but at that moment the situation seemed reversed.

'There, there.' With practised hands she stroked his back, and he felt the years fall away, and he was a child once more. Safe in his mother's hands. Her warm breath and loving voice in his ear, and assurances that everything would be all right. That the monsters under the bed were really only in his imagination, and that they would disappear if he told them to. But this time the monster was there to stay.

'Does Father know?' he said with his mouth against her shoulder. He knew better than to ask, but he couldn't help it. He felt her stiffen immediately, and he pulled away from the consoling embrace. The magic was broken, and she again sat facing him like a worn-out, grey little old lady, who had sided with his father at the moment when Niclas needed her most. His feelings were so ambivalent. He longed for her and loved her, but he was also filled with bitterness and contempt because she hadn't defended him when he needed her.

'He doesn't know that I'm here,' was all she said, and Niclas saw that mentally she had already walked out the door. But he couldn't let her go yet. If only for another moment, he wanted to keep her here with him, and he knew just how to do it.

'Do you want to see pictures of the children?' he asked softly, and she nodded.

He went over to his desk and pulled out the top drawer. He took out the photo album and handed it to her, careful not to look at it himself. He wasn't ready for that yet.

Deferentially she paged through the photographs, smiling sadly at each picture. What she had lost suddenly became incredibly tangible.

'How lovely they are,' she said with a grandmother's pride in

133

her voice. But the pride was mixed with sorrow that one of the children was now gone for ever.

'You took your wife's surname?' she asked hesitantly, clutching the album tightly on her lap.

'Yes,' said Niclas, his eyes fixed on some point behind her. 'I didn't want to keep his name.'

She just nodded sadly. 'Shouldn't you be getting back to your work?' she added uneasily, looking at him sitting behind the desk.

Niclas plucked aimlessly at the papers before him and swallowed hard to force back the last of his tears.

'I saw no alternative if I wanted to survive,' he continued.

His mother contented herself with that explanation, but the concern in her eyes increased. 'Just don't forget about the ones you still have left,' she said softly, hitting the tender spot in his chest with frightening precision.

But he felt as though he were two people. One person who wanted to be home with Charlotte and Albin and never leave them again, and one who wanted to escape into work, away from the pain that was made worse by sharing it. Above all he didn't want to see his own guilt mirrored in Charlotte's face. That was why his flight instinct had at last won the battle. All this he wanted to tell his mother. He wanted to put his head in her lap, grown man that he was, and tell her everything and then hear her assurances that everything would be all right. But the moment passed, and after placing the photo album on the desk she got up and headed for the door.

'Mother?'

'Yes?' She turned round.

Niclas held out the photo album to her. 'Take this, we have lots more pictures.'

Asta hesitated but then accepted it, as if it were a precious but fragile piece of jewellery. She slipped it carefully into her handbag.

'It's probably best if you hide them properly,' he said quietly with a wry smile, but she had already closed the door behind her.

He stared up at the ceiling and gave the wall a light kick. He couldn't comprehend how it could have turned out this way.

Why him? And why hadn't he objected when it might still have been possible?

The posters on the wall reminded him of who he wanted to be. Normally the heroes surrounding him could motivate him to fight harder, make a greater effort. Today they were just making him mad. They never would have stood for this shit. They would have refused at once. Done what had to be done. That was why they were where they were today. That's why they were heroes. He himself was just a little shit, and he would never be anything else. Just as Rune had always said. He hadn't wanted to believe him when he said that. He had dug in his heels and thought that by God, he was going to show Rune that he was wrong. He would show Rune that he was a hero, and then he'd be sorry, sorry about all those harsh words. All the humiliations. Then he would be the one who had the upper hand, and Rune would have to beg on his bended knee to get even a minute of his time.

The worst thing was that at first he had liked Rune. When his mum first met him he'd thought he was cool as hell. He drove a big American car and had mates who drove trendy choppers, and sometimes they let him ride on the bitch seat. But then they'd gotten married and that's when it all started to go haywire. Suddenly Rune and his mum had to show that they were proper Svenssons, with a house, a Volvo, and even a fucking caravan. The mates with the choppers disappeared, and instead they hung out with other ordinary Svenssons and had dinner parties with couples on Saturday nights. And of course they had to have their own kid. He'd heard Rune say that once to one of the boring neighbour couples. That they needed to have a kid of their own. Naturally he loved Sebastian, he said, but then added in a serious tone of voice that it still wasn't the same thing as having his *own* kid. So when Rune and his mum never managed to produce their own kid, Rune took it out on his stepson. Sebastian had to endure Rune's frustration over the fact that he and his wife never had a kid of their own. And when Mum died of cancer a few years ago, it only got worse. Now Rune was truly saddled with a kid that wasn't his own. He was always pointing this out, no matter how much Sebastian tried to show that he was grateful not to be shipped off to some horrible foster home when his mother died. Rune insisted on taking care of the boy as if he *were* his own. But sometimes Sebastian thought that if this was Rune's idea of how to take care of his own kid, then it was just as well that he and Mum had never had one.

Not that Rune beat him or anything. No, a decent, average Svensson like Rune would never do that. But somehow it would almost have felt better if he had. Then Sebastian would have had something more tangible to hate him for. Instead he now abused him only mentally – something that couldn't be seen on the outside.

As he lay staring at the ceiling Sebastian realized in an instant of clarity why he'd landed in his present situation. In spite of everything he loved his stepfather. Rune was the only father he'd ever known, and Sebastian had never wanted anything but to please him and in the end to be loved in return. And that was exactly why he was in deep shit. He understood this. He wasn't stupid. But what good did it do him to be smart? He was still stuck.

'What the hell are you saying?' Kaj's face turned beet-red, and he looked as though he was going to rush like a raging bull over to the neighbours' house. Patrik discreetly blocked his way and raised his hands in a calming gesture.

'Could we just sit down and talk this over in peace and quiet?'

Fury seemed to prevent the words from registering in Kaj's brain. Patrik and Gösta exchanged a glance. Suddenly it didn't seem so unbelievable that he might have attacked Lilian. But it was dangerous to get stuck thinking along certain lines, and until they had heard Kaj's version of the matter it was best not to draw any conclusions.

After Patrik's words had had a few seconds to sink in, Kaj turned round and stomped into the house. He evidently was expecting Patrik and Gösta to follow him, which they did after taking off their shoes. When they entered the kitchen they found Kaj facing them, leaning on the counter with his arms belligerently crossed over his chest. He freed one hand for a moment and pointed at the kitchen chairs. He obviously wasn't planning to sit down.

'What did that old biddy say now? That I hit her? Is that what she claims?' The colour again rose in his face, and for an instant Patrik was worried that the man would have a heart attack right in front of them.

'We've received a report of assault, yes,' Gösta said calmly, beating Patrik to it.

'So she reported me, that bitch!' Kaj yelled, and small drops of sweat began to appear at his greying temples.

'Officially, Lilian has not filed a complaint – not yet,' Patrik added. 'We wanted a chance to talk to you in peace and quiet first, so we could get to the bottom of this whole thing.' He glanced at his notebook and went on. 'So you went over to Lilian Florin's house about an hour ago?'

Kaj nodded reluctantly. 'I just wanted to hear what the hell she meant by reporting me as a suspect in the killing of that kid. She's done a lot of despicable things over the years, but something so . . .' More drops of sweat appeared, and his rage made him stumble over his words.

'So you walked right into her house?' Gösta asked. He too was starting to look a bit worried about Kaj's health.

'Yeah, what the hell, if I'd knocked she never would have let me in. I just wanted to have a chance to catch her off-guard. Ask her who the hell she thought she was messing with.' A note of anxiety now crept into Kaj's voice for the first time.

'And then what happened?' Patrik was jotting down notes as Kaj talked.

'That's all there was to it!' Kaj threw out his hands. 'I probably yelled at her a bit, I willingly admit it, and she told me to get out of her house. Since I'd said what I came to say, I left.'

'So you didn't hit her?'

'I probably wanted to give her a punch in the nose, but I'm not that fucking stupid.'

'Is that a no?' Patrik asked.

'Yeah, that's a no,' Kaj replied sullenly. 'I didn't touch her, and if she claims I did then she's lying. Which wouldn't surprise me in the least.' Now he was starting to sound really worried.

'Is there anyone who can corroborate your story?' said Gösta.

'No, there isn't. I saw Niclas drive off this morning and I made sure to go over there right after Charlotte left with the little boy in the pushchair.' He wiped his brow with one hand and wiped the sweat on his trouser leg.

'Well, I'm afraid it's your word against hers, unfortunately,' said Patrik. 'And Lilian has marks on her arm.'

Kaj was deflating with each word that Patrik said. His initial aggressiveness had been replaced by resignation. Then he suddenly straightened up.

'What about her husband? He was in the house. Damn, I forgot all about him. He's like a ghost. No one ever sees Stig anymore. But he must have been at home. Maybe he saw or heard something.'

The thought gave him renewed courage, and Patrik looked at Gösta. Imagine, that they hadn't thought of Stig. They hadn't even talked to him about Sara's death. Kaj was right. Stig had been virtually invisible as far as the investigation was concerned up till now. They'd completely forgotten about him.

'We'll go and talk to him as well,' said Patrik. 'Then we'll see what develops. But if he has nothing to add, things won't look too good for you if Lilian decides to press charges . . .'

He didn't need to explain his reasoning. Kaj was well aware of the possible consequences.

Charlotte was walking around town aimlessly. Albin was sleeping peacefully in his pushchair. Ever since she'd stopped taking the sedatives she had barely been able to bring herself to look at him. And yet she did what she had to do. She changed him, dressed him and fed him, but mechanically, without any feeling. Because what if it should happen again? Imagine if something happened to him too. She didn't even know how she could go on living without Sara. She put one foot before the other, forcing herself to move forward. But she actually wanted nothing more than to sink down into a little heap in the middle of the pavement and never get up again. Yet she couldn't allow herself to do that, nor could she allow herself to sink into the fog of medication again. Because, despite everything, Albin was still here. Even though she couldn't look at him, she felt in every nerve in her body that she still had one child who was very much alive. And for his sake she had to keep on breathing. But it was just so hard.

And then there was Niclas, who had retreated to work. It was only three days since their daughter was murdered, and he was already back in his office at the clinic, treating colds and minor injuries. Maybe he was even chatting casually with the patients, flirting with the nurses, and enjoying seeing himself in the role of the almighty doctor. Charlotte knew that she was being unfair. She knew that Niclas was suffering as much as she was. She just wished that they could have shared the pain, instead of each of them trying separately to find a reason to keep breathing for another minute, and then another and another. It wasn't what she wanted, but she couldn't help feeling anger and contempt because he had abandoned her now when she needed him most. On the other hand, perhaps she shouldn't have expected anything else. When had she ever been able to lean on him? When had he ever been anything but an overgrown child who counted on her to take care of all the dreary chores that shaped the daily lives of most people? But not his. He was supposed to have the right to play his way through life. To do only what was fun and enjoyable. It had surprised her that he'd even completed his medical studies. She had never believed that he would last long enough to get through all the obligatory stages and exhausting shiftwork. But the potential rewards had probably been tempting enough to keep him motivated. He wanted to be respected by others. A happy and successful person. At least outwardly.

The only reason she had stayed with him was because she would occasionally catch glimpses of that other man. The one who was vulnerable and could show what he was feeling. The one who dared reveal his true self and didn't have to keep his charm turned up to the max at all times. It was those glimpses that had made her fall in love with Niclas, though that now felt like a lifetime ago. In recent years those occasions had come less and less frequently, and she no longer knew who he was or what he wanted. Sometimes, in her weaker moments, she had wondered whether he actually wanted to have a family at all. To be brutally honest with herself, she believed that if given the choice he would have preferred a life without the obligations of a family. But he had to be getting something out of it, or else she didn't think he would have stayed as long as he had done. During the recent dark days she'd hoped in moments of selfishness that what had happened might at least bring her and Niclas closer together. But she had been very wrong about that. They were now farther from each other than ever before.

Without even noticing, Charlotte had walked towards Fjällbacka Campground and now stood in front of Erica's house. It had meant a great deal that her friend had come by yesterday, but Charlotte still had doubts. She had spent her whole life trying to take up as little space as possible, never demanding anything for herself, never causing any trouble. She understood how her grief affected other people, and she wasn't sure that she wanted to dump more of that burden on Erica. At the same time she really needed to see a friendly face. She wanted to talk to someone who wouldn't either turn away or, as in her mother's case, take the opportunity to tell her what she should have done.

Albin had begun to squirm, and she cautiously lifted him out of the pushchair. Still half asleep, he looked around and then gave a start when Charlotte knocked on the front door. A middle-aged woman she didn't know opened the door.

'Hello?' said Charlotte uncertainly, but then realized that this must be Patrik's mother. A vague memory from the distant time before Sara's death floated up to the surface and reminded her that Erica had mentioned that her mother-in-law was coming to visit.

'Hello, are you looking for Erica?' said Patrik's mother. Without waiting for a reply she stepped aside to let Charlotte into the hall.

'Is she awake?' Charlotte asked cautiously.

'Yes she is, she's nursing Maja. I've stopped counting how many times she's done that today. Well, I suppose I don't really understand modern customs. In my day children were fed every four hours, and never more than that, and that generation certainly has nothing to complain about.' Patrik's mother babbled on, and Charlotte nervously followed her. After people had been tiptoeing around her for several days, it felt odd to hear someone speaking in a normal tone of voice. Then she saw it dawn on Erica's mother-in-law who she must be, and the ease vanished from both her voice and her movements. She clapped her hand to her mouth and said, 'Forgive me, I didn't realize who you were.'

Charlotte didn't know what to reply to that. Her only response was to hold Albin closer.

'I really apologize . . .' Erica's mother-in-law was shifting anxiously from one foot to another, and she seemed to want to be anywhere else but in Charlotte's presence.

Was this how it was going to be from now on? thought Charlotte. People shrinking away as if she had the plague, whispering and pointing behind her back and saying, 'There's the woman whose daughter was murdered,' but without daring to look her in the eye. Maybe it was out of nervousness, because they had no idea what to say, or maybe it was from some sort of irrational fear that tragedies were contagious and might spread to their own lives if they got too close.

'Charlotte?' Erica called from the living room, and the older woman was obviously relieved to have an excuse to leave. Slowly and a bit hesitantly Charlotte went in to see Erica, who was sitting in her easy chair breast-feeding Maja. The scene felt both familiar and yet oddly remote. How many times in the past two months had she come in and encountered the same scene? But that thought also conjured up an image of Sara in her mind's eye. The last time Charlotte was here, Sara had come along. From a purely intellectual point of view she knew that it was only last Sunday, but she still had a hard time comprehending it. She saw before her how Sara had bounced up and down on the white sofa, with her long red hair flying about her face. She remembered admonishing her. Telling her sharply to stop. It all felt so petty now. What harm would it have done if she jumped on the cushions a bit? The thought made her suddenly dizzy, and Erica had to jump up and help her sit down in the nearest easy chair. Maja shrieked when Erica's breast was so brusquely snatched out of her mouth, but Erica ignored her daughter's protests and put her in the bouncing cradle.

With Erica's arms around her Charlotte dared to voice the question that had nagged at her subconscious ever since the police arrived with the news of Sara's death on Monday. She said, 'Why didn't they get hold of Niclas?'

141

STRÖMSTAD 1924

Anders had just finished work on the plinth of the statue when the foreman called to him from over in the quarry. He sighed and frowned; he didn't like having his concentration being disturbed. But of course he had to obey, as usual. Carefully he put his tools into his toolbox next to the granite block and went to hear what the foreman had to say.

The fat man was nervously twirling his moustache.

'What have you gone and done now, Andersson?' he said, half in jest, half concerned.

'Me? What is it?' said Anders, removing his work gloves and giving the man a bewildered look.

'The front office is calling for you. You have to go down there. Right now.'

Damn it all, Anders swore silently. Was there something else that had to be changed on the statue now, at the eleventh hour? Those architects, or 'artists', or whatever they chose to call themselves, had no idea what they were doing when they sat in their studios and redrew their sketches. Then they expected the stone-cutter to be able to make the changes just as easily in stone. They didn't understand that from the beginning he had planned the directions of the cleavages and marked the places where he had to cut, based on the original drawing. A change in the sketch would change his entire starting point, and in the worst case the stone might crack so that all the work had been done in vain.

But Anders also knew that it was no use to protest. It was

the client who made the decisions. He was merely a faceless slave who was expected to perform all the hard work that the person who had designed the statue could not or would not do himself.

'Well, I suppose I'll have to go down there and hear what they want,' said Anders with a sigh.

'It might not be anything major,' said the foreman, who knew precisely what Anders feared and was showing some sympathy for a change.

'Well, no use putting it off,' replied Anders as he slouched off towards the road.

A while later he knocked awkwardly on the door of the office and stepped inside. He wiped off his shoes as best he could, but realized that it didn't make much difference, since his clothes were full of granite dust and chips, and his hands and face were dirty. But he'd been compelled to come down here on short notice, so they would have to take him as he was. He plucked up his courage and followed the man from the front office into the director's private office.

A hasty look around the room made his heart sink to his stomach. He understood at once that this summons had nothing to do with the statue. Much more serious matters were about to be discussed.

There were only three people in the room. The director sat behind his desk and his entire visage radiated controlled rage. In one corner sat Agnes staring hard at the floor. And in front of the desk sat a man Anders did not know, looking at him with poorly concealed curiosity.

Unsure of how to act, Anders stepped about a yard into the room and took up an almost military stance. No matter what was to come, he would take it like a man. Sooner or later they would have ended up in this situation; he just wished he could have chosen the circumstances.

He sought Agnes's eyes, but she stubbornly refused to look up and kept staring at her shoes. His heart ached for her. She must find all this incredibly difficult. But they still had each other, and after the worst of the storm subsided they could begin building their life together.

144

Anders turned his gaze from Agnes and calmly regarded the man behind the desk. He waited for Agnes's father to speak. It took a very long time before that happened, and the hands of the clock seemed to move unbearably slowly. When August Stjernkvist finally spoke, his voice had a cool, metallic tone.

'I understand that you and my daughter have been meeting in secret.'

'Circumstances have forced us to it, yes,' replied Anders calmly. 'But I have never had anything but honourable intentions with respect to Agnes,' he went on, looking Stjernkvist in the eye. For a second he thought he saw surprise in the director's face. This was apparently not the reply he had anticipated.

'I see, well.' Stjernkvist cleared his throat to gain time and decide how to handle this statement. Then his anger returned.

'And how had you intended to do that? A rich girl and a poor stonecutter. Are you so stupid that you believed that was even possible?'

Anders reeled at the scornful tone in the man's voice. Had he acted stupidly? All his decisiveness started to give way before the contempt bombarding him, and he realized at once how absurd the idea sounded when said aloud. Obviously that could never be possible. He felt his heart slowly breaking into bits and desperately sought out Agnes's glance. Was this going to be the end? Would he never see her again? She still didn't look up.

'Agnes and I love each other,' he said quietly, hearing how he sounded like a condemned man offering his last words of defence.

'I know my daughter considerably better than you do, boy. And I know her considerably better than she thinks I do. Of course, I did spoil her and allowed her greater freedom than she probably should have had, but I also know that she's a girl with ambitions. She never would have sacrificed everything for a future with a labourer.'

The words stung like fire, and Anders wanted to scream that he was wrong. Her father was not describing the Agnes he knew, not at all. She was good and kind, and above all she loved him just as passionately as he loved her. She was certainly prepared to make the sacrifices necessary for them to be able to live together. With sheer force of will he tried to make her look up and tell her father how things really stood, but she remained silent and dismissive. Gradually the ground began to give way beneath him. Not only was he about to lose Agnes, he understood quite well that given these conditions he wouldn't be allowed to keep his job either.

Stjernkvist spoke again, and now Anders thought he could sense pain behind the anger. 'But things have suddenly taken on a new light. Under normal circumstances I would have done everything I could to stop my daughter from ending up with a stonecutter. But the two of you have already seen to that by presenting me with an accomplished fact.'

In bewilderment Anders wondered what he was talking about.

Stjernkvist saw his puzzled expression and continued. 'She's expecting a child, of course. You two must be complete idiots not to have thought of that eventuality.'

Anders gasped for breath. He was inclined to agree with Agnes's father. They had indeed been idiots. He had been just as convinced as Agnes was that the precautions they had taken were fully sufficient. Now everything was changed. His feelings were swirling about, making him even more confused. On the one hand, he couldn't help feeling happy that his beloved Agnes would be bearing his child; on the other hand he was ashamed before her father and understood his rage. He too would have been furious if anyone had done such a thing to his daughter. Anders waited tensely for the director to go on.

Mournfully, August Stjernkvist said, still refusing to look at his daughter, 'Naturally there is only one solution. You will have to get married, and to that end I have called in Judge Flemming today. He will marry you at once, and we will deal with the formalities afterwards.'

Over in her corner Agnes now looked up for the first time. To Anders's astonishment he saw no joy in her eyes, but only desperation. Her tone of voice was entreating when she spoke. 'Father dear, please don't force me into this. There are other ways to solve the problem, and you can't force me to marry him. After all, he's only a simple . . . worker.'

The words felt like the lash of a whip against Anders's face. He seemed to see her for the first time, as if she had metamorphosed into someone else before his eyes.

'Agnes?' he said, as if begging her to remain the girl he loved, even though he already knew that all his dreams were now crashing down around him.

She ignored him and continued desperately appealing to her father. But August wouldn't condescend to give her even a glance. He looked only at the judge and said, 'Do what you need to do.'

'Please, Father!' Agnes shrieked, throwing herself to her knees in a dramatic plea.

'Silence!' said her father turning his cold eyes on her at last. 'Don't make yourself ridiculous. I don't intend to tolerate any hysterical ploys from you. You've made your bed, and now you have to lie in it!' he shouted. His daughter shut up at once.

With a pained look on her face, Agnes reluctantly got to her feet and let the judge carry out his task. It was an odd wedding, with the bride sullenly standing a few yards from the bridegroom. But the reply to the judge's question was 'yes' from each of them, although with much reluctance from one side and much confusion from the other.

'So, now that's done,' August asserted after the businesslike ceremony was completed. 'Of course I can't have you working here any longer,' he said. Anders merely bowed his head to confirm that this was what he expected. His new father-in-law went on, 'But no matter how badly you have behaved, I can't leave my daughter penniless; I owe her mother that much.'

Agnes looked at him tensely, still with a small hope that she wouldn't have to lose everything.

'I have arranged a position for you at the quarry in Fjällbacka. One of the other cutters can finish the statue. I've also paid the first month's rent for a room with a kitchen in one of the barracks. After that month you'll have to manage on your own.'

Agnes let out a whimper. She put her hand to her throat as if she were about to choke, and Anders felt as though he were aboard a ship that was slowly sinking. If he still harboured any hopes of building a future with Agnes, they were crushed for good when he saw the contempt with which she regarded her new husband.

'Dear, beloved Father, please,' she again entreated. 'You can't do this to me. I would rather take my own life than move into a stinking hovel with that man.'

Anders grimaced at her words. Had it not been for the child he would have turned on his heel and left, but a real man took care of his obligations no matter how difficult the circumstances. That had been imprinted on him since he was a boy. So he remained standing in the room that now felt suffocatingly small and tried to imagine his future with a woman who obviously found him repulsive. She was now his companion for life.

'What's done is done,' said August to his daughter. 'You have the afternoon to gather up whatever possessions you can carry, then the carriage leaves for Fjällbacka. Choose your belongings wisely. You probably won't have much use for your party dresses,' he added spitefully, showing how deeply his daughter had wounded him. His soul would never recover from this.

When the door closed behind them the silence was thundering. Then Agnes looked at Anders with so much hatred that he had to dig in his heels so as not to flinch. An inner voice whispered to him to flee while there was still time, but his feet wouldn't budge. They felt as if they were nailed to the floor.

A premonition of bad times ahead made him shudder.

Morgan saw the police officers arrive and then leave again. But he didn't waste time wondering what business they had in his parents' house. He wasn't one to brood.

He stretched. It was now late afternoon and he had been sitting almost the whole day at his computer, as usual. His mother worried about what it would do to his back, but he saw no reason to be concerned about that before something actually happened. Of course his back had started to be rather hunched, but he felt no pain. As long as the problem was merely one of appearance it was nothing that his brain registered. For someone who wasn't normal anyway it didn't matter if he was a little hunchbacked as well.

It was a relief to be able to sit in peace. Now that the girl was gone, that disturbing element had vanished. He had really not liked her. Really. She was always coming in to bother him when he was most engrossed in his work, and she pretended not to hear when he told her to leave. The other children were afraid of him. They contented themselves with pointing their fingers behind his back the few times he showed himself outside the walls of the house. But not her. She kept intruding, demanding attention and refusing to be scared off when he yelled at her. Sometimes he'd been so frustrated that he had stood there screaming with his hands over his ears in the hope that it would make her leave. But she had only laughed. So it was really great that she wouldn't be coming back. Not ever.

Death fascinated him. There was something about the finality of it that kept his brain preoccupied with death in all its forms. The games he most enjoyed were the ones that had a lot of death in them. Blood and death.

Occasionally he had considered taking his own life. Not so much because he no longer wanted to live, but because he wanted to see what it was like to be dead. In the past he had made known his intentions. Said straight out to his parents that he was thinking of killing himself. Just as a matter of sharing information. But their reactions had made him keep such thoughts to himself nowadays. There had been a tremendous row, followed by more visits to the psychologist, at the same time that they, or rather his mother, had begun to watch him around the clock. Morgan had not liked that.

He didn't understand why everyone was so afraid of death. All the incomprehensible emotions that other people seemed to possess became more intense and numerous as soon as the talk turned to death. He really couldn't understand it. Death was a state of being, just like life. Why should one be better than the other?

Most of all he would have liked to be present when they cut into the girl at the post-mortem, be allowed to stand by and watch. See what it was that other people found so terrifying. Maybe the answer would be there when they opened her up. Maybe the answer would be in the faces of the people who cut her open.

Sometimes he dreamed that he was lying in a morgue himself. On a cold metal table, with nothing to hide his naked body. In his dreams he saw the steel gleaming just before the pathologist made the straight cut along his thorax.

But he never told anyone about these thoughts. Then they might think he was truly crazy, not merely different from everyone else, which was a label that he'd learned to live with over the years.

Morgan went back to the code on the computer screen. He enjoyed the calm and the silence. It was really great that she was gone.

Lilian opened the door before they had a chance to knock. Patrik suspected that she had been watching for them ever since they left. In the hall stood a pair of shoes that hadn't been there before, and Patrik assumed they belonged to Lilian's friend Eva who'd come over to lend her moral support.

'So,' said Lilian. 'What did he have to say in his defence? Can we finish that report now, so that you can take him in?'

Patrik took a deep breath. 'We'd just like to have a little talk with your husband first, before we proceed with a report. There are still a few things that seem unclear.'

For a second he saw uncertainty pass over her face, but she regained her belligerent expression at once.

'That's absolutely out of the question. Stig is ill. He's upstairs in bed resting and can't be disturbed under any circumstances.' Her voice sounded strained with a hint of nervousness to it. Patrik could see that Lilian had also forgotten about Stig as a potential witness. So it was even more important that they be allowed to talk with him.

'Unfortunately it can't be helped. I'm sure he could see us for a minute or two,' said Patrik in the most authoritative voice he could muster, taking off his jacket at the same time to emphasize his intent.

Lilian was just about to open her mouth to protest when Gösta said in his most official police tone of voice, 'If we aren't allowed to speak to Stig, it might be considered a matter of obstruction of justice. It wouldn't look good in the official report.'

Patrik was doubtful whether his colleague's assertion would hold in the long run, but it seemed to have the desired effect on Lilian, who furiously strode toward the stairs. When it looked as though she planned to go upstairs with them, Gösta placed a firm hand on her shoulder.

'We can find our way, thanks.'

'But . . .' Her eyes flickered, searching for some other valid protests, but she finally had to give up.

'Well, don't say that I didn't warn you. Stig is *not* doing well, and if he gets worse because you go stomping in and asking a lot of questions, then . . .'

They left the statement hanging as they went up the stairs. The guest room lay directly to the left, and since Lilian had left the door open, it wasn't hard to locate her spouse. Stig was ensconced in the bed, but he was awake and had turned his head towards the door in anticipation. Judging by how well Lilian's excited voice was now carrying up from the kitchen, he had no doubt heard that they were on their way up. Patrik entered the room before Gösta and had to force himself not to gasp. The man lying in bed was so frail and emaciated that his bones under the covers seemed to jut out in relief. His cheeks were sunken, and his skin had a grey, unhealthy colour. His hair had turned prematurely white, making him look considerably older than he was. There was a nauseating odour of illness in the room, and Patrik had to suppress a desire to breathe only through his mouth.

Dubiously he reached out a hand to Stig to introduce himself. Gösta did the same, and then they looked around the tiny room for a place to sit down. It felt altogether too officious to stand towering over Stig as he lay there in his sickbed. Stig raised a greyish hand and pointed to the edge of the bed.

'Unfortunately this is all I can offer you.' His voice was dry and feeble, and Patrik was again shocked at how utterly exhausted he looked. This man looked far too ill to be at home. He should be in hospital. But it was none of his business, and there was a doctor living in the house, after all.

Patrik and Gösta sat down cautiously on the edge of the bed. Stig grimaced a little when the bed bounced, and Patrik hurried to apologize, afraid that they had caused him pain. Stig waved off the apology.

Patrik cleared his throat. 'First of all, I'd like to start by offering my condolences for the loss of your granddaughter.' Again he heard how formal his voice sounded, a tone that he himself despised.

Stig closed his eyes and seemed to collect himself to reply. The words had obviously stirred up emotions that he was struggling to overcome.

'Technically, Sara was not really my grandchild – her grandfather, Charlotte's father, died eight years ago – but in my heart she always was. I've cared about her from when she was a little baby until . . .' he paused, 'now at the end.' He closed his eyes again, but when he opened them he seemed to have regained his composure.

'We've talked a bit with the rest of the family,' said Patrik, 'to find out exactly what happened that morning. I wonder whether you might have heard anything in particular. For example, do you know what time Sara left the house?'

Stig shook his head. 'I take strong sleeping pills and don't usually wake up before around ten. And by then she was already . . . gone.' He closed his eyes once more.

'When we asked your wife whether she could think of anyone who may have wanted to harm Sara, she named your neighbour, Kaj Wiberg. Do you agree with that assessment?'

'Did Lilian say that Kaj murdered Sara?' Stig looked at them sceptically.

'Well, not in so many words, but she hinted that there were reasons why your neighbour might wish your family ill.'

Stig let out a long sigh. 'Well, I've never understood what it is with those two. The feud was already going on before I came into the picture, before Lennart died. To be honest, I don't know who cast the first stone, and I daresay that Lilian is just as capable of keeping the feud going as Kaj is. I've tried to stay out of it as much as possible, but it's not easy.' He shook his head. 'No, I don't really understand why they carry on the way they do. I know my wife as a warm, sympathetic woman, but when it comes to Kaj and his family she seems to have a blind spot. You know, sometimes I think that she and Kaj actually enjoy the whole thing. That they live for the sake of the battle. But that sounds absurd. Why would anyone voluntarily keep it up the way they do, with legal action and everything? And it's cost us plenty of money. Kaj can afford it, but we're not as well off, retired as we both are. No, why would anyone want to keep on fighting like this?'

The question was purely rhetorical. Stig wasn't expecting an answer.

'Have they ever come to blows?' Patrik asked with interest.

'Good Lord, no,' Stig said emphatically. 'They aren't that crazy.' He laughed.

Patrik and Gösta exchanged a glance. 'Did you hear that Kaj was over here earlier today?'

'Yes, I could hardly avoid hearing it,' said Stig. 'There was a frightful commotion down in the kitchen, and he was shouting and carrying on. But Lilian threw him out with his tail between his legs.' He looked at Patrik. 'I don't really understand some people. I mean, regardless of what problems they've had with each other, one would think that he'd show a little sympathy, considering what's happened. With Sara, I mean.'

Patrik agreed that sympathy should have been the prevailing response in recent days, but unlike Stig he didn't put all the blame on Kaj. Lilian had also displayed an alarming lack of respect for the situation. He felt a nasty suspicion taking shape in his mind. He continued his questions, wanting to have it confirmed. 'Did you see Lilian after Kaj was here?' He held his breath.

'Of course,' said Stig, who seemed to wonder why Patrik was asking. 'She came upstairs with some tea and told me how shamelessly Kaj had behaved.'

Now Patrik was beginning to understand why Lilian had looked so uneasy when they told her they wanted to talk to Stig. She had made a tactical error in forgetting about her husband.

'Did you notice anything different about her?' Patrik asked.

'Different? How do you mean? She looked a little upset, but that's no wonder.'

'Nothing to indicate that she'd been slapped in the face?'

'Slapped in the face? No, absolutely not. Who's making that accusation?' Stig looked bewildered, and Patrik almost felt sorry for him.

'Lilian claims that Kaj assaulted her when he was here. And she showed us injuries, including on her face, to prove it.'

'But she didn't have any injuries on her face after Kaj was here. I don't understand . . .' Stig stirred restlessly, which evoked another grimace of pain.

Patrik's expression was stern as he signalled with his eyes to Gösta that they were done.

'We're going to go downstairs and have another talk with your wife,' he said, trying to get up as carefully as possible.

'Yes, but who could have . . .?'

They left Stig lying there with a confused look on his face. Patrik suspected that he would probably be having a serious talk with his wife after they left. But first they were going to have a serious talk with her.

He was seething inside as they went downstairs. It was no more

154

than three days since Sara had died, and Lilian was already trying to use her death as a weapon in a petty feud. It was so . . . callous that he could hardly conceive it was possible. What incensed him most was the fact that she was wasting police time and resources when they needed to focus all their energy on finding the person who had murdered her only grandchild. The fact that Lilian hadn't given a thought to the consequences was so despicable and perverse that he could barely find words to describe her actions.

When they entered the kitchen he saw from Lilian's expression that she knew the battle was lost.

'We just got some interesting information from Stig,' Patrik said ominously. Lilian's friend Eva looked at them curiously. She had no doubt swallowed Lilian's story hook, line and sinker, but in a few minutes she might well see her friend in a new light.

'I don't understand why you persist in bothering someone who's sick in bed, but the police clearly have no consideration for anyone nowadays,' Lilian sputtered in an abortive attempt to regain control.

'You're certainly right about that,' said Gösta, calmly sitting down on one of the kitchen chairs facing Lilian and Eva. Patrik pulled out a chair next to him and sat down too.

'It was a good idea that we had a word with Stig as well, because he made a remarkable statement. Perhaps you'd be willing to help out by explaining it.'

Lilian didn't ask what sort of statement her husband had made. She waited in furious silence for them to continue. It was Gösta who spoke next.

'He said that you came up to his room after Kaj left, and that there were no signs that anyone had struck you. Nor did you mention it to him. Can you explain that?'

'I suppose it takes a while before the marks are visible,' Lilian muttered in a brave attempt to salvage the situation. 'And I didn't want to worry Stig, considering his condition. I'm sure you understand.'

They understood more than that. And she knew it.

Patrik took over. 'I hope you realize the seriousness of fabricating false accusations.'

'I didn't fabricate anything,' said Lilian, flaring up. In a somewhat calmer tone she said, 'Well, maybe I . . . exaggerated a bit.

But only because he was on the verge of attacking me. I could see it in his eyes.'

'And the injuries you showed us?'

She said nothing, nor did she need to. They had already worked out that Lilian had inflicted them on herself before they arrived. For the first time Patrik began to wonder whether there was actually something wrong with her mind.

Obstinately she said, 'But it was only because you needed a reason to take him in for questioning. Then you could have searched in peace and quiet for proof that he or Morgan murdered Sara. I know it was one of them, and I just wanted to help put you on the right track.'

Patrik gave her an incredulous look. Either she was more single-minded than anyone he'd ever met, or she was simply a little crazy. In any case, they needed to put a stop to these idiocies.

'In future we'd appreciate it if you let us do our job. And leave the Wiberg family alone. Is that understood?'

Lilian nodded, but they could see that she was furious. During the whole conversation her friend had watched her with astonishment. Now she made a point of leaving at the same time Patrik and Gösta did. That friendship had no doubt suffered a shock.

They didn't discuss Lilian's story on the way back to the station. The whole thing was much too depressing.

Stig felt a pang of unease as he lay in bed. He knew that Lilian would be angry now, but he didn't quite know what he could have done differently. She had looked completely normal when she came up to his room. He just didn't understand all this nonsense about Kaj assaulting her. Why would she lie about something like that?

The footsteps on the stairs sounded as angry as he had feared. For an instant he wanted to pull the covers over his head and pretend to be asleep, but he thought better of it. Surely it couldn't be such a big deal. He had simply told the truth; Lilian had to realize that. And besides, the whole thing must have been a mistake.

The expression on her face said more than he wanted to know. Evidently she was furious with him, and Stig literally cringed under her gaze. He always found it extremely unpleasant when she was in one of these moods. He couldn't understand how someone like his Lilian, who was so amiable and warm, could occasionally be transformed into such a disagreeable person. Suddenly he wondered whether what the police had hinted at really might be true. Had she made up an accusation against Kaj? But he dismissed the idea. They just needed to straighten out this misunderstanding, and then he would grasp the situation.

'Can't you ever keep your big mouth shut?' She loomed over him, and her sharp tone of voice sent lightning bolts through his head.

'But my dear, I only told –'

'The truth? Is that what you wanted to say? That you simply told them the truth? How fortunate we all are to have such upright people as you, Stig. Honest, honourable people who don't give a damn whether they put their own wife in jeopardy. I thought you were supposed to be on my side.'

He felt saliva spray across his face and hardly recognized the distorted face hovering above him.

'But I'm always on your side, Lilian. I just didn't know . . .'

'Didn't know? Do I have to spell out everything for you, you stupid idiot?'

'But you didn't say anything to me . . . and the police are probably just imagining the whole absurd thing. I mean, you wouldn't make up things like that, would you?' Stig was struggling bravely to find some sort of logic in the rage that was directed at him. Only now did he notice the mark on Lilian's face that was starting to take on a purplish hue. His eyes narrowed and he gave her a searching look.

'What's that mark you have on your face, Lilian? You didn't have it when you came up to see me. Are you saying that what the police hinted at was right? Did you make up a story about Kaj hitting you when he was here?' His voice was incredulous, but he saw Lilian's shoulders droop a bit and needed no further confirmation.

'Why on earth would you do something so stupid?' Now their roles were reversed. Stig's voice was sharp, and Lilian sank down on the edge of the bed, burying her face in her hands.

'I don't know, Stig. I can see now that it was stupid, but I wanted them to start looking at Kaj and his family seriously. I'm positive that somehow they're mixed up in Sara's death. Haven't I always told you that man is totally lacking in scruples? And that weird Morgan, sneaking about in the bushes and spying on me. Why don't the police do something?'

Her body was shaking with sobs, and Stig summoned his last strength to sit up in bed despite the pain and put his arms around his wife. He stroked her back reassuringly, but his eyes were restless and searching.

When Patrik came home, Erica was sitting alone in the dark, thinking. Kristina had taken Maja out for a walk, and Charlotte had long since gone home. What Charlotte had said was worrying her.

When Erica heard Patrik open the front door she got up and went to meet him.

'Why are you sitting here in the dark?' He set a couple of grocery bags on the counter and began turning on lamps. The glare blinded her for a second before she got used to it. Then she sat down heavily at the kitchen table and watched her husband as he unpacked what he had bought.

'How pleasant things are here at home,' he said cheerfully, looking around. 'It certainly is nice that Mamma can come by and help out occasionally,' he went on, unaware that Erica was giving him the evil eye.

'Oh yes, it's just peachy,' she said acidly. 'It must be wonderful to come home to a clean and well-organized home for a change.'

'Yeah, it sure is!' said Patrik, still clueless that he was digging his own grave deeper with each passing second.

'Then maybe you should see about staying home in future, so things will be more orderly around here!' Erica yelled.

Patrik jumped from her sudden increase in volume. He turned round with an astonished look on his face.

'What did I say now?'

Erica got up from her chair and stormed out. Sometimes he was too stupid for words. If he didn't get it, she didn't have the energy to explain.

She sat down again in the dim light of the living room and looked out of the window. The weather outside precisely reflected how she felt inside. Grey, stormy, raw and cold. Deceptively calm periods with occasional strong storms. Tears began running down her cheeks. Patrik came and sat down beside her on the sofa.

'I'm sorry for being so dumb. It must not be that easy to have Mamma here in the house, is it?'

She could feel her lower lip quivering. She was so tired of crying. She felt she hadn't done anything else these past few months. If only she'd been prepared for how it would be. The contrast was so great to the joy she'd always believed she would feel when she had a baby. In her darkest moments she almost hated Patrik because he didn't feel the same way she did. The rational part of her was relieved because someone had to keep the family going. But she wished that for just a moment he could put himself in her situation and understand how she felt.

As if he was able to read her thoughts he said, 'I wish I could change places with you, I really do. But I can't, so you have to stop being so bloody brave and tell me what's going on with you. Maybe you should even go and talk with someone else, a professional. The people at the child care centre could probably help us out.'

Erica shook her head. Her depression would surely pass of its own accord. It had to. Besides, there were women who had it much worse than she did.

'Charlotte stopped by today,' she said.

'How's she doing?' Patrik said quietly.

'Better, whatever that means.' She paused. 'Are you getting anywhere?'

Patrik leaned back in the sofa and looked up at the ceiling. He heaved a deep sigh and said, 'No, unfortunately. We hardly know where to start. And besides, Charlotte's screwy mother seems to be more interested in finding more ammunition for her feud with her neighbour than in helping us with the investigation. It hasn't made our work any easier.'

'What's that all about?' Erica asked with interest. Patrik gave her a brief rundown of the day's events.

'Do you really think anyone in Sara's family could have had anything to do with her death?' Erica asked.

'No, I have a hard time believing that,' said Patrik. 'They all have plausible alibis for where they were that morning.'

'They do?' said Erica in an odd tone of voice. Patrik was about to ask what she meant when they heard the front door open and Kristina came in with Maja in her arms.

'I don't know what you've done to this child,' she said in annoyance. 'She was screaming the whole way back in the pram and refuses to settle down. This is what happens when you keep picking her up just because she frets a little. You're spoiling her. You and your sister never cried this much . . .'

Patrik interrupted her harangue by going over to take Maja. Erica could hear from Maja's cries that she was hungry, and she sat down with a sigh in the easy chair, undid her nursing bra, and plucked out a shapeless, milk-soaked pad. It was time again . . .

As soon as she entered the house Monica felt that something was wrong. Kaj's anger streamed towards her like sound waves through the air, and she promptly felt even more exhausted. What was it this time? She had tired of his hot temper long ago, but she couldn't recall that he'd ever been any different. They had been together since their early teens, and maybe back then his shifting moods had seemed exciting and attractive. She couldn't even remember any longer. Not that it mattered; life had run its own course. She got pregnant, they got married, Morgan was born, and then one day piled on top of another. Their sex life had been dead for years; she had long ago moved into her own bedroom. Maybe there was something more than this to life, but she had become accustomed to the way things were. Of course she had toyed with the thought of divorce from time to time. On one occasion, almost twenty years ago, she had even packed a bag in secret and was ready to take Morgan with her and leave. But then she'd decided to fix dinner for Kaj first, iron a few shirts, and run the washing machine so that she wouldn't leave a bunch of dirty clothes behind. Before she knew it she'd quietly unpacked her suitcase.

Monica went out to the kitchen. She knew she would find Kaj there because it was where he always sat when he was upset about something. Maybe because he could keep an eye on the usual cause of his agitation. Now he had pulled the curtain aside a crack and was staring at the house next door.

'Hi,' Monica said, but got no civilized greeting in reply. Instead he immediately launched into a long hate-filled tirade.

'Do you know what that bitch did today?' He didn't wait for an answer, nor did Monica intend to give him one. 'She called the police and claimed that I assaulted her! Showed them some fucking marks she'd inflicted on herself and said *I* was the one who hit her. She's off her bloody rocker!'

When Monica came into the kitchen she was determined not to get drawn into Kaj's latest dispute, but this was far worse than she'd expected. Against her will she felt anger rising up in her chest. But first she had to allay her fears. 'And you're quite sure that you didn't attack her, Kaj? You do have a tendency to fly off the handle . . .'

Kaj looked at her as if she'd lost her mind. 'What the hell are you saying? Do you really think I'd be so bloody stupid to play right into her hands like that? I wouldn't mind giving her a punch in the nose, but don't you think I know what she'd do then? Sure, I went over there and gave her a piece of my mind, but I didn't *touch* her!'

Monica could see that he was telling the truth, and she couldn't help looking spitefully towards the house next door. If only Lilian would leave them in peace!

'So, what happened? Did the cops fall for her lies?'

'No, thank God. They could tell she was lying. They were going to talk to Stig, and I think that he quashed the whole idea. But it was a close call.'

She sat down facing her husband at the kitchen table. His face was beet-red and he was drumming his fingers angrily on the table.

'Shouldn't we just throw in the towel and move away? We can't go on like this.' It was an appeal she had made many times before, but she always saw the same determination in her husband's eyes.

'Out of the question, I told you that. She's never going to drive me out of my home. I refuse to give her the satisfaction.'

He slammed his fist on the table to punctuate his words, but it wasn't necessary. Monica had heard it all before. She knew it was useless. And to be honest, she didn't want to hand Lilian the victory either. Not after all that woman had said about Morgan.

The thought of her son prompted her to change the subject. 'Have you looked in on Morgan today?'

Kaj reluctantly shifted his gaze from the Florins' house and muttered, 'No, should I have? You know he never leaves his room.'

'Okay, but I thought you might go over and say hi. Check on how he's doing.' She knew that this was wishful thinking, but she still couldn't help hoping. Morgan was his son, after all.

'Why should I?' Kaj snorted. 'If he wants company he can come over here.' He stood up. 'Is there anything to eat, or what?'

Silently she got up and began fixing dinner. Years ago it might have occurred to her that Kaj could have made dinner since he was home anyway. That thought no longer crossed her mind. Everything was the way it had always been. And would always be.

FJÄLLBACKA 1924

Not a word had been spoken during the trip to Fjällbacka. After spending so many nights whispering in each other's ears, they now had not a single word left for each other. Instead they sat stiff as tin soldiers, staring straight ahead, both of them brooding over their own thoughts.

Agnes felt as if the world had come crashing down around her. Was it really this morning she woke up in her big bed in her own elegant room in the magnificent villa where she had lived her whole life? How was it possible that she now sat here on this train, with a suitcase beside her, on her way to a life of misery with a man she no longer even wanted to acknowledge? She could hardly stand to look at him. On one occasion during the journey Anders had made an attempt to put a consoling hand on hers. She had shaken it off with such a disgusted expression that she hoped he wouldn't do it again.

Some hours later, when they stopped in front of the company shack that would be their shared home, Agnes at first refused to get out of the cab. She sat there unable to move, paralysed by the filth surrounding her and the noise from the dirty, snot-nosed kids who swarmed around the cab. This couldn't possibly be her life! For a moment she was tempted to ask the cab driver to turn round and drive her back to the train station, but she realized how futile that would be. Where would she go? Her father had made it crystal clear that he didn't want anything more to do with her. Taking some sort of domestic situation was something she would never have considered, even if she hadn't had the child in her belly. All paths were now closed to her, except the one leading to this filthy, wretched hovel.

With a lump in her throat she decided at last to get out of the cab. She grimaced when her foot sank into the mud. Even worse, she was wearing her lovely red shoes with the open toes, and now she felt the damp soak into her stockings and between her toes. Out of the corner of her eye, she saw curtains draw back to allow curious eyes to look out at the spectacle. She tossed her head. They could stare until their eyes popped out of their heads. What did she care what they thought? Simple servants is what they were. They had probably never seen a real lady before. Well, this was only going to be a brief sojourn. She would eventually find a way to get out of this predicament; she had never been in a position that she couldn't either lie or charm her way out of.

Decisively she picked up her bag and walked off towards the shack.

At the morning coffee break Patrik and Gösta told Martin and Annika what had happened the day before. Ernst seldom showed up before nine, and Mellberg thought it would undermine his role as chief to have coffee with the staff, so he stayed in his office.

'Doesn't she understand that she's shooting herself in the foot?' said Annika. 'She ought to want you to focus on searching for the killer instead of wasting time on such rubbish.' It was an echo of what Patrik and Gösta had already said to each other.

Patrik merely shook his head. 'Well, I don't know whether she can't think farther than the end of her nose, or whether she's simply crazy. But I think we should put this behind us now. Hopefully we managed to scare her a bit yesterday and she won't do it again. Do we have any other leads?'

No one said a word. There was an alarming lack of evidence and no leads to work with.

'When did you say we'd be getting the results from SCL?' Annika asked, breaking the tense silence.

'Monday,' said Patrik.

'Have the family been ruled out as suspects?' said Gösta, peering at everybody over his coffee cup.

Patrik was reminded at once of Erica's odd tone of voice last evening, when he brought up the family's alibis. There was something nagging at him too; now all he had to do was work out what it was. 'Of course not,' he said. 'Family members are always suspects, but there's nothing concrete to point in that direction.'

'What about their alibis?' said Annika. She often felt left out during the investigations, so she welcomed these opportunities to hear more about what was going on.

'Credible but not confirmed, I would say,' said Patrik. He got up to refill his coffee cup, then remained standing, leaning against the counter. 'Charlotte was sleeping in the downstairs flat because of a migraine. Stig stated that he was also asleep. He'd taken a sleeping pill and had no idea what was going on. Lilian was at home looking after Albin when Sara left the house, and Niclas was at work.'

'So none of them has an alibi that could be considered air-tight,' Annika said dryly.

'She's right,' said Gösta. 'We've probably been a little too cautious, not daring to press them harder. Their statements can definitely be called into question. Except for Niclas, none of their stories can be confirmed.'

There, that was it! Patrik realized what had been nagging at his subconscious. He began pacing back and forth excitedly. 'But Niclas *couldn't* have been at work. Don't you remember?' he said, turning towards Martin. 'We couldn't reach him that morning. It was almost two hours before he came home. We don't know where he actually was – or why he lied and said that he was at the clinic.'

Martin shook his head mutely. How could they have missed that?

'Shouldn't we question Morgan as well, the son of the family next door? True or not, reports were filed charging that he had sneaked about peeping in windows, ostensibly to see Lilian undressing . . . though I can't imagine why in God's name anyone would want to see that,' said Gösta, taking another sip of coffee as he looked at the others.

'Those reports are pretty old. And as you say, there isn't much evidence that they're true, especially considering what happened yesterday.' Patrik could hear that he sounded impatient. He wasn't at all sure that he wanted to waste time on investigating any more of Lilian's lies, old or new.

'On the other hand, we've already confirmed that we don't have very much to go on, so . . .' Gösta threw out his hands, and three pairs of eyes now regarded him with surprise. It wasn't like him to show any initiative in an investigation. But precisely because it was such a rare event, they thought they ought to pay attention. To bolster what he was saying, Gösta added, 'Besides, unless I'm mistaken, you can see the Florins' house from his cabin, so he actually might have noticed something that morning.'

'You're right,' said Patrik, once again feeling a bit stupid. He should have considered Morgan as a potential witness, at least. 'Okay, here's what we'll do: you and Martin talk to Morgan Wiberg . . .' he lowered his voice but forced himself to continue, 'and Ernst and I will take a closer look at Sara's father. We'll meet again this afternoon.'

'What about me? Is there anything I can do?' said Annika.

'Stay close to the phone. The case should have got a good deal of attention in the press by now, so if we're lucky we might get something useful from the public.'

Annika nodded and got up to put her coffee cup in the dishwasher. The others did the same, and Patrik went to his office to wait for Ernst to arrive. First things first. They had to have a talk about the importance of getting to work on time during an ongoing homicide investigation.

Mellberg could feel fate approaching by leaps and bounds. Only one day left. The letter was still in his top drawer. He hadn't dared look at it again. But he already knew the contents by heart. It amazed him that such contrasting emotions could be at war inside him. His first reactions had been disbelief and rage, suspicion and anger. But ever so slowly a feeling of hope had also emerged. It was this hope that had utterly surprised him. He had always considered his life to be nearly perfect, at least until he'd been transferred to this dump of a town. After that he was forced to admit that things may have taken a slight downturn. Yet other than the still elusive promotion he felt he deserved, he wasn't lacking for anything. It was true, the embarrassing little misadventure with Irina may have given him reason to believe that there were several more things he wanted from life, but he had quickly put that episode behind him.

He had always set great store by not needing anyone. The only person he'd ever been close to, and wanted to be close to, was his dear mother, but she was no longer among the living. The letter, however, implied that all this might change.

His breathing felt heavy and laboured. Dread was mixed with impatient curiosity. Part of him wanted the day to go faster, so that the certainty of tomorrow would replace all doubt. At the same time he wanted the day to pass so slowly that it practically stood still.

For a while he'd considered just saying to hell with everything. Toss the letter in his wastebasket and hope that the problem would disappear on its own. But he knew that would never work.

He sighed, put his feet up on the desk, and closed his eyes. He might as well wait patiently for what tomorrow would bring.

Gösta and Martin slipped discreetly past the big house, hoping that they wouldn't be noticed when they headed for Morgan's little cabin instead. Neither of them was in the mood for a confrontation with Kaj. They wanted a chance to speak with Morgan in peace, without his parents getting involved. Besides, he was an adult, so there was no reason for a parent to be present.

It took a long time before the door opened, so long that they weren't sure anyone was at home. But finally it did open, and a pale, blond man in his thirties stood before them.

'Who are you?' His voice was a monotone, and his face failed to show the inquiring expression that normally accompanied that sort of question.

'We're from the police,' said Gösta, introducing both of them. 'We're going around the neighbourhood interviewing the neighbours about the death of your neighbour's little girl, Sara.'

'I see,' said Morgan, still with the same expressionless face. He made no move to step aside.

'Could we come in and talk with you a bit?' said Martin. He was starting to feel a little uncomfortable in the presence of this strange young man.

'I'd rather not. It's ten o'clock, and I work from nine to quarter past eleven. Then I eat lunch between quarter past eleven and twelve, and then I work again from noon to quarter past two. After that I have coffee and rolls at the house with Mamma and Pappa until three o'clock. Then I work again until five, and after that I have dinner. Then the news is on channel 2 at six o'clock, then on channel 4 at six thirty, then on channel 1 at seven thirty, and then it's on channel 2 again at nine. After that I go to bed.'

He was still speaking in the same monotone, hardly seeming to take a breath during the whole speech. His voice was also a bit too high and shrill, and Martin exchanged a hasty glance with Gösta.

'It sounds like you have quite a busy schedule,' said Gösta, 'but you see, it's important for us to talk with you. So we'd really appreciate it if you could give us a few minutes of your time.'

Morgan seemed to mull over this question for a moment, but then decided to acquiesce. He stepped aside and let them in, but it was obvious he didn't appreciate this interruption of his routine.

Martin was taken aback when they entered. The cabin consisted of one small room, which seemed to serve as both workroom and bedroom, and there was also a little kitchen nook. The place looked clean and neat, except for one thing. There were piles of magazines everywhere. Narrow paths had been cleared between the stacks to facilitate movement between the various parts of the room. One path led to the bed, one to the computers, and one over to the kitchen. Otherwise the floor was completely covered. Martin glanced down and saw that the magazines were mostly about computers. Judging by the covers the collection before them had been amassed over many years. Some magazines looked new, while others seemed well-worn.

'I see that you're interested in computers,' Martin said.

Morgan merely looked at him without confirming the obvious in his observation.

'What sort of work do you do?' asked Gösta to fill in the awkward pause.

'I design computer games. Mostly fantasy,' replied Morgan. He went over to the computers, as if seeking protection. Martin noticed that he moved with a clumsy, lurching gait that threatened to knock over one of the stacks of magazines as he passed. But somehow he managed to avoid doing so, and he sat down at a computer without causing an accident. He gave Martin and Gösta a vacant stare as they stood there in the midst of all those magazines. They were wondering how to proceed in questioning this odd individual. There was something not quite right about him, but they couldn't quite put a finger on it.

'How interesting,' said Martin. 'I've always wondered how anyone managed to create all those fantastical worlds. It must take a heck of an imagination.'

'I don't actually create the games. Other people do that, I just code them. I have Asperger's,' Morgan added matter-of-factly. Martin and Gösta exchanged another bewildered glance.

'Asperger's,' said Martin. 'Unfortunately I don't know what that is.'

'No, most people don't,' said Morgan. 'It's a form of autism, but it's most often accompanied by normal to high intelligence. I possess high intelligence. Extremely high,' he added without seeming to attach any emotion to the statement. 'Those of us who have Asperger's have a hard time understanding such things as facial expressions, metaphors, irony, and tone of voice. The result is that we have problems interacting socially.'

It sounded as though he were reading from a book, and Martin had to make a real effort to follow Morgan's lecture.

'So I can't create the computer games myself, since that would require me to imagine other people's feelings. On the other hand, I'm one of the best programmers in Sweden.' The words were a simple statement of fact, not coloured by either boasting or pride.

Martin couldn't help being fascinated. He had never heard of Asperger's before, and hearing Morgan explain it made him genuinely interested. But they were here to do a job, and they had better get on with it.

'Is there somewhere we could sit down?' he said, looking about the room.

'On the bed,' replied Morgan, nodding to the narrow bed standing against the far wall. Cautiously Gösta and Martin made their way between the stacks of magazines and sat down carefully on the edge of the bed. Gösta spoke first.

'We assume you know what happened on Monday at the Florins'. Did you see anything peculiar that morning?'

Morgan did not reply, but looked at them blankly. Martin realized that 'anything peculiar' might be too abstract, so he tried to reformulate the question in a more concrete way. He couldn't even imagine how difficult it would be to function in society without being able to interpret all the implied messages in human communication.

'Did you notice when the girl left the house?' he said tentatively, hoping that was precise enough for Morgan to answer.

'Yes, I saw when the girl left the house,' said Morgan and then fell silent, unsure whether there was anything more to the question.

Martin was starting to get the hang of things and said more precisely, 'What time did you see her leave?'

'She went out at ten after nine,' said Morgan, still in the same high, shrill tone of voice.

'Did you see anyone else that morning?' Gösta asked.

'Yes.'

'Who did you see that morning, and at what time?' said Martin in an attempt to anticipate Gösta. He sensed that his colleague was starting to get impatient with their odd interviewee.

'At a quarter to eight I saw Niclas,' Morgan replied.

Martin was taking notes of everything he said. He didn't doubt for a second that the times were exact.

'Did you know Sara?'

'Yes.'

Gösta now began to squirm, and Martin hurried to place a warning hand on his arm. Something told him that an emotional outburst would not have a beneficial effect as they tried to get as much information as possible out of Morgan.

'How did you know her?'

The question elicited nothing but an empty stare from Morgan, and Martin rephrased it. He had never realized before how difficult it was to be precise when speaking, or how much he normally relied on the other person to understand the essence of what he was saying.

171

'Did she come here sometimes?'

Morgan nodded. 'She interrupted my routines. Knocked on the door when I was working and wanted to come in. Touched my things. Once she got angry when I told her to leave, and she knocked over some of my stacks.'

'You didn't like her?' said Martin.

'She interrupted my routines. And knocked over my stacks,' said Morgan, and that was about as close as he could come to showing any emotion about the girl.

'What do you think of her grandmother?'

'Lilian is a nasty person. That's what Pappa says.'

'She says that you sneaked about outside their house and looked in the windows. Did you do that?'

Morgan nodded without hesitation. 'Yes, I did. I wanted to have a look. But Mamma got mad when I said that. She told me that I mustn't do that.'

'So you stopped doing it?' said Gösta.

'Yes.'

'Because your mamma said that you mustn't?' Gösta's tone was sarcastic, but Morgan didn't notice.

'Yes, Mamma always talks about what one should and shouldn't do. We practise things to say and things to do. She teaches me that even if somebody says one thing, it can mean something completely different. Otherwise I might say or do the wrong thing.' Morgan looked at his watch. 'It's ten thirty. I should get back to work now.'

'We won't bother you any longer,' said Martin, getting to his feet. 'Please excuse us for disturbing your routine, but as police officers we can't always take such things into account.'

Morgan seemed content with that explanation and had already turned round to the computer screen. 'Pull the door closed behind you,' he said, 'or it will blow open.'

'What an odd duck,' said Gösta as they slipped through the garden to the car they had parked a block away.

'I thought it was fascinating, I really did,' said Martin. 'I've never heard of Asperger's before, have you?'

Gösta snorted. 'No, that's not something we had back in my day.

172

There are so many weird diagnoses nowadays. Personally I think the term "idiot" goes a long way.'

Martin sighed and got into the driver's seat. Gösta was certainly short on empathy, that's for sure.

Something was tugging at Martin's subconscious. Something that made him wonder whether they had actually asked the right questions. He struggled with his intractable memory but finally had to give up. Maybe he was just imagining things.

The clinic lay shrouded in a grey mist, and there was a single car in the car park. Ernst was still sulking about being admonished by Patrik for arriving late. He climbed out of the car and strode over to the main entrance. In annoyance, Patrik slammed the car door a bit too hard and trotted after him. It was like dealing with a little kid.

They passed the pharmacy counter and turned left into the reception area. There was no one else in sight, and their footsteps echoed in the deserted corridor. Finally they located a nurse and asked for Niclas. She informed them that he was with a patient, but he would be free in ten minutes, and she asked them to sit down and wait. Patrik was always fascinated by how similar all clinical waiting-rooms seemed. The same dismal wooden furniture with ugly upholstery, the same meaningless art on the walls, and always the same boring magazines. He leafed absentmindedly through something called *Care Guide* and was surprised at how many different ailments he'd never heard of. Ernst had sat down as far away as he could, nervously tapping his foot on the floor. Occasionally Patrik caught him shooting dirty looks his way, but it didn't bother him. Ernst could think whatever he liked, as long as he did his job.

'The doctor is free now,' said the nurse. She showed them into an office where Niclas sat behind a desk cluttered with papers. He looked exhausted. He stood up and shook hands with them, even attempting a welcoming smile. But the smile never reached his eyes but hardened into an anxious grimace.

'Are there any developments in the investigation?' he asked.

Patrik shook his head. 'We're working full-tilt, but so far without much progress. But we're bound to have a breakthrough,' he said, hoping to sound reassuring. But inside him the doubts were getting worse. He was far from sure that they would be successful this time.

'What can I do for you?' said Niclas wearily as he ran his hand over his blond hair.

Patrik couldn't help reflecting that the man before him looked like a model for the cover of one of those romance novels about beautiful nurses and handsome doctors. Even now his charm shone through, and Patrik could only imagine how attractive he must seem to women. According to what he'd heard from Erica, over the years that had presented problems in his marriage to Charlotte.

'We have a few questions regarding your activities last Monday morning,' Patrik began. Ernst was still sulking and he ignored Patrik's glances attempting to get him to participate.

'Oh yes?' said Niclas, apparently unmoved, but Patrik thought he noticed his gaze shift slightly.

'You told us that you were at work.'

'Yes, I drove here at quarter to eight, as usual,' said Niclas, but his nervousness was unmistakable.

'That's what we don't quite understand,' said Patrik in a last attempt to involve Ernst. But his colleague just stared obstinately out of the window facing the car park.

'We tried to get hold of you for a couple of hours that morning. And you weren't in. Of course we could check with the nurse,' said Patrik, gesturing towards the door. 'I presume she wrote down your office hours and can see whether you were here that morning.'

Now Niclas was squirming uneasily in his chair, and beads of sweat had appeared at his temples. But he was still struggling to look unmoved, and Patrik had to admit that he was doing a fairly good job of it. In a calm voice Niclas said, 'Oh, I remember now. I'd taken time off to drive out and look at some houses that were for sale. I didn't mention it to Charlotte because I wanted to surprise her.'

The explanation would have seemed plausible if it weren't for the tension that Patrik sensed beneath the calm tone of voice. He didn't believe for a moment what Niclas was saying.

'Could you be a little more precise? Which houses did you go to look at?'

Niclas gave a nervous laugh and seemed to be trying to think of a way to gain time. 'I'd have to check on that, I don't really recall,' he said hesitatingly.

'There aren't that many houses for sale here right now. You must at least remember what neighbourhoods you were in.' Patrik pressed him harder with his questions, and he saw Niclas growing more and more nervous. Whatever he had done that morning, he hadn't been looking at houses.

A moment of silence followed. It was obvious that Niclas's brain was working overtime in an attempt to salvage the situation. But then Patrik saw him give up and his whole body slumped. Now maybe they were getting somewhere.

'I don't . . .' Niclas's voice broke and he started over. 'I don't want Charlotte to hear about this.'

'We can't promise anything. Things have a tendency to come out sooner or later, but we're giving you an opportunity to present your version before we hear anyone else's.'

'You don't understand. It would destroy Charlotte completely if . . .' His voice broke again, and even though Patrik had no idea where this was going, he couldn't keep from feeling a certain sympathy for Niclas.

'As I said, I can't promise anything.' He waited for Niclas to conquer his anxiety and continue. Images of sweet, gentle Charlotte came to him, and suddenly his sympathy was mixed with repugnance. Sometimes he was ashamed to have to listen to the males of the species.

'I . . .' Niclas cleared his throat, 'I was with someone.'

'And who might that be?' asked Patrik. By now he had completely given up hope of bringing Ernst into the conversation. But his colleague suddenly turned from the window and regarded the subject of the interview with great interest.

'Jeanette Lind.'

'The woman who owns the gift shop on Galärbacken?' Patrik asked. He could vaguely recall a petite, curvaceous, dark-haired woman.

Niclas nodded. 'Yes, that Jeanette. We . . .' once again the same hesitation, 'we've been seeing each other for a while.'

'How long is a while?'

'A couple of months. Three, maybe.'

'How did the two of you manage that?' Patrik's curiosity was genuine. He had never understood how people in affairs could make time to meet. Or how they dared. Especially in a town as small as Fjällbacka, where a car parked for five minutes outside someone's house was enough to start the rumours flying.

'Sometimes at lunch, sometimes I said I was working late. Once I pretended I had an urgent house call.'

Patrik had to restrain himself from going over and punching this guy. But his personal feelings were irrelevant. They were here only to investigate the matter of his alibi.

'And last Monday morning you simply took a couple of hours off to drive over and see . . . Jeanette.'

'That's right,' said Niclas in a gruff voice. 'I said I had to make some house calls that I'd been putting off for a while, but that I'd be available on my mobile if anything urgent came up.'

'But you weren't. We tried to get hold of you through your nurse on repeated occasions, and you didn't answer your mobile.'

'I forgot to charge it. It died just after I left the clinic, but I didn't even notice.'

'And what time did you leave the clinic to meet your lover?'

That last word seemed to affect Niclas like a slap in the face, but he didn't object. Instead he ran his hands through his hair again and said wearily, 'Just after nine thirty, I think. I had telephone consultations between eight and nine, and then I did some paperwork for about half an hour. So between nine thirty and twenty to, I would think.'

'And we got hold of you just before one. Was that when you came back to the clinic?' Patrik was struggling to keep his voice neutral, but he couldn't help imagining Niclas in bed with his lover at the same time as his daughter lay dead in the sea. However one looked at it, Niclas Klinga was not presenting an attractive picture of himself.

'Yes, that's correct. I had to start seeing patients at one, so I got back around with about ten minutes to spare.'

'We're going to have to talk to Jeanette to verify your story. You realize that, don't you?' Patrik said.

176

Niclas nodded dejectedly. He repeated his entreaty once again: 'Try to keep Charlotte out of this: it would break her completely.'

You should have thought of that earlier, Patrik thought, but he didn't say it out loud. Niclas had probably had the same thought many times over the past few days.

FJÄLLBACKA 1924

It was so long ago that he had felt any joy in his work that those days seemed like a distant, pleasant dream. Day-to-day toil had made him lose all enthusiasm, and he now worked mechanically on whatever task was at hand. Agnes's demands never seemed to end. Nor could she make the money last, as the other stonecutter families managed to do, even though they often had a large brood of children to feed. Everything he brought home seemed to run through her fingers, and he often had to go hungry to the quarry because there was no money for food. And yet for once he brought home every öre he earned. Poker was the biggest amusement among the stonecutters. The games laid claim to both evenings and weekends, often ending when the men went home foolish with empty pockets. Their wives had long since resigned themselves and let the bitterness carve furrows in their faces.

Bitterness was a feeling that was beginning to take its toll on him too. Life with Agnes, which had seemed a beautiful dream less than a year ago, had turned out to be a form of punishment. The only thing he had done wrong was to love her and plant a child inside her, and yet he was being punished as if he'd committed the ultimate mortal sin. He couldn't even feel happy about the child in her belly anymore. Her pregnancy had not progressed free of pain, and now that she was in the last stage, things were worse than ever. During her entire pregnancy she had complained of aches and pains of one sort or another, and refused to take care of everyday chores. This meant that he not only worked from

179

early morning to late evening in the quarry, but he also had to handle all the chores that a housewife should do. It was not made any easier knowing that the other cutters by turns laughed at him and felt sorry for him because he was forced to carry out a woman's duties. Most often he was simply too exhausted to even care what others said behind his back.

Nevertheless, Anders was looking forward to the birth of the child. Maybe maternal love would make Agnes stop seeing herself as the centre of the world. A baby needed to be the centre of attention, and that would probably be a useful experience for his wife. Because he refused to give up the idea that they could make this marriage work. He was not a man who took his promises lightly. Now that they had forged a legally recognized bond, it was not something to be merely dissolved, no matter how hard their situation might be.

Naturally he would occasionally look at other women at the compound, women who worked hard and never complained. He thought that he'd been dealt an unfair hand in life, but at the same time he realized in all honesty that he had brought this situation upon himself. And consequently he had lost the right to complain.

With heavy steps he trudged home along the narrow track. This day had been just as monotonous as all the others. He had spent it cutting paving stones, and one shoulder was aching, where the same muscle had been subjected to far too much strain. Hunger was tearing at his stomach as well; there had been nothing at home that he could take with him in his lunch sack. If Jansson in the shack next door hadn't taken pity on him and shared his sandwich, Anders wouldn't have had a thing to eat all day. No, he thought, starting now, he was done entrusting his wages to Agnes. He would simply have to take charge of buying the groceries, just as he had taken over her other chores. He could stand to go without food himself, but he had no intention of letting his child starve. It was high time he began introducing some different routines at home.

He sighed and paused for a moment before he opened the flimsy wooden door and went inside to his wife.

From behind the glass window of the reception, Annika had a good view of everyone who came and went. But today it was quiet. Only Mellberg was still in his office, and no one had come to the police station on any urgent errand. But her office was hopping with activity. The publicity in the media had produced results, prompting a welter of calls, but it was still too early to say whether anything was worth following up. Nor was it her job to decide. She merely wrote down all the information, along with the name and phone number of the informant. The notes were then passed to the investigator in charge. In this case it was Patrik who would be the lucky recipient of a huge dose of gossip and baseless accusations, which in her experience made up most of the calls.

But this case had generated more buzz than usual. Anything having to do with children usually stirred up emotions among the public, and nothing aroused stronger feelings than murder. But it was not a pleasant picture she derived from the general populace when she took the calls. Most noticeable was the fact that the modern tolerance for homosexuals had not taken root outside the big cities. She was now getting lots of tips about men who were suspicious individuals simply because of confirmed or suspected homosexuality. In most cases the arguments that were advanced were laughably simple-minded. It was enough for a man to have a non-traditional profession for Annika to be told that he must be 'one of those perverts'. According to small-town logic, that alone was enough to accuse him of all sorts of things. So far she had received multiple tips about a local hairdresser, a part-time florist, and a teacher who had apparently committed the outrageous error of favouring pink shirts. Most suspect of all was a male day-care aide. Annika counted ten calls about this latter individual, and she put them all aside with a sigh. Sometimes she wondered whether time moved forward at all in small towns.

The next call proved to be different. The woman on the other end of the line wanted to remain anonymous, but the tip she provided was undoubtedly of interest. Annika straightened up and wrote down exactly what the woman told her. This one was going on the top of the stack. A shiver ran down her back because she sensed that she'd just heard something crucial to the case. It was so seldom that she had any part in what could break a case wide open that she couldn't help feeling a certain satisfaction. This could be one of those moments. The phone rang again and she picked up the receiver. Another tip about the florist.

Reluctantly Arne placed the hymnals on the pews. Usually this task made him feel good, but not today. Newfangled inventions! A music service on Friday evening, and it was far from God-fearing music. Cheerful and lively and altogether heathen! Music should only be played in church during Sunday worship service, and then preferably traditional hymns from the hymnal. Nowadays anything at all could be played, and in some instances people had even taken to applauding. Well, he had to be glad that here it wasn't yet as bad as in Strömstad, where the pastor brought in one pop artist after another. This evening at least it was only some youths from the local music college who would appear, not silly Stockholm women touring the country with hummable tunes that they were just as happy to play in the house of God as for drunks in the public parks.

It was going to be hymns in any event, and with meticulous care Arne hung up the numbers on the board to the right of the choir. When he had finished posting the numbers he took a step back to make sure they all hung straight. He took pride in every detail being perfect.

If only he would be allowed to create the same order among

human beings, everything would be so much better. Instead of thinking up their own idiocies, people could listen to him and learn. It was all in the Bible, after all. Everything was described in the smallest detail, if only one took the trouble to read what the Scriptures said.

He was again struck full force by the sorrow of not living his life as a pastor. After cautiously looking around to ensure that he was all alone, he opened the gate to the choir and stepped reverently up to the altar. He glanced up at the emaciated and wounded Jesus hanging on the cross. This was what life was all about. Studying the blood seeping out of Jesus's wounds, observing how the thorns cut into his scalp, and then bowing one's head in respect. He turned round and gazed out over the empty pews. In his mind's eye they were filled with people, his congregation, his audience. He tentatively raised his hands in the air and intoned in a crisp, echoing voice: 'May the Lord let his countenance shine upon you . . .'

He pictured the people being filled by his words. He saw them receiving the blessing into their hearts and looking at him with faces beaming. Arne slowly lowered his hands and stole a glance at the pulpit. He had never dared step up there, but today it was as if the Holy Spirit were filling him. If his father hadn't stood in the way of his calling, he could have approached the pulpit with the full right of a pastor. From that platform, elevated above the heads of the congregation, he could have preached God's word.

He tentatively moved towards the pulpit, but when he put his foot on the first step he heard the heavy church door creak open. He removed his foot and went back to his chores. The bitterness he felt ate into his breast like acid.

The shop was not open except during the summer months and on holiday weekends, so Patrik and Ernst had to look for Jeanette at the workplace where she made her living the other nine months of the year. She was a waitress at one of the few lunch spots in Grebbestad that was open in the winter, and Patrik felt his stomach rumble as they walked inside. But it was still too early for lunch, so the restaurant was empty of patrons. A young woman was slowly making the rounds of the tables, setting them up.

'Jeanette Lind?'

She looked up and nodded. 'Yes, that's me.'

'Patrik Hedström and Ernst Lundgren. We're from the Tanumshede police station. We'd like to ask you a few questions if that's all right.'

She nodded curtly but quickly lowered her gaze. If she had any powers of deduction she probably knew why they were there.

'Would you like some coffee?' she asked, and both Patrik and Ernst nodded eagerly.

Patrik watched her as she walked over to the coffee-maker. He recognized her type. Small, dark and curvaceous. Big brown eyes and hair with a natural wave that reached well below her shoulders. Certainly the prettiest girl in her class, maybe even in her whole grade level at school. Popular and always going with one of the older, cooler guys. But when the school years were over, the heyday of such girls came to an end as well. And yet they stayed in their home towns, aware that there at least they retained a bit of star status, while in any of the nearby cities they would suddenly seem mediocre in comparison with the hordes of other pretty girls. He judged that Jeanette was a lot younger than he was, and also much younger than Niclas. Twenty-five at most.

She placed a coffee cup in front of each of them and tossed her hair back as she sat down at the table. In her teens she had undoubtedly practised that move hundreds of times in front of the mirror. Patrik had to admit that by now she had the flirtatious gesture down pat.

'All right, shoot, or whatever it is they say in American films.' She gave them a wry smile and her eyes narrowed slightly as she stared at Patrik.

Against his will he had to admit that he could understand what it was that Niclas saw in her. He too had spent many years pining for the cutest girls in school. Boys were all alike. But he had really never had a chance. Short, thin and with decent grades, he had qualified as one of the average guys. He could only admire from afar the tough guys who cut maths class to hang out in the smoking area with a cigarette hanging from the corner of their mouth. Although over time, of course, he had already got to know many of those boys well in his professional capacity.

Some of them could even call the drunk tank at the station their second home.

'We were just speaking with Niclas Klinga and . . .' he hesitated, 'your name came up.'

'Yes, I'm sure it did,' said Jeanette, obviously not embarrassed in the least about the context in which her name must have been mentioned. She looked at Patrik calmly and waited for him to continue.

Ernst was sitting quietly as usual, and now took a cautious sip of his hot coffee. The looks he gave Jeanette belied the fact that he was old enough to be her father. Patrik glared angrily at his colleague and had to restrain a desire to kick him in the shin underneath the table.

'Well, he says that you were together Monday morning, is that correct?'

She tossed her hair again in her practised way and then nodded. 'Yes, that's true. We were at my place. I had the day off on Monday.'

'What time did Niclas arrive at your house?'

She examined her fingernails as she considered what to say. They were long and well manicured. Patrik wondered how she could do her work with such long nails.

'Sometime around nine thirty, I think. No, actually, I'm sure of it, because I had set the alarm clock for nine fifteen and I was in the shower when Niclas arrived.'

She giggled, and Patrik began to feel some distaste for her. Before him he saw Charlotte, Sara and Albin, but such images apparently didn't bother Jeanette.

'And how long did he stay?'

'We had lunch at noon, and he had an appointment at one o'clock at the clinic, so he probably left my place about twenty minutes before that, I should think. I live up on Kullen, so it's not far to his office from there.' Another little titter.

Now Patrik really had to control himself to keep from showing the disgust he felt. But Ernst didn't seem to have any such objections to Jeanette. His gaze grew more enthralled the longer they sat there.

'And Niclas was at your house the whole time? He didn't leave to run an errand?'

'No,' she said calmly, 'he didn't go anywhere, I can assure you of that.'

Patrik looked at Ernst and asked, 'Do you have anything to add?' His colleague responded by shaking his head, so he gathered up his notes.

'We'll be coming back with more questions, I'm sure, but that's all for now.'

'Well, I hope I've been of some help,' she said, getting up. She hadn't uttered a word about the fact that her lover's daughter had died. That a child had been murdered while she was rolling around in bed with the father. There was something indecent about her obvious lack of sympathy.

'Yes, thank you,' he said curtly, putting on his jacket he'd hung over the back of his chair. As they went out the door he saw that she'd gone back to setting the tables. She was humming some tune, but he couldn't hear what it was.

Charlotte paced aimlessly back and forth in the cellar flat where they had been living for the past few months. The pain in her chest made her restless and forced her to keep moving. She felt guilty that she hadn't been able to take care of Albin properly. Instead she had left him largely in the care of her mother-in-law; in the midst of her grief there was just no room for the baby. In his smile and his blue eyes she saw only Sara. He looked so much like she had looked at the same age; it hurt to see how similar they were. It also pained her to see what an anxious and timorous child he was. It was as if Sara had sucked up all the energy that should have been divided between the two children, leaving nothing for him. And yet Charlotte knew better than that. The secret chafed in her breast. She hoped that she could make amends.

Charlotte regretted what she had said to Erica yesterday. Right now she and Niclas needed to stick together; her suspicions were just making everything worse. She could see that he was suffering, and if this tragedy couldn't bring them back together, there was really no hope for them.

Since she'd emerged from her sedated fog, Charlotte had hoped that Niclas would be the man she always knew he could be. Tender, considerate and loving. She had seen glimpses before, and it was

186

this side of him that she loved. Now she wanted nothing more than to be able to lean on him; she wanted him to be the stronger one. But it hadn't turned out that way. He had shut himself off, gone back to work as quickly as he could, leaving her here among the broken pieces of their life.

Her foot struck something. Charlotte started to bend down but stopped abruptly. She'd asked Niclas to move all Sara's things out of sight, and he'd spent a whole morning putting everything in boxes and taking them up to the attic. But he'd missed one thing. Sara's old teddy bear lay halfway under the bed, and that was what Charlotte had felt with her foot. She gently picked it up and then had to sit down on the edge of the bed when everything started spinning before her eyes. The teddy bear felt grubby in her hands. Sara had refused to let them wash it, so it looked like it had been through a street fight. The bear also gave off an odd smell, and presumably it was this smell that absolutely mustn't be lost in the washing machine and replaced by the scent of laundry detergent. One eye was missing from the bear, and Charlotte touched the threads that had once held the button eye in place. It had been two hours since she'd last wept, the longest dry spell since the police had brought the news of Sara's death. Now the sobs began rising in her chest again. Charlotte hugged the teddy bear and lay down on her side on the bed. Then her grief took over.

'Will wonders never cease?' Pedersen said on the telephone. 'For the first time in the history of the world we got an analysis result back sooner than they predicted.'

'Hold on, I just have to pull over,' said Patrik, looking for a suitable spot. Ernst pointed to a little forest track on their side of the highway that would do.

'All right, I'm not a danger to traffic anymore. So, what did the tests show?' he said. It was clear from his tone of voice that he wasn't expecting much. They'd probably only managed to identify what Sara had eaten for breakfast. As for the water in her lungs, Patrik had done a little investigating on his own and found out that there wasn't much hope of identifying exactly what brand of soap was involved. Pedersen confirmed this at once.

'As I said before, the water was ordinary tap water, and the particular mixture of substances found in the water shows without any doubt that it was from the Fjällbacka area. Unfortunately the traces of soap couldn't be linked to any specific brand.'

'Well, that's not much to go on,' Patrik sighed. He was discouraged and once again felt the case slipping out of his hands.

'No, not as far as what was found in her lungs,' said Pedersen with a mysterious tone of voice. Patrik sat up straighter in the driver's seat.

'What else have you got?' he said, holding his breath as he waited for the answer.

'All right, here goes, even though I don't know what it means,' the M.E. replied. 'Analysis of the contents of the girl's stomach confirms what the family said she ate for breakfast, but . . .' Then he paused and Patrik almost screamed with impatience. 'There was something strange in her stomach. It seems as though the girl had eaten ashes.'

'Ashes?' said Patrik with a gobsmacked look on his face.

'Yes,' Pedersen said, 'and since we found them in the stomach, the lab did another check of the water in her lungs and found minute traces of ash there too. We missed them in the first analysis.'

'But how the hell could she have got ashes inside her body?' Out of the corner of his eye Patrik saw Ernst give a start and turn to stare at him.

'It's impossible to say for certain, but after looking at the data and going over the post-mortem report again, my theory is that someone forced the ashes into her orally. We did find traces in her mouth and oesophagus as well, even though most of it was flushed out by the water.'

Patrik didn't say a word, but his thoughts were tumbling round in his head. Why in the world would anyone have forced the girl to eat ashes? He tried to collect himself and focus on what he ought to ask about.

'But why would she have ashes in her lungs, if she had been forced to swallow them?'

'Once again, it's only speculation on my part, but it's possible the ashes went down the wrong way when they were stuffed in her mouth. If she was already in the bathtub when she was force-fed the ashes, some could have ended up in the water. And when she was drowned, the ash in the water could have then got into her lungs.'

With alarming clarity Patrik could see the whole scene before him. Sara in a bathtub, an unknown, menacing figure forcing a handful of ashes into her mouth and then holding her nose and mouth shut to force her to swallow. The same hands that later held her head underwater until bubbles stopped rising to the surface and everything was still.

A rustling sound came from the woods outside the car and broke the oppressive silence. In a low voice he said to Pedersen, 'Can you fax all this to us?'

'Already done. And the lab will be doing more tests on the ashes to see if they can find anything useful there. But they didn't want to wait for the results; they thought it was better to give us this information right away.'

'Yes, they were right about that. When do you think we can get more info on the ashes?'

'By the middle of next week, I should think,' said Pedersen. Then he added quietly, 'How's it going? Are you getting anywhere?'

It was unusual for the M.E. to ask questions about the investigation, but it didn't really surprise Patrik. Sara's death seemed to have affected so many people, even the most jaded. He thought for a moment before he replied.

'Not really, I'm afraid. To be honest, we don't have much to go on. But hopefully this will give us a lead. Not that I can see how at the moment, but it's an odd enough piece of information that it might break open the case.'

'Yes, let's hope so,' said Pedersen.

Patrik then gave Ernst a brief rundown of what he'd found out. They both sat in silence for a while, as the rustling continued in the bushes outside the car. Patrik was half-expecting to see a bull elk come rushing towards them, but it was probably just some birds or squirrels rummaging about in the fallen red leaves of autumn.

'What do you think, is it time to take a closer look at the Florins' bathroom?'

'Shouldn't we have done that already?' asked Ernst.

189

'Could be,' Patrik replied bitterly, well aware that Ernst had a point. 'But we didn't, so it's better to do it late than never.'

Ernst didn't answer. Patrik took out his mobile and made the necessary calls to summon backup and the technical team from Uddevalla. With Ernst's words ringing in his ears, he made his request sound as urgent as he could and was promised that the team would come out that very afternoon.

With a sigh Patrik started the car and put it in reverse. In his head whirled thoughts of ashes. And death.

FJÄLLBACKA 1924

Agnes hated her life. Even more than she'd thought possible on the day when she'd arrived at her new home. Never in her wildest dreams could she have imagined that everything would be so impoverished and miserable. And as if the physical setting weren't bad enough, her body had swollen up and made her ugly and awkward. She sweated all the time in the summer heat, and her hair, before so carefully coiffed, hung in lank strands. She wished for nothing more than that the creature who had transformed her into this repulsive figure would come out; at the same time she was terrified of the process of childbirth. The mere thought of it made her feel faint.

Living with Anders was also an affliction. If only he'd had a little steel in his backbone! Instead his mournful puppy-dog eyes followed her everywhere, begging for a crumb of attention. She knew that the other women despised her because she didn't spend all day scrubbing her filthy home like they did. Nor did she wait hand and foot on her ungrateful husband. But how could they expect her to act the same way? She was so much better than they were, after all, coming from a superior social class and with such a fine upbringing. It was unreasonable of Anders to demand that she get down on all fours and scour the wretched wooden floor or run to the quarry to bring him lunch. Besides, he had the nerve to complain about the way she handled the few coins he brought home. In her condition she shouldn't have to do anything, and she always craved some fine delicacy when she went to the grocer's. It shouldn't cause such a terrible fuss just because she allowed herself some treat, instead of spending all the money on butter or flour.

Agnes sighed and propped up her swollen feet on the stool in front of her. Many an evening she had sat here by the single small window and dreamt of how different her life might have been. If only her father hadn't been so bull-headed. Occasionally she had considered setting off for Strömstad and throwing herself on her knees before her father to beg for his mercy. If only she had believed that there was the slightest chance this gesture would succeed, she would have done it long before. But she knew her father, and she knew in her heart that it would do no good. She was stuck where she was, and until she thought up some way to extricate herself from her current situation, she would simply have to bide her time.

She heard footsteps on the front porch. With a sigh she realized that it must be Anders coming home. If he expected dinner to be on the table, he was going to be disappointed. Considering the pain and suffering she'd been enduring to bear his child, he should be fixing dinner for her instead. Not that there was much food in the house. The money always ran out a week after he got paid, and it was another week until the next payday. But since he was on such a good footing with the Jansson couple next door, surely he could go over and beg a loaf of bread from them and maybe something he could use to make soup.

'Good evening, Agnes,' said Anders, timidly opening the door. Despite the fact that they had been married more than six months, no homely atmosphere had developed, and he looked bewildered as he stood in the doorway.

'Good evening,' she snorted, frowning at his filthy appearance. 'Do you have to track all that dirt inside? At least take off your shoes.'

Obediently he removed his footwear and set them on the porch steps. 'Is there anything to eat?' he asked, which made Agnes glare at him as though he had just sworn the worst of all oaths.

'Do I look like I can stand around cooking for you? I can hardly stay on my feet, and you expect your dinner to be hot on the table as soon as you come home. And how am I supposed to pay for dinner? You don't bring home enough money for us to eat proper meals, and right now there isn't a single öre left. And the grocer won't give us any more credit, that old skinflint.'

Anders grimaced at the mention of credit. He hated to be in debt, but over the past six months since he and Agnes had moved in, she had bought plenty of things on tick.

'Well, I think we should have a talk about that . . .' He drawled his words and Agnes began to smell a rat. This didn't sound promising.

Anders went on. 'It's probably best if I take care of the money from now on.'

He didn't look her in the eye when he said it, and she could feel the rage building up inside of her. What did he mean? Was she now going to be robbed of the only joy she had left in life?

Vaguely aware of the storm that his words had provoked, Anders said, 'It's already hard for you to go down to the grocer, and when the baby is born it'll be hard for you to get away at all, so it's probably just as well that I take care of that chore.'

She was so furious that she couldn't say a word. Then her temporary muteness vanished and she told him exactly what she thought of the idea. She could see that he was squirming with discomfort because half the compound could hear what she was saying and the names she called him, but she didn't give a damn. She couldn't care less what these labourers thought of her, but she would damn well see to it that Anders didn't miss what she thought about him, not for a moment.

Despite her cursing he refused to give in, to her great surprise. For the first time he stood firm and let her yell herself out. When she had to pause to catch her breath, he calmly said that she could yell until her lungs exploded, but that was how things were going to be from now on.

Agnes felt herself starting to hyperventilate, and her rage made her see red. Her father had always relented when she began to retch and gasp for breath, but Anders simply gazed at her in silence and made no attempt to console her.

Then she felt a sharp pain in her belly, and she fell silent in horror. She wanted to go home to her father.

Monica felt the fear as a kick in the stomach.

'Have the police been here?'

Morgan nodded but didn't take his eyes off the screen. She knew that it was actually the wrong time to talk to him. According to his schedule he should be working now, so nobody could talk to him. But she couldn't help herself. Worry was spreading through her body, making her shift from one foot to the other. She wanted to go over and give her son a good shake, make him say more without her having to ask detailed questions about everything, but she knew it was hopeless. She would have to do this with her usual patience.

'What did they want?'

He still refused to look away from the screen, and he replied without his fingers for an instant slowing down as they flew over the keyboard. 'They asked about the girl that died.'

Her heart skipped not only one beat but several. In a hoarse voice she said, 'So what did they ask about?'

'Whether I'd seen her when she left in the morning.'

'Had you?'

'Had I what?' Morgan replied absentmindedly.

'Seen her?'

He ignored the question. 'Why are you asking me now? You know that it doesn't fit into my schedule. You usually come here when I'm not working.' His high, shrill voice contained no hint of whining; he was merely stating a fact. She had deviated from their usual routines, interrupted his rhythm, and she knew that it must be confusing him. But she couldn't help it. She had to know.

'Did you see when she left?'

'Yes, I saw when she left,' he said. 'I told the police about it, answered all their questions. Although they interrupted my routine too.'

Now he turned halfway towards her and looked at her with his intelligent but peculiar gaze. His eyes were always the same. They never changed, never showed any emotion. At least not recently. By now he had learned to have some control over his life. When he was younger he could succumb to enormous outbursts of rage in frustration over things he couldn't control, or choices he was unable to make. It could involve anything from deciding which day he would take a shower to choosing what he wanted to eat for dinner. But Monica and Morgan had both learned to deal with it. Now life was compartmentalized and the choices already made. He showered every other day, he had four different dishes that she alternated according to a rolling schedule, and breakfast and lunch were always the same. His work had also become something of a salvation for him. It was something he was good at, something that gave him an outlet for his high intelligence and that suited the special temperament of someone with Asperger's.

It was extremely rare that Monica came to see him at the wrong time in his schedule. She couldn't recall the last time she had done so. But now she had already disturbed him, so she might as well continue.

She followed one of the paths through the stacks of magazines and sat down on the edge of the bed.

'I don't want you to talk to them anymore unless I'm with you.'

Morgan just nodded. Then he turned all the way round to face her. He was now sitting astride the chair backwards, with his arms crossed and resting on the back.

'Do you think I could have seen her if I asked to?'

'Seen who?' asked Monica, surprised.

'Sara.'

'What do you mean?' Monica could feel the room spinning.

196

The stress of the past few days had upset her equilibrium, and Morgan's question made her lose her self-control.

'Why would you want to see her?' She couldn't keep the anger out of her voice, but as usual he didn't react to it. She wasn't even sure that he understood that her raised voice meant she was angry.

'To see how she looks now,' he replied calmly.

'Why?' Her voice rose even higher, and she could feel her fists clenching. The fear had her in a tight grip, and every word from Morgan felt like another step towards the darkness that terrified her.

'To see how dead she looks,' he said with his gaze fixed on her.

Monica was having a hard time breathing. It felt as though the walls of the little cabin were closing in on her. She couldn't stand it any longer. She had to get some air.

Without saying a word she rushed out the door and slammed it behind her. The raw, cold air stung her throat as she took long, deep breaths. After a while she could feel her pulse begin to slow.

She cautiously peered through one of the windows. Morgan had turned round. His hands were flying over the keyboard. She pressed her face to the glass and looked at the back of his neck. She loved him so much it hurt.

There was nothing that gave Lilian as much pleasure as cleaning house. The rest of the family claimed she was manic, but that didn't particularly bother her. As long as they stayed away and didn't try to help, she was happy.

She began with the kitchen, as usual. Every day the same routine. Wipe off all surfaces, vacuum, mop the floor, and once a week take everything out of the cupboards and cabinets and wipe them inside. When she was done with the kitchen she cleaned the hall, the living room, and the veranda. The only room on the ground floor that she couldn't clean at the moment was the little guest room where Albin was asleep. She would have to do it later.

She dragged the vacuum cleaner up the stairs. Stig had wanted to buy her a smaller model; she had politely but firmly declined. She'd had this one for fifteen years and it still worked like new. Much better than the newer models that broke down every fifteen minutes. But it was definitely heavy. She was panting a bit by the time she reached the upstairs hall. Stig was awake and turned his head towards her.

'You're going to wear yourself out,' he said in a feeble voice.

'Better than sitting and twiddling my thumbs.'

It was an old ritual they went through. He would tell her to take it easy, and she would come back with some snappy response. He would certainly change his tune if she stopped taking care of everything in the house and transferred some of the responsibility to the others. Without her this house would go downhill fast. Everything would just crumble away. She was the glue that kept it all together, and they knew it. If only they would show a little gratitude sometimes. No, instead they all kept nagging her to take it easy. Lilian could feel the old familiar irritation building up. She went into Stig's room. He looked a little paler today, she saw.

'You look worse,' she said, helping him to lift his head far enough off the bed so that she could pull out the pillow. She fluffed it up and placed it under his head again.

'I know. Today is not a good day.'

'Where does it hurt the most?' she asked, sitting down on the edge of the bed.

'Everywhere, it feels like,' said Stig faintly, attempting a smile.

'Can't you be more precise than that?' Lilian said, annoyed. She plucked at the knots on the bedspread and gave him an imperious look.

'My stomach,' said Stig. 'It's churning about somehow, and there's a sharp pain sometimes.'

'Well, Niclas is going to have to take a look at you tonight when he comes home. You can't lie here in this condition.'

'Just no hospital.' Stig waved his hand to fend off the idea.

'That's for Niclas to decide, not you.' Lilian plucked little bits of lint from the bedspread and looked around the room, searching. 'Where's the breakfast tray?'

He pointed to the floor. Lilian leaned over him and looked.

'You haven't eaten a thing,' she said crossly.

'Couldn't face it.'

'You've got to eat or you'll never get well, you know that. Now I'm going downstairs to fix you some tomato soup. You have to get some nourishment inside you.'

198

He merely nodded. There was no point in arguing with Lilian when she was in this mood.

Furiously she stomped down the stairs. Why did she always have to do everything?

The reception was empty when Martin and Gösta came back to the station. Annika must have taken an early lunch. Martin saw that there was a big pile of note papers in Annika's handwriting on the desk. Probably tips that had started coming in from the public.

'Are you going to lunch soon?' Gösta asked.

'Not quite yet,' said Martin. 'Can we eat at noon?'

'I'll probably starve to death by then, but it beats eating alone.'

'Okay, it's a deal,' said Martin and went into his office. He'd had a brainstorm on the way back from Fjällbacka. After checking in the telephone book he found what he was searching for.

'I'm looking for Eva Nestler,' he told the receptionist who answered. He was told that there were calls ahead of him, and he waited patiently in the phone queue. As usual, some off-putting canned music was playing, but after a while he started thinking that it sounded pretty good. Martin glanced at the clock. He'd been waiting for almost a quarter of an hour. He decided to give it five more minutes, then he'd hang up and try again later. Just then he heard Eva's voice in the receiver.

'Eva Nestler.'

'Hello, my name is Martin Molin. I don't know if you remember me, but we met a couple of months ago in connection with an investigation of suspected child abuse. I'm ringing from the Tanumshede police station,' he hastened to add.

'Yes, I remember. You work with Patrik Hedström,' said Eva. 'I've mostly been in contact with Patrik, but I recall meeting you as well.' There was a moment's silence. 'What can I help you with?'

Martin cleared his throat. 'Are you familiar with something called Asperger's?'

'Asperger's syndrome. Yes, I'm familiar with it.'

'We have a . . .' he fell silent and wondered how to express himself. Morgan wasn't quite classifiable as a suspect, rather as a person of interest. He started over. 'We've encountered Asperger's in a case we're working on right now, and I'd like a little more information about what it involves. Do you think you could help me?'

'Well,' said Eva hesitantly, 'I think I'd need a little time to refresh my knowledge.' Martin could hear her paging through something that must be an appointment diary. 'I'd actually set aside an hour after lunch to do some errands, but for the police . . .' She paused. 'Otherwise I don't have a slot free until Tuesday.'

'Right now would be fine,' Martin hurried to say. He'd actually hoped to be able to do it on the phone, but it wasn't much trouble to drive over to Strömstad.

'So I'll see you in about 45 minutes then?'

'Of course,' said Martin. Then a thought occurred to him. 'Should I bring you some lunch?'

'Sure, why not? A little return on my taxes wouldn't hurt. I'm just joking,' she added quickly, in case Martin misunderstood.

'No problem,' Martin laughed. 'Any special requests for what sort of food your tax should generate?'

'Something light would be good, maybe a salad. Most people try to slim down for summertime, but I seem to be doing the opposite. I'm trying to lose weight for winter instead.'

'A salad it is,' said Martin and hung up.

He took his jacket and stopped outside Gösta's door.

'Hey, we'll have to skip lunch today. I have to drive up to Strömstad and talk to Eva Nestler, the psychologist we usually consult.' Gösta's expression forced him to add, 'Of course, you can come along if you like.'

For a moment Gösta looked as though he wanted to do just that. Then the skies opened up outside and he shook his head.

'Heck no. I'm staying inside in this weather. I guess I'll give Patrik and Ernst a ring and see if they can bring back something edible.'

'You do that. I'm off now.'

Gösta had already turned his back and didn't reply. Martin hesitated a moment inside the front doors before he turned up his collar and jogged over to his car. Even though it wasn't parked very far away, he still managed to get soaked.

Half an hour later, he was parked by the river a stone's throw from Eva's office. It was located in the same building as the Strömstad police station, and he assumed they had a good deal to do with each other. The police often had occasion to avail themselves of a psychologist's services, for example when a victim of abuse needed professional help after an investigation was concluded. There weren't many practising psychologists in the county; Eva was one of the few. She had an excellent reputation and was considered highly skilled. Patrik had nothing but good things to say about her, and Martin hoped she could also help him.

In reality he wasn't quite sure why he wanted to consult her. Morgan was not a suspect, after all, but Martin's curiosity had been aroused by what lay behind his strange behaviour and character. Asperger's was something altogether new for Martin, and it couldn't hurt to know more about it.

He shook the rain off his jacket before he hung it in the cloakroom. His shirt underneath was also damp, and he shivered a bit. In a paper bag he had two salads that he'd bought at Coffee and Buns, and Eva Nestler's receptionist had apparently been forewarned of his arrival. She merely nodded in the direction of the door with Eva's nameplate. He knocked discreetly and heard a voice call out, 'Come in.'

'Hello, that was fast.' Eva glanced at the clock. 'I hope you didn't break any speed limits on the way over here.' She feigned a disapproving look and he laughed.

'No, no danger of that. Besides, I happen to know that the police are busy with other things today,' he whispered conspiratorially with a wink. He recalled that he'd liked Eva the first time he met her. She had a special talent for making people relax in her company. It must be a gift particular to people in her profession.

Martin set out the lunch on a little table in her office.

'I hope prawn salad will do.'

'That's perfect,' replied Eva, getting up from her chair behind the desk and sitting down on one of the four chairs around the table.

'Actually I'm only fooling myself,' she said as she poured the entire contents of the little container of dressing on the salad. 'After all this liquid fat has covered the veggies, I might as well

have ordered a hamburger. But a salad feels better psychologic-
ally. That way I might be able to convince myself that I can
indulge in a piece of cake tonight.' She laughed so hard her breasts
jiggled.

Martin could see from her plump figure that she probably
convinced herself of that quite often, but she was elegantly dressed
and her grey hair was cut short in a style that looked modern yet
suitable for her age.

'So, you wanted to know more about Asperger's syndrome,' she
said.

'Yes, I encountered it for the first time yesterday, and at this
stage I'm mostly just curious,' said Martin as he impaled a prawn
on his fork.

'Well, I do know something about it, but I've never actually
had a patient with that diagnosis, so I had to read up on the subject
before you came. What is it you want to know, more specifically?
There's plenty to say about it.'

'Let's see,' Martin said, giving it some thought. 'Maybe you
could tell me a bit about what characterizes someone with
Asperger's, and how you can tell that's what it is.'

'First of all, it's a diagnosis that hasn't been in use until quite
recently. It probably appeared about fifteen years ago, but it was
first documented back in the forties by Hans Asperger. It's a
functional disorder. Some researchers now claim he may have had
the malady himself.'

Martin nodded and let Eva continue.

'It's a form of autism, but the person most often has normal to
high intelligence.'

Martin recognized this from what Morgan had said.

Eva went on, 'What makes it hard to describe Asperger's
syndrome is that the symptoms can vary from one individual to
another, and they're divided into several groups. Some people
withdraw inside themselves, more like classic autism, while others
are extremely outgoing. And Asperger's is seldom discovered early.
Parents may be concerned that their child's behaviour is abnormal
in some way, without being able to say exactly what's wrong. And
as I said, the problem is that it can vary considerably from one
child to another. Some Asperger's children start talking unusually

202

early, some unusually late, and the same is true of starting to walk and lots of other developmental areas. Normally the problem doesn't show up before school age, but that's also when it can be wrongly diagnosed as ADHD or DAMP.'

'And how does the problem manifest itself then?' Martin was so fascinated that he was neglecting his lunch. Before he applied for the police academy he had toyed with the idea of studying psychology, and sometimes he wondered whether he might have made the wrong choice. Nothing was as interesting as the human psyche in all its myriad forms.

'The most obvious symptoms are probably the difficulties that arise with social interaction. The children consistently behave in an improper fashion. They don't understand social rules, and they may have a tendency to blurt out the truth, which obviously makes it hard to get along with other people. There is also a strong egocentricity. They have a hard time relating to other people's feelings and experiences and care only about themselves. Often they don't have much need to be with other people. If they do play with other children they either try to decide everything or they completely submit to the other children's will. The latter is more common among girls with the syndrome. Another clear indication is if the child develops a special interest that becomes an obsession. Children with Asperger's have the capacity to become incredibly detail-oriented, and they often learn everything about their special interest. For adults it's often exciting to watch the child develop his knowledge, but Asperger children have such one-track minds and are so often consumed by their special passion that others soon lose interest. When the children reach school age, obsessive thoughts and actions start becoming noticeable. They have to do things in a certain way, and they also force people around them to do things that way.'

'What about language?' asked Martin, recalling Morgan's odd way of expressing himself.

'Yes, language is another strong indicator.' Eva scraped the last of her salad from the plastic bowl and then continued. 'It's one of the big difficulties that people with Asperger's syndrome encounter in their daily lives. When we humans communicate, we usually express much more than what our words say. We use body language and facial expressions, we modify the intonation of a sentence, use different emphasis, and vigorously employ similes and metaphors. All these things present difficulties for someone with Asperger's. An expression such as "we'll probably have to skip coffee" could be understood as meaning that one should jump over a coffee cup. When speaking, they also have a hard time understanding hearing how they sound to other people. Their voice could be very soft, almost a whisper, or very loud and shrill. Often it is droning and monotonous.'

Martin nodded. Morgan's voice fit with that latter description.

'The person I met also had an odd way of moving. Is that common?'

Eva nodded. 'Motor function is also a distinct sign. It can be awkward, stiff, or extremely minimalistic. Stereotypy also occurs frequently.'

She could see from Martin's expression that she needed to explain that last term.

'That means stereotypical movements that are repeated, such as small waves of the hand.'

'If the person with Asperger's has trouble with motor skills, does it apply to everything he does?' Martin remembered how Morgan's fingers flew smoothly over the keyboard.

'No, not really. It's common that in conjunction with his special interest, or if he's doing something that particularly fascinates him, he can have very high-functioning fine-motor skills.'

'What are the teen years like for kids with this syndrome?'

'Well, that's a whole other story. But would you like some coffee before we go on? It's a lot of information to take in. Are you going to take notes, by the way, or is your memory that good?'

Martin pointed to the little tape recorder he'd placed on the table. 'My assistant will take care of that. But I won't say no to a cup of coffee.' His stomach was grumbling a little. Salad was not what he usually ate for lunch, and he knew he'd have to stop at a hot-dog stand on the way back.

After a while Eva came back with a cup of steaming hot coffee in each hand. She sat down and continued her lecture.

'Where were we? Oh yes, the teen years. Once again that's a time when it's rather difficult to diagnose a person with Asperger's if he or she hasn't been diagnosed previously. So many of the usual problems of adolescence come up, but they're often amplified and made more extreme by Asperger's. Hygiene, for example, is a big problem. Many are careless with their daily hygiene. They don't feel like taking a shower, brushing their teeth, or changing clothes. Going to school becomes problematic. They have a hard time grasping the importance of making an effort in school, and problems also continue in social interactions with schoolmates and other contemporaries. This makes it difficult and sometimes impossible for them to work in groups, which are becoming more prevalent in secondary school and the gym. Depression is common, as well as antisocial behaviour.'

Martin pricked up his ears at this. 'What would you include in that category?'

'Things such as violent crimes, break-ins, and arson.'

'So there's an increased tendency for persons with Asperger's to commit crimes of violence?'

'Well, it's not that those suffering from Asperger's as a whole are more inclined to violence, but the percentage is definitely higher than in the general population. As I said before, they have a strong ego fixation and difficulty understanding and involving themselves in other people's feelings. Lack of empathy is a strong personality trait. To simplify somewhat, one might say that common sense is a concept that is lacking in someone with Asperger's.'

'If a person with Asperger's . . .' Martin hesitated, 'was implicated in a homicide investigation, would there be a reason to pay closer attention to him?'

Eva took his question seriously and paused to ponder her reply.

'I can't answer that. Of course there are, as I said, certain characteristics in the diagnosis that lower the barrier that prevents most people from committing acts of violence. At the same time it's an exceedingly small percentage of people with Asperger's who go to the extreme of committing murder. Yes, I do read the papers, so I know what case you're talking about,' she said, cradling her coffee cup pensively in her hands. 'It's my personal opinion that it would be extremely risky to go down that road, if you know what I mean.'

Martin nodded. He knew exactly what she meant. It had

happened many times before that people ended up being wrongly accused simply because they were different. But knowledge is power, and he still felt it had been very valuable to get an insight into Morgan's world.

'I'd really like to thank you for taking the time to talk with me. I hope the errands you had to postpone because of me weren't urgent.'

'No, not at all,' said Eva, getting up to show him out. 'A little badly needed renewal of my wardrobe is all. In other words, nothing that can't wait till next week.'

She accompanied him to the cloakroom and waited while he put on his jacket, which was actually dry by now.

'I'm glad I don't have to go out in this crummy weather,' said Eva. They peered out of the window at the rain that was still pouring down and making big puddles on the square.

'Yes, it's looking like it's going to be autumn forever,' replied Martin, holding out his hand to say goodbye.

'Thanks for the lunch, by the way. And do call if you have any more questions. It was a pleasure to be able to brush up on a particular subject. I don't often get a chance to do that.'

'Right. Well, I'll give you a ring if I need to. Thanks again.'

FJÄLLBACKA 1924

The delivery was more horrible than Agnes could ever have imagined. She had been in the throes of labour for almost forty-eight hours and was close to dying, before the doctor finally leaned his whole weight on her belly and forced the first child out into the world. For there were two. The second boy soon followed, and they proudly showed her the babies after they had been washed and wrapped in warm blankets. But Agnes turned away. She didn't want to see the creatures that had destroyed her life and had brought her so near death. As far as she was concerned, they could give those babies away, or toss them in the river or do whatever they liked with them. Their tiny, shrill voices tore at her ears. After being forced to listen to that sound for a while, she covered her ears and bellowed at the woman holding them to take them away. In horror the nurse obeyed, and Agnes could hear people starting to whisper around her. But the shrieks faded, and now she just wanted to be allowed to sleep. Sleep for a hundred years, to be wakened by a kiss from a prince who would take her away from all this misery and from the two demanding little monsters that her body had expelled.

When she awoke she thought at first that her dream had been granted. A tall, dark figure stood leaning over her, and for a moment she thought she saw the prince she'd been waiting for. But then reality came crashing down on her. She saw that it was Anders's stupid face bending towards her. The sight of the loving expression on his face made her sick. Did he think that things between them would be different now, just because she had squeezed out two sons for him? She would be happy if he could take them away and let her have her freedom back. For a brief moment she noticed how that thought aroused a jubilant feeling in her breast. She was no longer huge and shapeless and pregnant. She could leave if she liked, find the life she deserved, the life where she belonged. Then she realized how impossible that would be. Since there was no chance of returning to her father, where would she go? She had no money of her own and no way of obtaining any, other than selling herself on the streets. Even her present life was better than that. The hopelessness of her situation made her turn her head away and sob. Anders gently stroked her hair. If she could have managed it she would have raised her arms to shove his hands away.

'They're so beautiful, Agnes. They're just perfect.' His voice was quivering a little.

She didn't reply, just stared at the wall and shut out everything else. If only somebody would come and take her away from here.

Sara still hadn't come back. Mamma had explained that she wasn't going to, but Frida hadn't believed her. She thought it was just something Mamma was saying. Sara couldn't simply disappear like that, could she? If so, Frida regretted that she hadn't been nicer to her. She wouldn't have fought so much with Sara when she took her toys, but just let her have them. Now it was probably too late.

She went over to the window and looked up at the sky again. It was grey and dirty-looking. Sara wouldn't like living there, would she?

Then there was the whole secret about the old man, too. Of course she'd promised Sara to keep quiet. But Mamma said that she should always tell the truth, and not saying anything was almost the same as lying, wasn't it?

Frida sat down in front of her dollhouse. It was her favourite toy. It had belonged to her mamma when she was little, and now it was Frida's. She had a hard time imagining that Mamma was once the same age as Frida was now. Mamma was so . . . grown-up, after all.

The dollhouse showed clear traces of being from the '70s. It was supposed to represent a two-storey brick house and it was furnished in brown and orange. The furniture was the same as when her mother had played with the dollhouse. Frida thought all the pieces were super, but it was a shame that there weren't more pink and blue things in the dollhouse. Blue was her favourite colour. And pink had been Sara's favourite. Frida thought it was odd. Everyone knew that pink and red clashed, and Sara had red hair, so she shouldn't have liked pink. But she did anyway. That was how she always was. Contrary, sort of.

There were four dolls that went with the house. Two child dolls and a mamma and a pappa doll. Now she took the two child dolls, both girls, and set them facing each other. Usually she wanted to be the one in green, because she was the nicest-looking, but now that Sara was dead she could be the green one. Frida would have to be the doll in the brown dress.

'Hi, Frida, do you know that I'm dead?' said the green Sara doll.

'Yes, Mamma told me,' said the brown one.

'What does she say about it?'

'That you've gone to heaven and won't be coming over to play with me anymore.'

'How boring,' said the Sara doll.

Frida nodded her doll's head. 'Yes, I think so too. If I knew you were going to die and wouldn't come over to play with me anymore, you could have had whatever toys you wanted and I wouldn't have complained.'

'What a shame,' said the Sara doll. 'That I'm dead, I mean.'

'Yes, what a shame,' said the one in brown.

Both dolls were silent for a moment. Then the Sara doll said in a serious tone of voice, 'You didn't say anything about the man, did you?'

'No, I promised.'

'Because it was our secret.'

'But why can't I tell? The old man was nasty, wasn't he?' The brown doll's voice sounded shrill.

'That's why. The old man said that I mustn't tell. And you have to do whatever nasty old men say.'

'But you're dead, so the old man can't do anything, can he?'

The Sara doll had nothing to say to that. Frida carefully put the dolls back in the house and went over to stand by the window again. Imagine that everything had to be so hard, just because Sara had died.

*   *   *

Annika was back from lunch and called out to Patrik when he and Ernst returned. He merely waved, in a hurry to get to his office, but she insisted. He stopped in the doorway with a curious expression on his face. Annika peered at him over the top of her glasses. He looked exhausted, and the rain had given him the appearance of a drowned cat besides. But between the baby and the murder of a child he probably didn't have much energy left to take care of himself.

She saw the impatience in Patrik's eyes and hurried to tell him what she wanted to report. 'I got a number of calls today, because of the media coverage.'

'Anything of interest?' said Patrik without much enthusiasm. It was so seldom they got anything useful from the public that he didn't have very high hopes.

'Yes and no,' said Annika. 'Most of them are from the usual gossips who ring up to pass on hot tips about their sworn enemies and all sorts of people, and in this case the homophobia has really been rampant. Apparently, any man who works with flowers or cuts hair is automatically suspected of being homosexual and capable of doing horrid things to children.'

Patrik was shifting from one foot to the other, and Annika rushed on. She took the top note from the pile and handed it to him.

'This one seems like it might be something. A woman rang, refused to give a name, but said we ought to take a look at the medical records of Sara's little brother. That's all she would say, but something told me there might be something to it. Could be worth following up on, anyway.'

Patrik didn't look nearly as interested as she had hoped. On the other hand he hadn't heard the urgency in the voice of the woman who rang. Her tone differed markedly from the poorly disguised malice of those who loved to spread gossip.

'Yes, it could be worth checking out, but don't get your hopes up. Anonymous tips don't usually pan out.'

Annika started to say something, but Patrik held up his hands.

'Yeah, yeah, I know. Something told you that this one is different. And I promise to follow up on it. But it'll have to wait a while. We have more pressing things to deal with right now. There's a

211

meeting in the lunchroom in five minutes, then I'll tell you more.' His fingers beat a quick tattoo on the door frame, and Patrik walked off with her note in his hand.

Annika wondered what new information had come up. She hoped it would be something that broke the case open. The mood at the station had been way too gloomy lately.

Niclas could find no peace and quiet to work. The image of Sara's face wouldn't leave him alone, and the visit from the police this morning had brought all his feelings of anxiety to the surface. Maybe it was right what everyone said, maybe he'd gone back to work too soon. But for him it had been a means of survival. It helped him to put aside the thoughts he didn't want to think about and instead focus his attention on ulcers, corns, three-day fever, and ear infections. Nothing mattered as long as he didn't have to think about Sara. Or Charlotte. But now reality had mercilessly intruded, and he felt himself rushing towards the abyss. It didn't help that his anxiety was self-inflicted. To be honest, which was unusual for him, he couldn't really understand why he did the things he did. Something inside seemed to keep driving him forward in a hunt for something that lay just out of reach. Despite the fact that he already had so much – or at least used to have so much. Now his life was in pieces, and nothing he said or did could change it.

Niclas leafed listlessly through the records in front of him. He always hated paperwork, and today he was having serious trouble concentrating. During his first appointment after lunch he had even been brusque and impolite to the patient. Normally he was charming with everyone, no matter who came in. But today he hadn't had the energy to pamper yet another old lady who came to see him about her imaginary pains. The patient in question had been something of a steady customer at the clinic, but now it was doubtful she would be back. His candid opinion on the state of her health had not been to her taste. Oh well, such things no longer seemed important.

With a sigh he began to gather up all the medical records. He was suddenly overwhelmed by the feelings he'd been trying to suppress for so long, and with a single motion he swept everything off his desk. The papers fluttered lazily to the floor and landed in one big heap. Niclas suddenly couldn't get his doctor's coat off fast enough. He flung it to the floor, pulled on his jacket and ran out of his office as if pursued by the Devil himself. Which he was, in a sense. He stopped briefly to tell his nurse with forced composure to cancel all his appointments for the afternoon. Then he rushed out into the rain. A tear found its way into his mouth, and the salt called up an image of his daughter, floating in a grey sea while whitecaps danced on the surface around her head. It made him run even faster. His tears merged with the rain as he fled. Most of all he was fleeing from himself.

The coffee-maker chugged and wheezed but produced the same black tar as usual. Patrik chose to stand next to the drainboard, while the others took their cups and sat down. Everyone was present except Martin, and he was just about to ask if anyone had seen him when he came dashing in, out of breath.

'Sorry I'm late. Annika rang and said there was a meeting. I was on my way and –'

Patrik held up his hand. 'We'll deal with that later. Right now I have some things I want to discuss.'

Martin nodded and sat down at the foot of the table, giving Patrik a curious look.

'We got the results of the analysis of Sara's stomach and lung contents. And they found something odd.'

The mood grew palpably tense around the table. Mellberg was looking attentively at Patrik, and even Ernst and Gösta seemed interested for a change. Annika was taking notes as usual so she could send out minutes to everyone after the meeting.

'Someone forced the girl to eat ashes.'

If a needle had dropped to the floor it would have sounded like thunder, it was so quiet in the room. Then Mellberg cleared his throat. 'Ashes? Did you say ashes?'

Patrik nodded. 'Yes, they were found in her stomach and her lungs. Pedersen's theory is that someone forced them into her mouth when she was already in the bathtub. Some of the ashes landed in the water, and when she was drowned she ended up with ashes in her lungs.'

'But why?' Annika said in amazement, forgetting for once to take notes.

'Yes, that's the question. And we also need to ask how this information can lead us forward. I already rang and ordered an examination of the Florin family's bathroom. Wherever we find ashes, that's the crime scene we're looking for.'

'But do you really think that someone in the family . . .' Gösta didn't finish his sentence.

'I don't think anything,' said Patrik. 'But if some other potential crime scene turns up, we'll have to go over it with a fine-toothed comb as well, especially if the search this afternoon doesn't produce anything. The Florins' home is still the last place she was seen, so we might as well start there. Or what do you think, Bertil?'

The question was rhetorical. Mellberg hadn't been involved in the investigation at all, but everyone knew that he liked to encourage the illusion that he was in control.

Mellberg nodded. 'Sounds like a good idea. But why wasn't a forensic examination of their home already done?'

Patrik had to control himself not to grimace. It was bad enough that Ernst had pointed out the same thing a moment earlier, but to have to hear it from Mellberg just made matters worse. It was easy to be smart in hindsight. If Patrik were to be completely honest, until now they hadn't any valid reason to do anything but a cursory inspection of the house. He didn't think he could even have obtained a warrant. But he chose not to point this out. Instead he replied as vaguely as possible: 'I think now we have something concrete to look for, it's a better time. In any case, the team from Uddevalla will be there at four o'clock. I intend to participate, and I'd like to take you along too, Martin, if you have time.'

Patrik glanced cautiously at Mellberg when he said this. He hoped that he wouldn't persist in forcing Ernst on him. He was in luck. Mellberg didn't say a word. Maybe the whole issue was forgotten by now.

'Sure, I can come along,' said Martin.

'All right, then. The meeting is adjourned.'

Annika had intended to tell everybody about the call she'd

received, but they had already stood up so she decided to wait. Patrik had the information, and she was sure he'd deal with it as soon as he could.

The handwritten note was in fact in Patrik's back pocket. Forgotten.

Stig heard the footsteps on the stairs and steeled himself. He'd heard Niclas and Lilian's voices downstairs and knew they were talking about him. He carefully pushed himself up to a half-sitting position. It felt like a thousand knives slicing into his stomach, but by the time Niclas came into the room Stig's face was without expression. The image of his father in hospital, helpless and small, languishing in a cold, clinical hospital bed, filled his thoughts. He swore once again that it would never happen to him. His condition was only temporary. It had passed before and it would pass again.

'Lilian says that you're feeling worse today.' Niclas sat down on the edge of the bed, and put on his most concerned doctor's expression. Stig saw that his eyes were rimmed in red. And it was no wonder if the boy had cried. Losing a child. Stig himself missed the little girl so much it hurt. He realized that Niclas was waiting for an answer.

'Oh, you know how women are. Blowing everything all out of proportion. I didn't sleep very well last night, that's all, but now I feel better.' The pain forced him to clench his jaws, and it was a strain not to show how he was really feeling.

Niclas gave him a suspicious look but then took out some paraphernalia from a large doctor's bag he had brought along.

'I'm not sure I believe you, but let's start by taking your blood pressure and checking your vitals. Then we'll see.'

He fastened the blood-pressure cuff round Stig's skinny arm and pumped it up until it was tight. He watched the gauge as it fell and then removed the cuff.

'150 over 80, not too bad. Unbutton your shirt and I'll have a listen to your chest.'

Stig obeyed and unbuttoned his shirt with fingers that were oddly stiff and unwilling. The cold stethoscope against his chest made him gasp for breath, and Niclas said gruffly, 'Long, deep breaths.'

Each breath hurt, but he managed through sheer willpower to do as Niclas asked. After listening for a moment, Niclas removed the stethoscope from his ears. He looked Stig straight in the eye.

'Well, there's nothing definite to go on, but if you're feeling worse then it's important that you let me know. Shouldn't we do a proper check-up on you? If I send you down to Uddevalla they can do some tests and see whether there's anything wrong that I'm missing.'

With a shake of his head, Stig showed his aversion to the suggestion. 'No, I'm feeling pretty good now. It's not necessary to waste time and money on me. I've probably just picked up some bug, but I'll get better soon. It's happened before, right?' A tone of entreaty slipped into his voice.

Niclas shook his head and sighed. 'Well, just don't say I didn't warn you. One can't be too careful when the body starts signalling that something's wrong. But I'm not going to force you. It's your health, so it's up to you – although I'm not looking forward to going downstairs and confronting Lilian, I must say. She was practically ready to ring for the ambulance when I came home.'

'Yes, she's a real hothead, my Lilian,' Stig chuckled, but fell silent quickly when the knives again stuck him in the stomach.

Niclas closed up his bag and gave Stig a suspicious look. 'Do you promise to tell me if there's something wrong?'

Stig nodded. 'Absolutely.'

As soon as he heard Niclas's footsteps going down the stairs he slid painfully back into a recumbent position. The pain would soon pass. Just so he stayed out of the hospital. He had to avoid that at all costs.

Lilian's face showed a broad range of emotions when she opened the door. Patrik and Martin stood in front, with a three-man team of technicians, or rather two men and one woman, behind them.

'What's this crowd for?'

'We have a warrant to examine your bathroom.'

Patrik had a hard time meeting her gaze. It was strange how often his profession made him feel like an insensitive shithead.

Lilian's gave them a look as hard as granite. But after a moment she stepped aside and let them in.

'Don't make a mess in there, I just cleaned,' she snapped.

The comment made Patrik once again regret that he hadn't ordered this done sooner. Judging from what he'd seen of the Florins' home earlier in the week, she cleaned house almost constantly. If there had been any viable evidence in the room, it was surely gone by now.

'We have a bathroom down here, with a shower, and one upstairs with a tub.' Lilian pointed up the stairs. 'Take off your shoes,' she commanded, and everyone obeyed. 'And don't bother Stig. He's resting.' With undisguised fury she went into the kitchen and began noisily clattering as she washed the dishes.

Patrik and Martin exchanged a look and led the techs upstairs. Careful to stay out of the way, they let the team get started on the bathroom and waited outside in the hall. The door to Stig's room was closed, and they spoke in low voices.

'Do you really think this is necessary?' said Martin. 'I mean, there's nothing to indicate that the killer was a family member, and . . . well, they're going through a difficult enough time as it is.'

'You're quite right, of course,' replied Patrik, almost whispering. 'But we can't rule anyone out simply because it makes us feel uncomfortable. Even if the family doesn't understand, we're doing this with their best interests in mind. If we can eliminate them from the list of suspects, we can devote more energy to other lines of inquiry. Don't you agree?'

Martin nodded. He knew that Patrik was right. It was all just so damned unpleasant. Footsteps on the stairs made them turn round, and they met Charlotte's inquiring glance.

'What's going on here? Mother said that you showed up with a whole army to look at our bathroom. Why?' Her voice rose a bit and she made an attempt to go past them. Patrik stopped her.

'Could we sit down for a moment and talk, please?'

Charlotte cast one last glance at the techs behind them and turned to go back downstairs. 'We'll sit in the kitchen,' she said, with her head turned away from Martin and Patrik. 'And I want Mother to hear what you have to say too.'

Lilian was still angrily clattering the dishes when they entered

217

the kitchen. Albin was sitting on a blanket on the floor, watching his grandmother's activities with big, serious eyes. He gave a start like a scared rabbit each time she raised her voice.

'If you're going to be taking things apart, I presume you'll put everything back the way it was.' Lilian's voice was like frost.

'I can't promise anything; they might need to take some things apart. But I can assure you they'll be as careful as possible,' said Patrik, taking a seat.

Charlotte picked Albin off the floor and sat down on one of the kitchen chairs with the boy on her lap. He snuggled into his mother's arms. She had lost weight, and she had dark circles under her eyes. She looked like she hadn't slept in a week – which she may not have done. He saw that she was trying to control a quivering lower lip when she asked, 'So, why is there a gang of police in the house all of a sudden? Why aren't they out looking for Sara's murderer instead?'

'We simply want to rule out all possibilities, Charlotte. The thing is, we . . . we have some new information. I wonder, can you think of any reason at all why someone would have wanted to make Sara eat ashes?'

Charlotte looked at him as though he'd lost his mind. She held on tighter to Albin, making him whimper. 'Eat ashes? What do you mean?'

He told her what the M.E. had said, and saw her face grow paler with every word.

'Only a crazy person would do something like that. So I understand even less why you're spending time *here*.' The last word sounded like a scream, and affected by his mother's anxiety Albin began to scream too. She hushed him at once and soothed him enough that he stopped, but she didn't take her eyes off Patrik.

He repeated what he'd said to Martin a little while ago. 'It's important for us to eliminate the family from the investigation. There is absolutely nothing to indicate that anyone in your family had anything to do with Sara's death. But we wouldn't be doing our job if we didn't do everything we could to investigate that possibility. As you know, it has happened in other cases. I'm afraid we can't always be as considerate as we'd like.'

Lilian gave a snort as she stood at the sink. Her whole body posture showed what she thought of Patrik's little speech.

'I do understand, of course I do,' said Charlotte. 'Just so you don't waste time when you could be spending it more effectively.'

'We're working full steam ahead, examining all possibilities, I can assure you of that.' On impulse Patrik leaned over the table and placed his hand on hers. She didn't pull away but met his gaze with great intensity, as if she wanted to look into his soul and with her own eyes see whether he was telling the truth. Patrik didn't flinch. And what she saw was evidently satisfactory, for she lowered her eyes and nodded.

'All right, I suppose I'll have to trust you. But it's lucky for you that Niclas isn't at home.'

'He was here a while ago,' said Lilian without turning round. 'He looked in on Stig but then left again.'

'Why did he come home? And why didn't he tell me that he was here?'

'You were sleeping, I think. And I have no idea why he came home in the middle of the afternoon. He must have needed a break. Well, I did tell him that I thought it was too soon for him to go back to work, but that boy is so conscientious that it's beyond all understanding. One certainly has to admire –'

Lilian's comments were interrupted by a demonstrative sigh from Charlotte, so she went back to washing dishes with even greater frenzy. Patrik could practically feel the tension reverberating in the room.

'In any event, he ought to hear about this. I'll ring the clinic.'

Charlotte set Albin down on his blanket on the floor and rang from the wall phone in the kitchen. No one said a word while she was on the phone. Patrik wanted nothing more than to get out of there. After a few minutes, Charlotte hung up.

'He wasn't there,' she said in disbelief.

'He wasn't there?' Lilian turned round. 'Then where is he?'

'Aina didn't know. She said that he'd taken the rest of the afternoon off. She assumed he went home.'

Lilian frowned, still turned towards the others in the kitchen. 'Well, he wasn't here more than fifteen minutes. He looked in on

Stig for a moment, then he left. And I got the impression he was going back to work.'

Patrik and Martin exchanged a look. They had their own theory about where the grieving father had gone.

The technician in charge stuck his head in the doorway to the kitchen. 'This is probably going to take a couple of hours. You'll have the results as soon as we're finished.'

Patrik and Martin got up, feeling a bit out of sorts, and nodded awkwardly to Charlotte and Lilian.

'Then we'll be on our way. And if you think of anything that might be linked to ashes, you know where to find us.'

Charlotte nodded, her face pale. Standing next to the sink Lilian pretended she was deaf and didn't even condescend to look at them.

They left the house in silence and walked towards the car.

'Could you give me a lift home?' asked Patrik.

'But you left your car down at the station. Won't you need it this weekend?'

'I just can't face going back there right now. And I still plan to come in and work a little on Saturday or Sunday. I can take the bus in and then drive my car home.'

'I thought you promised Erica to take the whole weekend off,' Martin ventured.

Patrik grimaced. 'Yeah, I know, but I hadn't counted on being saddled with a homicide investigation.'

'I'll be working this weekend, so tell me if there's anything I can do.'

'That's great, but I think I need to go over everything by myself in peace and quiet.'

'Well, you're the only one who knows what you need to do,' said Martin, getting into the car. Patrik got in on the passenger's side – but he wasn't so sure that Martin was right.

Finally she was going to get her mother-in-law out of the house. Erica could hardly believe it. All the admonitions, all the know-it-all comments and underhanded complaints had completely demolished her reserves of patience. She was counting the minutes until Kristina would get into her little Ford Escort and drive back home. If Erica had been suffering from a lack of confidence as a mother before her mother-in-law arrived, it was even worse now. Apparently nothing she did was right. She didn't know how to dress Maja the right way, or how to feed her correctly; she was too blunt, she was too clumsy, she was too lazy, she ought to rest more. There was no end to her shortcomings, and as Erica sat there with her daughter on her lap she felt as though she might as well give up. She would never manage all of this. At night she dreamt that she left Maja with Patrik and took a long trip. Far, far away. Somewhere that was calm and peaceful, with no screaming babies or responsibilities or demands. Somewhere she could curl up and be a little girl again, and someone else would take care of her.

At the same time she had a competing feeling inside that was steering her in the opposite direction. A protective instinct, and a certainty that she would never be able to leave the child she held in her arms. It was just as unthinkable as chopping off a leg or an arm. They were one now, and they would have to get through all this together. And yet she'd begun to think about what Charlotte had been urging her to do, before the terrible nightmare of Sara's death. Charlotte had said she should talk to someone, someone who understood how she was feeling. Maybe feeling like this wasn't normal. Maybe it wasn't supposed to be this way.

Sara's death was what made her begin to rethink things. It had put her own depression into perspective, made her see that she, unlike Charlotte, was going through a dark spell that could be dissipated. Charlotte would have to live with her grief for the rest of her life. But Erica might be able to do something about her situation. Before she went to talk to anyone, she ought to try Anna Wahlgren's baby care recommendations. If she could get Maja to sleep somewhere other than right on top of her, that would be progress. She just needed to muster some courage before she started that project. And get her mother-in-law out of the house.

Kristina came into the living room and gave Erica and Maja a worried look. 'Are you nursing her again? It can't have been more than two hours since last time.' She didn't wait for an answer but continued, 'In any case I've tried to put a little order in things here. All the laundry is washed, and it was quite a load, let me tell you. There are no dishes left to do, and I've given everything a good dusting. And by the way, I cooked some hamburgers and put them in the freezer, so you'll have something to eat besides those horrible frozen dinners. You have to eat properly, you know, and that goes for Patrik too. He works hard all day long, and then he has to take care of Maja large parts of the evening, so he needs all the nourishment he can get. I must say I was quite shocked when I saw him. He looked dreadfully pale and worn out.'

The litany went on and on, and Erica had to clench her teeth to resist the impulse to put her hands over her ears and sing, like a little girl. Of course she'd had a few hours free when her mother-in-law was here, she couldn't deny that, but the drawbacks clearly outweighed the benefits. With tears threatening to spill, she stubbornly stared straight ahead at Ricki Lake on the TV. Why couldn't her mother-in-law just leave?

It seemed as though her prayer had been heard, for Kristina set a packed suitcase in the hall and began putting on her coat and shoes.

'Are you sure you'll be able to get along?'

Erica wearily shifted her gaze from the TV and even managed to squeeze out a little smile.

'Sure, we'll be fine.' After an almost Herculean effort she added, 'And thanks so terribly much for all the help.'

She hoped Kristina couldn't hear how false it sounded. Apparently not, for her mother-in-law nodded graciously and said, 'Well, it's just nice to be of some use. I'll come back soon.'

Get your arse out of here, woman, Erica thought feverishly, trying by sheer force of will to shove her mother-in-law out the front door. Miraculously it seemed to work, and when the door closed behind her Erica heaved a deep sigh of relief. But it didn't last long. In the silence after Kristina's departure, with Maja's rhythmic snuffling the only sound, thoughts of Anna popped up. She still hadn't got hold of her sister, and Anna hadn't tried to call either. In frustration she punched the number of Anna's mobile, but as so many times before in recent weeks she got only the voicemail. She left a brief message for the umpteenth time and then broke the connection. Why wasn't Anna answering? Erica started devising one plan after another to find out what had happened to her sister, but eventually she gave up as she was overcome by fatigue. It would have to wait until another day.

Lucas said he was going out to look for a job, but she didn't believe him for an instant. Not dressed as he was, slovenly and unshaven with his hair unkempt. She had no idea what he was doing instead. But Anna knew better than to ask. Questions were bad. Questions led to hard blows that left visible marks. Last week she hadn't been able to take the children to day-care. The marks on her face had been so obvious that even Lucas realized it would be folly to let her go out.

Her thoughts kept circling around how this was all going to end. Everything had gone downhill so fast that it made her head spin. The time in the elegant flat in Östermalm, with Lucas going off to his job as a stockbroker each day, well-dressed and calm, felt like a distant dream. She could remember that even back then she had wanted to escape, but it was hard to understand why. Compared with her life now it could hardly have been so bad. Of course she had received the occasional beating, but there were good times as well, and everything had been so nice, so orderly. Now she looked around the cramped two-room flat and felt hope-lessness settling over her. The children slept on mattresses on the floor of the living room, and their toys were strewn about every-where. She couldn't even face picking them up. If Lucas came home before she found the energy to clean up, the consequences would certainly be harsh. But she simply couldn't be bothered anymore.

What scared her the most was when she looked into Lucas's eyes and saw that something vital had disappeared. Something human that had slipped away, to be replaced by something much darker and more dangerous. He had lost almost everything, and nothing was as dangerous as a person who had nothing more to lose.

For a moment she thought about making an attempt to get out of the flat and call for help. Collect the children at day-care, ring Erica and ask her to come get them. Or ring the police. But she wouldn't get beyond the thinking stage. She never knew when

Lucas might come home, and if he arrived at the moment she was trying to escape her prison, she would never again get a chance to flee, or a chance to survive.

Instead she sat down in the easy chair by the window and looked out over the courtyard. She let the dusk slowly descend over her life.

FJÄLLBACKA 1925

The sound of the sledgehammer striking the chisel was accompanied by his whistling. After the boys were born, he regained the joy he used to feel in his work, and each day he went to the quarry with the certainty that he now had something to work for. The twins were everything he had ever dreamt of. They were only six months old, but already they controlled his whole world and comprised his whole universe. The image of their bald little heads and toothless smiles kept coming back to him as he worked. It brought a song to his heart and he longed for evening so he could go home to them.

The thought of his wife made his otherwise even-handed blows on the granite lose their rhythm for a moment. She still hadn't seemed to bond with the children, although now it was a long time since she had almost died giving birth. The doctor had said that for some women it could take a long time to recover from such an experience, and that in those cases months could go by before they bonded with the child, or in this case the children. But by now half a year had passed. And Anders had tried his best to make things easier for Agnes. Despite his long workdays, he always tended to the boys when they woke up at night, and since she refused to nurse them, he also helped with feeding them. And he was happy to change their nappies and play with them. At the same time he had to spend long hours at the quarry, so Agnes was forced to take care of them while he was away. This worried him. When he came home he often found that they hadn't been changed all day and they were crying desperately from hunger. He had tried to talk to his wife about it, but she just turned her head away and refused to listen.

Finally he had gone over to the Janssons and asked Karin, Jansson's wife, if she'd consider coming over occasionally to see how his family was doing at his place. She'd given him a searching look and then promised to do so. Anders was eternally grateful to her for this. Not that she didn't have enough to do with her own children. The eight kids took up almost all her time, and yet she promised without hesitation to look in on his two as often as she could. A stone had been lifted from his heart with that promise. Sometimes he thought he saw a strange gleam in Agnes's eyes, but it vanished so quickly that he convinced himself it was just his imagination. But sometimes he would picture that look as he stood and worked, and then he had to stop himself from throwing down his sledgehammer and running home, just to make sure that the boys were sitting there on the floor and playing, rosy-cheeked and healthy.

Lately he had taken on even more work than usual. Somehow he had to find a way to make Agnes more satisfied with her life, otherwise she would make all of them unhappy. Ever since they moved to the company compound she had nagged him to rent a place somewhere in town instead, and Anders had decided to do all he could to grant that wish. If it would make her even a bit more kindly disposed to him and the boys, his long hours of work would be more than worth it. He put aside every extra öre he could spare. Now that he had control of the household funds it was possible to save, even though it meant that their meals became rather monotonous. His mother hadn't taught him how to cook many dishes, and he always bought the cheapest ingredients he could find. Agnes reluctantly began to take on some of a wife's duties, and after some practice, what she cooked began to be actually edible, so Anders had some hope that he could give up responsibility for making dinner in the near future.

If they could only move into the town of Fjällbacka, where things were a little more lively, the situation might get brighter.

Maybe they could even have a real married life again, something she had denied him for over a year.

Before him the stone parted in a perfect cleavage right down the middle. He took it as a good omen – his plan was leading him in the right direction.

At precisely ten past ten, the train rolled in. Mellberg had already been waiting for half an hour. Several times he had been on the verge of turning the car around and driving back home. But that wouldn't have served any purpose. His whereabouts would have been asked about and soon the gossip would have started. It was just as well to confront this entire disagreeable situation head on. At the same time he couldn't ignore the fact that something resembling eagerness was stirring in his breast. At first he hadn't even been able to identify the feeling. It was so foreign to him to feel anticipation for something, anything, that it took him a long moment to work out what the bubbling sensation was. It came as a big surprise when he finally identified it.

Sheer nervousness made it impossible for him to stand still on the platform awaiting the train's arrival. He constantly shifted position, and for the first time in his life wished he smoked, so that he could have calmed his nerves with a cigarette. Before he left the house he had cast a wistful glance at the bottle of Absolut vodka, but managed to restrain himself. He didn't want to smell of liquor the first time they met. First impressions were important.

Then the thought popped into his head again and took root. What if what she had said wasn't really true? It was confusing not to know what he was even hoping for, whether he wanted it to be true or not. He had already vacillated back and forth many times, but right now he was leaning towards hoping that the letter was right. No matter how strange that felt.

A toot of the horn in the distance signalled that the train from Göteborg was approaching the station. Mellberg gave a start, which made the hair he had combed over the top of his scalp slide down over one ear. With a swift and practised motion he flipped the strands of hair back into place and made sure that they were properly positioned. He didn't want to disgrace himself right from the start.

The train came rolling in at such speed that at first Mellberg didn't think it was even going to stop. Maybe it would keep on going into the unknown and leave him standing there, with his feelings of eagerness and uncertainty. But at last the train slowed and with much screeching and general racket it came to a halt. He swept his eyes over all the doors. All at once it struck him that he didn't even know if he would recognize him. Shouldn't she have put a carnation in his buttonhole or something? Then he realized that he was the only one waiting on the platform, so at least the arriving passenger would be able to find Mellberg.

The door furthest back opened, and Mellberg felt his heart stop beating for a second. A lady of retirement age carefully climbed down the steps. The disappointment at seeing her got his heart started again. But then he emerged. And as soon as Mellberg saw him, all doubt was erased. He was filled with a quiet, strange, aching joy.

The weekends went by so fast, but Erica enjoyed having Patrik at home. Saturday and Sunday were the days she focused on. Then Patrik could take care of Maja in the mornings, and one of the nights she usually used the breast pump so that he could give Maja the milk. That meant that she got a whole night of blessed sleep, even though she paid a price by waking up with two aching, leaking breasts that felt like cannonballs. But it was worth it. She never would have imagined that nirvana was being allowed to sleep a whole night undisturbed.

But this weekend had felt different. Patrik had gone in to work a few hours on Saturday, and he was silent and tense. Even though she understood why, it annoyed her that he was unable to devote himself completely to her and Maja. Her disappointment in turn gave her a guilty conscience and made her feel like a bad person.

If Patrik's brooding might lead to Charlotte and Niclas finding out who had murdered their daughter, then Erica ought to be generous enough to excuse his lack of attention. But logic and rationality didn't seem to be her strong suit these days.

On Sunday afternoon the overcast weather that had lasted all week finally broke, and they went for a long walk in town. Erica couldn't help being amazed at how the appearance of the sun could suddenly transform their surroundings so completely. In the storm and rain Fjällbacka looked so barren, so implacable and grey, but now the town sparkled once again, wedged in at the base of the monolithic hill. No trace remained of the breakers that had crashed against the docks and caused temporary flooding of Ingrid Bergman Square. Now the air was clear and fresh, and the water lay placid and gleaming as if it had never looked any other way.

Patrik pushed the pram, and Maja for once had acquiesced to fall asleep in it.

'How are you doing, actually?' Erica asked, and Patrik jumped, as if he were far, far away.

'I'm the one who should be asking you that question,' Patrik said, sounding guilty. 'You have a hard enough time without worrying about me too.'

Erica stuck her arm in under his and leaned her head on his shoulder. 'We both worry about each other, okay? And to answer your question first, things have been better, I have to admit. But they've been worse too. So now answer my question.'

She recognized Patrik's state of mind. It had been the same during the last murder investigation he'd handled, and this time it was a child who was the victim. And on top of everything, she was the daughter of one of her own friends.

'I just don't know how to proceed anymore. I've felt that way ever since we began this investigation. I went over everything again and again when I drove in to the station yesterday, but I've run out of ideas.'

'Is it true that nobody saw anything?'

He sighed. 'Yes, all they saw was Sara leaving the house. After that there was no trace of her. It's as if she vanished in a puff of smoke and then suddenly turned up in the sea.'

'I tried to ring Charlotte a while ago and Lilian answered,' Erica said cautiously. 'She sounded unusually curt, even for her. Is there something I should know about?'

Patrik hesitated, but finally decided to tell her. 'We did a crime-scene search at their house on Friday. Lilian was a bit upset about it . . .'

Erica raised her eyebrows. 'I can imagine. But why did you do that? I mean, someone outside the family must have done it, don't you think?'

Patrik shrugged. 'Yes, more than likely. But we can't just assume that's true. We have to investigate everything.' He was starting to get irritated that everyone was questioning the way he did his job. He couldn't rule out investigating the family simply because the idea was unpleasant. It was just as important to scrutinize the family members closely as it was to examine everything that pointed to an outside perpetrator. With no clues leading in a specific direction, all directions were equally important.

Erica could hear his irritation, and she patted him on the arm to show that she meant no offence. She felt him relax.

'Do we need to get something for dinner?' They were walking past the old clinic that was now a day-care centre, and saw the Konsum supermarket sign up ahead.

'Something good.'

'Do you mean dinner or dessert?' said Patrik, turning down the little hill towards the Konsum car park. Erica shot him a look, and Patrik laughed.

'Both,' she said. 'What I was thinking . . .'

When they emerged from the market with plenty of goodies loaded onto the pram's undercarriage, Patrik asked in surprise, 'Did I imagine it, or was the woman behind us in the queue giving me a funny look?'

'No, you weren't imagining it. That was Monica Wiberg, the Florins' neighbour. Her husband's name is Kaj and they have a son named Morgan, who I hear is a little strange.'

Now Patrik understood why the woman had been staring at him with such anger. Of course he wasn't the officer who had questioned her son, but it was probably enough that he was a member of the same profession.

'He has Asperger's,' said Patrik.

'Who?' said Erica, who had already forgotten what they were talking about and was fully engrossed in arranging Maja's cap, which had twisted to one side as she slept, exposing her ear to the autumn chill.

'Morgan Wiberg,' said Patrik. 'Gösta and Martin went over to talk to him, and he told them himself that he has something called Asperger's.'

'What's that?' said Erica curiously, letting Patrik push the pram once Maja's ears were both properly covered by the warm cap.

Patrik told her some of what he'd learned from Martin on Friday. It had been a good idea to go out and meet the psychologist.

'Is he a suspect?' Erica asked.

'No, not the way things look at the moment. But he seems to be the last person who saw Sara, so it doesn't hurt to know as much about him as possible.'

'To make sure that you're not targeting him because he's a little odd.' She bit her tongue as soon as she said that. 'Sorry, I know that you're more professional than that. It's just that in small towns like this, people who are different are always the ones singled out whenever something bad happens. Blame it on the village idiot, that sort of thing.'

'On the other hand, unusual individuals have always met with greater respect in small communities than in the big cities. An eccentric character is just another part of the daily scene and is accepted as he is. In the big city he would end up considerably more isolated.'

'You're right, but that kind of tolerance has always rested on shaky ground. That's all I'm saying.'

'Yeah, well, in any case Morgan isn't being treated any differently from anyone else, I can assure you of that.'

Erica didn't reply but stuck her arm under Patrik's again. The rest of the walk home they talked about other things. But she could sense that his thoughts were somewhere else the whole time.

By Monday the fine weather that had prevailed the day before was gone. Now it was just as grey and bitterly cold as before, and Patrik huddled up in a big, thick woollen jumper as he sat at his desk. Last summer the air conditioning hadn't worked, and it was like working in a sauna. Now the raw damp seeped through the walls, making him shiver. A ring from the telephone made him jump.

'You have a visitor,' Annika's voice said on the line.

'I'm not expecting anyone.'

'A Jeanette Lind says she wants to see you.'

Patrik pictured the curvaceous little brunette in his mind and wondered what she wanted.

'Send her in,' he said, getting up to greet his unexpected visitor. They shook hands politely in the corridor outside his office. Jeanette looked tired and haggard, and he wondered what had happened since last Friday when he last saw her. Many evening shifts at the restaurant, or something more personal?

'Would you like a cup of coffee?' he asked, and she nodded.

'Have a seat, and I'll bring you some.' He pointed to one of his guest chairs.

A moment later he set two cups on his desk.

'So, how can I help you?' He put his forearms on the desk and leaned forward.

It took a few seconds before she replied. With her eyes lowered, she warmed her hands on the coffee cup and seemed to be pondering how to begin. Then she tossed back her thick, dark hair and looked him straight in the eye.

'I lied about Niclas being with me last Monday,' she said.

Patrik's expression didn't reveal his consternation, but inside he felt something leap in his chest.

'Tell me more,' he said calmly.

'I just told you what Niclas had asked me to say. He gave me the times and asked me to say that we'd been together then.'

'And did he say why he wanted you to lie on his behalf?'

'All he said was that everything would be complicated otherwise. That it was much simpler for everyone if I gave him an alibi.'

'And you didn't question that?'

She shrugged. 'No, I had no reason to do so.'

'Even though a child had been murdered, you didn't think there was anything remarkable in him asking you to give him an alibi?' Patrik said incredulously.

Jeanette shrugged again. 'No,' she said. 'I mean, Niclas would hardly have killed his own daughter, would he?'

Patrik didn't reply. After a moment he asked, 'Niclas hasn't said anything about what he was actually doing that morning?'

'No.'

'And you have no idea yourself?'

Once again the impassive shrug of her shoulders. 'I just assumed he took the morning off. He works hard, and his wife is always nagging him about how he should help around the house, even though she's at home all day long. He probably needed a little free time.'

'And why would he risk his marriage by asking you to give him an alibi?' said Patrik, trying in vain to read something in Jeanette's aloof expression. The only thing that revealed any emotion was the way she was nervously drumming her long nails on the coffee cup.

'I have no idea,' she said impatiently. 'He probably thought that of two evils, it was better to be discovered with a lover than to be suspected of the murder of his own daughter.'

Patrik thought that sounded far-fetched, but people reacted strangely under stress; he'd seen many different examples.

'If you thought it was okay to give him an alibi as late as last Friday, why have you changed your mind now?'

Her nails kept drumming on the coffee cup. They were extremely well-manicured, even Patrik could see that.

'I . . . I thought about it all weekend, and it doesn't feel right. I mean, a child is dead, isn't she? You should be told everything.'

'Yes, we should,' said Patrik. He wasn't sure that he believed her explanation, but it didn't matter. Niclas no longer had an alibi for Monday morning, and worse, he'd asked someone to give him a phoney one. That was enough to send a number of warning flags to the top of the mast.

'Well, I must thank you for coming here to tell me this,' Patrik said, getting to his feet. Jeanette held out a dainty little hand and held onto his a bit too long as they said goodbye. Unconsciously Patrik wiped his hand on his jeans as soon as she was outside the door. There was something about that young woman that made her really disliked. But thanks to Jeanette they now had a solid lead to go on. It was time to look more closely at Niclas Klinga.

All at once Patrik remembered the note that Annika had given him. In a slight panic he felt in his back pocket. When he fished out the little piece of paper he was extremely grateful that neither he nor Erica had got around to washing clothes this weekend. He read the note and then sat down to make some phone calls.

FJÄLLBACKA 1926

The two-year-olds were shouting noisily behind her and Agnes hushed them in annoyance. She had never seen the likes of those boys for making a racket. They were surely spending too much time over at the Janssons', picking up things from their snotty kids, Agnes thought. She chose to close her eyes to the fact that the neighbouring woman had pretty much brought up her sons as her own ever since they were six months old. But things were going to change now that they were moving into town. Agnes looked back with pleasure from her seat on the moving cart. Hopefully, she would never have to set eyes on that miserable shack again. Now she would come one step closer to the life she deserved. She was at least going to live among sensible people in surroundings that were bustling and lively. The house they were renting wasn't really much to brag about, though the rooms were cleaner and brighter, and even a few square yards bigger, than those in the shack. But at least the house was located in Fjällbacka. She could step off the front porch without sinking to her ankles in mud, and she could start cultivating acquaintances who were considerably more stimulating than those simple stonecutter wives, who did nothing but produce one kid after another. Finally she would have a chance to get to know other people with completely different outlooks. Agnes chose to ignore the fact that she herself might not be an interesting acquaintance for them, since she now belonged to the crowd of cutter wives she scorned. Or perhaps she thought they would see that she was different.

'Johan, Karl, calm down. Sit still in the cart, or else you can get off and walk,' said Anders, turning halfway round to the boys. As usual Agnes thought he was much too lenient with them. If it were up to her, he would have yelled at them much louder, and even followed up his scoldings with a box on the ears. But on that issue he was unwavering. No one would raise a hand to his boys. Once Anders had caught her giving Johan a slap, and he gave her such a talking-to that she never dared do it again. In everything else she could get Anders to do as she wanted, but when it came to Karl and Johan he had the last word. He had even chosen their names. If the names were good enough for kings, they were good enough for his sons, he'd said. Agnes had merely snorted. Such foolishness. But she didn't give a damn what the boys were called, so if he wanted to name them she had no objection.

Most of all it would be lovely to get away from that busybody Mrs Jansson. Sure, it had been convenient that she took care of the kids for her, but she did it of her own free will. At the same time her reproachful glances had got on Agnes's nerves. As if she were a bad person just because she didn't view it as her sole purpose in life to wipe the shit from kids' bottoms.

They couldn't drive all the way up to the house, which stood along one of the small, narrow lanes that led down to the sea. They had to carry their belongings the last bit. Anders would be making a couple more trips to fetch their rickety furniture. Agnes said hello to the old man who owned the house and would be their landlord, and then she stepped into their new home. She never thought she'd consider two small rooms in a tiny house to be a step up in life, but compared to the dark shack the new dwelling looked like a castle.

She swept in with her skirts rustling over the threshold, was pleased to find that the previous tenant had left the place clean and neat. She detested living in messy or dirty surroundings, but in the small space of the company shack it hadn't seemed such a great idea to clean house. Besides, she wasn't inclined to clean. But if she could wheedle Anders, the skinflint, into buying some nice curtains and a rug, this house might be acceptable.

The boys raced past her legs and ran around like crazy in the empty room, chasing each other. Agnes felt herself boiling inside when she saw how the mud they tracked in on their shoes was spread all over the clean floor.

'Karl! Johan!' she yelled, and the boys froze in terror. She pressed her fists to her sides to stop herself from dealing out a resounding slap. Instead she settled for grabbing her sons by the arms and dragging them out the front door. She permitted herself to give each of them a little pinch, and saw with satisfaction how their tiny faces dissolved in tears.

'Pappa!' Karl began to wail, and Johan soon joined in the chorus. 'I want Pappa!'

'Shut up,' Agnes hissed, looking around anxiously. A fine thing it would be to disgrace herself on the first day in their new home. But the boys had gone past the point where they could stop crying.

'Pappa!' they wailed in unison, and Agnes had to force herself to take deep, controlled breaths so she wouldn't do anything rash. Then the boys raised the ante.

'Karin, we want Karin,' they shrieked, as they lay down on the ground and began pounding their little fists.

They were damned cry-babies, just like their father. To think that they had the nerve to prefer that rotten bitch to their own mother. She felt her foot start to twitch with an urge to kick them in the soft parts round their stomachs. Fortunately at that moment Anders appeared at the top of the hill.

'What's going on here?' he said in his melodious Blekinge accent, and the boys were up on their feet like bolts of greased lightning.

'Pappa! Mamma's mean!'

'So what happened now?' he said in resignation, giving Agnes a disapproving glance. She silently cursed him. He didn't even know what had happened, and still he took his sons' side. She couldn't be bothered to explain, but turned on her heel and went into the house to gather up the bits of mud the boys had left behind. Behind her she heard them snuffling with their faces buried in Anders's coat. Like father, like sons.

Monica took a sick day on Monday. Only a week had passed since they found the girl, but it felt like years had been added to her life since then. She heard Kaj rummaging about in the kitchen and knew that it was only a matter of time. Sure enough, here it came.

'Monica-a-a-a. Where's the coffee?'

She closed her eyes and answered with forced politeness, 'In the tin in the cupboard above the stove. Where it's been for the past ten years,' she couldn't help adding.

She heard a muttered reply from the kitchen and got up with a sigh. She'd better go help him. She couldn't understand how a grown man could be so helpless. How he'd been able to run a business with thirty employees was beyond her comprehension.

'Let me,' she said, snatching the tin of coffee from his hand.

'What's got into you?' said Kaj in the same annoyed tone of voice.

Monica took a deep breath to calm herself down as she silently counted out spoonfuls of coffee. It wasn't worth starting a fight with Kaj on top of everything else.

'Nothing,' she said. 'I'm just a little tired. And I don't like it that the police were here talking to Morgan.'

'Well, what can we do about it?' said Kaj, sitting down at the kitchen table and waiting for the coffee to be served. 'He's a grown man, even if you refuse to believe it,' he added.

'You of all people ought to know how difficult things are for

Morgan. Where have you been all these years? Aren't you part of this family?' The irritation crept back into her voice, and she began slicing the Swiss roll with more energy than necessary.

'I've been part of this family as much as you have, thank you very much. On the other hand, I haven't been as inclined to coddle Morgan. Or drag him from one shrink to another. What good has that done? He just sits out there in his cabin all day long, getting weirder and weirder with each passing year.'

'I never coddled him,' said Monica between clenched teeth. 'I tried to give our son the best care he could get, considering what he's had to deal with. The fact that you chose to ignore him is something you'll have to live with. If you spent half the time with him that you spend on your exercise routines . . .'

She practically slammed the plate of Swiss roll onto the table and then stood leaning against the counter with her arms crossed.

'All right, all right,' said Kaj, trying to placate her as he stuffed a piece of cake in his mouth. He was in no mood for a fight either, this early in the morning. 'No need to drag that up again. At any rate, I agree with you that it's unpleasant having the police running in and out. Why don't they focus their attention on that damned bitch next door instead?'

Now that he was onto his favourite topic again, he pulled the curtain aside and looked over at the Florins' house.

'Seems quiet over there. I wonder what all those cars were doing there on Friday? And all the boxes and equipment they carried in?'

Monica dropped her guard reluctantly and sat down across from him. She took a piece of cake even though she knew she shouldn't. Her craving for sweets had already added some weight around her hips. But Kaj didn't seem to mind, so why should she make an effort?

'I have no idea, and it's not worth worrying about. The main thing is that they leave Morgan alone.'

The cold, sinking feeling in Monica's stomach refused to subside. With each day it got worse and worse. The sugar in the cake calmed her nerves for a while, but she knew that anxiety would soon overpower her again. In despair she looked at Kaj across the table. She considered telling him everything, but soon realized

242

how absurd that would be. Thirty years together and they had nothing in common. He was contentedly chewing another piece of Swiss roll, unaware of the wolves' claws ripping his wife apart inside.

'Shouldn't you be at work?' said Kaj and stopped chewing.

Typical. She should have left an hour ago, but he hadn't noticed until now that she'd stayed home.

'I called in sick. I'm not feeling well.'

'You look okay to me,' he said critically. 'A little pale, maybe. Well, you know I keep telling you to quit that job. It's crazy to keep slaving away there when you don't have to. We don't really need your salary.'

A violent rage flared up inside her. She jumped to her feet.

'I don't want to hear any more about that. I stayed at home for more than twenty years and did nothing but iron your shirts and fix dinner for you and your business associates. Don't I have the right to my own life?'

She snatched up the plate of cake, went over to the rubbish bin and demonstratively dumped in the last pieces on top of the coffee grounds and food scraps. Then she left Kaj gaping at the kitchen table. She couldn't stand looking at him for another second.

Mia parked the pram in back of Järnboden hardware store and made sure that Liam was asleep. She was just going to run in and buy a few things, and she didn't feel like dragging the pram inside. The wind was blowing hard, but it was worse at the front of the shop, the side facing the water. At the back the shop was protected against the wind by the stone mass of Veddeberget, and the car would be fine there for the five minutes she planned to be gone.

The bell over the door rang as she entered. The shop was filled with everything that do-it-yourself handymen and boat lovers could ever possibly need. She checked the shopping list Markus had given her to see what she was supposed to buy. He'd promised to put up the rest of the shelves in the nursery this weekend if she picked up the necessary hardware.

Mia was happy to be getting the nursery done at last. Months had flown by, and despite the fact that Liam was already six months old, his room still looked like it was under contruction. It was not like the cosy, snug children's room she had always dreamt of. The only problem was that she was depending on her boyfriend to fix up the room. She'd never held a hammer in her life and he was actually quite handy once he put his mind to it; unfortunately that didn't happen very often.

Sometimes she wondered whether the rest of her life would be like this. When they first met, she'd thought his philosophy was wonderful: always have a good time and never do anything boring. She had latched on to his lifestyle, and for almost a year they had lived a marvellously carefree life with lots of partying and spur-of-the-moment decisions. But eventually she had grown tired of all that. She felt the responsibilities of adult life growing more insistent – especially since she'd had Liam. In the meantime Markus kept on living in his little bubble; she felt like she now had two children to raise. He didn't contribute anything towards food and rent either. If she hadn't been living at home and getting money from her parents, they would have starved to death.

Markus was good at talking his way into jobs, that wasn't the problem. No, the problem was that no job ever lived up to his expectations, or his demands that everything always had to be cool, so he usually quit after a couple of weeks. Then he would loaf about for a while, living off her until he succeeded in charming his way into a new job. He slept most of the day as well, so he almost never helped out, either with the housework or with Liam. Instead he stayed up all night playing computer games.

To be honest, Mia had begun to tire of the way they were living. She was twenty years old and felt like forty. She kept hearing herself harping and nagging, and sometimes to her horror she sounded just like her mother.

Mia sighed as she walked down one aisle of shelves. She looked at the list. Nails and some of the other things he needed she found quite easily, but she had to ask for help to find the screws. When she was finished at last and about to pay Berit at the checkout, she glanced at the clock. A quarter of an hour had flown by while she was ticking off the items on the list, and she felt sweat starting to trickle from her armpits. She hoped Liam hadn't woken up. She hurried to the door with her purchases, and as soon as she stepped outside she heard his piercing screams, just as she had feared. But they sounded different from the way they were when he was angry, hungry, or upset. This was a scream of sheer panic, and it echoed shrilly off the rock wall of Veddeberget.

Mia's maternal instinct told her that something was wrong, and she dropped her bags and ran to the pram. When she looked down at him her heart stopped for an instant as she tried to understand what she was seeing. Liam's face was black with something that looked like ashes, or soot. In his open, shrieking mouth she also saw a clump of ashes, and he kept sticking out his tongue in an attempt to get rid of the nasty stuff. The inside of the pram was coated with the black powder, and when Mia lifted up her panic-stricken son and pressed him to her breast, her coat became covered with it too. Her mind could still not form any sensible theory of what had happened, but with Liam in her arms she ran back inside Järnboden. All she knew was that someone had done something to her son. As the clerk rang for help, Mia tried desperately to get the ashes out of Liam's mouth using a paper napkin.

Only an insane person would have done something like this.

By two o'clock they had all the information they needed. Annika had done the legwork, and Patrik thanked her in a low voice as he gathered up all the pages that had come in by fax in a steady stream. He knocked on Martin's door but walked in without waiting for him to answer.

'Hello,' said Martin, and managed to make the casual greeting sound like a question. He knew what Patrik and Annika had been working on, and he only needed to see Patrik's face to know that their efforts had paid off.

Patrik didn't reply to the greeting but sat down in the chair in front of Martin's desk and placed the faxes on his desktop without commenting.

'I presume you've come up with something,' said Martin, reaching for the stack of paper.

'Yes, after we succeeded in getting a warrant, it was like opening Pandora's box. There's all sorts of information. See for yourself.'

Patrik leaned back in the chair and waited for Martin to finish skimming through the printouts.

'This doesn't look good,' said Martin after a while.

'No, it doesn't,' said Patrik, shaking his head. 'A total of thirteen times Albin was taken to the clinic with some sort of injury. Broken leg, cuts, burns, and God knows what else. It's like reading a textbook on child abuse.'

'And you think it's Niclas and not Charlotte who did all this?' Martin nodded at the stack of faxes.

'First of all, there's no proof that it is actually child abuse. No one has found any reason to start asking questions before now, and theoretically he might just be the unluckiest kid in the world. That said, both you and I know that's very unlikely. It's possible that someone abused Albin on repeated occasions. Whether it's Niclas or Charlotte, well, that's impossible to say for sure. But at the moment Niclas is the one we have the most questions about, so I'm assuming he's the more likely candidate, at least.'

'Could it be both of them? There have been cases like that, as you know.'

'Absolutely,' said Patrik. 'Anything is possible, and we can't rule it out. But considering the fact that Niclas lied about his alibi – and also attempted to get someone else to lie for him – I'd like to bring him in for a serious talk. Are we agreed on that?'

Martin nodded. 'Yes, definitely. Let's get him in here and present this information to him and then see what he has to say.'

'Good, that's what we'll do, then. Should we go over there right away?'

Martin nodded. 'I'm ready if you are.'

An hour later they had Niclas sitting across from them in the interview room. He looked obdurate, but he hadn't protested when they fetched him from the clinic. It was as though he had no energy to make any objections. At no time during the trip to the station had he asked why they wanted to talk to him. Instead he had stared out at the passing landscape and let the silence speak for itself. For a brief moment Patrik felt a pang of sympathy. It looked as though Niclas's brain had only now registered the fact that his daughter was dead, and for the present he was devoting all his energy trying to cope with that knowledge. Then Patrik remembered the contents of the physician's reports, and his sympathy was quickly and effectively extinguished.

'Do you know why we want to talk with you?' Patrik began calmly.

'No,' Niclas replied, studying the tabletop.

'We've received some information that is . . .' Patrik paused for effect, 'disturbing.'

No response from Niclas. His whole body slumped forward, and his hands resting on the table were trembling slightly.

'Don't you want to know what sort of information we have?' said Martin kindly, but Niclas didn't respond to that either.

'Then we'll tell you,' Martin went on, glancing at Patrik to take over, who cleared his throat.

'First of all, it turned out that the statement you gave us about where you were on Monday morning was not correct.'

Here Niclas looked up for the first time. Patrik thought he saw a glint of surprise, which disappeared just as rapidly. In the absence of any verbal reply, Patrik continued.

'The person who gave you an alibi has retracted her statement. In plain Swedish: Jeanette has now told us that you were not with her at all, as you claimed, and she also says that you asked her to lie about it.'

No reaction from Niclas. It seemed as though all emotion had drained out of him, leaving behind only a vacuum. He showed no anger, astonishment, consternation, or any of the feelings that Patrik had expected. He waited him out, but silence prevailed.

'Would you like to comment?' Martin coaxed him.

Niclas shook his head. 'If that's her story . . .'

'Perhaps you'd like to tell us where you were during the hours in question.'

Niclas merely shrugged. Then he said in a low voice, 'I have no intention of making any statement. I don't even understand why I'm here and being asked these questions. It's my daughter who is dead. Why would I have harmed her?' He raised his eyes and looked at Patrik, who saw a suitable avenue to the next question.

'Perhaps because you have a habit of abusing your children. At least Albin.'

Now Niclas gave a start, and he stared at Patrik with his mouth open. A slight quiver of his lower lip was the first indication of

247

emotion they'd seen. 'What do you mean?' said Niclas uncertainly, and his eyes flicked between Patrik and Martin.

'We know,' Martin said calmly, leafing demonstratively through the stack of papers before him. He had made copies of the faxes so that both he and Patrik had a set.

'What is it you think you know?' said Niclas, and his voice contained a hint of defiance. But he couldn't prevent his gaze from returning to the papers in front of Martin.

'Thirteen times Albin has been treated for various types of injuries. What does that tell you as a doctor? What conclusion would you draw if someone came in thirteen times with a child who had burns, cuts and broken bones?'

Niclas pressed his lips together.

Patrik went on. 'Well, you didn't take him to the same clinic every time. That would have been tempting fate, wouldn't it? But when we gathered reports from the hospital in Uddevalla and the clinics in the region, it makes a total of thirteen times. Is he an unusually accident-prone child, or what?'

Still no reply from Niclas. Patrik looked at his hands. Were those hands capable of injuring a little child?

'Perhaps there's an explanation for this,' said Martin in a deceptively gentle voice. 'I mean, I can understand that things can just get to be too much sometimes. You doctors work long hours and are worn-out and stressed. Sara was also a very demanding girl, and having a little baby as well might have been enough to break even the best of us. All the frustrations that need to get out, that have to find an outlet. In spite of everything, we're only human, aren't we? And that could explain why there haven't been any more reports of "accidents" since you moved to Fjällbacka. Getting some help around the house, a less stressful job, and everything suddenly feels easier. There's no longer a need to vent your frustrations.'

'You know nothing about me or my life. Don't flatter yourself that you do,' Niclas said with unexpected acrimony, staring down at the tabletop. 'I'm not going to talk to you about this anymore, so you can just as well cut out the psychobabble.'

'You mean you have no comment at all to any of this?' said Patrik, waving his copies of the reports.

'No, I don't. I already told you that,' replied Niclas stubbornly continuing to study the top of the table.

'You realize that we have to turn over this data to social welfare, don't you?' said Patrik, leaning towards Niclas. Once again they saw only a slight quiver of his lip.

'Do what you have to do,' said Niclas in a thick voice. 'Do you intend to hold me here, or can I go now?'

Patrik stood up. 'You can go. But we're going to have more questions for you.'

He escorted Niclas to the main entrance, but neither of them made any move to shake hands.

Patrik went back to the interview room, where Martin was waiting.

'What do you think of that?' said Martin.

'I don't really know. To start with I expected a stronger reaction.'

'Yeah, he seems utterly shut off from the outside world. But I assume it might be the way grief has affected him. According to what you told me, he threw himself back into work as if nothing had happened. Besides, he was forced to be strong at home when Charlotte collapsed. If she's feeling better now, maybe his grief has caught up with him. What I'm saying is that we can't assume that he might have done something, in spite of the odd way he was behaving. The circumstances are really rather extraordinary.'

'Yeah, you're right,' said Patrik with a sigh. 'But we also can't ignore certain facts. He did ask Jeanette to lie about his alibi, and we still don't know where he actually was that morning. And I wasn't born yesterday – these reports clearly show that Albin was abused. If I were to guess who the most likely perpetrator is, it would definitely be Niclas.'

'So we're going to file a report with social welfare, as you said?' asked Martin.

Patrik hesitated. 'We really ought to do it immediately, but something tells me we should wait a few days, until we know more.'

'Okay, you're the boss,' said Martin. 'I just hope you know what you're doing.'

'To be honest, I don't have a damned clue,' said Patrik with a wry smile. 'Not a damned fucking clue.'

* * *

249

Erica gave a start at the knock on the door. Maja was lying on her back in her baby gym, and Erica had been sitting in a corner of the sofa lost in an exhausted torpor. She jumped up and went to open the door. When she saw who was standing outside, she raised her eyebrows a bit in astonishment.

'Hello, Niclas,' she said, but made no move to let him in. They had only met a few times, and she wondered why he had decided to drop by.

'Hello,' he said uncertainly, and then fell silent. After what felt like a very long time he said, 'May I come in for a moment? I need to talk with you.'

'Of course,' said Erica, still feeling puzzled. 'Come in and I'll put on some coffee.'

She went to the kitchen and made coffee while Niclas hung up his coat. Then she picked up Maja from the floor because she had started to fuss, and poured the coffee with her free hand before she sat down at the kitchen table.

'I certainly recognize that,' Niclas said with a laugh as he sat down facing Erica. 'All mothers seem to have the ability to do anything with one hand as easily as two. I don't know how you manage it.'

Erica smiled back at him. It was incredible how much Niclas's face changed when he laughed. But then he turned serious again, and his face closed up.

He sipped his coffee as if to gain time. Erica was filled with curiosity. What did he want from her?

'You're probably wondering why I'm here,' he said as if reading her mind. Erica didn't reply. Niclas took another swallow from his cup and then went on, 'I know that Charlotte has been here and talked to you.'

'I can't discuss what we –'

He held up his hand. 'No, I'm not here to pry about what Charlotte might have told you. I'm here because you're the closest friend she has in this town, and from what I saw when you came over, you're a good friend. And Charlotte will be needing a friend now.'

Erica gave him a quizzical look. At the same time she had an awful premonition about what he was going to say. She felt a little hand against her cheek and looked down at Maja, who was staring up at her contentedly, reaching for a lock of her hair. To be honest she didn't know whether she wanted to hear any more. Something inside her wanted to stay inside the cocoon she'd been living in the past few months. Even though it often felt as if she were suffocating, at the same time it was safe and familiar. But she repressed the impulse to shrink from what he was going to tell her. She shifted her gaze from Maja to Niclas and said, 'I'll help you in any way I can.'

Niclas nodded but then seemed to hesitate. After turning the coffee cup in his hands for a while, he took a deep breath and said, 'I've betrayed Charlotte. I've betrayed my family in the worst possible way. But there's something else. Something that has been undermining us, making us drift apart. Things that we now have to confront. Charlotte doesn't know about my cheating yet, but I'll have to tell her, and then she's going to need you.'

'Tell me,' said Erica softly, and with obvious relief Niclas began pouring out everything in one incoherent and unpleasant mass.

When he finished, the relief on his face was evident. Erica didn't know what to say. She caressed Maja's cheek, as if to defend herself against a reality that was too ugly and horrible. Part of her wanted to stand up and tell him to go to hell. Another part of her wanted to hug him and pat his back consolingly. Instead she said, 'You have to tell Charlotte everything. Go home right now and tell her everything you told me. And I'll be here if she needs to talk. Then . . .' Erica paused, unsure of how to say it, 'then the two of you have to get a grip on your life. If Charlotte, and I'm saying *if* she can forgive you, then you'll have to make it your responsibility to see to it that the two of you can go on. The first thing you have to do is to arrange things so that you both get out of that house. Charlotte was already being driven crazy by Lilian, and I know that since Sara died it's only got worse. You two have to have your own home. A home where you can find your way back to each other again, where you can grieve for Sara in peace. There you can become a family.'

Niclas nodded. 'Yes, I know you're right. I should have taken care of that long ago, but I was so involved in my own troubles that I didn't see . . .'

He bent forward and stared hard at the tabletop. When he looked up his eyes were filled with tears. 'I miss her so much, Erica. I miss her so much that it feels like I'm falling apart. Sara is gone, Erica. It's only now that I understand it. Sara is gone.'

The tears ran down his cheeks and dripped onto the table. His whole body was shaking, and his face was contorted almost beyond recognition. Erica reached across the table and took his hand in hers. For a long time they sat together as he sobbed out his pain.

That weekend it happened again. A couple of weeks had passed since the last time, so Sebastian had begun to hope that it was all just a dream, or that it had ended once and for all. But then those moments returned. The moments of loathing, denial and pain.

If only he knew how to fight it. Whenever it happened he felt his lack of will paralyse his body, and he had to let himself float along.

Sebastian wrapped his arms around his knees as he sat at the top of Veddeberget. From this high up he could look out over the bay. It was cold and windy, but somehow beautiful. For once it felt the same outside as in. Although some rain would have made things even better. Because that was precisely the way he felt inside. As if it was raining. Pouring down and flushing away all that was good and whole. As if it were running down a gigantic drain.

And Rune had chewed him out, on top of everything else. Yelled and screamed and said he damn well didn't see that Sebastian was making enough of an effort. That he had to do better. That he wasn't going to have any future if he didn't work harder, because he certainly didn't seem to have a good head for studying. But he had tried. As much as he could under the circumstances. It wasn't his fault that everything turned to shit.

His eyes were stinging. Angrily he wiped them with the sleeve of his jumper. The last thing he wanted was to sit here blubbering like some cry-baby. Especially when it was all his own fault. If he'd only been a little stronger, then it wouldn't have had to happen. Not the first time. Not the second time either. Not over and over and over again.

Now the tears were running down his cheeks, and he rubbed

them so hard with the rough sleeve of his jumper that red streaks appeared on his face.

For a moment he had an impulse to put an end to it all. It would be so easy: a few steps to the edge, then he could jump. In a couple of seconds it would all be over, and no one would really care. Rune would surely be relieved. Then he wouldn't have to take care of somebody's else's kid. Maybe he could even meet someone else and have the son he really wanted.

Sebastian stood up. The thought was still tempting. He walked slowly over to the cliff and looked down. It was a steep drop. He tried to imagine how it would feel. To fly through the air, utterly weightless for a few moments, and then the thud when his body hit the ground. Would he feel anything at all in that instant? Testing, he stuck one foot over the edge of the cliff and let it hang free in the air. Then the thought struck him that he might not die from the fall. What if he survived, but as a cripple or something like that? A drooling vegetable for the rest of his life. Then Rune really would have something to grumble about. Although he would no doubt bundle him off to some nursing home as quickly as possible.

With his foot hanging over the edge Sebastian hesitated. Then he sat down again and slowly scooted back. With his arms hugging his chest he gazed out towards the horizon. Far, far away.

As soon as Niclas walked in the door she threw herself over him.

'What happened? Aina rang and said that the police came and got you at work, is that true?' Lilian's voice was anxious, bordering on panic-stricken. 'I haven't said anything to Charlotte,' she added.

Niclas waved her off, but Lilian wasn't that easy to dismiss. She followed close on his heels as he walked to the kitchen, bombarding him with questions. He ignored her and went straight to the coffee-maker and poured himself a big cup of coffee. The machine was shut off and the coffee was hardly more than lukewarm, but it didn't matter. He needed coffee, or a big glass of whisky, but it was probably best if he stuck to the non-alcoholic alternative.

He sat down at the table, and Lilian followed his example as she scrutinized him. What sort of idiotic ideas had the police come up with now? Didn't they know that Niclas was someone to be respected, a doctor, a successful man? Once again she was amazed that her daughter had had such luck, that she had made such a catch. Of course, they were only teenagers when they started going out together, but Lilian had seen immediately that Niclas was a man with a future, and so she had encouraged the relationship. She ascribed it to luck that Niclas chose Charlotte above all the other girls who were running after him. She was pretty cute, of course, when she made an effort, but even as a teenager she had put on a few too many kilos, and worst of all she had no ambitions. And yet Charlotte had won what her mother had wished for most of all. Lilian had worn her son-in-law's success like a star on her chest, but now everything was at risk. She was terrified of the gossip-mongers in town, who would instantly start spreading rumours if it came out that the police had taken Niclas in for questioning. His eyes were completely red from crying too, so they must have given him a hard time.

'Well, what did they want?'

'They just had a few questions,' Niclas said dismissively, drinking the now lukewarm coffee in big gulps.

'What sort of questions?' Lilian refused to give up. If she was going to have to run the gauntlet whenever she ventured into town, she at least wanted to know what it was all about.

But Niclas ignored her. He got up and put the empty coffee cup in the dishwasher.

'Is Charlotte downstairs?'

'She's resting,' said Lilian, not bothering to conceal her anger at not getting an answer.

'I'm going down to talk to her.'

'What do you want to talk to her about?' Lilian still wouldn't let up. But by now Niclas had had enough.

'That's between me and Charlotte. I already told you it was nothing special. I assume I'm allowed to speak with my own wife without informing you, aren't I? Erica is right, it's time for Charlotte and me to get a place of our own.'

Lilian shrank back with every syllable. Niclas had always treated her with respect, so his words now felt like slaps in the face. Especially after all she had done for him. For him and Charlotte.

The injustice of it all made her blood boil, and she searched for something caustic to say, but found nothing until he was already halfway down the stairs. She sat down at the kitchen table again. Her thoughts were tumbling about in her head. How could he speak to her that way? She had never had anything but their best interests in mind. She had constantly made sacrifices and put her own interests last. They were like leeches, sucking all the energy out of her. Lilian could see it so clearly now. Stig, Charlotte, and now Niclas as well. They were all exploiting her. They took and took from her outstretched hand, without ever giving anything in return.

Charlotte sat thinking about her father. It was strange, but during the eight years that had passed since his death, she had thought about him less and less. The memories had turned into vague, out-of-focus images of a few specific moments. But since Sara died, she remembered him as clearly as if he'd passed away yesterday.

They had been very close, she and Lennart. Much closer than she and her mother had ever been. Sometimes it had almost felt as if they shared the same soul. He had always been able to make her laugh. Her mother seldom laughed, and Charlotte couldn't remember a single instance when they had laughed together. Her father had been the diplomat of the family, always mediating and trying to explain things. For instance, why Lilian kept badgering her daughter, why nothing Charlotte did was ever good enough. Why she could never live up to her mother's expectations. On the other hand, she had never disappointed her father. In his eyes she had been perfect; she knew that.

It came as a shock when he fell ill. The disease progressed so slowly, so gradually, that it took a long time before they even noticed it was happening. Sometimes Charlotte wondered if she could have forestalled his death if she'd been more observant. Seen the signs earlier. But at the time she and Niclas were living in Uddevalla, and she was expecting Sara. She'd been so wrapped up in her own life. When she eventually noticed that he wasn't feeling well, she had for once joined forces with Lilian and wrangled with him until he went in for a medical exam. But by then it was too late. After that, everything happened so fast.

Only a month later he was dead. The doctors said that he'd contracted a rare disease that attacked the nervous system and gradually broke down his body. They also said that it wouldn't have helped if he had come in earlier. But Charlotte still felt guilty.

She wondered whether she could have kept his memory more alive if she'd had more room in which to grieve for him. But Lilian had taken up all the space there was. She'd laid claim to all mourning rights and demanded that her grief take precedence over everyone else's. A torrent of people had passed through their home in the weeks after Lennart had died, and for them Charlotte could just as well have been part of the furniture. All condolences, all expressions of regret were directed towards Lilian, who held audience like a queen. At those moments Charlotte had hated her mother. The ironic thing was that just before they got the news of Lennart's diagnosis, she thought that her father was about to leave Lilian. The quarrels and bickering had escalated, and a separation seemed inevitable. But then Lennart fell ill, and Charlotte realized that her mother had cast all the old grudges aside and devoted herself wholeheartedly to her husband. It was only afterwards that Charlotte had got a bitter taste in her mouth from her mother's seemingly boundless need to be the centre of attention.

But the years passed and she put bitterness aside. Life held too much else for her to keep focusing on bad feelings towards her mother. Nor had she had the time to think about or mourn her father. This was no longer the case. Life had caught up with her, run her down, and left her aching all over by the side of the road. Now she had all the time in the world to think about the man who should have been here right now. Who would have known what to say, who would have stroked her hair and said that everything was going to be all right. Lilian, as usual, was worrying too much about herself to take the time to listen, and Niclas, well, he was just Niclas. Any hope she had harboured that might bring them closer to each other had been extinguished. It was as though he'd sealed himself up inside his own little cocoon. Of course he had never let her get very close, but now he was like a shadow figure slinking in and out of her life. He laid his head on the pillow next to hers every night, but then they lay there side by side, careful not to touch each other. Afraid that a sudden and unexpected contact of skin against skin might open wounds that would be better left alone. They had been through so much together. Against all odds they had maintained an illusion of unity, at least, but now she wondered whether they might have come to the end of the road.

Footsteps on the stairs roused her from these weighty thoughts. She looked up and saw Niclas. A glance at the clock showed that there were still a couple of hours left until he ought to be coming home from work.

'Hi, are you home already?' she said in surprise, starting to get up.

'Don't get up, we need to talk.' Her heart sank. Whatever it was he had to say, it wasn't going to be good.

FJÄLLBACKA 1928

Life in the house wasn't the big improvement she had hoped for. Who she was now still took precedence over the person she had once been. With each passing year her bitterness grew, and the life she had lived before she married seemed more like a distant dream. Had she really worn fine dresses, played the piano at elegant parties, had suitors compete to dance with her? Above all, was there actually a time when she could eat as much food and sweets as she liked?

She had inquired about her father and, to her satisfaction, heard that he was a broken man. He now lived alone in the big house and went out only to go to work. That pleased Agnes; at the same time she harboured a faint hope that he might take her back in his good graces if his life had turned sufficiently miserable. But the years passed and nothing happened, and that hope faded more and more.

The boys were now four years old and completely incorrigible. They ran wild around the neighbourhood, as small as they were, and Agnes had neither the desire nor the energy to discipline them properly. And Anders had even longer workdays now that he had to travel from town out to the quarry. He left before the boys woke up and came home after they had gone to bed. Only on Sundays could he spend a little time with them, and then they were so happy to have him home that they behaved like little angels.

They hadn't had any more children, Agnes made sure of that.

Anders had made some awkward attempts to bring up the subject, and his desire to be allowed into her bed, but she'd had no difficulty in saying no. The desire she once felt for him was utterly gone. Now she was merely disgusted, and she shuddered at the thought of feeling his dirty, lacerated fingers anywhere near her skin. The fact that he didn't protest against the enforced celibacy also increased her contempt for him. What some people would call consideration, she called spinelessness, and the fact that he still did most of the housework only reinforced that image. No real man would wash his children's clothes or make his own packed lunch. Yet she closed her eyes to the fact that the reason he did so was because she refused to do these tasks herself.

'Mamma, Johan hit me!' Karl came running over to where she sat on the front steps smoking a cigarette, a bad habit she had acquired in recent years. She defiantly asked Anders for money to buy cigarettes, always hoping that he would object.

Now she cast a cool glance the crying boy before her and then slowly blew a cloud of smoke in his face. He started to cough and rubbed his eyes. He pressed up against her in an attempt to find some solace, but like so many times before she refused to respond with affection. It was up to Anders to dole out endearments. He spoiled the boys so much that she didn't need to make them mamma's boys too. Brusquely she pushed Karl away and gave him a swat on the bottom.

'Don't blubber – just hit him back,' she said calmly, blowing another puff of smoke up into the clear spring air.

Karl gave her a look that contained all the sorrow he felt at being rejected once again. Then he lowered his head and slunk over towards his brother.

Not long ago the woman next door had actually had the nerve to come over and tell Agnes that she ought to keep a better eye on her kids. She'd seen them playing alone out on the wharf by the freight dock. Agnes had merely given the old crone a dirty look and then calmly told her to mind her own business. Considering that her oldest daughter had gone to the city and, according to rumour, made her living by showing herself off as God made her, she was hardly the one to tell Agnes how to take care of her children. The woman had put on a wounded expression and then walked off muttering something about 'poor boys', but she hadn't dared to come and knock on the door again, which was exactly as Agnes had intended.

She leaned back in the spring sunshine, reminding herself not to enjoy for too long the rays that felt so good on her face. She wanted to retain the white complexion that was the mark of a woman of the upper class. The only thing she had left from her former life was her looks, and that was something she exploited to the utmost, trying to put a little silver lining on her otherwise dreary existence. It was astonishing how much she could glean from the shopkeeper in exchange for acquiescing to an embrace or maybe more, provided there was enough to gain. In that way she'd been able to bring home sweets and extra food, though she shared none of it with her family. She'd even acquired a bit of fabric that she carefully hid from Anders. For the time being she had to be content with touching it occasionally, rubbing it against her cheek to feel its silky smoothness. The butcher had also dropped a few hints, but there were limits to what she would do just to get some extra fine cuts of meat. The shopkeeper was a relatively young man and good-looking, and not half bad when it came to exchanging kisses in the back room, but the butcher was a fat, greasy lout in his sixties. Agnes would need to get considerably more than a piece of rump steak for allowing those sausage fingers with dried blood under the nails to slip underneath her dress.

She knew that people were talking behind her back. But once she realized that she would never regain her former social status, she no longer cared. Let them talk. If she could find ways to indulge in some of the good things in life, she had no intention of letting the views of a bunch of narrow-minded workers prevent her from doing so. And if it also bothered Anders occasionally to hear what people were saying about his wife, then all the better. In Agnes's eyes it was his fault that she had ended up where she was, and it made her happy if she could cause him pain.

But the past few weeks something had been bothering her. She felt as though something was going on, but she wasn't part of it. Several times she had come upon Anders lost in thought, staring into space as if he were contemplating something important. On one occasion she had even asked him if he was thinking about

261

anything in particular, but he had denied it, though not very convincingly. He was involved in something, she was sure of it. Something that would affect her, but for some reason she was not allowed to know what it was. The whole thing was driving her crazy, but in this situation she knew her husband well enough to realize that it would do no good to push him to reveal anything before he was ready. He could be stubborn as a mule if he set his mind to it.

Pensively, she picked up the packet of cigarettes and got up to go inside. She wondered briefly where the boys could have run off to, but then shrugged her shoulders, leaving them to take care of themselves. For her part she intended to take a little midday nap.

The afternoon passed slowly. Patrik had spent far too much time poring over Albin's medical records. He wondered whether he'd made the right choice when he decided to wait to bring in the social welfare authorities. But something told him that he had to know more before he did that. Once the bureaucratic wheels began to turn, it would be hard to stop the process, and he knew that both the police and the doctors were reluctant to report suspected child abuse. There was always a risk that there was a natural explanation, but no one would be willing to consider that possibility after social welfare stepped in. Besides, there hadn't been any incidents since the Klinga family had moved to Fjällbacka. Apparently the situation had stabilized. But he couldn't be entirely sure, and if Albin was hurt again the responsibility would be on his shoulders.

The telephone rang and interrupted his gloomy thoughts.

'Patrik Hedström.'

'Hello, this is Lars Kalfors from the Göteborg police.'

'Yes?' said Patrik. The man sounded as though he was supposed to recognize his name, but he couldn't recall hearing it before. And he had no idea why someone from Göteborg would be calling him.

'We just sent over some information regarding an ongoing matter to you. It was marked for your attention, I believe.'

'Oh yes?' said Patrik, even more puzzled. 'Offhand I can't recall seeing any message from Göteborg on my desk. When was it sent, and what was it about?'

'I got in touch with you over three weeks ago. I work in the division dealing with the sexual exploitation of children, and we're tracking a child pornography ring. We stumbled on a person from your district, and that's why I contacted you.'

Patrik felt like an idiot, but he had no idea what the man was talking about. 'Who did you talk to here?'

'Well, you seemed to be on parental leave that day, so I was referred to a . . . let me see . . .' It sounded like the man was paging through his notes. 'Here it is. I talked with an Ernst Lundgren.'

Patrik felt anger clouding his vision and making him see red. In his mind's eye he pictured himself putting his hands around Ernst's neck and slowly starting to squeeze. With forced calm he said, 'We must have had a communications glitch here at the station. Maybe you should give me the information instead. Then I can look into what's happened.'

'Of course, I can do that.'

Kalfors gave him a broad outline of what their work had involved, and how they came to be working on the child pornography case that was now high priority. When he came to the bit where the Tanumshede police station might be able to contribute something, Patrik gasped. He forced himself to listen to the whole account, then promised they'd give the matter immediate attention. After that he offered the usual polite phrases. But as soon as he hung up he was on his feet. He crossed his office in two strides and yelled out into the corridor, 'ERNST!'

Erica was sitting on the sofa, trying to sort out her thoughts when a knock on the door made her jump again. She guessed who it was and went to open the door. Charlotte stood outside. She had no coat on and looked like she'd run the whole way from her house. Sweat was running down her forehead and she was shaking uncontrollably.

'My God, you look awful,' said Erica, but instantly regretted her choice of words and swept Charlotte into the warmth of the house.

'Is this a bad time?' Charlotte asked pitifully, and Erica shook her head.

'Of course not. You're welcome here anytime, you know that.'

Charlotte just nodded, still shivering with her arms hugging her body. Her hair was plastered to her head from sweat and the damp air, and a stray lock hung into her eyes. She looked like a soaking wet puppy that had been abandoned.

'Would you like some tea?' asked Erica.

Charlotte had a frantic look in her eye, mixed with the haunted expression that had been there ever since she had gotten the news about Sara. But she nodded gratefully in answer to Erica's offer.

'Have a seat, I'll be right back,' Erica said and went into the kitchen. She checked on Maja in the living room, who seemed content and merely cast an interested glance at Charlotte as she walked past.

'I'll get your sofa wet if I sit down,' said Charlotte, as if that would be the end of the world.

'Don't worry, it'll dry,' said Erica. 'Look, I only have wild strawberry tea, is that all right, or do you think it's too sweet?'

'That'll be fine,' said Charlotte. Erica suspected she would have said the same thing if she'd been offered horse-flavoured tea.

Erica soon returned carrying a tray with two big cups of tea, a jar of honey and two spoons. She set it on the table in front of the sofa and sat down next to Charlotte.

Cautiously Charlotte raised her cup and sipped the tea. Erica sat quietly next to her and did the same. She didn't want to force Charlotte into talking, but she felt an almost physical need for her friend to confide in her. Maybe she just didn't know where to start. Erica wondered whether Niclas had told Charlotte that he'd been over to see her. After another long silence when Maja's babble was the only sound, Charlotte answered that question.

'I know that he's been here. He told me. So you already know that he's been seeing someone else. Again, I should add.' A bitter laugh escaped Charlotte's lips, and the tears that she had been holding back finally poured out.

'Yes, I know,' said Erica. She also knew what her friend meant by 'again'. Charlotte had told her about Niclas's recurring affairs. But also that she'd believed they'd stopped since they decided to start over in Fjällbacka. He had promised that it would be a new start in that respect as well.

'He's been seeing her for several months. Can you imagine? For several months. Here, in Fjällbacka. And nobody caught them. He must have incredible damn luck.' Her laugh now had a hint of hysteria to it, and Erica put a consoling hand on her knee.

'Who is it?' Erica said quietly.

'Didn't Niclas tell you?'

Erica shook her head, so Charlotte said, 'Some little bitch who's twenty-five years old. I don't know who she is. Jeanette something.' Charlotte waved her hand. The subject had shifted; it was Niclas's betrayal that mattered.

'I can't tell you all the shit I've taken over the years. All the times I've forgiven him, hoping he would change, and said I would forget about it and then promised to continue on. And this time it was really going to be different. We would get away from all the stuff that had happened, go live in a different town, become new people, or so I assumed.' Then that ominous laugh again. But the tears kept pouring out.

'I'm terribly sorry, Charlotte.' Erica stroked her back.

'We've been together so many years. We've had two children, we've gone through more than anyone could imagine. We've lost a child, and now this.'

'Why is he telling you now?' said Erica, taking a sip of tea.

'Didn't he say?' Charlotte asked in surprise. 'You're not going to believe this. But he told me it was because the police took him in for questioning today.'

'They did?' Not that Patrik told her everything about his work, but she had no clue that they were particularly interested in Niclas. 'Why was that?'

'He said he didn't really know. But they'd found out about his affair with this girl, and that may have been why they wanted to check him out. But it's all cleared up now, he said. They know he'd never hurt his own daughter; they just wanted him to answer a few questions.'

'Are you sure that's the only reason?' Erica couldn't resist asking. She knew enough about Patrik's job to realize that it seemed like a rather thin excuse for bringing somebody in for questioning. Especially the victim's father. At the same time she began to question Niclas's motive for visiting her. After all, she was not only his wife's friend, she was also living with the detective who was in charge of the investigation.

Charlotte looked confused. 'Well, that was what he said, at any rate. But there was something . . .'

'Yes?'

'Oh, I don't know, except it feels like he didn't tell me everything, now that you mention it. But I was so focused on what he said about his lover that I was probably deaf and blind to everything else.'

Charlotte sounded so bitter that Erica wanted to take her in her arms and rock her like a baby. But she always felt a little uncomfortable when she got too physical with other people, so she made do with continuing to stroke Charlotte's back.

'And you have no idea what other reasons there could be?' Was she imagining things, or did a shadow suddenly cross Charlotte's face? But it vanished so quickly that she was unsure.

Charlotte's reply at least was swift and confident. 'No, I have no idea what it could be.' Then she fell silent and took a little sip of tea. She was calmer than when she arrived, and wasn't crying anymore. But the expression on her face was bleak, and if a broken heart could be visible on the outside, then that was how Charlotte's heart looked at the moment.

'How did you and Niclas actually meet?' Erica asked, more out of curiosity than for any therapeutic reason.

'Well, that's a fine mess of a story, I have to say.' For the first time her laugh sounded almost genuine. 'He was in the class ahead of me in gymnasium. I hadn't really paid too much attention to him, because I had a crush on one of his friends. But for some reason Niclas got interested in me and started to show it, so gradually I got interested in him too. We ended up going steady for a month or two, and then I was the one who actually got bored.'

'You broke up with him?'

'Don't sound so surprised, you might offend me.' She laughed and Erica joined in.

'Unfortunately I didn't stick to my decision for more than a couple of months. Then I went over to see him one evening, and the whole merry-go-round started up again. This time we were

267

together all summer, and then he went off on a drinking trip with his mates. When he returned he came up with some story, in case I heard from the others about how he'd disappeared on the last night. He claimed he'd drunk too much and passed out behind a bar but the truth came out pretty quickly and our relationship was finished for the second time. After that I was honestly relieved that I got away with just a few tears. Niclas started going through all the girls in Uddevalla as if every day were his last, and you wouldn't believe some of the stories I heard. I'm ashamed to admit that on a few occasions I was weaker in the flesh than in spirit, but those episodes left me with quite a bitter aftertaste. Looking back, it probably would have been better if the story had ended there, and Niclas had remained a simple teenage mistake. But even though I loathed so much of what he had done and who he had become, he stayed in the back of my mind for a long time. A couple of years later we met by accident and the rest is history, as they say. I suppose I should have known what I was getting myself into.'

'People change. The fact that he cheated on you as a teenager doesn't mean you should automatically assume he would do the same as an adult. Most people mature with time.'

'Not Niclas, apparently,' said Charlotte, letting the bitterness take over again. 'But I can't really bring myself to hate him. We've been through too much together, and sometimes I see glimpses of his true self. On some occasions I've seen him vulnerable and open, and it's because of those times that I love him. I also know about his family life, and what happened with his father when he was seventeen, so I probably saw all of that as some sort of mitigating circumstance. And yet it's hard to comprehend why he would want to hurt me so badly.'

'What are you going to do now?' Erica asked. She glanced over at Maja and couldn't believe her eyes when she saw that her daughter had fallen asleep on her own in the bouncer. That had never happened before.

'I don't know. I can't face dealing with it right now. And in a way it feels like it doesn't matter. Sara is dead, and nothing Niclas does or says can hurt anywhere near as much as that does. Niclas wants us to start over, find our own place and move out of Mamma and Stig's house as soon as we can. But I have no idea what to do right now . . .'

She bowed her head. Then she abruptly got to her feet.

'I have to go home. Mamma has spent enough time watching Albin today. Thanks for letting me unload all this on you.'

'You're always welcome here, you know that.'

'Thanks.' Charlotte gave Erica a quick hug and then vanished as quickly as she'd come.

Erica wandered back into the living room. In amazement she stopped in front of the bouncer and looked down at her sleeping daughter. Maybe there was hope for her life after all. Unfortunately she didn't know whether Charlotte could say the same thing.

Morgan had come to his favourite part of the computer game he was working on. The part where the first blow of the sword fell. The man's head rolled, and according to the script there should be plenty of extreme effects. His fingers raced across the keyboard, and on the screen the scene emerged at lightning speed. He admired and envied the people who could write the stories, which he then was commissioned to transform into virtual reality. If there was anything he lacked in his life, it was the imagination that others had, allowing them to burst all boundaries and let ideas flow freely. Naturally he had tried. Sometimes he'd even been forced to give it a go himself. Writing compositions in school, for instance. Those had been a nightmare. Sometimes the pupils were given a topic, or just an image, and from that they were expected to spin a whole web of events and characters. He'd never got further than the first sentence. Then his mind just seemed to shut down. It was blank. The paper lay empty before him, absolutely screaming to be filled with words, but none came. The teachers had berated him. At least until Mamma went and talked to them, after his parents had received the diagnosis. Then the teachers merely regarded his attempts with curiosity, observing him as if he were an alien life-form. They didn't know how right they were. That was how he felt as he sat at his school desk, with the blank paper in front of him and the sound of his classmates' scratching pens all around. An alien life-form.

When Morgan discovered the world of computers he'd felt at home for the first time. This was something that came easy to him, that he could master. If he was an odd piece of the puzzle then he had finally found another piece that was a perfect fit.

When he was younger he had gone in for code languages just as manically. He had read everything he could find about the subject and could reel off what he'd learned for hours on end. There was something about numbers and letters being used in ingenious combinations that had appealed to him. But once his interest in computers took over, overnight he lost his fascination with codes. The knowledge was still there, and whenever he liked he could pull out everything he'd ever learned about the topic, but it simply didn't interest him anymore.

The blood running down the edge of the sword made him think of the girl again. He wondered whether her blood had congealed inside her now that she was dead. Whether it was just a dense mass filling her blood vessels. Maybe it had also turned the brown colour of dried blood; he'd seen it once when he'd tried cutting himself on the wrist. In fascination he'd stared at the blood trickling out, watching the way the flow gradually slowed, coagulated and began to change colour.

His mother had been shocked when she came into his room that time. He'd tried to explain that he just wanted to see what it was like to die, but without a word she'd shoved him into the car and driven him to the medical clinic. Although actually it wasn't necessary. It hurt to cut himself, so he hadn't made a deep cut and the blood had already coagulated. But his mother still got hysterical anyway.

Morgan didn't understand why death seemed to be such a scary concept for normal people. It was only a state of being, just like living. And sometimes death seemed much more tempting to him than life. So sometimes he envied the girl. Because now she knew. Knew the solution to the riddle.

He forced himself to concentrate on the computer game again. Sometimes thinking about death could make several hours vanish before he knew it. And that screwed up his schedule.

*   *   *

Looking surly, Ernst sat in front of Patrik, refusing to meet his gaze. Instead he studied his unpolished shoes.

'Answer me, damn it!' Patrik yelled at him. 'Did you get a call from Göteborg about child pornography?'

'Yes,' Ernst replied grumpily.

'And why didn't we ever hear about it?'

There was a long silence.

'I repeat,' said Patrik in an ominously low voice, 'why didn't you report it to us?'

'I didn't think it was that important,' said Ernst evasively.

'You didn't think it was that important!' Patrik's tone was ice-cold and he slammed his fist on the desk so hard that his keyboard jumped.

'No,' said Ernst.

'And why not?'

'Well, there was so much else going on at the time . . . And it felt a bit improbable, I mean, that's the sort of thing they're into in the big cities.'

'Don't talk nonsense,' said Patrik without being able to conceal his contempt. He'd got up from his chair and was now towering behind his desk. His rage made him look four inches taller. 'You know very well that child pornography has nothing to do with geography. It happens in small towns too. So stop talking bullshit and tell me the real reason. And believe me, if it's what I think, you're going to be in serious hot water!'

Ernst looked up from his shoes and glared defiantly at Patrik, but he knew it was time to lay his cards on the table.

'I just didn't think it sounded plausible. I mean, I know the guy, and it didn't seem like something he'd be involved in. So I thought the Göteborg cops must have made a mistake, and an innocent person would have to suffer if I passed on the information. You know how it is,' he said, glaring at Patrik. 'It wouldn't change anything if they rang again after a while and said, "Oh, excuse us, but there's been a mistake here and you can forget about that name we gave you" – his name would still be mud in this town. So I thought I'd wait a while and see what happened.'

'*You'd wait a while and see what happened*!' Patrik was so furious that he had to force himself to enunciate each syllable to keep from stammering.

'Well, I mean, you have to agree this whole thing is unreasonable. He's well known for all the work he does with young people. He does plenty of good things, I have to tell you.'

'I don't give a shit what sort of good things he does. If our colleagues in Göteborg ring and say that his name came up in an investigation of child pornography, then we *have* to check it out. That's our fucking job! And if you two are best mates –'

'We aren't best mates,' Ernst muttered.

'. . . or friends or whatever the fuck, then it makes no difference at all, don't you see that? You can't sit there and make decisions about what's going to be investigated or what's not, based on who you know or don't know!'

'After all the years I've spent on the force –' Ernst couldn't finish his sentence before Patrik cut him off.

'After all the years you've spent on the force you should bloody well know better! And you didn't think to say anything when his name came up in a murder investigation? Wouldn't that at least have been a good time to tell us about the call?'

Ernst had gone back to studying his shoes and didn't feel like getting drawn into an argument. Patrik sighed and sat down. He folded his hands and gave Ernst a sombre look.

'Well, there isn't much we can do about it now. We've received all the data from Göteborg and will be bringing him in for questioning. We've also got a warrant to search his home. You'd better pray on bended knee that he hasn't got wind of this and managed to clean out all the evidence. And Mellberg has been informed. I'm sure he'll want to have a talk with you.'

Ernst didn't say a word when he got up from his chair. He knew that he had probably committed the worst blunder of his career. And in his case that was saying a lot.

'Mamma, if I promised to keep a secret, how long do I have to keep it?'

'I don't know,' replied Veronika. 'You shouldn't really ever tell anyone's secret, should you?'

'Hmm,' said Frida, drawing circles in her yoghurt with her spoon.

'Don't play with your food,' said Veronika, wiping off the drainboard with annoyance. Then she stopped in the middle of what she was doing and turned to her daughter.

'Why do you ask, anyway?'

'Dunno,' said Frida with a shrug.

'You certainly do know. Now tell me, why do you ask?' Veronika sat down on a kitchen chair next to her daughter and gazed at her thoughtfully.

'If you shouldn't ever tell someone's secret, then I can't say anything, can I? But –'

'What do you mean?' Veronika coaxed her cautiously.

'But if somebody you promised something to is dead, do you still have to keep the secret? What if you say something and then the person who's dead comes back and gets really mad?'

'Sweetheart, is it Sara who made you promise to keep something secret?' Frida kept drawing circles in her bowl of yoghurt. 'We talked about this before, and you have to believe me when I say that I'm really sorry, but Sara is never coming back. Sara is in heaven and she's going to stay there for ever and ever.'

'For ever and ever, for all the eternities of eternity? A thousand million million years?'

'Yes, a thousand million million years. And as far as the secret goes, I don't think Sara would be mad if you only told it to me.'

'Are you sure?' Frida looked nervously up at the grey sky she could see out of the kitchen window.

'I'm completely sure.' Veronika placed a hand on her daughter's arm to reassure her.

After a moment of silence as Frida apparently pondered what her mother had told her, she said hesitantly, 'Sara was super-scared. There was a nasty old man who scared her.'

'A nasty old man? When was that?' Veronika waited tensely for her daughter's reply.

'The day before she went to heaven.'

'Are you sure that's when it was?'

Upset that her mother would doubt her, Frida frowned. 'Ye-e-es, I'm absolutely sure. I know all the days of the week. I'm not a baby.'

273

'No, no, I know that. You're a big girl, and of course you know what day it was,' Veronika said soothingly.

Then she cautiously tried to coax out more information. Frida was still sulking over her mistrust, but the temptation to share the secret was finally too strong.

'Sara said that the old man was really disgusting. He came and talked to her when she was playing down by the water and he was mean.'

'Did Sara say that he was mean?'

'Mm-hmm,' said Frida, thinking that was enough of an answer.

Veronika continued patiently. 'What exactly did she say? How was he mean?'

'He grabbed her by the arm so it hurt. Like this, she said.' Frida demonstrated by taking a hard grip with her right hand on her upper left arm. 'And then he said dumb things too.'

'What kind of dumb things?'

'Sara didn't understand all of it. She just said that she knew it was nasty. It sounded like "double pawn" or something like that.'

'Double pawn?' said Veronika, looking bewildered.

'I told you it was dumb and Sara didn't understand. But it was nasty, that's what she said. And he didn't talk regular with her, he yelled at her. Really loud. So it made her ears hurt.' Now Frida demonstrated by holding her hands over her ears.

Carefully Veronika took her hands away and said, 'You know, this may be a secret that you'll have to tell other people besides me.'

'But you said . . .' Frida sounded upset and her eyes once again nervously sought out the grey sky outdoors.

'I know I said that, but you know what? I really think that Sara would want you to tell this secret to the police.'

'Why?' asked Frida, still looking worried.

'Because when somebody dies and goes to heaven, the police want to know all the secrets that person had. And people usually want the police to know all their secrets too. It's the job of the police to find out everything.'

'So they're supposed to know all the secrets?' said Frida in amazement. 'Do I have to tell them about the time I didn't want to eat all my sandwich and hid it under the sofa cushion?'

Veronika couldn't help smiling. 'No, I don't think the police need to know that secret.'

'I don't mean while I'm alive, but if I die, would you have to tell them about that?'

The smile vanished from Veronika's face. She shook her head. The conversation had taken an unpleasant turn. Gently she stroked her daughter's blonde hair and whispered, 'You don't have to worry about that, because you're not going to die.'

'How do you know that, Mamma?' asked Frida.

'I just know.' Veronika got up abruptly from her chair and with her heart clenched up so hard that she had difficulty breathing, she went out to the hall. Without turning round, so that her daughter couldn't see her tears, she called in a voice that came out unnecessarily brusque, 'Put on your coat and shoes. We're going to talk to the police right now.'

Frida obeyed. But when they went out to the car she involuntarily flinched beneath the heavy grey sky. She hoped that Mamma was right. She hoped that Sara wouldn't be mad.

FJÄLLBACKA 1928

Lovingly he dressed the boys and combed their hair. It was Sunday, and he was going to take the boys out for a walk in the sunshine. It was hard to get their clothes on because they were jumping up and down with joy at being able to go out with their father, but at last they were dressed and ready to set off. Agnes didn't answer when the boys called goodbye to her. It cut Anders to the quick to see once more the thirsting, disappointed look in their eyes when they looked at their mother. She didn't seem to understand it, but they longed for her – longed to smell her close to them and to feel her arms around them. The idea that she might be aware of this but deliberately denied them was a possibility he didn't even want to imagine, but it was a thought that kept intruding more and more often. Now that the boys were four years old, he could only surmise that there was something unnatural about the way she related to them. At first he'd thought that it was because of the difficult childbirth, but as the years passed she still hadn't seemed to bond with them.

He himself never felt so rich as when he walked off down the hill with a little child's hand firmly gripped in each of his own. The boys were still so small that they would rather run than walk. Sometimes he had to jog to keep up with them, even though his legs were so much longer than theirs. People smiled and tipped their hats when they came scurrying along the main street. He knew that they made a pleasant sight – the father, big and tall in his Sunday best, and the boys, also as finely dressed as a stonecutter's sons could be, and with their tousled blond hair that was exactly the same shade as his own. They even had his brown eyes. Anders was often told how they were his spitting image, and he swelled with pride every time. Sometimes he permitted himself a sigh of gratitude that they didn't take after Agnes either in appearance or manner. Over the years he'd noticed a hardness in her, which he sincerely hoped the children wouldn't inherit.

When he passed by the village shop he hastened his steps and carefully avoided looking in that direction. Naturally he had to go there now and then to buy the things they needed, but since he'd heard what people were saying he tried to limit his visits as much as possible. If only he believed that there was no truth to what the gossips were saying, he could have walked in there with his head held high. The worst thing was that he didn't doubt the rumours for a minute. And even if he had doubted, the shopkeeper's superior smile and bold tone of voice would have been enough to convince him. Sometimes Anders wondered if there was any limit to how much he had to take. If it hadn't been for the boys he would have cleared out long ago. But the twins forced him to look for another option to leaving his wife, and he believed that he had found it. Anders had a plan. It had taken a year of hard work to carry it out, but now he was getting close. As soon as some last pieces fell into place he would be able to offer his family a new beginning, a chance to make everything right. Maybe he would then be able to give Agnes more of what she longed for so that the darkness that seemed to be growing inside her heart would disappear. He thought he could already see how their new life would look and how it would offer all of them so much more than this one here.

He squeezed the boys' hands extra hard and smiled at them when they tilted their heads back to look up at him.

'Pappa, could we get a cola?' said Johan in the hope that his father's good mood would make him favourably disposed to such a request. And it did. After pondering for a moment Anders nodded his assent, and the boys whooped and jumped up and down in anticipation. Buying a couple of colas would necessitate a visit to the village shop, of course, but it would be worth it. Soon he would be done with all that.

Gösta sat in his office, slumped at his desk. The mood had been tense to say the least since Ernst's screw-up had been revealed. Gösta shook his head. His colleague had made any number of mistakes over the years, but this time he'd gone too far in ignoring how a police officer should carry out his job. For the first time Gösta believed that Ernst actually might be fired because of his actions. Not even Mellberg could back him up after this.

Despondently he looked out of the window. This was the time of year he hated most. It was even worse than winter. He still had the memory of summer fresh in his mind, and he could still reel off the scores of pretty much every round of golf he'd played. By the time winter arrived at least a merciful forgetfulness had begun to roll in, and he sometimes wondered whether he'd really made those perfect shots on the golf course, or whether it was all just a beautiful dream.

The telephone interrupted his ruminations.

'Gösta Flygare.'

'Hi, Gösta, it's Annika. Look, I've got Pedersen on the line and he's looking for Patrik, but I can't get hold of him right now. Could you talk to Pedersen?'

'Sure, put him on.' He waited a couple of seconds. Then he heard the click on the line and the medical examiner's voice.

'Hello?'

'Yes, I'm here. It's Gösta Flygare.'

'I heard that Patrik was out on a job. But you're working on the investigation of the murder of the little girl too, aren't you?'

'Everyone at the station is, more or less.'

'Good, then you can take down the information we just got in, but it's important that everything be sent on to Hedström.'

Gösta wondered for a second whether Pedersen had heard about Ernst's fiasco, but then realized it was impossible. He probably just wanted to emphasize that the head of the investigation should get all the information. And Gösta had no intention of making the same mistake as Lundgren, that's for sure. Hedström was going to hear about everything, even the slightest clearing of his throat.

'I'll take notes, and you'll fax me as usual, right?'

'Of course,' said Pedersen. 'We've got the analysis of the ashes now. That is, the ashes the girl had in her stomach and lungs.'

'I'm familiar with the details,' said Gösta, who couldn't keep a hint of irritation from sneaking into his reply. Did Pedersen think he was simply some bloody errand boy at the station, or what?

If he heard Gösta's annoyance, Pedersen ignored it and went on calmly, 'Well, we've found out a few interesting things. First, the ashes aren't exactly fresh. The contents, at least certain portions, might be characterized as . . .' he paused, 'rather old.'

'Rather old?' said Gösta, still sounding peevish. But he couldn't deny that he was curious. 'What exactly does "rather old" mean? Are we talking Stone Age, or the Swinging Sixties?'

'Well, that's the snag. According to SFL it's incredibly difficult to pin down. The best estimate I could get was that the ashes are somewhere between fifty and a hundred years old.'

'Hundred-year-old ashes?' said Gösta, astonished.

'Yes, or maybe fifty. Or somewhere in between. But that wasn't the only remarkable thing they found. There were also fine particles of stone in the ashes. Granite, to be precise.'

'Granite? Where the hell are the ashes from then? It couldn't have been a piece of granite that burned, could it?'

'No, stone doesn't burn, as we all know. The stone must have been in fine particles from the start. They're still working on analysing the material to be able to say something more definite. But . . .'

Gösta could hear that something big was brewing. 'Yes?' he said.

'What they can tell, at this point, is that it seems to be a mixture. They've found remnants of wood mixed in with . . .' he paused but then went on, 'organic matter.'

'Organic matter? Are you saying what I think you are? Are they ashes from a human body?'

'Well, that's what further analyses will show. It's not yet possible to determined whether they're human or the remains of some animal. And it's not certain they'll even be able to determine that, but SFL is going to try. And as I said, in any case it's mixed with other substances: wood and granite.'

'I'll be damned,' said Gösta. 'So somebody saved these old ashes.'

'Yes, or found them somewhere.'

'That's right, it could be that too.'

'So this should give you a little to go on,' said Pedersen dryly. 'Hopefully we can find out more in a few days, such as whether there are actually human remains in the ashes. Until then this will have to do.'

'Yes, it will,' said Gösta, already imagining his colleagues' faces when he told them what he'd found out. The question was how in the world the information could be used.

He put down the receiver and went over to the fax machine. What was whirling in his head was the news of the granite particles Pedersen had mentioned. They should provide a lead.

But the thought slipped away.

Asta groaned as she straightened up. The old wooden floor had been laid when the house was built and could only be cleaned with soap and water. Although her body would probably last for a while yet, with every year that passed it got harder for her to kneel down and scrub.

She looked around the house. For forty years she had lived here. She and Arne. Before that he had lived here with his parents, who had remained living with the newlyweds. Suddenly both parents passed away within the space of a few months. She was ashamed of even thinking it, but those had been hard years. Arne's father had been as gruff as a general, and his mother wasn't much better. Arne had never discussed it with her, but she gathered from random comments that he'd been beaten a lot when he was

281

little. Maybe that's why he'd been so hard on Niclas. A boy who thinks he's loved with the whip will probably dispense love with the whip when that day comes. Although in Arne's case it had been a belt, of course. The big brown belt that hung on the inside of the pantry door and was used whenever their son had done something that didn't suit his father. But who was she to question the way Arne had brought up their son? Certainly it had broken her heart to hear her son's muffled screams of pain, and she had used a gentle hand to wipe away his tears when the ordeal was over, but Arne had always known best.

Laboriously she climbed up on a kitchen chair and took down the curtains. She couldn't see any dirt on them yet, but as Arne always said, if anything ever gets dirty it should have been cleaned long ago. She stopped abruptly, with her hands raised above her head, just as she was about to lift off the curtain rod. Hadn't she done the same thing on that horrible day? Yes, she believed she had. She had stood there changing the curtains when she heard raised voices coming from outside in the garden. Naturally she was used to hearing Arne's angry voice, but what was unusual was that Niclas had also raised his voice. It was so inconceivable, and the possible consequences so dire, that she hurried to jump down from the chair and run out to the garden. They were standing facing each other, like two combatants. Their voices, which had sounded loud from inside the house, now hurt her eardrums. Incapable of stopping, she had run up to Arne and grabbed his arm.

'What's going on here?' She could still hear how desperate her voice had sounded. And as soon as she took hold of Arne's arm she knew it was the wrong thing to do. He fell silent and turned towards her with eyes that were completely empty of emotion. Then he raised his hand and slapped her hard. The silence that followed was ominous. They had stood utterly still, like a three-headed stone statue. Then she saw as if in slow motion how Niclas drew his arm back, clenched his fist, and aimed it at his father's head. The sound of his fist slamming into Arne's face had abruptly broken the eerie silence and set everything in motion again. In disbelief Arne put his hand up to his cheek and stared at his son. Then Asta saw Niclas's arm draw back and fly at Arne again.

After that it seemed it would never stop. Niclas moved like an automaton, punching him over and over. Arne took the blows without seeming to understand what was happening. Finally his legs gave out and he fell to his knees. Niclas was breathing hard. He looked at his father on his knees before him, with blood running out of his nose. Then he turned and ran.

After that day she was not allowed to mention Niclas's name again. He was seventeen years old.

Asta climbed down carefully from the chair with the curtains in her arms. Lately she'd had so many disquieting thoughts, and it was probably no accident that the memories of that day were intruding just now. The girl's death had stirred up so many feelings, so much that she'd tried to forget over the years. A realization of how much she'd lost because of Arne's stubbornness had come sneaking up on her, awakening emotions that would only make life more difficult for her. But as soon as she went to visit her son at the clinic she'd begun to question much of what she'd taken for granted over the years. Maybe Arne didn't know everything after all. Maybe Arne wasn't the one who could decide how everything should be, even for her. Maybe she could start making her own decisions about her life. The thoughts made her nervous, and she pushed them aside until later. Right now she had curtains to wash.

Patrik knocked on the door with an authoritative rap. He was already having to work to keep his expression neutral. Inside of him he felt repugnance welling up and giving him a foul taste in his mouth. This was the lowest of the low, the most loathsome type of person he could imagine. The only consolation, and this was not something Patrik would ever say out loud, was that once this type of person ended up behind lock and key, he wouldn't have it easy in prison. Paedophiles were at the bottom of the pecking order and were treated accordingly. And rightfully so.

He heard footsteps approaching and took a step back. Martin stirred tensely beside him, and standing behind them were several colleagues from Uddevalla, including some who could provide invaluable expertise in these cases – computer expertise.

The door opened and Kaj's thin form appeared. As always he

was formally dressed, and Patrik wondered if he even owned any casual clothes. For his part he always slipped on a pair of worn-out jogging trousers and a cosy sweatshirt the minute he got home.

'What is it this time?' Kaj stuck his head out of the door and frowned when he saw two police cars parked in his driveway. 'Is it really necessary for you to advertise your presence like this? The old lady next door is probably rubbing her hands together with glee. If you have something to ask me you could just pick up the phone, or send over one person instead of a whole troop!'

Patrik studied him for a moment, wondering whether Kaj really felt so secure that uniformed policemen showing up at his door didn't arouse any thoughts that he'd been found out. Or maybe he was simply a good actor. Well, they would soon see.

'We have a warrant to search the premises. And we request that you accompany us to the station for questioning.' Patrik's voice was extremely formal and revealed none of the emotions he was feeling.

'A warrant to search my house? What the hell? Is it that damned woman who thought this up? I swear I'm going to . . .' Kaj stepped outside onto the porch and seemed to consider heading over to the Florins' house. Patrik held up his hand, and Martin blocked his way.

'This has nothing to do with Lilian Florin. We have information that implicates you in child pornography.'

Kaj stiffened. Now Patrik realized that he hadn't been acting earlier. He really hadn't considered that possibility. Stammering, he tried to regain his composure.

'Wha . . . what in . . . what are you saying, man?' But his protest sounded powerless, and the shock had made his shoulders slump.

'As I said, we have a warrant to search the premises, and if you'd be so kind as to come with us in one of the cars, we intend to continue this conversation in peace and quiet at the station.'

The bitter taste of gall in his mouth forced Patrik to keep swallowing. He wanted to throw himself at Kaj and shake him, ask him how, why, what it was that enticed him about children, young boys, that he couldn't get in an adult relationship. But there would be plenty of time for those questions. The most important thing right now was to secure the evidence.

284

Kaj seemed to be utterly paralysed, and without replying or taking along a jacket, he followed them down the stairs and compliantly got into the back seat of one of the police cars.

Patrik turned to his colleagues from Uddevalla. 'We'll take him in and begin the questioning. You do what you have to do here, and ring if you find anything we can use. I know I don't have to point this out, but I'll say it anyway: take all the computers and don't forget that the warrant includes the cabin on the property. I know there's at least one computer in there.'

His colleagues nodded and entered the house with determined expressions.

With a sense of elation Lilian leisurely walked past the police cars as she made her way home. It was as if her dreams had been answered. An entire phalanx of officers outside the neighbours' house, and on top of that, Kaj wearing a downhearted expression had been forced to get in the back of one of the police cars. A feeling of joy surged through her. After all these years of trouble with him and his family, his behaviour had finally caught up with him. God knows that she herself had always behaved correctly. Could she help it that she wanted everything to be done with decorum? Could she help it that he had done things that deviated from the spirit of neighbourliness, so that she was then forced to answer in kind? And people had the nerve to claim that she was belligerent. Oh yes, she'd heard the gossip going around town. But she denied any responsibility for the trouble between them. If Kaj hadn't kept it up by bothering them and doing stupid things, she wouldn't have made a fuss. In normal circumstances no one was as gentle and easy-going as she was. And she felt absolutely no guilt in telling the police about that peculiar son of theirs. Everybody knew that sooner or later, people like that who had something wrong in the head would present problems. Even though she may have exaggerated Morgan's Peeping Tom behaviour in her statement to the police, she'd only done it to prevent further problems. People like that could come up with anything if they were allowed to run riot, and it was common knowledge that they had an overactive sex drive.

But now everybody would get to see how things really stood.

It wasn't outside *her* house that the police were swarming. She paused outside her front door to watch the show with her arms crossed and a malevolent smile on her lips.

When the police car with Kaj drove off, she reluctantly went inside. She pondered for a moment whether to go over there as a concerned citizen and ask what was going on. But the police disappeared inside Kaj's house before she even finished that thought, and she didn't want to seem like such a busybody that she would go over and knock on the door.

As she took off her shoes and hung up her jacket she wondered whether Monica knew what was going on. Maybe she ought to ring her at the library and tell her, like a good neighbour, of course. But Stig's voice from upstairs interrupted her before she made up her mind.

'Lilian, is that you?'

She went upstairs. He sounded feeble today. 'Yes, darling, it's me.'

'Where have you been?'

He looked up at her pitifully as she entered his bedroom. What a weak little soul he was now. A feeling of tenderness rose up inside her when she realized how dependent he was on her care. It warmed her heart to feel so needed. It was like when Charlotte was a child. What a feeling of power that had been to be responsible for such a helpless little life. Actually she had liked that period the best. Gradually, as Charlotte grew up, she had slipped more and more out of her mother's hands. If Lilian had been able to do so, she would have frozen time and stopped her from growing up altogether. But the harder she tried to hold on to her daughter, the more she had pulled away. Instead, Charlotte's father had quite undeservedly received all the love and respect that Lilian thought *she* deserved. She was Charlotte's mother, after all. A father should have lower status than a mother. She was the one who'd given birth to her, and during the first years she was the one who'd satisfied all her daughter's needs. Then Lennart had taken over, reaping the fruits of all her labours. He had turned Charlotte into a daddy's girl. After Charlotte moved out and it was just the two of them, he'd started talking about divorce, as if Charlotte were the only one who counted in all those years.

The memory made the anger rise up in her throat, and she

forced herself to smile at Stig. At least he needed her. And so did Niclas, to some extent, even though he didn't know it himself. Charlotte had no idea how good she had it. Instead she was always grumbling that her husband never helped out, that he didn't do his part when it came to the children. Ungrateful, that's what she was. But Lilian had also begun to feel deeply disappointed with Niclas. He would come home and snap at her and talk about moving. But she knew quite well where these whims came from. She simply hadn't thought he'd be so easily influenced.

'You look so stern,' said Stig, reaching for her hand. She pretended not to notice and instead carefully smoothed out the bedspread.

Stig always took Charlotte's side, so Lilian couldn't say anything to him about what she'd just been thinking. Instead she told him, 'There's an awful commotion next door. Police officers and police cars everywhere. This is no fun, let me tell you, having such people living so close.'

Stig sat up with a start. The movement made him grimace and grab his stomach. But his face was filled with hope. 'It must be about Sara. Do you think they've found out anything about Sara?'

Lilian nodded. 'Yes, it wouldn't surprise me. Why else would they send out a whole contingent?'

'It would be a blessing for Charlotte and Niclas if we could have an end to all this.'

'Yes, and you know how it has been upsetting me too, Stig. Now maybe I can have peace in my soul again.'

She let Stig pat her hand, and his voice was as loving as usual when he said, 'Of course, darling. You have such a kind heart, this has been a terrible time for you.' He turned her hand over and kissed her palm.

She let him hold her hand for a second longer, but then pulled it back. Brusquely she said, 'It's nice to hear someone worrying about me for a change. Let's just hope that we're right, and that they took Kaj away because of Sara.'

'What else do you think it could be?' Stig sounded surprised.

'Well, I don't know. I didn't really think about it. But I of all people know what he's capable of –'

'When is the funeral?' Stig interrupted.

Lilian got up from the side of the bed. 'We're still waiting to hear when we can get the body back. Probably next week sometime.'

'Please don't use the word "body". It's our Sara we're talking about.'

'She's actually my grandchild, not yours,' Lilian snapped.

'I loved her too, and you know it,' said Stig gently.

'Yes, dear, I know. Forgive me. All this is just so hard for me, and nobody seems to understand.' She wiped away a tear, noticing the remorse on Stig's face.

'No, I'm the one who should ask for forgiveness. That was stupid of me. Can you forgive me, darling?'

'Of course,' said Lilian magnanimously. 'And now I think you should rest and not think so much about all this. I'll go downstairs and make some tea and bring you a cup. Then maybe you can sleep for a while afterwards.'

'What have I done to deserve you?' said Stig to his wife with a smile.

It wasn't easy for Mellberg to concentrate on work. Not because he had ever prioritized that part of his life, but he usually was able to get at least a little bit done. And the situation that Ernst had provoked should have taken up a larger part of his thoughts. But since last Saturday nothing was the same. Back home in his flat the boy was playing video games. The new ones that he'd bought him yesterday. Mellberg had always kept a tight control on his wallet and yet he had suddenly felt an irresistible urge to be generous. And video games were clearly what stood at the top of the list, so video games it would be. Mellberg had bought an Xbox and three games, and even though he'd been shocked at the price, he hadn't balked.

Because the boy was his, after all. Simon, his son. If he'd had any doubts before, they were swept aside as soon as he saw him step off the train. It was like seeing himself as a young lad. The same well-fed physique, the same strong facial features. The emotions aroused in him were astonishing. Mellberg was still shocked that he was capable of such deep feelings. He had always taken pride in the fact that he didn't need anyone. Well, with the possible exception of his mother.

She had always pointed out that it was a sin and a shame that such excellent genes as his weren't going to be passed on. And on that she'd undoubtedly had a point. It was one of the foremost reasons that he wished that his mother could have met his son. To show her that she was right. All it took was a glance at the boy to see that he'd inherited many of his father's characteristics. The apple certainly didn't fall far from the tree. The boy's mother had said in her letter that he was lazy, unmotivated, insubordinate, and did miserably in school. But that said more about her child-rearing ability than about the boy. He just needed to spend a little time with his father, a manly role model. It was surely only a matter of time before he'd make a man out of him.

Naturally he thought that Simon at least could have said 'thank you' when he gave him the video games, but the poor boy was probably so shocked to get anything as a gift that he didn't know what to say. Lucky that Mellberg was such a good judge of people. It wouldn't be productive to force anything at this stage; he knew that much about raising children. Although he had no practical experience in the subject, he had to admit, but how hard could it be? It was probably only a matter of using common sense. The boy was a teenager, after all, and people said that was going to be difficult, but in Mellberg's opinion it was simply a matter of finding the appropriate language: slang for peasant farmers and Latin for scholars. And if there was anyone who knew how to talk to people on their level, it was him. He was convinced that he would have no problem at all.

Voices out in the corridor announced that Patrik and Martin were back. Hopefully with that paedophile jerk in tow. This was one interrogation he intended to participate in, for a change. And this time he'd be forced to put away the kid gloves.

FJÄLLBACKA 1928

It began like any other day. The boys had run over to the neighbours' in the morning, and she'd been lucky that they stayed there
until evening. The old woman had even felt sorry for the boys
and fed them, so she got out of fixing lunch, even though it usually
only entailed making a couple of open sandwiches. This turn of
events had put her in such a good mood that she condescended
to mop the floor. So when evening came she felt sure of getting
some well-earned praise from her husband. Even though she didn't
particularly care what he thought, she still craved attention and
she looked on praise as a luxury.

By the time she heard Anders coming up the front steps, Karl
and Johan were already asleep, and she was sitting at the kitchen
table reading a women's magazine. She looked up at him distract-
edly and nodded, but then gave a start. He didn't look as tired
and downhearted as he usually did when he came home; he had
a gleam in his eye that she hadn't seen in a long time. A vague
feeling of uneasiness awoke inside her.

He sank down on one of the wooden chairs facing her, folded
his hands and rested them on the worn tabletop.

'Agnes,' he said, and then stopped. The silence lasted long
enough for the unpleasant feeling in her stomach to grow into a
lump. He obviously had something on his mind, and if there was
anything she had learned in her life, it was that surprises were
seldom good.

'Agnes,' he said again, 'I've been thinking a lot about our future, and about our family, and I've come to the conclusion that we need a change.'

All right, so far she was following him. She just couldn't envision what he'd be able to do to change her life for the better.

Anders continued with obvious pride. 'So that's why I've taken on as much extra work as I could this past year, and I put away all the money so I could buy us a one-way ticket.'

'A ticket? Where to?' asked Agnes, with her uneasiness rising. She also felt annoyed at the realization that he had withheld money from her.

'To America,' Anders said, seeming to expect a positive reaction. Instead Agnes felt the shock turn her face numb. What had that idiot gone and done now?

'America?' was all she could say.

He nodded eagerly. 'Yes, we're leaving next week, and you'd better believe I had to pull some strings to arrange everything. I've been in touch with some of the Swedes who went over there from Fjällbacka, and they assured me that there's plenty of work for someone like me. A man who's skilled can make himself a good future "over there".' This last he said in English with his broad Blekinge accent, evidently proud that he already knew two words in his new language.

Agnes wanted to lean forward and slap him right across his grinning, happy face. What was he thinking? Was he so naïve that he actually believed she would get on a boat to a foreign land together with him and his brats? To end up in an even more dependent position, in an unfamiliar country, with a strange language and strange people? Certainly she hated her life here, but at least there was the possibility that she might someday get out of the hellhole she'd ended up in. Although to be honest she had toyed with the idea of travelling to America herself, but alone, without him and the kids as a shackle round her leg.

But Anders didn't see the horror in her face. Overjoyed, he took out the tickets and placed them on the table. In desperation Agnes regarded the four pieces of paper, spread out like a fan before him. She wanted to shrivel up and cry.

She had a week. A miserable week left to get out of this situation somehow. She forced herself to give Anders a smile.

Monica had driven to Konsum to buy groceries, but suddenly she set down the shopping basket and walked out the door without buying a thing. Something was telling her she had to get home. Her mother and grandmother had been the same way. They could sense things, and she too had learned to listen to her inner voice.

She floored the gas pedal of her little Fiat as she took the road around the mountain, past the Kullen neighbourhood. When she came round the curve on the road up to Sälvik, she saw the police car parked outside their house and knew she had been right to heed her instincts. She parked right behind the police car and got out cautiously, terror-stricken at what she might encounter. Each night for the past week she'd had exactly the same dream. Police officers coming to their home and uncovering the very thing she'd done her utmost to put out of her mind. Now it was reality, not a dream, and she approached the house with reluctance. Trying to postpone the inevitable. Then she heard Morgan wailing, and she began to run. Up the garden path, out to his little cabin. He was standing in front of the door to the cabin screaming at two policemen. With his arms outstretched he was trying to block the entrance.

'Nobody can come into my house! It's mine!'

'We have a warrant,' said one policeman in an attempt to reason with him. 'We have to do our job, so please let us in.'

'No, you're just going to mess things up!' Morgan spread his arms even wider.

'We promise to be careful and disturb as little as possible. On the other hand, we may have to take a few things with us – if you have a computer in there, for instance.'

Morgan interrupted the policeman with a loud bellow. His eyes flicked back and forth and his body had started to twitch uncontrollably.

'No, no, no, no, no,' he chanted. He looked ready to defend his computers with his life, and Monica believed this was quite close to the truth. She hurried over to the group.

'What's going on? Can I help?'

'Who are you?' asked the policeman standing closest to her, but he didn't take his eyes off Morgan as he spoke.

'I'm Morgan's mother. I live here.' She pointed to the main house.

'Could you please explain to your son that we have a warrant to enter the cabin and look around? We're also permitted to take any computer equipment that may be in there.'

At the mention of the computers Morgan began to shake his head violently and again chanted, 'No, no, no, no . . .'

With great calm Monica walked up to him. As she fixed her gaze on the police officers, she put her arm round her son and stroked his back.

'Could you please tell me first why you're here? Then I'm sure I can help you.'

The younger of the two officers looked embarrassed and lowered his eyes. The older one who was certainly more hardened answered her calmly, 'We've taken in your husband for questioning, and we also have a warrant to search the premises.'

'May I ask why?' She could hear that she sounded unnecessarily cool, but to see those officers standing there trying to get past Morgan without giving her a reasonable explanation was not something she intended to accept.

'Your husband's name has come up in connection with possession of child pornography.'

Her hand stroking Morgan's back stopped short. She tried to speak but all that came out was a wheeze.

'Child pornography?' She cleared her throat to try and regain control of her voice. 'You must be mistaken. My husband, involved in child pornography?'

Thoughts began to tumble round in her head. Things she'd always wondered about, always pondered. But most overwhelming was a feeling of relief. They hadn't come because of what she feared most.

She took a few seconds to collect herself and then turned to Morgan.

'Now listen to me. You have to let them go inside the cabin. And you have to let them take the computers. You have no choice, it's the police. It's their right.'

'But what if they mess things up? And what about my schedule?' The shrill pitch of his voice wasn't the usual monotone, but displayed unusual sensitivity.

'I'm sure they'll be careful, just as they said. And you have no choice.' She stressed this last sentence and could feel him begin to calm down. It was always easier for Morgan to handle situations in which he had no choice.

'Do you promise not to mess things up?'

The policemen nodded, and Morgan slowly took a step away from the door.

'And you have to be careful with the files on the computers. I have a lot of jobs stored there.'

Again they nodded, and now he stepped out of the way and let them go inside.

'Why are they doing this, Mamma?'

'I don't know,' Monica lied. Relief was still the dominant emotion inside her. But slowly the realization of what the officers had said began to sink in. A feeling of disgust began to form in her stomach and work its way upwards. She took Morgan by the arm and led him to the front of the house. She kept turning her head to look back with concern towards the cabin.

'Don't worry, they promised to be careful.'

'Are we going inside the big house?' said Morgan. 'I don't usually go in the big house this time of day.'

'No, I know that,' said Monica. 'But today we have to do something totally different. We can't bother the policemen. So you have to come with me to Aunt Gudrun's house.'

He looked confused. 'But we only go there at Christmas. Or when one of them has a birthday.'

'I know,' Monica said patiently. 'But today we have to make an exception.'

He pondered this for a moment and then decided that there was logic in what she said.

As they walked towards the car Monica saw out of the corner of her eye the curtain drawn aside in the Florins' kitchen. Lilian stood in the window watching them. She was smiling.

'So, Kaj. This is certainly not a pleasant situation.' Patrik sat facing him, with Martin next to him and Mellberg sitting discreetly on a chair in the corner. To Patrik's great relief he had voluntarily offered to play a passive role in the interrogation. Patrik would have preferred not to have him there, but he was the chief, after all.

Kaj didn't answer. He dropped his chin to his chest, giving Patrik and Martin a close-up view of the top of his head. His hair had thinned over the years so that his pink scalp shone through the wisps of black hair.

'Do you have any explanation for why your name appears on an order list for child pornography? And don't give me that old story that it must be a mistake. Your name and address are both on the list, so there's no question that you were the one who placed the order.'

'Somebody must be trying to frame me,' Kaj muttered into his lap.

'Oh, really?' said Patrik, his voice dripping with sarcasm. 'Then perhaps you can tell us why anyone would go to the trouble of trying to put you in jail. What sort of arch-enemies have you made over the years?'

Kaj didn't answer. Martin slammed the palm of his hand on the table to get his attention, which made Kaj jump.

'Didn't you hear the question? Who would be interested in sending you to jail?'

Still no reply, so Martin continued. 'That's not so easy to answer, is it? Because there isn't anyone.'

There were a number of printouts in front of Patrik and Martin. Patrik leafed through them for a moment in silence, pulling out a few pages and gathering them into a pile.

'You must realize that we have plenty of material about you. We have names of others who . . .' he searched for the right term – 'share the same interest and who you've been in contact with. We have information on when you ordered material from them, we know that you've submitted material yourself, and we also have records of chat sessions that our colleagues in Göteborg have been skilled enough to get their hands on. There are a number of talented computer guys over there, you understand. And they weren't stopped by the elaborate firewalls that you all set up so that no one could hack into your little group and eavesdrop on the cheery topics that you discuss. Nothing is foolproof, you know.'

Now Kaj looked up and his eyes flitted restlessly from Patrik to the printouts in front of him. His whole world was tumbling down as the second hand ticked on the wall clock behind him. Patrik saw that he was shaken by the revelation that someone had been able to get into files they had thought were completely protected. Now Kaj was clearly wondering exactly how much they knew. It was just the right time to press him further.

'At this very moment we're going through your whole house. And our colleagues aren't amateurs. There is no hiding place they haven't seen before. No brilliant secret cubby-holes that they can't find. And your computer will be sent to Uddevalla to be examined by some guys who are real hackers. You know, guys who could get into banks on the Internet and move a little money around if they felt like it and if they didn't happen to be on the side of the law.'

Patrik thought he might be exaggerating the skills of his colleagues a bit, but Kaj didn't know that. And he could see that the tactic was working. Little beads of sweat had begun to appear on Kaj's brow, and he could feel rather than see Kaj's legs start to shake uncontrollably.

'And even though you may be an amateur when it comes to computers, perhaps Morgan has told you that just because you've deleted a file, that doesn't mean it's gone. Our computer guys can restore most of everything, as long as there hasn't been damage to the hard drive.'

Martin took up where Patrik had left off. 'As soon as they've had a chance to go through your computer, we'll have a little talk.

297

Then we'll know precisely what you've been up to. Göteborg and our own staff are working full speed to try and identify the children who appear in the material the police confiscated. The information we have so far indicates that your favourite victims are young boys. Is that correct? Well, is it true, Kaj? Do you prefer boys with no hair on their chest – young, innocent lads?'

Kaj's lower lip was quivering, but he still said nothing.

Patrik leaned forward and lowered his voice. Now he had reached the moment that was the real point of the interrogation.

'But what about girls? Does it work with little girls too? Pretty tempting with one living so close by, right next door in the neighbours' house. Must have been almost irresistible. Especially since it would be a chance to get back at Lilian. What a feeling. Right under her nose, to avenge all those years of injustice. But something went wrong, didn't it? How did it happen? Did the girl start to struggle, say that she was going to tell her mamma, so you had to drown her to make her shut up?'

Mouth agape, Kaj looked first at Patrik, then at Martin. His eyes were big and shiny. He shook his head.

'No, I had nothing to do with that. I never touched her, I swear!'

The last words came out like a shriek, and Kaj looked as though he would have a heart attack at any moment. Patrik wondered if he ought to interrupt the questioning, but decided to continue a bit longer.

'And why should we believe you? We have proof that you have a sexual interest in children, and we'll soon know if there's evidence that you've actually assaulted anyone. A seven-year-old girl living in the house next door to yours was found drowned. That's an odd coincidence, don't you think?'

He didn't mention that no trace of sexual assault had been found on Sara. But as Pedersen had said, that didn't necessarily mean that one hadn't taken place.

'But I swear I had nothing to do with the girl's death! She's never been inside our house, I swear it!'

'That remains to be seen,' said Martin grimly, casting a glance at Patrik. He saw the same 'bloody hell' expression in his eyes that he felt in his own. Patrik gave a slight nod and Martin got up to go make a phone call. They had forgotten to order a team of techs to check the bathroom. When that mistake was corrected and he'd been promised an immediate response, he went back in the interrogation room. Patrik was still asking about Sara.

'So you really expect us to believe it when you say that you were never once tempted to . . . take an interest in the neighbour's girl. She was a sweet girl, too.'

'I didn't touch her, I told you. And I wouldn't call her sweet. A bloody child of Satan is what she was. Sneaking into the garden in the summertime and pulling up all Monica's flowers. No doubt her fucking grandmother put her up to it.'

Patrik was shocked at how fast Kaj's nervousness vanished and his hatred of Lilian Florin took over. Even under these circumstances the feelings were so ingrained that for a moment they made Kaj forget why he was sitting there. Then Patrik saw reality sink in again, and his shoulders slumped as he hunched over the table.

'I didn't kill the little girl,' said Kaj quietly. 'And I never touched her, I swear.'

Patrik again exchanged a look with Martin and then made a decision. They probably weren't going to get much further right now. Hopefully they'd have more material once the search was completed of Kaj's house and computer. And if they were really lucky, the techs would find something when they examined the bathroom.

Martin took Kaj back to his cell, and Mellberg left right after that. Patrik remained where he was. He looked at the clock. By now he'd had enough too. He intended to drive home and kiss Erica and bury his nose in Maja's little neck and drink up the scent of her. That was probably the only thing that could get rid of the cloying feeling he had after sitting locked in a small room with Kaj. A sense of inadequacy also made him long for the security of home. He just couldn't screw this case up. People like Kaj shouldn't be allowed to go free. Especially not if they had a little girl's death on their conscience.

He was just about to go out the front door when Annika stopped him. 'You have visitors; they've been waiting quite a while. Gösta wants to talk to you ASAP. And I got a tip that you ought to take a look at right away.'

Patrik sighed and let the door glide shut. It seemed he'd have to give up his plan to go home. Now it looked as though he'd have to ring Erica instead and tell her he'd be late. That was a conversation he wasn't looking forward to.

Charlotte's finger hesitated in front of the doorbell. Then she made up her mind, took a deep breath, and pressed the button. She heard it ring inside. For a second she considered turning on her heel and fleeing, but she heard footsteps inside and forced herself to stand still.

She vaguely recognized the woman who opened the door. The town was small enough that they'd probably run into each other, and she saw that the other woman knew exactly who she was. After a brief moment of hesitation Jeanette opened the door and stepped aside.

Charlotte was surprised at how young Jeanette looked. Twenty-five, Niclas had said when she pressed him. She didn't know why she wanted to know such details. It was like a primitive need, an urge to know as much as possible. Maybe it was because she hoped somehow to understand what he was looking for that she couldn't seem to give him. And maybe that was precisely why she'd been inexorably drawn here. She had never before confronted the women from any of his affairs. She had wanted to see them but never dared. But after Sara's death everything changed. It was as though she were invulnerable. All terrors had vanished. She had already been struck by the worst possible thing that could happen to a person. So much of what had previously paralysed and terrified her now seemed like insignificant obstacles. Not that it was easy to come here, she wouldn't say that. But she had done it. Sara was dead, so she had done it.

'What do you want?' Jeanette looked at her warily.

Charlotte felt big in comparison with this other woman who was probably no more than five foot three. At five foot nine Charlotte felt like a giant. Jeanette had also not had her figure altered by two pregnancies. Charlotte couldn't help noticing that her breasts in the tight top didn't need a bra to look perky. In her mind's eye Charlotte pictured Jeanette naked, in bed with Niclas, who was caressing her perfect breasts. She shook her head to get rid of the image. She had already spent far too much time on that sort of self-torment over the years. But the images no longer bothered her as much. She had worse images than that in her head – images of Sara, floating in the water.

Charlotte forced herself back to reality. In a calm voice she said, 'I just want to talk a little. Could we have a cup of coffee?'

She didn't know whether Jeanette had expected her to show up or whether she found the situation so surreal that she couldn't really take it in. At any rate, Jeanette's face showed no surprise. She simply nodded and went into the kitchen, with Charlotte following.

Curious, she looked around the flat. It was close to what she'd imagined. A little two-room place with a lot of pine furniture, frilly curtains, and souvenirs of trips abroad as the primary decoration. Jeanette apparently saved every öre she earned to be able to take party trips to the sunshine, and those trips were probably the high point of her life. Except when she was fucking married men, that is, Charlotte thought bitterly as she sat down at the kitchen table. She wasn't feeling as self-assured as she hoped she looked. Her heart was pounding hard, making her very nervous. But she'd just looked the other woman in the eye, seeing for the first time what sort of person could make a roll in the hay weigh heavier than marriage vows, children and decency.

To her surprise Charlotte was disappointed. She had always imagined Niclas's lovers to be in a whole different class. Sure, Jeanette was cute and curvy, she couldn't ignore that, but she was so – she searched for the right word so *insipid*. She radiated no warmth, no energy. From what Charlotte could see of her and her home, this woman didn't seem to have either the capacity or ambition to do anything other than just go with the flow in life.

'Here,' said Jeanette peevishly, setting a coffee cup in front of Charlotte. Then she sat down across the table and began nervously sipping her coffee. Charlotte noticed that she had long, perfectly manicured nails. Yet another thing that didn't exist in the world of mothers of small children.

'Are you surprised to see me here?' said Charlotte, observing with ostensible calm the woman facing her.

Jeanette shrugged her shoulders. 'Dunno. Maybe. I haven't thought that much about you.'

At least she's honest, Charlotte thought. Whether it was from boldness or sheer stupidity, she couldn't tell yet.

'Did you know that Niclas told me about you?'

Once again the same nonchalant shrug. 'I knew it would come out sooner or later.'

'How did you know that?'

'People talk so much in this town. There's always somebody who's seen someone somewhere, and then they feel compelled to pass it on.'

'Sounds like this isn't the first time you've played this game,' said Charlotte.

A little smile tugged at the corners of Jeanette's mouth. 'I can't help it if the best ones are already taken. Not that it usually bothers them much.'

Charlotte's eyes narrowed. 'So Niclas didn't worry about it either? That he was married and had two kids?' The word 'had' stuck in her throat and she felt her emotions once again well up and threaten to take over. With an effort she pushed them back.

Her hesitation apparently made Jeanette realize that she might have certain human obligations. Stiffly she said, 'I'm really sorry about your daughter. About Sara.'

'Don't speak my daughter's name, thank you,' said Charlotte with an icy cold that made Jeanette shrink back. She lowered her eyes and stirred her coffee.

'Instead answer my question: did Niclas worry about sleeping with you when he had a family at home?'

'He didn't talk about you,' said Jeanette evasively.

'Never?'

'We had other things to do rather than talk about you,' Jeanette let slip, before she again realized that out of sheer decency she ought to watch what she said.

Charlotte looked at her with disgust. But she felt even more disgust and contempt for Niclas, who clearly had been ready to throw away everything they shared for this – a stupid, narrow-minded girl who thought that the world lay at her feet simply because she'd once been chosen as the class Lucia in high school. Yes, Charlotte knew the type. Too much attention during her most impressionable years had swelled Jeanette's ego to enormous proportions. Hurting other people, taking what didn't belong to her, had no meaning for girls like her.

Charlotte stood up. She was sorry she'd come. She would have preferred to keep the image of Niclas's lover as a beautiful, intelligent, passionate woman. Someone she could harbour some understanding for as a competitor. But this girl just seemed cheap. The thought of Niclas with Jeanette turned her stomach, and she could feel the little respect she still had for him slowly vanishing into nothingness.

'I'll find my way out,' she said, and left Jeanette sitting at the kitchen table. On the way out she happened to bump into a ceramic donkey with 'Lanzarote 1998' painted on it that was standing on the hall bureau. It shattered into a thousand bits on the floor. An ass for an ass, thought Charlotte, treading with glee on the remains before she shut the door behind her.

FJÄLLBACKA 1928

It was a Sunday when catastrophe struck. The boat to America was supposed to sail from Göteborg on Friday, and they had already done most of the packing. Anders had sent Agnes into town to buy some last items that he thought they would need 'over there', and for once he had entrusted her with some money.

She had her basket full of purchases when she turned the corner and began to walk up the hill. She could hear people shouting in the distance, and she quickened her steps. The smoke reached her a few houses away from theirs, and she saw that it was thicker farther up the hill. Agnes dropped the basket and ran. The first thing she saw was the fire. Huge flames were shooting out of the windows of the house, and people were running back and forth like chickens with their heads cut off. The men and some of the women were carrying buckets of water. The rest of the women held their hands to their heads, screaming in panic. The fire had spread to a number of houses and seemed to be taking over more and more of the neighbourhood. It spread with incredible speed. Agnes observed the scene with her mouth agape and her eyes wide with shock. Nothing could have prepared her for this sight.

A thick black smoke began to settle like a lid over the houses, turning the air at ground level greyish and hazy, like a fog. Agnes still stood as if frozen to the spot when one of the neighbour women came up to her and grabbed her by the arm.

'Agnes, come with me, don't just stand there staring at it.' She tried to pull her along, but Agnes wouldn't budge. Her eyes filled with tears from the smoke as she stared at the flaming ruin of their home. It seemed to be the one burning brightest of all.

'Anders . . . the boys . . .' she said tonelessly. The neighbour woman now tugged desperately at the sleeve of her blouse to get her to leave the scene.

'We don't know anything yet,' said the woman, who Agnes vaguely recalled was named Britt, or maybe Britta. She went on, 'Everybody was told to gather at the market square. Maybe your family are already down there,' she said, but Agnes could hear the doubt in her voice. The woman knew as well as Agnes that she wouldn't find any of them there.

Slowly she turned round and felt the heat from the fire warming her back. Listlessly she followed Britt or Britta down the hill, allowing herself to be led to the square, where the wailing of the women rose to the heavens. But they all fell silent when Agnes appeared. The rumour had already spread; while they were crying over their lost homes and possessions, Agnes could cry over her husband and her two little boys. All the mothers looked at her with aching hearts. Regardless of what they may have said or thought about her before, at this moment she was a mother who had lost her children, and they pressed their own little ones close.

Agnes kept her gaze fixed on the ground. She did not cry.

They stood up as Patrik came towards them. Veronika held her daughter's hand tight and wouldn't let go even when Patrik led them to his small office. He pointed to the two chairs and they sat down.

'So, how can I help you?' asked Patrik, smiling reassuringly at Frida when he noticed her anxious expression. She looked up at her mother, who nodded.

'Frida has something to tell you,' said Veronika, nodding again to her daughter.

'Actually it's a secret,' said Frida in a faint voice.

'Oh, a secret,' said Patrik. 'How exciting.' He could see that the girl was extremely uncertain about whether to tell him or not, so he went on, 'But you know, the job of the police is to listen to everyone's secrets, so it doesn't really count if you tell a secret to the police.'

That made Frida's face light up. 'So you get to know all the secrets in the world, then?'

'Well, maybe not all of them,' said Patrik. 'But almost all. So what sort of secret do you have?'

'There was a disgusting old man who scared Sara,' she said, now talking fast to get the words out. 'He was super-nasty and said that she was "double pawn" and Sara got really scared. But I wasn't allowed to tell anybody, because she was afraid the old man would come back.'

She caught her breath. Patrik felt his eyebrows arch. Double pawn?

'What did the old man look like, Frida? Can you remember?'

She nodded. 'He was super-old. A hundred at least. Like Grandpa.'

'Her Grandpa is sixty,' said Veronika, and couldn't help smiling.

Frida went on. 'His hair was all grey and his clothes were all black.' She seemed about to continue but then slumped down in her chair. 'That's all I remember,' she said downhearted, and Patrik winked at her.

'That's excellent. And it was a good secret to tell the police.'

'So you don't think that Sara will be mad when she comes back from heaven, because I told you?'

Veronika took a deep breath to explain again the realities of death to her daughter, but Patrik interrupted.

'No, because you know what I think? I think that Sara is having much too good a time in heaven to want to come back, and I'm sure she doesn't mind whether you told the secret or not.'

'Are you sure?' said Frida sceptically.

'I'm sure,' said Patrik.

Veronika got up. 'Well, you know where we live if you need to ask anything else. But I really think Frida doesn't know any more than that.' She hesitated. 'Do you think it might be . . .?'

Patrik just shook his head and said, 'Impossible to say, but it was great that you came in and told me about this. All information is important.'

'Could I ride in a police car?' said Frida, giving Patrik a pleading look.

He laughed. 'Not today, but I'll see if we can arrange it some other time.'

She seemed content with that, and preceded her mother into the corridor.

'Thanks for coming,' said Patrik, shaking hands with Veronika.

'I do hope you catch the man who did this soon. I hardly dare let her out of my sight,' she said, reaching out to stroke her daughter's hair.

'We'll do our best,' said Patrik with more confidence than he felt, and accompanied them to the front entrance.

As the door closed behind them he pondered what Frida had said. A disgusting old man? The description she'd given didn't match Kaj. Who could it be?

He went over to Annika sitting behind her glassed-in counter. After glancing at the clock he said wearily, 'You had some tips I was supposed to look at?'

'Yes, here they are,' she said, shoving a sheet of paper towards him. 'And don't forget that Gösta wants to talk to you too. He's probably about to go home, so you'd better get hold of him right away.'

'Some people sure have it easy, being able to go home,' he sighed. Erica hadn't been happy when he called, and his guilty conscience was nagging him.

'He probably goes home when you tell him he can go home,' said Annika, peering over the top of her glasses at Patrik.

'In theory you're right, but in practice it's probably best for Gösta to go home and get some rest. He doesn't contribute much when he's sitting here grumbling.'

It sounded harsher than Patrik intended, but sometimes he got so tired of having to drag his colleagues along with him. Two of them, at any rate. Oh well, he could at least be thankful that Gösta was far too lacking in initiative to present the problems that Ernst did.

'I suppose I'd better go find out what he wants.'

Patrik picked up the piece of paper with the tip information and headed for Gösta's office. He stopped in the doorway long enough to see Gösta shut down a game of solitaire on his computer. The fact that his colleague was sitting there wasting time while Patrik was working like a Trojan made him so irritated that he had to clench his teeth. He couldn't have this discussion with Gösta now, but sooner or later . . .

'So, there you are,' said Gösta, sounding put out, and Patrik wondered whether 'sooner' might be the best option.

'I had something important to take care of,' Patrik said, making an effort not to sound as critical as he felt.

'Well, I have some things to tell you too,' said Gösta, and Patrik heard to his surprise a certain eagerness in his colleague's voice.

'Shoot,' said Patrik in English, then realizing from Gösta's quizzical look that English expressions probably weren't his strong suit. Unless they were golf-related, of course.

Gösta told him about the conversation with Pedersen, and Patrik listened with growing interest. He took the faxes that Gösta handed him and sat down to study them.

'Yep, these are undeniably interesting,' he said. 'The question is, how do we proceed from here?'

'Well,' said Gösta, 'I've been thinking the same thing. The information might help us link somebody to the murder if we find the right person. But until then it doesn't give us much to go on.'

'And they couldn't say for sure whether the organic remains were animal or human?'

'No,' said Gösta, shaking his head. 'But within a few days we might get the answer to that.'

Patrik looked thoughtful. 'Tell me again, Gösta, what did Pedersen say about the stone?'

'That it was granite.'

'Pretty damn common here in Bohuslän, in other words,' said Patrik ironically, running his hand dispiritedly through his hair. 'If only we could work out what role the ashes played, I bet we'd also know who murdered Sara.'

Gösta nodded in agreement.

'Well, we aren't going to get any further right now,' said Patrik, getting to his feet. 'But it was damned interesting information. Why don't you head home now, Gösta, and we'll start fresh tomorrow.' He even managed to force a smile.

Gösta didn't need to be told twice. Within two minutes he'd shut down the computer, gathered up his things, and was on his way out the door. Patrik wasn't quite as fortunate. It was already quarter to seven, but he went in and sat down at his desk to read through the notes Annika had given him. A moment later, he grabbed the telephone.

Sometimes Erica felt as though she were standing outside the real world, encased in a tiny little bubble that kept shrinking. Now it was so small that she felt she could touch its walls if she reached out her hand.

Maja was sleeping at her breast. Once again Erica had tried to lay her down and get her to sleep by herself, but Maja woke up a few minutes later, protesting loudly at the enormous indignity of finding herself in a cot. And just when she was sleeping so

310

soundly at her mother's breast. Erica had considered trying out the suggestions in *The Baby Book* but so far she hadn't got beyond the thinking stage. So as usual she had given up and quieted the baby's cries by putting Maja to her breast and letting her sleep there. Often she would sleep for an hour or two, provided Erica didn't move much and she wasn't disturbed by loud noises from the telephone or the TV. So Erica had now been sitting for half an hour like a paving stone in the easy chair, with the telephone unplugged and the TV on mute. Of course there was nothing good on at this time of day, so she watched an episode of a dumb American soap opera that TV4 apparently had bought by the thousands. She hated her life.

Feeling guilty, she looked at the little downy head resting happily on the nursing pillow. The baby's mouth was half open and her eyelids fluttered now and then. Erica's despair had nothing to do with lack of motherly love. She loved Maja fiercely and sincerely. At the same time she felt as if she'd been invaded by an alien parasite that sucked all joy out of her and forced her into a shadow existence that had nothing in common with the life she'd lived before.

Sometimes she felt such bitterness against Patrik as well. He could make small guest appearances in her world and then slip out into the real world like a normal person; he didn't understand how it felt to be living her life right now. But in more clear-headed moments she realized that she wasn't being fair. Because how could he understand? He wasn't physically bound to the baby in the same way she was, nor emotionally either, for that matter. For better or worse, the bond between mother and daughter was so strong in the beginning that it functioned as both a shackle and a lifeline.

One of her legs had gone to sleep, and Erica cautiously tried to change position. It was risky, she knew that, but the pain in her leg was too much. Maja started to squirm, opened her eyes and immediately began searching for food with her mouth wide open. With a sigh Erica stuck in her nipple again. So far Maja had only slept for half an hour, and Erica knew that it wouldn't be long before she fell asleep again. Sitting motionless like this, her bottom was going to get a real workout today too. No, damn it all, she thought in the next instant. This time she was going to make Maja sleep alone!

It turned into a battle of wills. In one corner, Erica, seventy-two kilos. In the other, Maja, six kilos. With a firm grip Erica rolled the pram over the threshold between the living room and the hall. A whole arm's length, in, out. She wondered how anyone could sleep in a pram that shook like there was an earthquake going on, but according to *The Baby Book* that was exactly what was needed. Give the baby plain and clear instructions that 'now you're going to sleep, Mamma has the situation under control'. Although by fifteen minutes into the experiment Erica wouldn't exactly describe her situation as 'under control'. Although Maja, according to all calculations, should have been extremely tired, she screamed to high heaven, furious at being denied the right to the pacifying warmth of her mother's body. For a moment Erica was tempted to give up and sit down and nurse her daughter to sleep, but then she thought better of it. No matter how angry Maja was about the new regime, and how much her shrieks cut to Erica's heart, Maja would be better served by a mother who felt happy and had the energy to take care of her. So she persevered. Each time Maja cried in protest, Erica firmly rolled the pram back and forth. If Maja quieted down and seemed about to go to sleep, Erica would carefully stop the pram. According to Anna Wahlgren it was important to stop moving the pram just before the baby fell asleep so she would do so under her own power. And hallelujah! Half an hour later Maja was sound asleep in the pram. Cautiously Erica wheeled her into the workroom, closed the door, and sat down on the sofa with a blissful smile on her face.

Her good humour held on, even when it was eight o'clock and Patrik still hadn't come home. Erica hadn't had the energy to go round and turn on the lamps, so as the twilight gradually turned to night, the house had grown ever darker. Now the only light came from the TV screen. She lazily watched one of the many reality shows that were on in the evening as she fed Maja once again. To her shame, she had to admit being hooked on far too many of these shows and Patrik had taken to muttering about being inundated with petty intrigues and people greedy for media attention. His time watching sports programmes had been considerably curtailed, but as long as he wasn't the one who had to sit and nurse Maja all evening, he agreed to let Erica be the boss of the remote control. Now she turned up the volume, amazed at how a bunch of cute girls were willing to prance and preen themselves for the sake of a vain and foolish young man who tried to convince them that he was marriage material. It was obvious to all the TV viewers that he considered his participation in the programme as a way to increase his pick-up success at the trendiest clubs in Stockholm. Erica actually agreed with Patrik that the programme was an intelligence-free zone, but once she started watching it she couldn't stop.

A sound from the front door made her turn the volume back down. For an instant her old fear of the dark took over, but then she pulled herself together and realized that it must be Patrik finally coming home.

'You've sure got it dark in here,' he said, turning on a couple of lamps before he went over to Erica and Maja. He leaned over and kissed Erica on the cheek, stroked Maja's head gently, and then plopped down on the sofa.

'I'm really sorry to be so late,' he said. Despite Erica's childish feelings earlier that day, her annoyance drained out of her at once.

'It doesn't matter,' she said. 'We managed fine, the two of us.' She was still euphoric at getting some brief moments to herself when Maja was sleeping in the pram in the workroom.

'No chance of watching a little hockey, is there?' Patrik cast a wistful glance at the TV without having noticed Erica's unusually good mood.

Erica just snorted in reply. What a dumb question.

'That's what I thought,' he said and stood up. 'I'm going to make myself a couple of sandwiches. Would you like some?'

She shook her head. 'I ate a while ago. But a cup of tea would be nice. She'll probably have had her fill soon.' As if Maja understood what Erica said, she let go and looked up in contentment. Erica gratefully straightened her clothes, set Maja in the bouncer, and went to join Patrik in the kitchen. He was at the stove stirring O'Boy cocoa powder into a saucepan of milk. She went to stand behind him, putting her arms round him to hug him tight.

It felt so good, and she realized how little physical contact they'd had since Maja was born. She was mostly to blame for that, she had to admit.

'How was your day?' she asked. That was something else she hadn't done in a long time.

'Terrible,' he said, taking butter, cheese and caviar out of the fridge.

'I heard that you brought Kaj in,' she said cautiously, unsure of how much Patrik would want to tell. She had decided not to say anything about the visits she'd had that day.

'The gossip has spread like wildfire, I presume?' said Patrik.

'You could say that.'

'So what are people saying?'

'That he must have had something to do with Sara's death. Is it true?'

'I don't know.' Patrik seemed tired as he poured the hot chocolate into a cup and fixed a couple of open sandwiches. He sat down facing Erica and began to dunk his cheese and caviar sandwich into the hot chocolate. After a while he went on, 'But we didn't bring him in because of Sara's murder. There was another reason.'

He fell silent again. Erica knew better than to pry, but she couldn't help asking. In her mind's eye she saw Charlotte's listless gaze.

'But is there anything to indicate that he may have had something to do with Sara's death?'

Patrik dunked another sandwich in the chocolate and Erica tried not to look. She thought this habit was barbaric, to say the least.

'Yeah, there might well be. But we'll have to wait and see. We can't take the risk of narrowing our focus. There's something else we have to look at too,' he said, avoiding her eyes.

She stopped asking questions. Some grunts of protest from the living room indicated that Maja was getting tired of sitting all alone. Patrik got up and brought in the bouncer with their daughter in it. She gurgled gratefully and waved her hands and feet when Patrik set her on the kitchen table. The weariness in his face vanished, and his eyes took on that special gleam reserved for his daughter.

'Is this Pappa's little sweetie? Did Pappa's little darling have a good day? Is she the sweetest girl in the whole world?' he babbled with his face close to Maja's. Then Maja's face contorted, turned bright red, and after a couple of groans there was a noise from the lower regions and a dense stink spread round the table. Erica got up automatically to deal with the situation.

'I'll get it, you just sit,' said Patrik, and Erica gratefully sank back onto the kitchen chair.

When Patrik came back with a newly changed Maja in her pyjamas, she told him with great enthusiasm about the successful pram trick and how she had got Maja to fall asleep.

Patrik looked sceptical. 'She cried for forty-five minutes before she fell asleep? Is she really supposed to do that? On TV they said that if they cry, you're supposed to give them the breast. Can it really be good for her to have to cry like that?'

His lack of enthusiasm and understanding made Erica furious. 'Obviously the point is not for her to cry for forty-five minutes. It'll taper off in a few days, and besides, if you don't think it's a good idea, then you can stay home and take care of her! You're not the one who has to sit here nursing all day long. That must be why you don't see any need to make any changes!'

Then she burst into tears and dashed upstairs to the bedroom. Patrik sat there at the kitchen table, feeling like an idiot. He should think before he opened his mouth.

FJÄLLBACKA 1928

Two days later her father came to Fjällbacka. She was sitting in the little room where she had found a temporary roof over her head, waiting with her hands folded in her lap. When he came in she reflected that the gossip had been right. He looked terrible. His hair had thinned even more on top. A couple of years earlier he'd been pleasantly plump, but now his figure was bordering on fat, and his breathing was erratic. His complexion was flushed bright red from the exertion, but just underneath was a grey tinge that refused to yield to the red. He didn't look well.

He hesitated at the threshold with an expression of disbelief when he saw how small and dark the room was, but when he caught sight of Agnes he rushed forward to give her a big hug. She didn't return the embrace, but kept her hands in her lap. He had betrayed her, and nothing could change that fact.

August tried to get a reaction out of her but then gave up and released her. And yet he couldn't help caressing her cheek. She flinched as if he'd slapped her.

'Agnes, Agnes, my poor Agnes.' He sat down on the chair next to her but refrained from touching her again. The sympathy on his face turned her stomach. It was too late for that now. Four years ago she had needed him, yearned for paternal care and concern. Now it made no difference.

She studiously avoided looking at him as he urgently spoke to her, his words occasionally catching in his throat.

'Agnes, I know that I was wrong and that nothing I can say

317

will change that. But let me help you now that you're in such terrible straits. Come back home, and let me take care of you. Things can be like they were before, everything can be like before. What has happened is horrible, but together we can put it all behind you.'

His voice rose and sank in imploring waves that shattered against the hard shell of her heart. His words felt like a reproach.

'Dear Agnes, please come home. You can have anything you want.'

She saw out of the corner of her eye how his hands trembled, and his beseeching tone of voice gave her more satisfaction than she could have ever imagined. And she *had* imagined it; she had dreamt about it many times during the dark years that had passed.

She slowly turned to face him. August took this as a sign that she accepted his entreaties and eagerly tried to take her hands. Without expression she abruptly pulled her hands away.

'I'm leaving for America on Friday,' she said, enjoying the dismayed expression on August's face.

'A . . . aa . . . merica,' August stammered, and Agnes saw beads of sweat break out on his upper lip. Whatever he had expected, it wasn't this.

'Anders had bought tickets for all of us. He dreamt about a future for us there. I intend to honour his wish and go there myself,' she said dramatically, shifting her eyes away from her father to look out of the window. She knew that her profile was beautiful in the backlight, and her black clothing emphasized the pallor she had so carefully guarded.

People had been tiptoeing around her for two days. A small room had been put at her disposal, with the promise that she could stay as long as she liked. All the talking behind her back, all the contempt they had previously directed at her, all that was as if it had been swept away with the wind. The women brought her food and clothing. Everything she wore now was either borrowed or a gift. She had nothing of her own left.

Anders's cutter mates at the quarry had also come by. Dressed in their Sunday best and newly scrubbed, they stood with their caps in hand and looked at the floor. They shook her hand and mumbled some words about Anders.

Agnes couldn't wait until she could get away from this patched, threadbare crowd. She longed to go aboard the boat that would take her to another continent. She wanted to let the sea air blow away the filth and decay that lay like a membrane over her skin. For a couple more days she had to tolerate their sympathy and their pathetic attempts to show goodwill. Then she would set off and never look back. But first there was what she wanted to get from the bloated, red-faced man sitting next to her, this man who had abandoned her so cruelly four years ago. Now she would see to it that he paid, and paid dearly, for each and every one of the four years that had passed.

Her father continued to stammer, still in shock over the news she had just announced. 'But, but, how will you make a living over there?' he asked with concern, wiping the sweat from his brow with a little handkerchief that he pulled out of his pocket.

'I don't know,' she replied with a melodramatic sigh, allowing a worried shadow to glide across her face. It was gone in an instant, but there was still enough time for her father to notice.

'Won't you change your mind, my heart? Come stay with your old father instead.'

She shook her head, waiting for him to offer another suggestion. In that respect he did not disappoint her. Men were so easy to see through.

'Won't you at least let me help you, then? Some money to get you started, and an allowance so you can manage? Couldn't I do that much for you? Otherwise I'll worry to death about you, all alone and so far away.'

Agnes pretended to ponder the idea for a moment, and August hastened to add, 'And surely I can see to it that you have a better ticket for the crossing. A private stateroom in first class. That sounds a little better than travelling squeezed in with a bunch of other people.'

She nodded graciously and said after a pause, 'Well yes, I suppose I could let you do that. You can give me the money tomorrow. After the funeral,' she added, and August flinched as though he'd burned himself.

He tentatively tried to find the right words. 'The boys,' he began in a trembling voice, 'did they look like our side of the family?'

319

They had been the spitting image of Anders, but in a stony voice Agnes said, 'They looked precisely like the pictures of you when you were little. Like small copies of you. And they often asked why they didn't have a grandfather like the other children.' She saw how her words twisted like a knife in his breast. One lie after another, but the more his conscience weighed on him, the more he would fill her purse.

With tears in his eyes her father got up to take his leave. In the doorway he turned round to look at Agnes one last time. She decided to throw him a little scrap and nodded graciously. As she predicted that small gesture made him happy, and he gave her a smile with his eyes shining.

With hatred Agnes watched him go. She would allow someone to betray her only once. After that there were no second chances.

Patrik sat in the car and tried to focus on the first task of the day. He thought it important to follow up as soon as possible on the call he had made just before he left work yesterday evening. But he was having a hard time forgetting the stupid words he'd said to Erica last night. To think that it could be so difficult. He'd always believed that raising a child was easy. Well, maybe a lot of work, but not as anxiety-ridden as it had been during the past two months. He sighed, feeling dejected.

Not until he parked outside the brown-and-white blocks of flats by the southern road into Fjällbacka was he able to concentrate on the present and forget his problems at home. The flat he was heading for was in the first block, second stairwell, and he took the stairs up to the first floor. The sign on the door said 'Svensson & Kallin'. He knocked cautiously. He knew that the couple living in the flat had a young child, and he was painfully aware of how unwelcome a stranger would be if he woke the kid. A young man of about twenty-five opened the door. Although it was already nine-thirty he looked sulky, as if he'd just got up.

'Mia, it's for you.'

He stepped aside without greeting Patrik and shuffled into a small room off the hall. Patrik looked into the room that was probably intended as a guest room, but now it was set up as a game room, with a computer, several joysticks, and piles of games strewn across a desk. A game of 'shoot to kill as many enemies as possible' was running on the computer. The young man, who Patrik assumed

321

was either Svensson or Kallin, started playing as if he had entered another world.

The kitchen was to the left down the hall, and Patrik stepped inside after depositing his shoes by the front door.

'Come in, I'm feeding Liam.'

The little boy sat in a white highchair, being fed porridge and some sort of fruit purée. Patrik waved to him and was rewarded with a mushy smile.

'Have a seat,' said Mia, pointing to a chair across from them.

He did as she said and took out his notebook.

'Could you tell me exactly what happened yesterday?'

A light trembling of her hand holding the spoon showed how upsetting the events of the previous day had been for her. She nodded and related briefly what had happened. Patrik took notes, but it was the same information that Annika had received the day before when Mia had called in her report.

'And you saw no one in the vicinity of the car?'

Mia shook her head. Liam, who apparently thought his mother was playing a game, shook his head frenetically too, which made it considerably more difficult to feed him the porridge.

'No, I didn't see anybody. Either before or after.'

'You parked the pram in the rear, you said?'

'Yes, it's more secluded there, and I thought it would be a safer place to leave him. I wanted to take him inside with me, but he was asleep, and it seemed more trouble than it was worth to drag the pram into the store. I was just going to be gone a couple of minutes.'

'And then when you came out, you saw a dark substance in the pram and on Liam.'

'Yes, he was screaming like crazy. His whole mouth must have been stuffed full, but he'd managed to spit out most of it. The inside of his mouth was coloured black.'

'Did you take him to a doctor?'

Again she shook her head, and Patrik saw that he'd hit a nerve.

'No. I probably should have, but we were in a hurry to get home, and he seemed to be doing all right, except that he was scared and angry, so I . . .'

Her voice trailed off and Patrik hurried to say, 'I'm sure it's not dangerous. You did the right thing. The boy does look like he's feeling fine.'

Liam waved his arms, as if to confirm what was said and then opened his mouth wide for the next spoonful of porridge. There was obviously nothing wrong with his appetite, as evidenced by his plump double chin.

'The shirt I called about yesterday, did you . . .'

She got up. 'No, I didn't wash it, just as you asked me. And it's full of that black stuff. Looks like ashes, I think.'

She went to get the shirt. Liam stared longingly at the spoon, which she'd put down beside the bowl. Patrik hesitated for a second, then moved to the chair Mia had been sitting on and took up where she left off. Two spoonfuls went smoothly, but then Liam decided to demonstrate his car sounds, flubbering his lips so that Patrik's hair and face were sprayed with mush. Just then Mia came back with the shirt. She couldn't help laughing.

'Look at you. I should have warned you, or at least given you a raincoat and a sou'wester. I'm really sorry.'

'No problem,' said Patrik wiping off a little mush from his eyelashes with a smile. 'My baby is just two months old, so it's good for me to get a little practice.'

'Go ahead and practice,' said Mia, who sat down and let him continue the feeding. 'Here's the shirt,' she said, placing it on the table.

Patrik looked at it. The whole front was black and filthy.

'I'd like to take this with me. Do you mind?'

'Not at all. Take it. I'd have just thrown it away anyway. I'll put it in a plastic bag for you.'

Patrik took the bag and got up. 'If you think of anything else, just ring the station,' he said, handing her his card.

'I certainly will. I just don't understand why anyone would do something like this. What do you think the shirt might tell you?'

He just shook his head in reply. Patrik couldn't say anything about the reason for his interest. As yet nothing had leaked out to the press about the ashes they'd found in connection with Sara's murder. He glanced at Liam. Thank goodness it hadn't gone as far in his case. The question was whether murder had never been the intention; maybe something had interrupted the person who did this. But until they had the ashes on the shirt analysed, they couldn't say whether it was connected to Sara's death or not. Although he was already willing to bet that they would find a connection. This was no coincidence.

When Patrik got back in his car he took his mobile out of his jacket pocket. He hadn't heard from the team that did the search of Kaj's house yesterday, and he thought that was a little strange. He'd had too much on his mind yesterday to worry about it, but now he wondered why they hadn't reported back to him. Swearing, he saw that he'd turned off his phone on his way in to interrogate Kaj and then forgotten to turn it back on. The voicemail icon was flashing. He punched 133 and listened tensely to the message. With a glint of triumph in his eyes he flipped the phone shut and stuffed it back in his pocket.

Patrik had again chosen the kitchen as their meeting place. It was the biggest room in the police station, and he also thought the proximity to freshly brewed coffee would be an asset, given the situation. Annika had dashed off to the bakery down the street and bought a big bag of hazelnut balls, coconut mocha squares and chocolate oatmeal balls. Patrik didn't have to twist anyone's arm; as he stood at the easel with the tablet everyone was munching on some high-calorie treat.

He cleared his throat. 'As you know, yesterday was quite eventful.'

Gösta nodded and reached for another hazelnut ball. But Mellberg was too fast for him. The chief was already well into his third pastry and looked like he'd welcome a fourth. Ernst sat off by himself, and everyone carefully avoided looking at him. Ever since his disastrous mistake had come to light, a sort of doomsday shadow had hovered over him. Nobody knew when the axe would fall. All such matters had to be deferred as long as they were involved in the most intensive phase of the homicide investigation. But everyone knew it was only a matter of time. Including Ernst.

All eyes were directed at Patrik. He went on. 'I think I'll sum up what we have so far. Most of this you already know, but it might be good to get an overview of where we stand.'

He cleared his throat one more time, took his pen and began writing notes on the big tablet as he talked.

'First of all, we brought in the father, Niclas, for questioning and asked him about his alibi. We still don't know where he was on Monday morning, and the question is, why did he try to concoct a fake alibi? We also suspect child abuse, based on the information we received from the clinic about the injuries that his son Albin had sustained. The question is whether Sara was also subjected to abuse and whether it could have escalated to murder.'

He drew a point on the tablet, wrote 'Niclas' next to it, and then drew lines to the two words 'alibi' and 'suspected abuse'. Then he turned back to his colleagues.

'Then Sara's playmate Frida came in yesterday with her mother, and the girl reported that someone she called a "nasty old man" had given Sara a real fright the day before she died. He had behaved in a threatening manner towards her and also called her "double pawn". Is there anyone who can explain what that might mean?'

Patrik looked inquiringly at the group. At first no one answered. They sat quietly and seemed to be making an effort to work out what such an odd phrase could mean.

Annika looked at them, shook her head at their obtuseness, and then said, 'He probably said "Devil's spawn".'

It was so obvious that they all looked as if they wanted to slap their foreheads.

'Yes, of course,' said Patrik, also cursing his stupidity. 'That makes it sound like we're dealing with some religious fanatic. And Frida described the individual as an older man with grey hair. Martin, could you check with Sara's mother and see whether that matches anyone they know?'

Martin nodded.

'Then we got an interesting report yesterday. A young mother parked a pram behind Järnboden with her sleeping son inside. Then she went into the shop to buy something. When she came out she started screaming, because the inside of the pram was covered with some black substance that the boy also had in his mouth. It seemed as though someone had tried to force him to swallow the stuff. I drove over and talked with the boy's mother this morning, and she gave me the shirt that the boy was wearing.

The whole front of it is covered with something that could well be ashes.'

Silence descended over the table. No one chewed, no one slurped coffee. Patrik continued, 'I've already sent it off for analysis, and something tells me it's the same type of ashes we found in Sara's stomach. We have a very precise time for when this . . . assault occurred, so it might be worthwhile to check alibis. Gösta, you and I will handle that.'

Gösta nodded and picked the last shreds of coconut from his plate.

The tablet was now covered with notes and arrows, and Patrik paused for a second with his pen hovering. Then he made one more point and wrote 'Kaj' next to it. It was obvious to all that he'd now reached the part of the summation that he judged the most important.

'After we talked with our colleagues in Göteborg, it came to our attention that Kaj Wiberg is implicated in an investigation of a paedophile ring.'

They all made an even greater effort not to look at Ernst, and he squirmed a bit in his seat.

'We brought Kaj in for questioning yesterday and also conducted a search of his home, with the help of our colleagues from Uddevalla. The interview produced nothing concrete, but we view it as a first step and will continue our talks with Kaj. Using the material we're getting from Göteborg we'll also see whether we can identify any victims locally. Kaj, as you know, has taken an active role for many years in working with youths in Fjällbacka, so it's not entirely far-fetched to believe that assaults occurred during his years here.'

'Is there anything to indicate that he might be linked to Sara's murder?' Gösta asked.

'I'll get to that in a moment,' replied Patrik evasively, and Martin shot him an astonished look. They hadn't had any luck developing any connection during the interrogation.

'The search of Kaj's house may have given us our first big breakthrough in the investigation.'

The tension increased palpably, and Patrik couldn't resist drawing it out a bit for the sake of effect. Then he said, 'When they searched Kaj's house yesterday, the officers found Sara's jacket.'

They all gasped.

'Where did they find it?' asked Martin, looking a bit miffed that Patrik hadn't told him about this.

'That's just the thing,' said Patrik. 'It wasn't in the main house, but out in the cabin on the lot where their son Morgan lives.'

'Jesus Christ,' said Gösta. 'I could have sworn that weirdo was mixed up in it. People like that –'

Patrik cut him off. 'I agree that it looks bad, but I don't want us to get locked into that theory yet. First of all, we don't know whether it was the father or the son who put the jacket there; it could just as well have been Kaj trying to hide it. Second, there are too many other unresolved issues – for example, Niclas's attempt to construct a false alibi – so we can't completely ignore them. We have to keep working on *all* the points I've put up here on the tablet. Any questions?'

Mellberg spoke up. 'Excellent work, Hedström. It looks good. And by all means check out those other things you wrote down as well.' He gestured idly at the board. 'But I'm inclined to agree with Gösta. That Morgan boy doesn't seem quite right, and if I were you,' he said, holding his hand theatrically to his chest, 'I'd pull out all the stops to clamp down on him. But it's clear, you're responsible for the investigation, and you're the one who decides.' Mellberg said this in a way that made it obvious to everyone that he thought Patrik would do best to follow his advice.

Patrik didn't reply, which Mellberg interpreted to mean his message had hit home. He nodded contentedly. Now it was only a matter of time before the case was solved.

Resolutely Patrik went back into his office and got to work on the day's tasks. The old fart could believe what he liked, but Patrik had no intention of dancing to *his* tune. Naturally the fact that they'd found the jacket in Morgan's cabin had also made him want to draw certain conclusions, but something – whether it was instinct, experience or merely a hunch – told him that not everything was as it seemed.

FJÄLLBACKA 1928

Standing with her back to the Swedish coastline she closed her eyes and felt the breeze against her eyelids. This was what freedom felt like.

The boat to America had sailed from Göteborg on the dot, and the wharf had been full of people saying goodbye to their loved ones with both hope and sorrow. None of them knew whether they would ever see one another again. America was so far away that most people who went there never returned and were heard from only by letter.

But there had been no one to say goodbye to Agnes. That was precisely the way she wanted it. She was leaving her old life behind and setting off towards a new land. With her father's cheque in her pocket and a fine cabin in first class, she felt for the first time in years that she was on the right track.

For a moment her thoughts drifted to Anders and the boys. The church had been filled to the brim for the funeral, and loud sniffles had risen towards the roof in a sorrowful chorus. But she had not wept. Behind the veil of her hat she had looked at the three coffins near the altar. One big one and two small. The white coffins were covered with flowers and wreaths. The largest wreath was from her father. She had forbidden him to come.

Not that there had been much to put in the coffins. The fire had raged with such consuming heat that almost nothing was left. So the coffins contained only a few remains. The pastor had suggested urns instead, considering the state of the remains, but

Agnes had wanted it this way. Three coffins that could be lowered into the ground.

Some of Anders's workmates had carved the headstone. One stone for all three, with their names elegantly engraved.

They had been the sole victims of the fire. Otherwise only property had been destroyed, but the destruction had been extensive. The whole lower part of Fjällbacka, the part closest to the sea, was now charred and in ruins. Many houses were gone, and burnt pilings stuck up out of the water where docks used to be. But few had complained about the loss of their homes. Whenever they had the desire to cry about what they had lost, they thought of Agnes and what had been taken from her. Everyone from that part of town had turned up at the funeral, and their hearts ached when they pictured in their minds the little blond boys walking hand in hand with their father.

But their mother shed nary a tear. When the funeral was over she went back to her temporary lodgings and packed the few belongings that had been given to her. Charity. Being forced to accept alms was so distasteful to her that it made her feel sick, but she would never be at the mercy of other people's kindness again.

As she stood on the top deck of the ship, no one would guess that until quite recently she had lived a life of poverty. New clothing had been hastily acquired, and her baggage was the most elegant that money could buy. With pleasure she stroked her hand over the soft fabric of her dress. What a difference from the worn, faded clothes that had been her lot for four years.

All that was left of her old life was a blue wooden box that she had carefully stowed in the bottom of her luggage. The box itself was not important, but its contents were. She had sneaked out the night before and filled it to remind her never again to let anything stand in the way of the life she deserved. She had made the mistake of trusting one man, and it had cost her four long years. After the way her father had betrayed her, she was determined never to let another man do the same. And she would see to it that her father would pay dearly for his actions. Loneliness was the highest price, but she also intended to make sure that his money flowed in her direction. She had earned it. And she knew precisely which buttons to push to keep his guilty conscience alive. Men were so easy to manipulate.

She was roused from her reverie by the sound of someone clearing his throat. She was so startled that she jumped.

'Ah, excuse me, I hope I didn't frighten you, Madam?'

An elegantly dressed man smiled suavely and held out his hand to her.

Agnes scrutinized him with a quick and practised eye before she returned his smile and placed her gloved hand in his. He had an expensive, tailored suit and hands that had never seen manual labour. In his thirties and with a pleasant, yes, even attractive appearance. No ring on his ring finger. This passage might be much more pleasant than she'd anticipated.

'Agnes, Agnes Stjernkvist. And it's Miss, not Madam.'

Erica's friend Dan had come to visit. Even though they'd spoken on the phone a couple of times, he still hadn't been to the house to have a look at Maja. But now his huge body filled the hall, and he took the baby from Erica with the ease of an experienced father.

'Helllllo, baby girl. What a little beauty we have here,' he cooed, lifting her towards the ceiling. Erica had to stifle an impulse to snatch her daughter back, but Maja didn't look like she minded the situation at all. And considering that Dan had three daughters of his own, he probably knew what he was doing.

'So how's little Mamma doing?' he said, giving Erica one of his bear-hugs. Once upon a time they had been an item, but the romance was long since over and for many years now they had been close friends. Their friendship had suffered a real setback two winters ago, when they had both gotten mixed up in a murder investigation under unpleasant circumstances, but the passage of time had healed the rift. After Dan got a divorce from his wife Pernilla, though, they hadn't seen each other very often. Dan had jumped into the single life and all that involved, while Erica went in the opposite direction. He had gone through a series of unsuitable girlfriends, but at the moment he was single and on the loose. Erica thought he looked happier than he had in a long time. The divorce had taken its toll on him, and he often lamented not being with his daughters more than every other week, but he seemed to have grown used to the situation and moved on.

'I wondered whether you'd like to take a walk with us,' said Erica. 'Maja is starting to get tired, and if we take a stroll she'll probably fall asleep in the pram.'

'A short one, then,' Dan muttered. 'It's pretty chilly out there, and I was looking forward to getting inside where it's warm.'

'Just until she goes to sleep,' Erica cajoled her friend, and he reluctantly put his shoes back on.

She kept her promise. Ten minutes later they were back inside and Maja was sleeping peacefully under the rain hood of the pram.

'Have you got a baby alarm?' Dan asked.

Erica shook her head. 'No, I'll have to look in on her from time to time.'

'You should have said something. I could have tried to dig up our old one.'

'I hope you'll be coming over more often now,' said Erica, 'so you can bring it next time.'

'All right. I'm sorry for taking so long to come over and say hi,' he said. 'But I know how the first few months are, so I –'

'You don't have to apologize,' said Erica. 'You're completely right. I haven't felt ready to have visitors until now.'

They sat down on the sofa. Erica had set out coffee and buns that were warm from the oven. Dan helped himself.

'Mmm,' he said. 'Did you bake these?' He couldn't help a hint of amazement from creeping into his voice.

Erica gave him a dirty look. 'If that were the case, you wouldn't sound so surprised. But no, it wasn't me. My mother-in-law baked them when she was here,' she had to admit.

'I thought it must be something like that. These aren't burnt enough to be yours,' Dan teased her.

Erica couldn't come up with a witty retort. He was right. She had never been much of a baker.

After a pleasant chat that enabled them to get caught up with what had been happening in their lives lately, Erica stood up.

'I just have to go check on Maja.'

She cautiously cracked open the front door and looked down into the pram. That's funny, Maja must have slid down under the covers. She detached the rain hood as quietly as she could and pulled back the blanket. Panic struck her full-force. Maja wasn't in the pram!

Martin's spine creaked as he sat down, and he stretched his arms above his head to straighten out his vertebrae. All that lugging of cartons and moving of furniture had made him feel like an old man. Suddenly he realized that a few hours at the gym occasionally might be a good idea, but it was too late to make up for lost time now. Anyway, Pia always said she liked his lanky body, so he saw no reason to make any changes. But his back did hurt like hell.

The new place had turned out fine, he had to admit. Pia was the one who decided where to put everything, and the result was much better than anything he'd ever been able to come up with in his bachelor flats. He just wished he could have kept a few more of his own things. Only his stereo, TV and a 'Billy' bookshelf from IKEA had passed muster. The rest of his possessions had been sent off to the dump without mercy. He was saddest to part with the old leather sofa he'd had in his living room. He agreed that it had probably seen better days, but the memories . . . ah, what memories.

On second thought that might be precisely the reason that Pia had been so firm about tossing it in favour of a 'Tomelilla' model from IKEA. He'd actually been allowed to keep an old pine kitchen table, but Pia had quickly bought a tablecloth to cover every inch of its surface.

Well, those were only tiny bits of sand in the machinery. So far there hadn't been anything negative about living together. He loved coming home to Pia every evening, cuddling up with her on the sofa and watching something worthless on TV with Pia's head in his lap. And he loved slipping into the new double bed and falling asleep together. Everything was just as wonderful as he'd dreamt it would be. He knew that he probably ought to be sad that the wild partying of his bachelor days was over, at least that's what some of his mates said, but he didn't miss it any more than he missed a huge hangover. And Pia, well, she was simply perfect.

335

Martin wiped the foolish newly-in-love smile off his face and looked up the Florin family's number to phone them. He hoped it wouldn't be that terrible harpy who answered. Charlotte's mother reminded him of a caricature of a mother-in-law.

He was in luck. Charlotte herself answered. He felt a pang of sympathy when he heard how listless her voice sounded.

'Yes, hello, this is Martin Molin from Tanumshede police station.'

'What's this about?' Charlotte asked cautiously.

Martin was well aware that a call from the police aroused both misgivings and hopes, so he hastened to say, 'Well, I just wanted to check on something with you. We got a tip that somebody threatened Sara the day before she . . .' he stammered, 'died.'

'Threatened her?' said Charlotte, and he could almost see her puzzled expression. 'Who said that? Sara didn't tell us anything about it.'

'Her playmate, Frida.'

'But why didn't Frida say anything about it before now?'

'Sara made her promise not to say anything. Frida said it was a secret.'

'But who would threaten her?' Only now did Charlotte perk up enough to ask the relevant question.

'Frida didn't know who he was. But she described the man as older with grey hair and black clothes. And he apparently called Sara "the Devil's spawn". Does any of this ring a bell?'

'It certainly does,' said Charlotte through clenched teeth. 'It most certainly does.'

The pain had intensified over the past few days. It felt like a hungry animal tearing at his stomach with its claws.

Stig turned carefully onto his side. No position was really comfortable. No matter how he lay, it hurt somewhere. But it hurt most of all in his heart. He was thinking about Sara more often. About the way they'd had long, serious talks about everything under the sun. School, friends, her precocious meditations on everything that went on around her. He didn't believe the others had ever taken the time to see that side of her. They had focused only on her awkward, loud, and troublesome traits. And Sara had reacted to their image of her by becoming even more difficult, making even more noise, and smashing things. A vicious circle of frustration that none of them knew how to handle.

But in the hours she spent with him she had found peace. He missed her so much it hurt. He had seen so much of Lilian in her. Lilian's strength and decisiveness. Her brusque manner that concealed such enormous concern and love.

As if she could read his mind, Lilian came into the room. Stig had been so deeply immersed in his reverie that he didn't even hear her footsteps on the stairs.

'Here's a little lunch for you. I was out buying some fresh rolls,' she chirped, and he felt his stomach turn over at the mere sight of what was on the tray.

'I'm not that hungry right now,' he attempted, but at the same time he knew how fruitless any protests would be.

'You have to eat something if you want to get better,' said Lilian in her stern nurse's voice. 'Here, I'll help you.'

She sat down on the edge of the bed and took a bowl of kefir from the tray. She carefully raised a spoon and moved it to his lips. He reluctantly opened his mouth and let her feed him. The feeling of kefir running down his throat nauseated him, but he let her have her way. She meant well, and basically he knew she was right. If he didn't eat he'd never be healthy.

'How do you feel now?' Lilian asked as she took one of the rolls with butter and cheese and held it to his mouth so he could take a bite.

He swallowed and replied with a forced smile, 'I think it's a little better, actually. I slept quite well last night.'

'That's nice to hear,' said Lilian, patting his hand. 'There's no sense playing with your health, and you have to promise that you'll tell me if it gets worse. Lennart was just like you, stubborn as hell, and he refused to let anyone examine him until it was too late. Sometimes I wonder if he'd still be alive if I'd insisted more . . .' With a sad look she gazed into the distance, her hand holding the spoon poised in mid-air.

Stig stroked her other hand and said gently, 'You have nothing to reproach yourself for, Lilian. I know you did everything you could for Lennart when he was sick, because that's the sort of person you are. You are not to blame for his death. And I'm feeling better, believe me. I've got better on my own before. If I just have a chance to rest up, I'm sure it will pass. It's probably just "burn-out", like they talk so much about these days. Don't worry about me. You have so many other worse things to worry about.'

Lilian sighed and nodded. 'Yes, you're probably right. It's a lot for me to bear right now.'

'Yes, you poor thing. I wish I were feeling healthy so I could offer you more support in your grief. I'm also grieving terribly about the girl. I can't even imagine how you must feel. And how is Charlotte doing, by the way? It's been a couple of days since she's come upstairs to see me.'

'Charlotte?' said Lilian, and for a moment he thought he saw an ill-humoured glint in her eye. But it vanished so fast he convinced himself that he'd imagined it. Charlotte was everything to Lilian, after all. She was always saying how she lived for her daughter and her family.

'Well, Charlotte is feeling better than at first, anyway. Even though I think she should have kept taking those sedatives. I don't understand why people have to try to muddle through on their own, when there are such good drugs they could take. And Niclas was certainly willing to write her a prescription, but he refused to write any for me. Did you ever hear anything so stupid? I'm grieving too, and I'm just as upset as Charlotte. Sara was my granddaughter, wasn't she?'

Lilian's voice had again taken on that sharp, annoyed tone. But just as Stig felt an annoyed frown forming on his brow, she changed her tune and was once again the loving, caring wife that his illness had really made him appreciate. He could hardly expect her to be her usual self, after all that had happened. The stress and the sorrow were affecting her too.

'Now that you've eaten something you need to rest,' said Lilian as she got up.

Stig stopped her with a little wave. 'Have you heard any more about why the police took Kaj in for questioning? Does it have anything to do with Sara?'

'No, we haven't heard anything yet. We'll probably be the last to know,' Lilian snorted. 'But I hope they throw the book at him.'

She turned on her heel and walked out the door, but he still had time to glimpse a smile on her face.

NEW YORK 1946

Life 'over there' hadn't turned out the way she'd expected. Bitter lines of disappointment were etched round her mouth and eyes, but Agnes was nevertheless still a beautiful woman at the age of forty-two.

The first years had been wonderful. Her father's money had ensured her a very comfortable lifestyle, and the contributions she received from her male admirers had improved it significantly. She had lacked for nothing. The elegant apartment in New York was the frequent setting for joyous parties, and the beautiful people had no trouble finding their way to her home. Offers of marriage had been numerous, but she had bided her time, in the hunt for someone even richer, more stylish, more sophisticated. In the meantime, she had not denied herself any form of amusement. It was as though she had to compensate for the lost years and live twice as fast and hard as everyone else. There had been a feverish eagerness in the way she loved, partied, and spent money on clothes, jewellery, and furnishings for her apartment. Those years felt so distant now.

When the Kreuger crash came in 1932, her father lost everything. A few foolish investments and the fortune he had amassed was gone. When the telegram arrived she had felt such consuming rage at his idiotic behaviour that she tore the piece of paper to bits and stamped on them. How dare he lose everything that one day was supposed to be hers? Everything that would have been her security, her life.

She sent a long telegram back in which she told him in exhaustive detail what she thought of him and how he had destroyed her life.

When a week later a telegram arrived with the news that he had put a pistol to his temple, Agnes had merely crumpled it up and tossed it in the wastebasket. She was neither surprised nor upset. As far as she was concerned, he deserved nothing less.

The years that followed had been hard. Not as hard as those with Anders, but a struggle for survival all the same. Now the only way she could live was at the benevolence of men. When she no longer had any financial resources of her own, her wealthy, urbane suitors were gradually replaced by beaux of lesser social status. Offers of marriage ceased altogether. Instead the propositions were of an entirely different nature, and as long as the men paid she didn't object. It also seemed that something inside of her had been damaged by the difficult childbirth, so she was unable to get pregnant, but that increased her value among her occasional partners. None of them wanted to be bound to her by a child, and she herself would have rather jumped off a building than go through that atrocious experience again.

Agnes had been forced to give up the beautiful apartment; the new one was much smaller, darker, and far from the centre of town. She no longer hosted parties in her home, and she'd had to pawn or sell most of her possessions.

When the Second World War came, everything that had been bad got even worse. And for the first time since she boarded the boat in Göteborg, Agnes longed for home. Her homesickness gradually grew to resolve, and when the war finally ended she decided to go back to Sweden. In New York she had nothing of value, but in Fjällbacka there was something that she could still call her own. After the big fire, her father had bought the lot where the house she'd lived in had stood, and he had had a new one built on the same site – perhaps in the hope that one day she would return home. The house was in her name, so it was still there, even though everything else he had owned was gone. It had been rented out for all these years, and the income had been placed in an account in the event she ever came back. Several times over the years she had tried to gain access to the money, but she was always

342

told by the administrator that her father had stipulated that she would get the money only if she moved back to her homeland. At the time she had cursed what she viewed as an injustice, but now she reluctantly had to admit that perhaps it hadn't been so stupid after all. Agnes calculated that she would be able to survive on that money for at least a year, and during that time she had set her mind on finding someone who could support her.

In order for that plan to succeed, she was forced to stick to the story she had created about her life in America. She sold everything she owned and spent every öre on a dress of elegant quality and a set of fine luggage. The bags were empty – she hadn't had enough money to fill them with anything – but no one would notice that when she came ashore. She looked like a successful woman, and she had also elevated her position to that of the widow of a wealthy man with business dealings of an indefinite nature. 'Something in finance,' she intended to say, with a blasé shrug of her shoulders. She was sure it would work. People back in Sweden were so naïve and so easily impressed by people who had been to the promised land. No one would think it was odd that she came home in triumph. No one would suspect a thing.

The wharf was full of people. Agnes was shoved here and there as she carried a suitcase in each hand. The money hadn't been enough for a first-class or even a second-class ticket, so she would stick out like a peacock among the grey masses in third class. In other words, she didn't have to fool anyone on the boat by pretending to be a fine lady. As long as she disembarked in Göteborg, nobody would know how she had made the voyage.

She felt something soft nuzzling her hand. Agnes looked down to see a little girl in a white frilly dress looking at her with tears running down her cheeks. The crowd swelled around her, surging back and forth, and no one paid any attention to the little girl who must have lost her parents.

'Where's your mommy?' said Agnes in the language she now mastered almost perfectly.

The girl cried even harder, and Agnes vaguely recalled that children of her age might not have started to talk yet. In fact she seemed to have just learned to walk and looked as though she might fall beneath the tramping feet all around her.

343

Agnes took the girl by the hand and looked around. No one seemed to be looking for her. Nothing but rough work clothes wherever she looked, and judging by her clothing the girl definitely seemed to belong to a different social class. Agnes was about to call for help when she had an idea. It was bold, incredibly bold, but brilliant. Wouldn't her story about the rich husband who died and widowed her for the second time take on additional veracity if she also had a small child with her? And even though she remembered how much trouble the boys had been, it would probably be entirely different with a little girl. She was sweet as sugar, that girl. Agnes could dress her in pretty clothes, and tie ribbons in those lovely locks. She was a regular little darling. The thought was appealing to Agnes more and more, and in the blink of an eye she made up her mind. She took both suitcases in one hand and the girl by the other and strode towards the ship. No one reacted when she embarked, and she stifled a desire to look back over her shoulder. The trick was to look as though the child naturally belonged to her, and the girl had even stopped crying out of sheer amazement and willingly followed along. Agnes took that as a sign that she was doing the right thing. Her parents were surely not nice to her, since she went with a stranger so easily. Given a little time, Agnes would be able to give the girl everything she wished for, and she knew that she would be an excellent mother. The boys had just been too difficult. This little girl was different. She could feel it. Everything was going to be different.

Niclas came home as soon as she rang. Because she hadn't wanted to say what it was about, he dashed in the front door with his heart in his throat. On the stairs he saw Lilian coming down with a tray, and she looked surprised.

'Why are you home?'

'Charlotte rang me. You don't know what it's about?'

'No, she never tells me anything,' Lilian snapped. Then she gave him an ingratiating smile. 'I was just out buying fresh buns, they're in a bag in the kitchen.'

He ignored her and took the stairs down to the cellar flat in two strides. It wouldn't surprise him if Lilian was standing with her ear to the door right now, trying to hear what they were saying.

'Charlotte?'

'I'm in here, changing Albin.'

He went to the bathroom and saw her standing at the changing table with her back to him. Even from her posture he could see that she was angry, and he wondered what she'd found out now.

'What was it that was so important? I had patients waiting.' The best defence was a good offence.

'Martin Molin rang.'

He searched his memory for the name.

'The policeman in Tanumshede,' she clarified, and now he remembered. The young, freckled chap.

'What did he want?' he said tensely.

Charlotte, who now had finished changing and dressing Albin, turned toward Niclas with their son in her arms.

'They discovered that someone had threatened Sara. The day before she died.' Her voice was ice-cold and Niclas waited nervously for her to continue.

'Yes?'

'The man who threatened her was described as an older man with grey hair and black clothes. He called her the "Devil's spawn". Does that sound like anyone you know?'

Rage coursed through his veins in a fraction of a second.

'Bloody hell,' he cried and ran up the stairs. When he tore open the door to the ground floor he almost knocked Lilian unconscious. He had guessed right: the old biddy had been standing there listening. But it wasn't even worth getting excited about now. He put on his shoes without bothering to tie them, grabbed his jacket and ran out to the car.

Ten minutes later he stopped with a screech outside his parents' house after driving much too fast through town. The house stood on the side of the hill, right above the mini-golf course, and it looked exactly the same as it did when he was a boy. He shoved open the car door and jumped out without bothering to shut it. Then he rushed right up to the front entrance. For a second he paused, then he took a deep breath and knocked hard on the door. Niclas hoped his father was at home. No matter how un-Christian he was, it wasn't proper to do what he intended to do in a church.

'Who is it?' called the familiar, stern voice from inside the house. Niclas tried the door handle. As usual, the door wasn't locked. Without hesitating he stepped inside and called out.

'Where are you, you cowardly old devil?'

'What in the world is going on?' His mother came into the hall from the kitchen holding a tea towel and a plate. Then he saw his father's austere figure emerge from the living room.

'Ask him.' Niclas pointed a trembling finger at his father, whom he hadn't seen other than from a distance since he was seventeen years old.

'I don't know what he's talking about,' said Arne, refusing to speak directly to his son. 'Of all the nerve, coming in here and

346

standing there cursing and screaming. That's enough now. Get out of here.'

'You know damn well what I'm talking about, you old bastard.' Niclas saw to his satisfaction how his father flinched at his choice of words. 'And how cowardly can you be, threatening a little girl! If you're the one who killed her I'll make sure that you never walk again, you bloody fucking . . .'

His mother looked back and forth between the two men and then raised her voice. This was so unusual that Niclas abruptly shut up, and even his father closed his mouth without replying.

'Now can one of you be so good as to tell me what this is all about? Niclas, you can't just barge in here and start screaming, and if it's something to do with Sara, then I have a right to know.'

After taking a couple of deep breaths Niclas said through clenched teeth, 'The police found out' – he could hardly bring himself to look at his father – 'that he yelled and screamed and threatened Sara. The day before she died.' Fury took over again and he shouted, 'What the bloody hell is wrong with you? Scaring a seven-year-old out of her wits and calling her the "Devil's spawn" or some such nonsense. She was seven years old, don't you get it, seven years old! And I'm supposed to believe that it was a coincidence that you threatened her the day before she was found murdered! Is that right?'

He took a step towards his father, who hastily backed up.

Asta now stared at her husband. 'Is the boy telling the truth?'

'I don't have to stand here and answer to anyone. I answer only to the Lord,' said Arne bombastically, turning his back to his wife and son.

'Don't even try that. You answer me now!'

Niclas looked in astonishment as his mother followed Arne into the living room with her hands on her hips, ready for a fight. Arne too seemed shocked that his wife dared defy him. He was opening and closing his mouth without any sound coming out.

'Answer me,' Asta continued, backing Arne farther into the room as she came closer. 'Did you see Sara?'

'Yes, I did,' said Arne defiantly in a last attempt to assert the authority he'd taken for granted for forty years.

'And what did you say to her?' Asta seemed to grow a foot

taller before their eyes. Niclas thought she was terrifying, and from the look in his father's eyes he could see that he thought the same thing.

'I had to see whether she was made of sterner stuff than her father. If she'd taken after my side of the family.'

'Your side,' Asta snorted. 'Oh yes, that would be something. Sanctimonious fawners and stuck-up females, that's what you have on your side of the family. Is that supposed to be something worth emulating? So what was your conclusion?'

With a hurt expression on his face Arne said, 'Silence, woman, I come from God-fearing folk. And it didn't take long to work out that the girl was not made of good stock. Impudent and obstinate and noisy, not the way girls should be. I tried to talk to her about God, I did, and she stuck out her tongue at me. So I told her a few truths. I still believe I was within my full right to do so. Someone had obviously not bothered to raise the child properly; it was high time somebody took her in hand.'

'So you scared the wits out of her,' said Niclas, clenching his fists.

'I saw the Devil in her recoil,' Arne said proudly.

'You God-damned . . .' Niclas took a step towards him, but stopped when a hard knock was heard at the door.

Time stood still for a second and then the moment passed. Niclas knew that he had been standing at the edge of the abyss and then retreated. If he'd gone after his father, he wouldn't have been able to stop. Not this time.

He left the room without looking at either his father or his mother and opened the front door. The man outside seemed surprised to see him there.

'Oh, hello. Martin Molin. We've met before. I'm from the police. I'd like to have a word with your father.'

Niclas stepped aside without a word. He felt the officer watching him as he walked to his car.

'Where's Martin?' said Patrik.

'He drove over to Fjällbacka,' Annika said. 'Charlotte identified our nasty old man without much difficulty. It's Sara's grandfather, Arne Antonsson. A bit of a nut case according to Charlotte. He and his son have evidently not spoken to each other in years.'

'Just so Martin remembers to check his alibi, both for the morning when Sara was murdered and for the incident yesterday with the little boy.'

'The last thing he did was to double-check the time in question for yesterday. Between one and one thirty, wasn't it?'

'Exactly. I'm glad there's at least one person we can count on.' Annika's eyes narrowed. 'Has Mellberg talked to Ernst yet? I mean, I was surprised when he showed up this morning. I thought he would have been suspended at the very least, if not fired by now.'

'Yeah, I know, I thought that was what happened when he was allowed to go home yesterday. I was just as surprised as you were to find him sitting there as if nothing had happened. I'll have to speak to Mellberg. He can't just look through his fingers this time. If he does, I'm quitting!' A grim furrow had formed between Patrik's eyebrows.

'Don't talk like that,' said Annika in alarm. 'Have a talk with Mellberg. I'm sure he has a plan for how to deal with Ernst.'

'You don't even believe that yourself,' said Patrik, and Annika looked away. He was right. She seriously doubted it.

She changed the subject. 'When are we going to question Kaj again?'

'I was thinking of doing it now. But I'd prefer to have Martin present.'

'He took off not long ago, so it may be a while before he gets back. He tried to tell you, but you were on the phone.'

'Yeah, I was busy checking Niclas's alibi for yesterday. Which was airtight, by the way. Patient appointments from twelve to three o'clock. And I'm not just going by his appointment book; I had it confirmed by each of the patients he saw.'

'So, what does that mean?'

'If I only knew,' said Patrik, massaging the bridge of his nose with his fingers. 'It doesn't change the fact that he couldn't come up with an alibi for Monday morning, and it's still suspicious that he tried to conceal his whereabouts. But he wasn't the one involved yesterday, at any rate. Gösta was going to ring the rest of the family to hear where they were at that time.'

'I assume that Kaj will also have to answer that question in detail,' said Annika.

Patrik nodded. 'Yeah, you can bet on it. And his wife. And his son. I thought I'd have a talk with them after I interview Kaj again.'

'And in spite of everything, the killer could still be someone else entirely, someone we haven't even considered,' Annika said.

'That's the worst thing about it. While we're chasing our tails, the murderer is probably sitting at home laughing at us. But after yesterday I'm sure, at least, that he, or she, is still in the vicinity. And that it's probably someone from Fjällbacka.'

'Or else we already have the murderer in custody,' said Annika, nodding towards the jail.

Patrik smiled. 'Or else we already have the murderer in custody. Well, I don't have time to hang around here, I have to go talk to a man about a jacket . . .'

'Lots of luck,' Annika shouted after him.

'Dan! Dan!' Erica yelled. She could hear the panic in her voice, and it just made her more upset. She frantically rummaged through the covers in the pram, as if her daughter had somehow been able to hide in a corner. But the pram was empty.

'What is it?' said Dan, who came running, with an anxious look on his face. 'What's happened? Why are you yelling?'

Erica tried to speak, but her tongue felt thick and clumsy, and she couldn't get any words out. Instead she pointed with a trembling hand at the pram, and Dan hurried to look inside.

He gazed down at the empty space, and she saw the realization hit him like a hammer blow.

'Where's Maja? Is she gone? Where's . . .?' He didn't finish his sentence but looked about wildly. Erica was hanging on to him, panic-stricken. Now the words gushed out of her.

'We have to find her! Where's my daughter? Where's Maja? Where is she?'

'Shh, there, there. We'll find her. Don't worry, we'll find her.' Dan concealed his own panic so he could reassure Erica. He put his hands on her shoulders and looked her straight in the eye. 'Now we have to stay calm. I'll go out and look for her. You ring the police. It'll be all right.'

Erica felt her chest heaving spasmodically in an odd imitation of breathing, but she did as he said. Dan left the front door open, and a cold wind blew into the house. But that didn't bother her. She felt nothing other than paralysing panic that made her brain stop working. For the life of her she couldn't remember where she'd put the telephone. Finally she just ran round and round the living room rummaging under pillows and tossing things aside. At last she realized that it was in the middle of the living room coffee table. She flung herself over it and with stiff fingers punched in the number of the station. Then she heard Dan's voice outside.

'Erica, Erica, I found her!'

She dropped the phone and rushed to the front door, heading for his voice. In her stocking feet she ran down the steps and out on the driveway. The wet and the cold went right through to her skin, but she couldn't care less. She saw Dan running towards her from the front of the house; he was carrying something red in his arms. A terrific wail rose up and Erica felt relief wash over her like a storm swell. Maja was screaming, she was alive.

Erica ran the last few yards that separated her from Dan and grabbed Maja out of his arms. Sobbing she hugged her daughter close for a second before she went down on her knees, lay Maja on the ground, and tore open her red overalls to examine her. She looked unhurt and was now screaming to high heaven, flailing her arms and legs. Still kneeling, Erica lifted her daughter up and pressed her tight once again, as she let tears of relief mix with the falling rain.

'Come on, let's go inside. You'll both be soaked,' said Dan gently as he helped Erica to her feet. Without loosening her grip on the baby she followed him up the steps and into the house. The relief she felt was physical in a way that she never could have imagined. It was as though she'd lost a part of her body that was now re-attached. She was still sobbing, and Dan patted her reassuringly on the shoulder.

'Where did you find her?' she managed to say.

'She was lying on the ground in front of the house.'

Only now did they both seem to understand that someone must have put Maja there. For some reason this person had taken her out of the pram, sneaked round the house, and placed the sleeping baby on the ground. The panic that this realization aroused made Erica start to sob again.

'Shh . . . it's over now,' said Dan. 'We found her and she looks unharmed. But we'd better ring the police. You didn't have time to call them, did you?'

Erica shook her head.

'We have to ring Patrik,' she said. 'Can you do it? I never want to let her go again.' She hugged Maja tight. But now she noticed something she'd missed before. She looked at the front of Dan's jumper and held Maja out so she could examine her too.

'What's this here?' she said. 'What's all this black stuff?'

Dan glanced at the dirty overalls but said only, 'What's Patrik's number?'

In a shaky voice Erica told him the number of Patrik's mobile and watched as Dan punched in it. A hard lump of fear had formed in her stomach.

The days ran into one another. Anna's feeling of impotence was paralysing. Nothing Erica's sister said or did escaped him. Lucas was watching her every step, listening to every word.

The violence had increased too. Now he openly enjoyed seeing her pain and humiliation. He took what he wanted, when he wanted, and God help her if she protested or resisted. Not that she would even think of it now. It was so obvious that there was something wrong with his mind. All barriers were gone, and there was something evil in his eyes that aroused her survival instinct and told her to go along with his demands. If only she would be allowed to live.

For herself, she had shut down completely. It was looking at the children that pained her the most. They were no longer allowed to go to day-care, and spent their days in the same shadow existence as she did. Listless and clinging they regarded her with dead eyes, and it felt like an accusation. She took full blame for what was happening. She should have protected them. She should have kept Lucas out of their lives, precisely as she had intended. But a single instant of fear had made her give in. She allowed herself to be convinced that she was doing it for the children's sake, for their safety. Instead she had surrendered to her own cowardice. It was her habit of always taking what seemed the path of least resistance, at least at first glance. But this time she had gravely misjudged her options. She had chosen the narrowest, trickiest and most perilous path available, and she had compelled her children to come along as well.

Sometimes she dreamt about killing him. To anticipate him in what she now knew would be the inevitable conclusion. Occasionally she would watch him as he slept next to her, during the long hours of the night when she lay awake, unable to relax enough to escape into sleep. Then she would imagine with pleasure how one of the kitchen knives would slip into his flesh and slice through the fragile thread that bound him to life. Or she would feel the rope cutting into her hands as she cautiously looped it round his neck and pulled it tight.

But it went no further than wonderful dreams. Something inside her, maybe an inherent cowardice, made her lie still in bed while dark thoughts ricocheted around in her skull.

Sometimes she pictured Erica's baby before her in the night. The little girl she had not yet seen. She envied the child. She would be getting the same warmth, the same care that Anna herself had received from Erica when they were growing up, more as mother and daughter than as sisters. But back then she hadn't appreciated Erica. She had felt suffocated and inferior. The bitterness that she felt from their mother's lack of love had apparently made her heart so hard that it wasn't receptive to what her sister had tried to give her. Anna sincerely hoped that Maja would be better able to accept the enormous ocean of love that she knew Erica was capable of giving. Especially for her sister's sake. Despite their difference in age and the distance that separated them, Anna knew her sister so well. She knew that if there was anyone who was in desperate need of having her love reciprocated, it was Erica. The odd thing was that Anna had always viewed her as being so strong, and her own bitterness had been diluted by that feeling. Now that she herself was weaker than ever before, she saw her sister as she actually was. Scared to death that everyone would see what their mother had seen, what had made her see the two sisters as unworthy of love. If only Anna had one more chance, she would throw her arms around Erica and thank her for all those years of unconditional love. Thank her for the concern, for the scoldings, for the worried look in her eyes when she thought that Anna was on the wrong track. Thank her for everything that had previously made Anna feel suffocated and constricted. How ironic. She hadn't really known what it felt like to be suffocated and truly constricted. Not until now.

The sound of the key in the lock made her jump. The children also paused with alarm from listlessly playing on the floor.

Anna got up and went to meet him.

Schwarzenegger gazed down at him with concern through his dark sunglasses. The Terminator. If only Sebastian had been like him. Cool. Tough. A machine without the ability to feel.

Sebastian stared up at the poster as he lay on his bed. He could still hear Rune's voice, his phoney voice of concern. That tone of smarmy, feigned caring. The only thing he actually worried about was what people would say about *him*. What was it he had said?

'I've heard some terrible accusations made against Kaj. I have a hard time believing that it's anything but pure slander, but I still have to ask the question: did he on any occasion behave in an inappropriate manner towards you or any of the other boys? Peeked at you in the shower, or anything like that?'

Sebastian had laughed to himself at Rune's naïveté. 'Peeked at you in the shower . . .' That wouldn't have been so bad. It was the other thing that he couldn't live with. Not now, when everything was going to come out. He had an idea how things like that worked. They took their pictures and saved them and traded them, but no matter how well they hid them, they would all come out now.

It wouldn't take more than a morning, then it would be all over the school. The girls would stare at him, pointing and giggling. The boys would make jokes about queers and make stupid hand gestures as he walked by. Nobody would have the slightest sympathy for him. No one would see how big the hole in his chest was.

He turned his head a bit to the left and looked at the poster of Clint as Dirty Harry. He should have had a pistol like that. Or even better, a submachine gun. Then he could have done it the way those guys in the States did it. Run into the school in a long black coat and mow down everyone he saw. Especially the cool ones, who were going to treat him the worst. But he knew that it was nothing but a crazy idea. It wasn't in his nature to hurt anyone. It wasn't their fault, really. He had only himself to blame, and it was only himself he wanted to hurt. He could have put a stop to it, of course. Hadn't he ever said no? Not in so many words. Somehow he'd hoped that Kaj would see how it troubled him, how much he was hurting him, and stop of his own accord.

Everything had been so complicated. Because a part of him had liked Kaj. He'd been great, and at first Sebastian had got that fatherly feeling from him. The feeling he never got from Rune. He'd been able to talk to Kaj. About school, about girls, about Mamma and about Rune, and Kaj had put his arm round him and listened. It was only after a while that things had got so screwed up.

It was quiet in the house. Rune had gone off to work, pleased that he'd confirmed what he already thought he knew, that all the accusations against Kaj were utterly groundless. He would probably sit in the lunchroom and loudly complain about how the police made unfounded accusations.

Sebastian got up from the bed and prepared to leave. He stopped in the doorway and turned round. He looked at each and every one of them and gave them a curt nod, as if in greeting. Clint, Sly, Arnold, Jean-Claude and Dolph. The ones who were everything he was not.

For a moment he thought he saw them nod back.

The adrenaline was still pumping after the encounter with his father, and Niclas felt sufficiently belligerent to take on the next person with whom he had a score to settle.

He drove down Galärbacken and stopped short when he saw that Jeanette was in her shop, busily preparing to stay open on All Saints' Day. He parked the car and went inside. For the first time since they'd met he felt no tingle in his loins when he saw her. He felt only a sour, metallic distaste, both for himself and for her.

'What the hell do you think you're doing?'

Jeanette turned round and gave Niclas a cold look when he slammed the door behind him, making the 'Open' sign flutter.

'I don't know what you're talking about.' She turned her back to him and continued unpacking a box of knick-knacks to price and put up on the shelves.

'You certainly do. You know exactly what I'm talking about. You've been to the police and told them some cops-and-robbers story about how I forced you to lie and give me an alibi. How fucking low can you sink? Is it revenge you're after, or do you just enjoy making trouble? What the hell were you thinking? I lost my daughter a week ago. Can't you understand that I don't want to keep going behind my wife's back anymore?'

'You promised me,' said Jeanette with flashing eyes. 'You promised that we'd be together, that you'd divorce Charlotte, that we'd have kids together. You promised me a hell of a lot, Niclas.'

'So, why the fuck do you think I did that? Because you loved hearing it. Because you willingly spread your legs when you heard those promises about a ring and a future. Because I wanted to have a little fun with you in bed once in a while. I can't believe you're so fucking dumb that you believed me. You know the game as well as I do. You've had your share of married men before, I'm sure,' he said rudely, watching her flinch at each word, as if he'd slapped her. But he didn't care. He'd already crossed the line and had no desire to show a sensitive side or spare her feelings. Now only the pure, unadulterated truth was appropriate, and after what she'd done, she deserved to hear it.

'You fucking pig,' said Jeanette, reaching for one of the objects she was unpacking. In the next instant a porcelain lighthouse whistled towards his head, but it missed and hit the display window instead. With a deafening crash the pane shattered and big chunks of glass came sliding down. The silence that followed was so complete that it echoed off the walls. Like two combatants they stared at each other as mutual rage made their chests heave. Then Niclas turned on his heel and walked calmly out of the shop. The only sound was the glass crunching under his shoes.

Arne stood in helpless silence and watched while she packed. If Asta hadn't been so determined, the sight of him would have surprised her so much that she would have stopped what she was doing. Arne had never before been helpless. But her fury kept her hands at work, folding clothes and placing them in the biggest suitcase they owned. She didn't yet know how she was going to lug it out of the house, or where she would go. It didn't matter. She didn't intend to stay one more minute in the same house with him. Finally the scales had fallen from her eyes. That feeling of dissonance that she'd always had, the feeling that things might not be the way that Arne said, had finally taken over. He wasn't all-powerful. He wasn't perfect. He was merely a weak, pathetic man who enjoyed bullying other people. And then there was his belief in God. It probably didn't go very deep. Asta saw clearly now how he used the word of God in a way that strangely enough always matched his own views. If God was like Arne's God, then she wanted no part of his faith.

'But Asta, I don't understand. Why are you doing this?'

His voice was whiny like a little boy's, and she didn't even feel like answering him. He stood there in the doorway wringing his hands as he watched her remove one item of clothing after another from the drawers and wardrobes. She didn't intend to come back, so it was best that she take everything all at once.

'Where are you going to go? You have nowhere to go!'

Now he was begging her, but the extraordinary nature of the situation only made her shudder. She tried not to think of all the years she'd wasted; fortunately she was cast in a pragmatic mould. What was done was done. But she didn't intend to waste even one more day of her life.

Acutely aware that the situation was about to slip out of his grasp, Arne now attempted a more tried and true method. He thought he could gain control by raising his voice.

'Asta, you have to stop all this nonsense! Unpack your clothes at once!'

For an instant she did stop packing, but only long enough to give him a look that summed up forty years of oppression. She gathered all her wrath, all her hatred, and tossed it back at him. To her satisfaction she saw him recoil and then shrink before her gaze. When he spoke again it was in a quiet, pitiful voice. The voice of a man who realized that he'd for ever lost control.

'I didn't mean . . . I mean, of course I shouldn't have spoken to the girl that way, I realize that now. But she lacked all respect, and when she behaved so stubbornly towards me I could hear the voice of God telling me that I was compelled to intervene, and –'

Asta cut him off. 'Arne Antonsson. God has never spoken to you. He never will. You're too stupid and deaf for that. As for all that nonsense I've listened to for forty years about how you never had a chance to become a pastor because your father drank up all the money – you should know that it wasn't money that was lacking. Your mother kept a tight grip on the pursestrings and didn't let your father drink up more than was necessary. But she told me before she died that she had no intention of throwing their money away by sending you to seminary school. She may have been an unkind woman, but she had a clear head, and she could see that you weren't suited to be a pastor.'

Arne gasped for breath and stared at her as he slowly turned more and more pale. For a moment she thought he was having a heart attack, and felt herself softening inside against her will. But then she turned on her heel and marched out of the house. She slowly let the air seep out between her lips. She took no pleasure in destroying him, but in the end he'd given her no choice.

GÖTEBORG 1954

She didn't understand how she could keep doing so many things wrong. Once again she had ended up here in the cellar, and the dark seemed to make the wound on her bottom hurt that much more. It was the buckle on the belt that had torn open the wound. Mother only used the end with the buckle when she had been really bad. If only she could understand what was so terrible about taking a tiny little biscuit. They had looked so good, and the cook had made so many that nobody would notice if one was missing. But sometimes she wondered whether her mother sensed it when she was about to stuff something good in her mouth. Mother would come sneaking up behind her without a sound, just as her hand was going to close around something delicious. Then all she could do was steel herself and hope that Mother was having a good day so that it would be one of the milder punishments.

At first she had tried to give Father a beseeching look, but he always looked away. He would pick up his newspaper and go out to sit on the veranda while Mother dispensed whatever punishment she'd chosen. She no longer even tried to get any help from him.

She was shivering from the cold. Little rustling sounds became magnified in her mind as she pictured gigantic rats and enormous spiders, and she could hear them getting closer. It was so hard to keep track of time. She didn't know how long she'd been sitting down here in the dark, but judging by the growling in her stomach it must have been hours. She was nearly always hungry, which was why Mother kept reprimanding her so harshly. There seemed to be something inside her that constantly longed for food, cakes and candy, something that screamed to be filled with sweets. Right now she tasted instead the rough, dry, acrid substance that Mother always made her eat. A spoonful that was forced down her throat when the blows stopped and it was time for her to sit in the cellar. Mother said that what she was feeding her was Humility. Mother also said that she was punishing her for her own good. That a girl couldn't allow herself to get fat, because then no man would look at her and she would have to spend her whole life alone.

Actually she didn't understand what would be so terrible about that. Mother never seemed to look at Father with any joy in her eyes, and none of the men who kept swaggering round Mother's slim figure, giving her compliments and fawning over her, seemed to give her any great satisfaction. No, she would rather be alone than live in the icy cold that prevailed between her parents. Maybe that was why food and sweets tempted her so much. Maybe that was how she could acquire a thick protective padding over her skin that was so sensitive, both to Mother's constant reproaches and to the beatings. Even at such a young age she had known that she could never live up to her mother's expectations. Mother had made that quite clear. Even so, she had really tried. She had done everything that Mother said, trying especially hard to starve off the fat that kept collecting under her skin. But nothing seemed to help.

But she had begun to learn who was actually to blame for everything. Mother had explained that it was Father who demanded so much of them, and that was why Mother had to be so strict with her. At first it had sounded a bit strange. Father never raised his voice and seemed entirely too weak to make any demands on Mother, but the more often the claim was repeated, the more it began to sound like the truth.

She'd begun to hate Father. If only he stopped being so malicious and unreasonable, Mother would be nice and the beatings would stop and everything would be better. Then she would be able to stop eating, and become just as thin and beautiful as Mother, and Father would be proud of them both. Instead he made Mother sneak up to her room in tears in the evenings and in a whisper describe the various ways he tormented her. On those occasions she always said how painful it was for her to be the one who meted out the punishments. She called her darling, just like when she was small, and promised that things would be different. A person did what she had to do, said Mother and then gave her a hug, which was so unusual and unexpected that at first she sat as stiff as a stick, unable to respond to the embrace. Gradually she began to long for those occasions when her Mother put her thin arms round her neck and she felt her cheeks wet with tears against her own. Then she felt needed.

As she sat there in the dark she felt her hatred towards Father swelling like a huge monster inside her. In the daytime, up in the light, she had to hide this hatred of him behind smiles and curtseys, pretending everything was fine. But down here in the dark she could allow the monster out, letting it grow in peace and quiet. She actually got on well with the monster. It had turned into an old, dear friend, the only friend she had.

'You can come up now.'

The voice from upstairs was clear and cold. She opened herself up and drew the monster inside. There it would have to stay until she ended up in the cellar again. Then it could come out and resume growing again.

Patrik received the call just as he was supposed to escort Kaj to the interrogation room. He listened in silence and then went to get Martin. As he was about to knock on his door he remembered that Annika had said that Martin had gone to Fjällbacka, and he cursed to himself when he realized that he would have to take along Gösta instead. He didn't even consider Ernst. The mere thought of him made the rage rise up in his throat. If the guy knew what was good for him he would stay as far away from Patrik as humanly possible.

But he was in luck. Just as he was heading with heavy steps towards Gösta's office, he heard Martin's voice out in the reception and hurried out to find him.

'There you are. Damn, this is great. I thought you wouldn't get back in time. You have to come with me at once.'

'What happened?' said Martin, following Patrik, who hurried out the main entrance after giving a hasty wave to Annika behind the glass.

'A young man has hanged himself. He left a note that mentions Kaj.'

'Oh, shit.'

Patrik got behind the wheel of the police car and put on the blue light. Martin felt like an old lady as he automatically reached out for the handle above the door on the passenger side, but with Patrik in the driver's seat it was a matter of sheer survival instinct.

A mere fifteen minutes later they pulled up in front of the Rydén family's house in the part of Fjällbacka that for some reason was called 'The Swamp'. An ambulance was parked in front of the low brick house, and the EMTs were doing their best to lift a gurney out of the back. A little man with thinning hair in his forties was running back and forth on the driveway and seemed to be in a state of shock. As Patrik and Martin parked and climbed out of the car, one of the ambulance guys went over to the man, wrapped a yellow blanket round his shoulders, and seemed to be trying to talk him into sitting down. The man finally obeyed. With the blanket wrapped tight around him he sank down on a low kerb that marked the border between the driveway and the flower bed.

They had met the ambulance personnel before and didn't bother introducing themselves. Instead they simply greeted each other with a nod.

'So what happened?' asked Patrik.

'The stepfather came home and found his son in the garage. He hanged himself.' One of the EMTs nodded towards the garage door, which somebody had pulled down so that nothing inside could be seen from the street.

Patrik looked over at the little man sitting a few yards away. What that man had just seen was something no one should ever have to see. He was shivering now, as if from the cold, and Patrik recognized it as a sign of shock. But that was something for the EMTs to handle.

'Can we go inside?'

'Yes, we thought we'd just check with you before we lifted him down. He's been hanging there a couple of hours, so there was no reason to hurry. We're the ones who pulled down the garage door, by the way. It seemed unnecessary to let him hang there in public view.'

Patrik patted him on the shoulder. 'Quite right, good thinking. In case there's any connection with our ongoing homicide investigation, I've called the techs in too. So it was good that you didn't cut him down. They should be here any minute, and they'll no doubt want as few people as possible stomping around in there. I suggest that Martin and I go in and that you wait out here for the time being. Do you have the situation under control?' He nodded in the direction of the stepfather.

'Johnny will take care of him. He's in shock. But I'm sure you can talk to him in a little while. He told us that he found a note in the boy's room. He didn't bring anything out, so it's probably still up there.'

'Good,' said Patrik and headed slowly towards the garage door. He grimaced, steeling himself as he bent down to take hold of the handle and raise the door.

The sight was just as horrible as he'd expected. He could hear Martin gasp behind him.

For a moment it felt to Patrik as if the boy was staring right at them, and he had to stop himself from turning and running away. A choking sound behind him made him realize that he should have warned Martin how they needed to proceed in such cases. But now it was too late. He turned round in time to see Martin running out of the garage and over to a bush where he emptied his stomach.

He heard another vehicle pull up next to the police car and the ambulance and assumed it was the tech team arriving. He tried to move carefully so as not to draw the wrath of the team. Above all he didn't want to disturb any evidence if all was not as it seemed. But nothing he saw contradicted his assessment of suicide. A thick rope hung from a hook in the ceiling. The noose was around the boy's neck and a chair had been kicked over and lay on the floor. It looked like a kitchen chair brought from inside the house. The chair had a cushion upholstered in a lingonberry pattern, and its bright cheerfulness offered a sharp contrast to the macabre scene.

Patrik heard a familiar voice behind him.

'Poor devil, he wasn't very old, was he?' Torbjörn Ruud, chief of the technical team from Uddevalla, stepped into the garage and looked up at Sebastian.

'Fourteen,' said Patrik, and they were silent for a moment, faced with the incomprehensible fact that a boy of fourteen could find life so unbearable that death was the only way out.

'Is there any reason to believe that it's not a suicide?' asked Torbjörn as he prepared the camera in his hand.

'No, not really,' said Patrik. 'There's even a note, which I haven't seen yet. Although the note names a person involved in a homicide investigation, so I won't leave anything to chance.'

'The girl?' said Torbjörn, and Patrik nodded.

'Okay, then in other words we'll treat it as a suspicious death. Ask one of the others to take care of the note, so it's not handled by too many people before we get our mitts on it.'

'I'll do it right now,' said Patrik, relieved to have an excuse to leave the garage. He went over to Martin, who was self-consciously wiping his mouth with a paper napkin.

'Pardon me,' he said, gloomily looking at his shoes which had been sprayed by his lunch.

'It doesn't matter. I've done it myself,' said Patrik. 'But now the techs and then the ambulance guys will have to deal with the body. I'm going to check on that note, and you can go see whether it's possible to talk to the stepfather.'

Martin nodded and bent down to wipe off his shoes as best he could. Patrik waved to one of the techs from Uddevalla. She brought her bag of equipment and followed without a word.

The house was uncannily quiet when they went inside. The boy's stepfather had watched them as they went in the front door.

Patrik looked around.

'I'd guess it's upstairs,' said the tech. He thought her name was Eva. She was one of the techs who'd done the examination of the Florins' bathroom.

'Yeah, I don't see anything down here that looks like a boy's room, so you're probably right.'

They climbed the stairs and Patrik suddenly had a flashback to his own childhood home. The houses all seemed to have been built around the same time, and he knew the style well, with fibre wallpaper on the walls and light pine stairs with a wide banister.

Eva was right. At the top of the staircase was an open door that led to a room unmistakably that of a teenage boy. The door, the walls and even the ceiling were covered with posters, and it didn't take a genius to discover the common theme. The boy had loved action heroes. Anyone who struck first and asked questions later; they were all there. The men were dominant, of course, but a single woman had been granted a place in the collection – Angelina Jolie, as Lara Croft. Although Patrik suspected that her toughness wasn't the only reason that Sebastian had put her picture up on his wall – she had quite a pair, to be exact. And he couldn't blame the boy.

A white sheet of paper lying in the middle of the desk brought Patrik back to reality. They went over to take a look at the note. Eva put on a pair of thin gloves and took a plastic bag out of her equipment case. Carefully, with her thumb and forefinger holding one corner of the letter, she dropped it into the plastic bag and then handed it to Patrik. Now he could read it without destroying any fingerprints that might be on the paper.

Patrik glanced through the letter in silence. The words were so filled with pain that he almost lost his balance. But he cleared his throat to maintain his composure, and when he finished reading the note he handed it to Eva. He had no doubt that the letter was genuine.

Patrik felt overcome with anger and resolve. He couldn't offer Sebastian a Schwarzenegger who would mete out justice while wearing cool sunglasses, but he could definitely offer him the help of Patrik Hedström. He had to hope that would be enough.

His phone rang and he answered absentmindedly, still absorbed by his rage over the boy's meaningless death. He was mildly surprised to hear Dan's voice on the phone. Erica's friend usually never rang him directly. Patrik's astonished expression was soon replaced by dismay.

Since the adrenaline was still pumping through his veins, Niclas thought he might as well take on all the troublesome stuff at once, before his usual flight instinct kicked in. So much of what had gone wrong in his life could be blamed on the fact that he was afraid of conflict and turned weak when strength counted most. He was starting to realize that it was Charlotte he had to thank for the things that were still good in his life.

When he turned into the driveway at the house he forced himself to sit in the car for a minute and just breathe. He needed to think through what he was going to say to Charlotte. It was essential that he find exactly the right words. Ever since he'd been forced to confess to her that he'd had an affair with Jeanette, he'd felt the chasm between them widening more and more with each minute they were together. The cracks in their relationship had already existed, both before his revelation and before Sara's death, so it wasn't hard for them to grow. Soon it would be too late. The secret that they shared hadn't brought them together; instead it had merely hastened the process that was pushing them apart. That was where he thought they'd have to begin. If they weren't honest about everything starting right now, nothing would be able to save their marriage. And for the first time in ages, maybe ever, he was sure that was what he wanted.

Hesitantly he got out of the car. Something inside him was still telling him to run, to drive back to the clinic and bury himself in work, to find a new woman to embrace, to return to familiar territory. But he stifled that urge, quickened his steps and walked in the front door.

He could hear murmuring voices upstairs and knew that Lilian must be up in Stig's room. Thank goodness. He didn't want to face her barrage of questions again, and he closed the door as quietly as he could.

Charlotte looked up in astonishment when he came down to the cellar flat.

'You're home early.'

'Yes, I thought we should talk.'

'Haven't we talked enough?' she said indifferently and continued to fold the laundry. Albin was sitting next to her on the floor, playing with his toys. Charlotte looked worn out. He knew that she didn't get many hours of sleep at night; she lay in bed tossing and turning, although he'd pretended not to notice. He hadn't talked to her about it, hadn't caressed her cheek or taken her in his arms. The skin under her eyes had dark smudges, and he could see how she'd grown thin. How many times had he angrily muttered that she ought to pull herself together and lose some weight. Now he'd give anything for her to get back some of her former plumpness.

Niclas sat down on the bed next to her and took her hand. Her shocked expression told him that it was something he did far too seldom. He felt awkward and fumbling, and for a instant he wanted to flee again. But he kept her hand in his and said, 'I'm so dreadfully sorry, Charlotte. For everything. For all the years I've been distant, both physically and mentally; for everything I've blamed you for in my mind even though it was actually my own fault; for the affairs I've had; for the physical closeness I've stolen from you and given to others; for not finding a way for us to get out of this house sooner; for not listening to you; for not loving you enough. I'm sorry for all that and more. But I can't change the past, only promise you that everything will be different starting now. Do you believe me? Please, Charlotte, I have to hear that you believe me!'

She raised her eyes and looked at him. Tears welled up in her eyes and spilled out as she fixed her gaze on him.

'Yes, I believe you. For Sara's sake, I believe you.'

He simply nodded, unable to go on. Then he cleared his throat and said, 'Then there's one thing we have to do. I've thought about this, and we can't keep living with a secret. Monsters live in the dark.'

After a brief pause she nodded. With a sigh she leaned her head on his shoulder, and he felt as though she were falling into him.

They sat that way for a long time.

He made it home in five minutes. He hugged Erica and Maja long and hard, and then shook Dan's hand gratefully.

'What a stroke of luck you were here,' he said, adding Dan to the list of people he had to be thankful for.

'Right. But I don't understand it. Who would take it into their head to do something like this? And why?'

Patrik sat next to Erica on the sofa, holding her hand. After casting a hesitant glance at Erica he said, 'It probably has some connection with Sara's murder.'

Erica gave a start. 'What? Why do you think that? Why would . . .?'

Patrik pointed at Maja's overalls on the floor. 'That looks like ashes.' His voice broke and he had to clear his throat to go on. 'Sara had ashes in her lungs, and there was also a . . .' he searched for the right word, 'an attack on another small child. Ashes were again involved.'

'But what does it mean?' Erica looked bewildered. Nothing she was hearing made any sense.

'I don't know,' said Patrik wearily, passing his hand over his eyes. 'We don't understand it either. We've sent off the ashes we found on the other child's clothing to the lab, to see whether it has the same chemical composition as the ashes inside Sara, but we haven't got an answer back yet. And now I want to send off Maja's clothes too.'

Erica nodded mutely. Her panic had metamorphosed into a shocked, trance-like state. Patrik gave her a hug. 'I'll call in and tell them I'm staying home for the rest of the day. I just have to get Maja's clothes sent off so they can start the analysis as soon as possible. We have to catch whoever is doing this,' he said grimly. It was a promise he was making to himself as much as to Erica. His daughter was unhurt, true, but the mental cruelty behind the deed gave him an uneasy feeling that the person they were searching for was extremely disturbed.

'Can you stay until I get back?' he asked Dan, who nodded.

'Absolutely. I'll stay as long as you need me to.'

Patrik kissed Erica on the cheek and patted Maja tenderly. Then he picked up Maja's overalls, put on his jacket and hurried off. He wanted to get back home soon.

GÖTEBORG 1954

The girl was hopeless. Agnes sighed. So many hopes she'd had for her, so many dreams. She had been so sweet when she was little, and with her dark hair she was easily taken for her daughter. Agnes had decided to call her Mary. Partly because it would remind everyone of her years in the States and the status she'd accrued from living abroad, and partly because it was a lovely name for a charming child.

But after a couple of years something had happened. The girl had begun to swell out in all directions, and the fat covered her sweet features like a mask. It disgusted Agnes. By the time the girl was four her thighs were quivering and her cheeks drooped like on a Saint Bernard, but nothing seemed to stop her from eating. And God knows that Agnes had sincerely tried. But nothing did any good. They hid the food and put locks on the cupboards, but Mary was like a mouse who could always sniff out something that she could stuff into her mouth. Now, at the age of ten, she was a regular mountain of fat. The hours in the cellar didn't seem to have any deterrent effect; instead she always came up from there hungrier than ever.

Agnes simply didn't understand it. She had always placed enormous importance on her own appearance, not least because her looks made it possible for her to obtain the things she wanted in life. It was inconceivable that a girl would want to destroy her chances in that way.

Sometimes she regretted her decision to take the girl with her from the dock in New York. But only partly. It had actually worked exactly the way she'd imagined. Nobody could resist the rich widow with the delightful little daughter, and it had taken her only three months to find the man who could give her the lifestyle she deserved. Åke had come to Fjällbacka for a week in July to enjoy a little recreation; instead he was caught so efficiently by Agnes that he proposed after knowing her for only two months. With a becoming demureness she had accepted, and after a quiet wedding she and her daughter moved to Göteborg, where Åke had a huge flat on Vasagatan. The house in Fjällbacka had once again been rented out, and she heaved a sigh of relief at escaping the isolation that living in the little town involved.

Nor had she been happy about the fact that people still insisted on bringing up her past. It was so long ago, and yet Anders and the boys seemed to live so vividly in everyone's memory. She couldn't understand their need to keep harping on what had happened. One lady had even had the cheek to ask Agnes how she could bring herself to live on the very site where her family had been killed. By then she already had Åke dangling on the hook, so she had allowed herself the liberty to ignore the comment, simply turning on her heel and walking away. There would surely be talk about that, but it no longer mattered to her. She had achieved her goal. Åke had a prestigious position in an insurance firm and would be able to provide her with a comfortable life. Unfortunately, he didn't seem much interested in a social life, but she would soon change that. For the first time in years, Agnes would be the centre of attention at a glittering party. She wanted to have dancing, champagne, beautiful clothes and jewellery, and no one would ever be able to take those things from her again. She erased the memories of her past so effectively that it often felt merely like a distant and unpleasant dream.

But life had one more trick up its sleeve for her. The glittering parties turned out to be few, and she wasn't exactly swimming in beautiful jewels. Åke proved to be notoriously stingy, and she had to fight for every öre. He had also exhibited an unbecoming disappointment when, six months after the wedding, a telegram arrived, saying that all the assets she had inherited from her wealthy late husband had unfortunately been lost through a bad investment by the man appointed to administer them for her. She had sent it to herself, of course, but she was very proud of the theatrical performance she put on when it arrived, including the dramatic fainting scene. She hadn't counted on Åke reacting as strongly as he did, and it made her suspect that the prospect of acquiring her financial assets had played a greater role in convincing him to propose marriage than she'd thought. But what was done was done for both of them, and they now attempted to tolerate each other as best they could.

At first she had felt only a slight irritation at his miserliness and his absolute lack of initiative. What he enjoyed most was sitting at home, night after night, eating the dinner that was set before him on the table, reading the newspaper and perhaps a couple of chapters in a book, and then changing into his old-man pyjamas and slipping into bed just before nine. When they were newly-weds he had occasionally fumbled for her in the bed at night, but now to her relief his lovemaking had decreased to twice a month, always with the light off and without even bothering to remove his pyjama top. But Agnes had noticed that the morning after it was always easier to procure a modest sum for her own use, and she never let such an opportunity go to waste.

But as the years passed her irritation had grown to hatred, and she had begun to search for a suitable weapon to use against Åke. When she noticed that he was becoming attached to the girl, she realized that she'd found it. She knew that he was strongly opposed to her punishments, but also that he was afraid of conflict and too weak stand up in Mary's defence. And she found the greatest enjoyment in slowly but surely turning the girl against him.

Agnes was well aware of how much Mary longed for a little attention and tenderness. If she gave it to her at the same time as she dripped poison in her ear in the form of lies about Åke, she could practically see the venom spreading and taking hold. Then she could let it work in peace and quiet.

Poor Åke had no idea what he was doing wrong. He saw that the girl was growing more distant, and he could hardly fail to notice the contempt in her eyes. He probably suspected that Agnes was to blame, but he could never put his finger on exactly what she did to make the girl detest him so. He spoke with Mary as often as he could and even tried to buy her forgiveness by bribing her with the sweets he knew that she craved. But nothing seemed to help. Inexorably she slipped farther and farther away from him, and as the distance grew his bitterness towards his wife kept pace. Eight years after they married, Åke knew that he'd made a huge mistake, but he couldn't manage to get out of it. And even though Mary now refused to have anything to do with him, he still felt that he was her last chance at security. If he disappeared from her life, he couldn't imagine what his wife might do to the girl. He no longer had any illusions about her.

Agnes was well aware of all this. Sometimes her intuition was uncanny, and she could read people like an open book.

She was sitting at her dressing table, doing her make-up. Unbeknownst to Åke, she'd been having a passionate affair for the past six months with one of his closest friends. She pinned up her black hair, which had still not a trace of grey in it, and dabbed a little perfume behind her ears, on her wrists, and down her cleavage. She was dressed in black silk undergarments trimmed with lace; she still had a figure that would make many young girls envious.

She was looking forward to the rendezvous, which as usual would take place at Hotel Eggers. Per-Erik was a real man, unlike Åke, and she was pleased that he'd begun to talk more and more about leaving his wife. She wasn't so naïve as to believe such promises from a married man, but she knew that he appreciated her skills in bed more than was healthy. His chubby little wife simply couldn't compete.

But there was still the problem of Åke. Agnes's brain began working at high speed. In the mirror she saw her daughter's plump face and the big eyes hungrily watching her.

Despite having taken a long shower and changed his clothes, Martin thought he could still smell the odour of vomit in his nostrils from the day before. The suicide and then the call from Patrik telling him that someone had attacked Maja had shaken him, and he'd been filled with a feeling of helplessness. There were so many threads in this case, so many odd things happening all at once, that for the life of him he couldn't understand how they would ever make any sense of the mess.

Outside Patrik's door he hesitated. In view of what had happened he wasn't sure that Patrik would be working today. But sounds from inside his office told him that Patrik had already come in. He knocked cautiously.

'Come in,' Patrik called out.

'I wasn't sure you'd be here today,' Martin said. 'I thought you might be at home with Erica and Maja.'

'I wanted to stay home,' said Patrik. 'But more than that, I want to catch the psycho who's doing this.'

'But did Erica really want to be at home alone?' Martin said tentatively, unsure whether that was the right thing to say.

'I wanted somebody to come over and stay with them, but she insisted everything was fine. But I did ring and talk to her friend Dan, the guy who was at our house yesterday when it happened, and he promised to drop by and look in on them.'

'Did they get any prints?' Martin asked.

'Unfortunately no. It was raining, so all the tracks had been washed away. But I sent Maja's overalls with the ashes to the lab, so we'll see what that turns up. In my view, it's merely a formality; it would be much too big a coincidence if the ashes didn't match the other sample.'

'But why Maja?'

'Who knows?' said Patrik. 'Presumably it was a warning directed at me. Something I did, or didn't do, during the course of the case. Oh, I don't know,' he said in frustration. 'But the best we can do now is to keep working full speed ahead, so that we get this solved as soon as possible. Until then none of us can relax.'

'What do we do first, interrogate Kaj?'

'Yes,' Patrik said grimly, 'we interrogate Kaj.'

'You do realize that Kaj was in custody yesterday when –'

'Yeah, of course I do,' Patrik said, sounding annoyed. 'But it doesn't mean that he isn't mixed up in this somehow. Or that he won't have to answer to other things.'

'Okay, I was just checking,' said Martin, holding up his hands defensively. 'I'll just hang up my jacket and meet you there.' He headed for his office.

Patrik was gathering up his things to go to the interrogation room when the phone rang. He saw from the display that it was Annika and picked it up, hoping that it wasn't anything important. He was really looking forward to getting into it with the shithead they had in custody. Now more than ever.

'Yes?' He could hear that his tone was curt, but Annika had a thick skin and wouldn't be offended. At least he hoped not.

But Patrik ended up listening with increasing interest and then said, 'Okay, send them in.'

He dashed over to Martin's office. 'Charlotte and Niclas are here, looking for me. We'll have to wait a bit with the interrogation until I hear what they want.'

Without waiting for a reply he ran back to his office. A few seconds later he heard footsteps and a low murmur in the corridor. When Sara's parents stepped into the room, Patrik was shocked to see how Charlotte looked. In the short time since he'd seen her last she had aged considerably, and her clothes hung loosely on her body. Niclas, too, looked tired and worn out, but not as bad as his wife. They sat down in the visitors' chairs, and during the silence that followed Patrik had time to wonder what was so important that they would come here unannounced.

It was Niclas who spoke first. 'We . . . we lied to you. Or rather, there are some things we didn't tell you, and that's probably almost as bad as lying.' Patrik felt his interest rising, but decided to wait Niclas out. After a moment he went on.

'Albin's injuries. The ones you thought, or believed, that I gave him. It was, it was . . .' He seemed to be searching for words, and Charlotte took over for him.

'It was Sara.' Her voice sounded mechanical and empty of all emotion. Patrik recoiled in his chair. That wasn't what he was expecting to hear.

'Sara?' he said, baffled.

'Yes,' said Charlotte. 'You know already that Sara had problems. She had a hard time controlling her impulses and would get the most terrible attacks of rage. Before Albin was born she turned her anger on us, but we were big enough to defend ourselves and make sure she didn't hurt herself or us. But when Albin arrived . . .' Her voice broke and she looked down at her hands, which lay trembling in her lap.

'Everything escalated out of our control after Albin was born,' Niclas said. 'We thought, foolishly, that maybe it would be a positive influence on Sara to have a little brother. Someone she could feel responsible for and protect. But in hindsight that was probably naïve of us. She hated him and the time he demanded from us. She took all the opportunities she could to do him harm, and even if we tried to be there and watch them every second, it was impossible. She was quick . . .' He looked at Charlotte, who nodded feebly.

Niclas went on. 'We tried everything. A social worker, a psychologist, aggression management, medication. There was nothing we didn't try. We experimented with changing her diet, took away all sugar and all fast carbohydrates because some findings suggested that might have a positive effect. But nothing, absolutely nothing, seemed to work. Finally we were at the end of our rope. Sooner or later she was going to do serious harm to someone. We just didn't want to have to send her away. And where would we send her? So when this position at the clinic

377

in Fjällbacka was advertised, we thought that might be the solution. A complete change of scene, with Charlotte's mother and Stig close by to help relieve some of the pressure. It sounded perfect.'

Now it was Niclas's voice that broke. Charlotte put her hand on his and squeezed it. Together they had been to hell and back, and in a way they were still there.

'I'm truly sorry,' said Patrik. 'But I also have to ask: do you have any proof of what you're telling me?'

Niclas nodded. 'I understand that you have to ask. We brought a list of everyone we consulted about Sara. We also contacted them and told them that the police might ring them and ask questions. And we told them they didn't need to preserve patient confidentiality, but to tell the police everything.'

Niclas handed the list to Patrik, who didn't doubt for a moment the veracity of what he'd just heard. But it still had to be corroborated.

'Have you made any progress? With Kaj, I mean?' Charlotte asked hesitantly.

'We're in the process of interrogating him on various points. Unfortunately that's all I can tell you.'

Charlotte merely nodded.

Patrik saw that Niclas wanted to say something else, but that he was having a hard time. He waited him out.

'With regard to the alibi . . .' He glanced at Charlotte, who again nodded almost imperceptibly. 'I recommend that you have a talk with Jeanette. She lied when she said I wasn't there, to get back at me for ending our relationship. I'm sure that if you press her a bit, the truth will come out.'

Patrik was not surprised. He'd thought that something sounded phoney in Jeanette's account. Well, they could deal with her when the time came. If necessary. Hopefully the question of whether Niclas had an alibi or not would be superfluous after this afternoon's interrogation.

They got up and shook hands. Then Niclas's mobile rang. He took the call out in the corridor and a perplexed expression soon appeared on his face.

'The hospital? Now? Stay calm, we'll be right over.'

He turned to Charlotte, who was standing next to Patrik in the doorway.

'Stig has taken a turn for the worse. He's on his way to the hospital.'

Patrik gazed after them as they hurried off down the corridor. Hadn't they suffered enough?

Arne had taken refuge in the church. Asta's words were still whirling round in his head like an angry swarm of hornets. His whole world was falling apart, and the answers he'd hoped to find in the church had not yet materialized. Instead it was as if the stone walls were slowly closing in around him as he sat on the front pew. And didn't Jesus up there on the cross have a sneer on his lips that he'd never noticed before?

A sound behind him made him turn round. Some latecomer German tourists came in the door talking loudly and frenetically taking photographs. He had always been annoyed by tourists who came here at all seasons of the year, and this was the straw that broke the camel's back.

Arne stood up and screamed, with spittle spraying from his lips, 'Get out of here! At once! Out!'

Although they didn't understand a word of what he was saying, his tone left no room for doubt, and they slunk timidly out the door.

Pleased at having finally put his foot down, Arne sat back down on the pew, but Jesus's scornful smile promptly propelled him into a state of gloom again.

A glance at the pulpit infused him with new courage. It was time to do what he should have done long, long ago.

Life was so unfair. Hadn't he been forced to fight an uphill battle ever since he was born? He'd never got something for nothing. Nobody saw his true qualities. Ernst simply didn't understand what was wrong with everybody. What was the problem? Why were they always looking askance at him, whispering behind his back, stealing the opportunities that should have been his? That's how it had always been. Even in grade school they had ganged up on him. The girls had giggled and the boys had given him thrashings on the way home from school. Not even when his father fell and landed on a pitchfork did he get any sympathy. Instead he knew what the people in all the houses were saying with their tattling tongues. That his poor mother probably had something to do with it. They simply had no shame in what they said.

He'd always believed that things would be better as soon as he left school. When he got out in the real world. He had chosen to become a policeman because he would have a chance to show himself as the powerful man he was. But after twenty-five years on the force he had to admit that things hadn't quite gone the way he'd planned. Yet never before had he been in such deep shit as he was now. He just couldn't have imagined that Kaj would have had anything to do with such things. They played cards together, after all. Kaj was a great pal and one of the few people who actually wanted to hang out with him. And they'd heard stories about how unfounded accusations had destroyed the lives of innocent men. So when Ernst got a chance to do a mate a favour, of course he had done it. That was nothing to hold against him, was it? He'd had the best of intentions when he neglected to report that call from Göteborg, but nobody seemed to understand. And now everything had blown up in his face. Why did he always have such fucking bad luck? He was smart enough to realize that the boy's suicide yesterday was going to add insult to injury.

But as he sat there in his office, banished to solitude like a prisoner in Siberia, Ernst had a flash of genius. He knew precisely how he could turn the situation to his own advantage. He intended to become the hero of the day, and once and for all show that whippersnapper Hedström who was the most experienced cop on the force. Hedström had probably noticed how he'd rolled his eyes at the meeting, when Mellberg had pointed out that they probably ought to take a closer look at the village idiot. But one man's meat is another man's poison. If Hedström couldn't put two and two together to solve the murder, then Ernst would just have to jump in and do it for him. It was obvious to anyone that Morgan was the guilty party, and the fact that the girl's jacket was found at his home removed any remaining doubt.

What appealed to Ernst most was the brilliant simplicity of his plan. He would bring Morgan in for questioning, get him to confess in no time, and thereby arrest the murderer. At the same time he could show Mellberg that he, Ernst, certainly did listen to what a superior said, while Hedström was not only incompetent but also insubordinate. After that he would surely be taken into the chief's good graces again.

He got up and walked to the door, displaying more energy than usual. Now it was up to him to do some high-quality police work. He looked up and down the corridor to make sure that nobody was watching as he slipped out, but the coast was clear.

GÖTEBORG 1957

Mary felt nothing as she stood there in the pouring rain. Neither hatred nor joy. Only a cold emptiness that filled her whole body, from the outermost layer of skin down to the white bones of her skeleton.

Her mother was sobbing next to her. She was more stylish than usual. The black funeral dress looked good on her. No one could ignore the dramatic effect of her beauty. With a trembling hand she let a single red rose fall onto her husband's coffin and then threw herself sobbing into Per-Erik's arms. Just behind him stood his wife, sympathy written all over the plain features of her face, thanks to her total ignorance of how often her husband had slept with the woman who was now wetting his lapels with her tears.

Mary watched with an aching heart, wishing her mother had chosen instead to seek solace in her embrace. Dismissed once again. Rejected once again. Doubt descended on her with full force, but she forced herself to push it away. She couldn't start questioning everything now; if she did she would go under.

The rain was cold against her cheeks, but her face betrayed no emotion. With stiff legs she walked the few steps up to the hole in the ground and tried to make her fingers hold out the rose in her hand. The monster stirred inside her, coaxing her, making her raise her arm and hold the rose over the shiny black coffin down there in the hole. Then she saw her fingers as if in slow motion let go of the spiny stalk, and with unbearable slowness the flower floated down towards the hard surface. She thought she heard a loud echo when it struck the wood, but no one else seemed to react, so the sound must have been all in her head.

She stood there for what seemed like an eternity before she felt a light touch on her elbow. Per-Erik's wife smiled gently to her and nodded that it was time to go. Before them walked the rest of the funeral cortège, led by Agnes and Per-Erik. He had his arm around Mother's shoulders and she was leaning against him.

Mary glanced at the woman next to her and wondered scornfully how she could be so stupid and naïve not to see the aura of sexual tension surrounding the couple in front of her. Mary was only thirteen, but she could see it as clearly as the falling rain. Well, that stupid woman would soon find out what reality looked like.

Sometimes she felt so much older than thirteen. She regarded the foolishness of humanity with a contempt that far exceeded that of a normal thirteen-year-old – but then she'd had an excellent teacher. Mother had taught her that everyone was only interested in tending to their own desires, and that a person had to take care of getting what she wanted in life. Nothing should ever stand in the way, Mother had intoned, and Mary had been a splendid student. Now she felt wise and experienced and ready to be given the respect she deserved from Mother. After all, she had proven how far her love reached. Hadn't she made the ultimate sacrifice for her mother? Now she would get that love back with interest, she knew it. She would never again have to sit in the dark cellar and watch the monster grow.

Out of the corner of her eye she saw Per-Erik watching her with a concerned look on his face. She discovered that she had a broad smile on her lips and quickly stifled it. It was important to maintain appearances. That's what Mother always said. And Mother was always right.

The sound of the sirens could be heard from far away. Stig wanted
to sit up and protest, demand that they turn the ambulance around
and drive him home. But his limbs refused to obey him, and when
he tried to speak only a croaking sound came from his lips. Lilian's
worried face hovered above him. 'Shh, don't try to talk. Save your
energy. We'll be in Uddevalla soon.'

Reluctantly he gave up any attempt to struggle. He hadn't the
energy. The pain was still there, and now it was worse than ever.

It had happened so fast. In the morning he had felt quite well
and had even managed to eat a little. But then the pain level had
risen more and more, and finally it became unbearable. When
Lilian came upstairs with morning tea, he was no longer able to
speak, and she had dropped the tray in fright. Then the whole
circus started up. The sound of sirens outside, stomping on the
stairs, hands that carefully lifted him onto a gurney and loaded
him into an ambulance. Followed by a high-speed drive, though
he was only vaguely aware of it.

The fear of landing in hospital was even worse than the pain
he felt. In his mind he saw over and over the image of his father
as he lay in the hospital bed, so small and pitiful, so different from
the boisterous, happy man who used to lift him up in the air when
he was little and affectionately wrestled with him when he was
older. Now Stig knew that he was going to die. If he ended up in
hospital it was only a matter of time.

He wished he could raise his hand and stroke Lilian's cheek.

385

Such a brief time they'd had together. Sure, they'd had their quarrels and bad patches, when he thought they might even go their separate ways, but they had managed to find their way back to each other. Now she would have to find someone else to grow old with.

He would also miss Charlotte and the children. The child, he corrected himself, and felt a pang in his heart, a pain that was more than physical. It was the only positive thing he could see about what had happened. He was firmly convinced that there was life after death, a better place. Maybe he could meet the girl there and find out what actually happened on that morning.

He felt Lilian's hand on his cheek. Unconsciousness began to dissolve reality, and he gratefully shut his eyes. It would be pleasant at least to escape from the pain.

The wind whipped at him as he walked towards Morgan's little cabin. Ernst's enthusiasm had dissipated somewhat on the way over, but he was now excited again, now that he had his prey within reach.

An authoritative knock would launch his road to victory, and it was rewarded a few seconds later with the sound of footsteps inside. Morgan's thin face appeared in the doorway, and in his odd, monotone voice he said, 'What do you want?'

His direct question took Ernst by surprise, and he had to regroup mentally for a moment before he spoke. 'You have to come with me to the police station.'

'Why?' Morgan asked, and Ernst felt irritation creeping over him. What a bizarre person this guy was.

'Because we need to talk to you about a few things.'

'You took my computers. I don't have my computers anymore. You took them,' Morgan chanted, and Ernst saw an opportunity open up.

'Precisely, and that's why you have to come with me. So we can give you back your computers. We're finished with them, you see.' Ernst was incredibly pleased with his stroke of genius.

'Why can't you bring them here? You took them from here.'

'Do you want the computers or not?' Ernst exploded. His patience was now seriously starting to wear thin.

After a moment of hesitation and some internal deliberation, the prospect of getting his computers back conquered Morgan's reluctance to venture into uncharted territory.

'I'll come along. So that I can pick up my computers.'

'Fine. Good boy,' said Ernst, smiling to himself as Morgan went to fetch his jacket.

They sat in silence during the whole trip to the station. Morgan stared out of the window on his side, and Ernst saw no reason to engage in small talk. He was saving his ammunition for the official interview. Then he would no doubt get the idiot to talk.

Once they arrived at the station one tiny dilemma remained. How was Ernst going to get the interrogation subject inside without any of the others noticing what he was up to? Such a discovery would ruin his whole brilliant plan; that must not happen under any circumstances. Finally he came up with a fool-proof idea. From his mobile he rang to the reception, and in a disguised voice he told Annika that he had a package to deliver to the rear entrance. He waited a few seconds, keeping a tight grip on Morgan, then with his heart in his throat he led the way to the main entrance, hoping that Annika had hurried off to the other end of the station. It worked. She wasn't in her usual spot. Ernst quickly pulled Morgan past the reception and into the nearest interview room. He closed the door behind him and locked it, then permitted himself a little triumphant smile before he invited Morgan to sit down on one of the chairs. Someone had left a window half open to air the place out. It was unhooked and flapping in the breeze. Ernst ignored the noise. He wanted to get started as soon as possible before someone tried to poke their head in here.

'So-o-o, my friend, here we are.' Ernst made a big production out of turning on the tape recorder.

Morgan's eyes had begun to wander. Something told him that everything was not as it should be.

'You're not my friend,' he said matter-of-factly. 'We don't know each other, so how could you be my friend? Friends know each other.' After a moment's pause he went on. 'I'm supposed to pick up my computers. That's why I came here. You said that my computers were ready.'

'I did say that, yes,' said Ernst with a sneer. 'But you see, I lied. And you're right about one thing: I'm not your friend. Right now I'm your worst enemy.' A bit dramatic perhaps, but Ernst was cruelly pleased with that line. He recalled hearing it once in a film.

'I don't want to be here anymore,' said Morgan and began looking towards the door. 'I want my computers back and I want to go home.'

'You can forget about that. It'll be a long time before you're going to see your home again.' Damn, he was good. He really ought to write screenplays for American action films. He went on. 'We found her jacket in your cabin, and we have plenty of other forensic evidence showing you were the one who murdered her.' Pure lies, the latter statement, but Morgan didn't know that. And in this game there were no rules.

'But I didn't kill her. Even though I wanted to sometimes,' he added tonelessly.

Ernst felt his heart leap. This was going better than he'd ever imagined.

'It's no use trying to feed me those lies. We have other forensic evidence and we have the jacket, so we don't really need anything else. But it's clear, it would be better for you if you told me how you did it. Then maybe you won't have to do life in prison. You won't be able to have any computers in there.'

Now he saw for the first time a genuine emotion in the idiot's face. Good, it looked like panic was starting to set in. Then he'd be softened up soon. But to improve the situation even more he would try a little trick he'd learned from *NYPD Blue* and the other cop shows from the States that he followed slavishly. He would leave the guy to sweat it out all alone for a while. If he was given time to think about his situation he would confess quicker than Ernst could say 'Andy Sipowicz'.

'I have to go take a piss. We'll continue this conversation in a moment.' He turned his back on Morgan and started towards the door.

Morgan was now babbling incessantly in an entreating tone. 'I didn't do it. I can't sit in prison for the rest of my life. I didn't kill her. I don't know how the jacket ended up at my place. She was wearing it when she went into her house. Please, don't leave me here. Get my mamma, I want to talk to Mamma. Mamma can work all this out, please . . .'

Ernst quickly shut the door behind him so the idiot's babble wouldn't be heard out in the corridor. After a couple of steps Annika caught sight of him and gave him a suspicious look.

'What were you doing in there?'

'Oh, I was just checking something. I thought I left my wallet in one of the interview rooms.'

She didn't look as though she believed him, but let it go. The next second she looked out of the window and cried, 'What in the world?'

'What is it?' said Ernst, feeling a sudden pang of uneasiness in his stomach.

'A guy just climbed out one of the windows and now he's running towards the highway.'

'What the hell!' Ernst almost dislocated his shoulder as he slammed against the door, in his haste forgetting that it was always locked.

'Open the door, for God's sake!' he yelled at Annika, and she obeyed in fright. He tore open the second door and dashed out after Morgan. He saw Morgan look back and run even faster. In horror Ernst saw a black mini-van approaching at speed.

'No-o-o-o!' he shrieked in panic.

Then came the thud and everything was quiet.

Martin wondered what it was that Charlotte and Niclas had been in such a hurry to talk to Patrik about. He hoped it was something that would allow them to remove Niclas from the list of suspects. The thought that the murderer might be the girl's own father was too horrendous to contemplate.

He couldn't get a handle on Niclas. Albin's medical reports were pretty serious, and Niclas hadn't managed to convince him that he was innocent of inflicting injuries on the boy. And yet there was something that didn't fit. Niclas was a complex man, to say the least. He gave the impression of a kind and stable person when you sat eye to eye with him, but he seemed to have made a total mess of his private life. Although Martin had been no angel in his swinging single days, now that he was living with someone he couldn't understand how anyone could betray his better half like that. What did Niclas tell Charlotte when he came home after being with Jeanette? How could he make his tone of voice sound natural? How could he look her in the eye after rolling around in bed with his lover only a few hours earlier? Martin simply couldn't understand it.

Niclas had displayed a temperament that was difficult to pinpoint. Martin had seen the look in his eyes when he turned up at his father's house earlier in the day. Niclas looked like he'd wanted to kill his father. God knows what might have happened if Martin hadn't shown up.

And yet. Despite Niclas's contradictory nature Martin didn't believe that he knowingly and willingly would have drowned his own daughter. And what would have been his motive for doing so?

His thoughts were interrupted when he heard footsteps in the corridor and saw Charlotte and Niclas hurry past. He was curious to know what the rush was.

Patrik appeared in the doorway, and Martin raised his eyebrows as he gave his colleague an inquiring look.

'It was Sara who hurt Albin,' Patrik said, sitting down in the visitor's chair.

Whatever Martin was expecting, it certainly wasn't that. 'How do we know they're telling the truth? Couldn't Niclas be trying to divert attention from himself?'

'Yeah, he could be, of course,' said Patrik wearily. 'But I have to say that I believe them. Even though we do have to substantiate their story. They gave me names and phone numbers of people we can contact. And Niclas's alibi does seem to hold up after all. He claims that Jeanette lied when she said he wasn't with her, as a way to get back at him after he dumped her. And there too I'm inclined to take him at his word, although naturally we'll have to have a serious talk with Jeanette.'

'What a screwed-up . . .' said Martin, and he didn't have to finish his sentence before Patrik agreed.

'Yes, humanity has not shown its noblest side in this investigation,' he said, shaking his head. 'And apropos that very subject, should we get started on that interview now?'

Martin nodded, took his notebook and got up to follow Patrik, who was already on his way out the door. To his back he said, 'By the way, have you heard anything from Pedersen yet? About the ashes on the little boy's shirt?'

'No,' replied Patrik without turning round. 'But they were going to shift into high gear and analyse both the shirt and Maja's overalls ASAP. I'd be willing to bet that they'll find the ashes came from the same source.'

'Whatever that may be,' said Martin.

'Yeah, whatever that may be.'

They entered the interrogation room and sat down across from Kaj. No one said a word at first as Patrik calmly leafed through his papers. He saw to his satisfaction that Kaj was nervously wringing his hands, and that tiny drops of sweat had formed on his upper lip. Good, he was scared. That would make the questioning easier. And considering how much evidence they'd gathered from the search of the house, Patrik didn't feel worried in the least. If only they had evidence this good in all their investigations, life would be much easier.

Then his mood shifted. He'd come to a photostat of the boy's suicide note, and it was an abrupt reminder of why they did this job, and who the man before them was. Patrik clenched his fists in determination. He looked at Kaj, who averted his eyes.

'We actually don't need to talk to you. We have plenty of evidence from the search of your house to put you behind lock and key for a long, long time. But we still want to give you a chance to explain your side of the story. Because that's the way we are. Nice guys.'

'I don't know what you're talking about,' said Kaj in a quavering voice. 'This is a miscarriage of justice. You can't hold me here. I'm innocent.'

Patrik merely nodded sympathetically. 'You know, I almost believe you. And I might even do so if it weren't for these.' He took some photos out of his thick folder and pushed them over to Kaj. He was pleased to see Kaj first turn pale and then red. He gave Patrik a bewildered look.

'I told you we had skilled computer guys, didn't I?' Patrik said. 'And didn't I say that things don't disappear just because you delete them? You've been very efficient at erasing stuff from your computer, but unfortunately not efficient enough. We got hold of everything you downloaded and shared with your paedo-pals. Photos, email, video files. All of it. Lock, stock and barrel.'

Kaj opened and closed his mouth. It looked as though he was trying to shape words, but they stubbornly stuck to his tongue.

'Not so much to say now, is there? Two colleagues from Göteborg are coming here tomorrow and they'd like to talk to you as well. They consider our discoveries to be extremely interesting.'

Kaj didn't say a word, so Patrik continued, determined to shake him in some way. He detested the man in front of him; he detested everything he represented, everything he had done. But he didn't let it show. Calmly and in a matter-of-fact tone he went on talking to him as if discussing the weather, not child abuse. For a moment he considered taking up the matter of Sara's jacket directly, but decided at last to wait a while with that. Instead he leaned across the table, looked Kaj in the eye and said, 'Do you people ever think about the children who are your victims? Do you give them the slightest thought, or are you too wrapped up in satisfying your own needs?'

He hadn't expected a reply, nor did he get one. In the ensuing silence he went on, 'Do you know anything about what goes on inside a young boy's head when he comes up against somebody like you? Do you know what goes to pieces, what you steal from him?'

Only a slight twitch in Kaj's face showed that he'd heard him. Without taking his eyes off the man, Patrik took a sheet of paper and pushed it slowly across the table. At first Kaj refused to look down, but then he slowly lowered his gaze to the sheet of paper and began to read. With an incredulous expression on his face he looked at Patrik, who merely nodded grimly.

'Yes, that's precisely what it looks like it is. A suicide note. Sebastian Rydén took his life this morning. His stepfather found him hanging in the garage. I was there when they cut him down.'

'You're lying.' Kaj's hand shook as he picked up the letter. But Patrik could see that he knew it was true.

'Wouldn't it feel good to stop lying?' Patrik asked him softly. 'You must have cared for Sebastian, I'm sure of that – so do it for his sake. You can see what he wrote. He wanted it to end. You can end it.'

His tone was treacherously sympathetic. Patrik glanced quickly at Martin, who sat ready with his pen poised over his notebook. The tape recorder was humming like a little bumblebee in the room as well, but Martin was in the habit of always taking his own notes.

Kaj smoothed out the letter with his fingers and opened his mouth to say something. Martin held his pen, ready to start writing.

At that very instant Annika tore open the door.

'There's been an accident outside, hurry!'

Then she ran off down the hall. After a second of shocked silence, Patrik and Martin ran after her.

At the last moment Patrik remembered to lock the door. They'd have to resume with Kaj later. He only hoped that the moment hadn't passed them by.

Mellberg couldn't deny that he felt a bit worried. It had only been a couple of days, of course, but he didn't sense that they had any real father-son contact yet. Sure, maybe he should be a little more patient, but he really didn't think he was getting the appreciation he deserved. The respect due a father. The unconditional love that all parents spoke of, perhaps combined with a little healthy fear. The boy seemed absolutely indifferent. He loafed about on Mellberg's sofa all day long, eating enormous quantities of crisps and playing his video games. Mellberg couldn't understand where he'd got such a slacker attitude. It must be from his mother. Mellberg could remember being a bundle of energy as a youth. Even with the best effort he couldn't actually recall the achievements in sports he must have made – in fact he couldn't summon up a single memory of himself in any sort of sports context – but he ascribed that failing to the toll of time. His image of himself as a youth was definitely that of a muscular boy with a spring in his step.

He looked at the clock. Not yet noon. His fingers drummed impatiently on the desktop. Maybe he ought to go home instead and spend a little quality time with Simon. It would probably make the boy happy. When Mellberg thought about it, he realized that his son was probably just shy. Inside he was undoubtedly longing for his pappa, who had been absent for so long, to come and drag him out of his shell. That must be it. Mellberg sighed with relief. It was lucky that he understood kids, otherwise he probably would have given up by now and let the boy sit there on the sofa feeling miserable. But Simon would soon find how lucky he was in the father lottery.

With great enthusiasm Mellberg pulled on his jacket, thinking about what they might dream up as a suitable father-son activity. Unfortunately there wasn't much for two real men to do in this Godforsaken hole. If they'd been in Göteborg he could have taken his son on his first visit to a strip club, or taught him about roulette. As it was, he didn't quite know what they should do. Oh well, he'd think of something.

As he passed Hedström's door he thought that it was damned unpleasant about what happened to his daughter. It was another sign that you never knew when something might occur, and it was best to enjoy your children while there was still time. With that in mind he convinced himself that nobody would blame him for going home early today.

Whistling, he walked towards the reception, but stopped short when he saw doors flying open and his men running towards the front entrance. Something was going on, and as usual nobody had bothered to tell him.

'What's going on?' he shouted to Gösta, who wasn't as fast as the others and was bringing up the rear.

'Somebody's been run over right outside.'

'Oh shit,' said Mellberg, and he also started running as best he could.

Right outside the entrance he stopped. A big black mini-van stood in the middle of the street. A man who was probably the driver was wandering about holding his head. The air bag had deployed on the driver's side, and he looked uninjured but confused. In front of the vehicle a heap lay in the street. Patrik and Annika were kneeling next to it, while Martin tried to calm the driver. Ernst stood a bit to the side, with his long arms hanging down and his face as white as a sheet. Gösta joined him, and Mellberg saw them talking quietly with each other. Gösta's worried expression bothered Mellberg. He got an uncomfortable feeling in his stomach.

'Did anyone call an ambulance?' he asked, and Annika answered yes. Awkward and unsure what to do next, he went over to Ernst and Gösta. 'What happened? Do you know?'

An ominous silence from both of them told him that he wasn't going to like the answer. He saw that Ernst was blinking nervously, so Mellberg fixed his gaze on him.

'Well, is anyone going to answer, or do I have to drag it out of you?'

'It was an accident,' said Ernst in a shrill voice.

'Could you give me some details about this "accident"?' Mellberg asked, still glaring at his subordinate.

'I was just going to ask him some questions, and he flipped out. He was a total fucking psycho, that guy. I couldn't help it, could I?' Ernst raised his voice belligerently in a desperate attempt to take control of the situation that had so suddenly slipped out of his hands.

The ominous feeling in Mellberg's stomach grew. He looked at the heap lying in the street.

'Who is it lying under that vehicle, Ernst? Tell me.' He was whispering, almost snarling the words, and that more than anything else told Ernst what deep shit he was in.

Taking a deep breath he whispered, 'Morgan. Morgan Wiberg.'

'What the fuck are you saying?' roared Mellberg so loud that both Ernst and Gösta shrank back, and Patrik and Annika turned round.

'Did you know about this, Hedström?' asked Mellberg.

Patrik shook his head grimly. 'No, I didn't give any instructions for Morgan to be brought in for questioning.'

'So-o-o, you thought you'd show off a little.' Mellberg had lowered his voice to a treacherously calm tone.

'You said that we should look at the idiot first. And unlike certain colleagues,' Ernst nodded in Patrik's direction, 'I have complete confidence in your opinion and always listen to what you say.'

In a normal situation flattery would have been the proper path to take, but this time Ernst had made such a mess of things that not even compliments could make Mellberg favourably disposed towards him.

'Did I specifically say that Morgan should be brought in? Well, did I say that?'

Ernst seemed to hesitate for a moment, and then whispered, 'No.'

'All right then,' Mellberg yelled. 'Now where the hell is the fucking ambulance? Are they taking a coffee break on the way, or what?'

He felt his frustration flying in all directions, and it didn't help when Hedström said calmly, 'I don't think they need to hurry. He hasn't breathed since we got here. I think death was instantaneous.'

Mellberg shut his eyes. In his mind he saw his whole career slipping away. All the years of hard work . . . maybe not with the daily police work, but with navigating the political jungle and staying on good terms with those who had influence while stepping on those who might put obstacles in his way. All this rendered meaningless because of a stupid fucking hick cop.

Slowly he turned back to Ernst. In an icy voice he said, 'You are suspended pending investigation. And if I were you, I wouldn't expect to be coming back.'

'But, sir . . .' said Ernst, preparing to protest. He shut up abruptly when Mellberg raised his index finger in the air.

'Shut up,' was all he said, and with that Ernst knew that the game was lost. He might as well just go home.

GÖTEBORG 1957

Agnes stretched out lazily in the big bed. There was something about the glow right after making love with a man that made her feel alive and vibrant. She looked at Per-Erik's broad back as he sat on the edge of the bed pulling on his well-pressed suit trousers.

'Well, when are you going to tell Elisabeth?' she said, scrutinizing her red-painted fingernails for imperfections. She found none. The lack of a reply from him made her look up from her nails.

'Per-Erik?'

He cleared his throat. 'I think it's a bit early. It's hardly been a month since Åke died, and what would people say if . . .' he let the rest of the sentence remain unspoken.

'I thought that what we have meant more to you than what "people" might think,' she said with a sharpness he hadn't heard before.

'It does, darling, it does. I just think we ought to . . . wait a little,' he said, turning to caress her bare legs.

Agnes gave him a suspicious look. His expression was inscrutable. It bothered her that she could never really read him, the way she'd always been able to read other men. Yet that might be why, for the first time in her life, she felt that she'd met a man who could live up to her expectations. And it was about time. Of course she looked extremely good for fifty-three, but the years had brought unwelcome changes even for her. Soon she might not be able to rely on her looks any longer. The thought frightened her, and that's why it was so important for Per-Erik to keep all the promises he'd made to her. During the years their relationship had lasted, she had always been the one who was in control. At least that was how she viewed it. But for the first time Agnes felt a pang of doubt. Maybe she had let herself be duped. She hoped for his sake that wasn't the case.

Harald Spjuth was content with his life as a pastor. But as a human being he sometimes felt a little lonesome. Although he was forty years old, he had not yet found anyone to share his life with, and that was something that pained him deeply. Perhaps his pastor's collar had created an obstacle, because nothing in his personality indicated that he would have any difficulties in finding love. He was a genuinely pleasant and good person, even if those might not be the terms he would use to describe himself, since he was also both humble and shy. Nor could his looks be blamed for his loneliness. While he didn't exactly qualify as a cinema hero up on the silver screen, he had pleasant features and a full head of hair. He also possessed the enviable trait of never gaining an ounce despite his fondness for good food and the many coffee klatsches that life as a pastor in a small town entailed. And yet things hadn't really gone his way.

But Harald had not despaired. He wondered what his congregation would say if they knew how industrious he had been when it came to placing personals ads recently. After trying both square dancing and cooking courses with no success, he had sat down in the late spring and written his first classified ad. Since then things had just rolled along. He hadn't met the love of his life yet, but he had gone to several enjoyable lunch meetings and had acquired a couple of very nice pen pals in the bargain. At home on the kitchen table lay three more letters waiting for him to have time to read them. But duty first.

He'd been to visit some of the elderly folks who appreciated the opportunity to chat for a while and often passed by the parsonage on their way to church. Many of his more ambitious colleagues would probably have thought that the congregation was a trifle too small, but Harald was flourishing. The yellow parsonage was a lovely home, and he was always struck by how imposing the church was as he walked up the little hill on the tree-lined lane. When he passed the old church school that stood across from the parsonage, he reflected for a moment over the vitriolic debate that had flared up in town. An estate developer wanted to tear down the extremely dilapidated building and put up a block of flats. But the project had immediately generated a number of articles written in protest, as well as letters to the editor from people who wanted the building to be preserved as it was at any cost. In a way Harald could understand both sides, but it was still remarkable that most of the opponents were not year-round residents but summer visitors with residences in Fjällbacka. Naturally they wanted their retreat to remain as gloriously picturesque and cute as possible. They enjoyed wandering about town on the weekends and counted themselves fortunate that they had such a pleasant refuge far from the workaday world in the big city. The only problem was that a town that did not develop would die sooner or later; the image couldn't be frozen for ever. Flats were needed, and it was impossible to make everything in Fjällbacka a national landmark without affecting the very lifeblood of the town. Tourism was fine, of course, but there was a life after summertime as well, Harald reflected as he ambled up the hill towards the church.

Before he entered he was in the habit of stopping to look up at the tower, with his head tipped back as far as he could manage. In windy weather like today he had the illusion that the tower was swaying, and the imposing sight of thousands of tons of granite about to fall on him always made him feel respect for the men who had built the majestic church. Sometimes he wished that he had lived in those times and been one of the stonecutters of Bohuslän. Those men who lived in obscurity and yet had used their hands to create everything from the simplest roads to the most magnificent statues. But he was wise enough to know that this was all a romantic dream. Life had probably not been much fun for those men, and he appreciated the comforts of the present day far too much to fool himself into thinking he'd be better off without them.

After permitting himself a moment of daydreaming, he opened the port. Guiltily he caught himself crossing his fingers that Arne wouldn't be there. There was nothing really wrong with the fellow, and he did a good enough job, but Harald had to admit that he had a problem with the old adherents of Schartau's pietistic Lutheranism, and Arne was one of the worst. One would have to search far and wide to find another the likes of this gloomy man. He seemed to revel in misery and constantly sought the negative in everything. Sometimes when Arne was standing next to him, Harald could feel all joy in life being literally sucked out of him. Nor did he have much patience for the man's eternal harping about female pastors, either. If Harald had five Kronor for each time Arne had taken offence over his predecessor, he would be a rich man today. Honestly, he couldn't understand what was so terrible about a woman preaching God's word instead of a man. Whenever Arne launched into one of his tirades, Harald had to stifle a desire to say that it didn't require a penis to preach God's word, but he always bit his tongue just in time. Poor Arne would probably drop dead on the spot if he heard a pastor say anything like that.

Once inside the sacristy all hope vanished that Arne might have stayed securely at home. Harald heard his voice and thought that he was probably talking to some poor tourists who had run into the most conservative verger in the Swedish realm. For a moment Harald was tempted to sneak back out. Then he sighed and thought he should do the Christian thing and go in and rescue the poor creatures.

But there were no tourists in sight. Instead Arne was standing high up on the pulpit and preaching in a thunderous voice to the empty pews. Harald stared at him in disbelief, wondering what on earth had taken possession of the fellow.

Arne was waving his arms and working hard as if he were holding a sermon on the mount; he stopped only for a moment when he saw Harald come in the door. Then he went on as if nothing had happened. Now Harald also saw all the papers strewn beneath the pulpit. That was explained when Arne with sweeping gestures tore pages out of the psalmbook he held in his hand and let them float to the floor.

'What do you think you're doing?' said Harald indignantly, striding resolutely up the centre aisle of the church.

'I'm doing what should have been done a long time ago,' replied Arne belligerently. 'I'm ripping up the horrible new-fangled things. Ungodly is what they are,' he snorted and continued to rip out page after page. 'I don't understand why everything old suddenly has to be changed. It was all so much better before. Now all morality has been made lax, and people dance and sing whether it's Thursday or Sunday! Not to mention that they're copulating everywhere, outside the sanctity of marriage.'

His hair was standing on end, and Harald wondered once again whether poor Arne had completely lost his mind. He didn't know what had brought on this sudden outburst. Arne had of course been muttering much the same opinions year in and year out, but he had never ventured to do anything this bold before.

'You've got to calm down, Arne. Please come down from the pulpit and we'll have a talk.'

'Talk? Ha! That's all anyone does,' Arne spouted from his elevated position. 'That's what I'm saying, it's time for action instead! And this place is as good as any to begin,' he said as page after page continued falling to the floor like big snowflakes.

But now Harald flew into a temper. Standing here vandalizing his magnificent church! There had to be a limit to the man's nonsense!

'Come down from there, Arne, come down right now!' he shouted, which made the verger stop short. Never before had the pastor raised his voice. He was normally so gentle, so it had an effect.

'You have ten seconds to come down from there, or I'll come up and get you, big as you are!' Harald went on, now bright red in the face with rage. The look in his eyes left no doubt that he meant business.

Arne's belligerence was deflated as fast as it came on, and he docilely obeyed the pastor's command.

'All right, then,' said Harald in a considerably milder voice when

402

he went over to Arne and put an arm round his shoulders. 'Let's go over to the parsonage. I'll put on a pot of coffee, and we'll have a little of that coffee cake that Signe was so kind to bake. Then we'll have a talk, you and I.'

And they walked off down the centre aisle towards the door, the small man with his arm round the big man. Like an odd bridal couple.

Monica felt a bit dizzy when she got out of the car. She hadn't got much sleep the night before. The thought of the horrible thing Kaj was accused of doing had kept her awake till the wee hours.

The worst thing was actually the lack of any doubt. When she heard the police officer read off the allegations, she knew from the first moment that they were true. So many pieces of the puzzle finally fell into place. Suddenly there was an explanation for so much that had happened during their years together.

A feeling of disgust turned her stomach, and she leaned against the car and spat out a little gall onto the asphalt. She had fought off the nausea all morning. When she arrived at work, her boss had told her that she didn't have to work if she didn't feel like it, considering the circumstances. But she had refused to go home. The thought of sitting at home all day was repulsive. She would rather endure people's stares than walk about in his house, sit on his sofa, cook food in his kitchen. The thought that he had touched her, although not in a long, long time, made her want to flay the skin from her body.

But in the end she had no choice. After she'd tried to stay on her feet for an hour the boss had told her to go home, and this time he refused to take no for an answer. With a lump in her stomach she had slowly started driving home. By the time she got to the bottom of Galärbacken she was just creeping along. The driver of the car behind her had honked his horn in annoyance, but Monica couldn't have cared less.

If it hadn't been for Morgan she would have packed a bag and driven to her sister's house. But she couldn't abandon him. He would go crazy anywhere else than in his little cabin; the fact that they had taken his computers was enough of an upheaval in his world. Yesterday she had found him wandering restlessly among his stacks of magazines. He was lost without his anchors in the real world. She hoped that the police would give back his computers soon.

Monica took out the key to the front door and was about to unlock it when she stopped. She wasn't ready to go inside yet. A sudden longing to see her son made her stuff the key back in her pocket, go down the steps and take the path to Morgan's cabin. He would surely be annoyed that she was breaking the routines and showing up at his place, but for once she didn't care. She remembered how he had smelled as a baby, how that smell had made her want to move mountains for his sake. Now she felt a need to sniff the back of his neck once more, as big as he was, to hug him as if he were her rock, instead of vice versa, as it had been for all these years.

She knocked cautiously on the door and waited. There was no sound from inside, and she began to feel uneasy. Monica knocked again, a little harder this time, and waited tensely to hear the sound of footsteps inside. Nothing.

She tried the door, but it was locked. Fumbling, she reached above the door for the spare key and finally found it.

Where could he be? Morgan hardly ever went anywhere by himself. Never before had he gone anywhere without either taking her along or at least very properly telling her where he was going. Fear began prickling at her throat, and she half-expected to find him dead inside his cabin. That was what she had always dreaded. That one day he would stop talking about death and instead decide to seek it out. Maybe the loss of his computers and the encroachment into his world had made him finally decide to set off for the place from which there was no return.

But the cabin was empty. Anxiously she looked around, and her gaze quickly fell on a piece of paper lying on top of a pile of magazines near the door. She recognized Morgan's handwriting even before she read what he'd written, and her heart skipped a beat. She breathed a sigh of relief as soon as she read the note. She didn't realize until her shoulders relaxed how hard she'd been clenching her muscles.

'Computers ready. Went with the police to pick up,' it said on the paper, and her concern returned. It wasn't the suicide note she had feared, but there was something that didn't make sense. Why would the police come to collect him so that he could get his computers back? Wouldn't they have brought them along and delivered them directly?

Monica made up her mind in an instant. She dashed back to the car and drove off with a squeal of rubber. The whole way to Tanumshede she pressed the accelerator to the floor, and her hands clutched the steering wheel so hard that they began to sweat. When she passed the intersection by Tanum Tavern she heard sirens behind her and was overtaken by an ambulance driving at high speed. She unconsciously sped up and almost flew past Hedemyr's. At Mr Li's store she had to stop suddenly, and the strap of the seat belt locked hard against her chest. The ambulance had stopped right in front of the police station, and a queue of cars had formed from both directions because they couldn't get past what looked like the scene of an accident. When she craned her neck she could see a dark heap lying in the street. She didn't need to see any more to know who it was.

As if in slow motion she undid her seat belt and opened the car door, leaving it wide open after she climbed out. With a feeling of impending doom she walked very slowly towards the accident scene.

The first thing she saw was the blood. The red running from his head onto the asphalt and spreading out in a wide circle around his hair. The second thing she saw were his eyes. Wide open, dead.

A man was heading towards her. His arms ready to stop her. His mouth moved, said something. She ignored the man and continued straight ahead. She fell heavily to her knees next to Morgan. She placed his head on her lap and held it close, without caring about the blood that was still trickling out and now wetting her trousers. Then she heard the wail. She wondered who could sound so sad, so full of pain. Then she realized it was herself.

They had driven faster than the speed limit all the way to Uddevalla. Lilian had assured them that Albin was safe with Veronika and Frida, so they could drive directly to the hospital from the police station. Charlotte hoped that they wouldn't arrive too late. Her mother had sounded as if Stig's life hung by a thread, and she caught herself clasping her hands as if in prayer, although she was not a religious person.

Stig was the friendliest person she had ever met. She realized only now how fond of him she'd grown during the time they had lived with him and Lilian. She'd met him before that, of course, but it was always during such brief visits. She didn't really get to know him until they moved in. Much of her warm feeling was based on the fact that he and Sara had been so close. He'd been able to coax out the good from her daughter, favourable traits that Charlotte had always known existed but couldn't reach. Sara was never insolent to Stig, she never burst out in a rage, she didn't jump around like a crazy person, incapable of controlling her energy. With him she sat calmly on the edge of the bed and held his hand, telling him about her day at school. Charlotte had never ceased to be amazed at how Sara behaved when she was with Stig, and now she sincerely regretted not having told him that. She realized she had hardly even spoken to him since Sara died. She had been so immersed in her own grief that she hadn't even thought of his. He must have been heartbroken as he lay upstairs in his room, sick and in pain and with only his own thoughts to keep him company. She should have at least gone up to see him and have a talk.

As soon as the car stopped in the car park, Charlotte jumped out. She ran towards the entrance and didn't wait for Niclas. He knew his way around the hospital better than she did, so he would soon catch up.

'Charlotte!' Lilian came towards her with arms outstretched as she entered the waiting room. Her mother was sobbing, and everyone turned to look at her. People crying had the same effect on their fellow human beings as car crashes. Nobody could help looking.

Charlotte awkwardly patted her mother on the back. Lilian had never been particularly demonstrative, and physical contact with her felt unusual.

'Oh, Charlotte, it was dreadful! I went up to bring him some tea and he was completely out of it! I called his name and tried to shake him, but I got no response at all. And nobody can tell me what was wrong with him. He's in intensive care and they won't let me see him. Shouldn't I be allowed to be with him? And what if he dies!'

Lilian shrieked so loudly it was heard all over the room, and for a moment Charlotte was embarrassed to have everyone looking at them. Then she pulled herself together and reminded herself that her mother had always had a tendency towards the dramatic, but that didn't make her worry any less genuine.

'Sit down and I'll go see whether I can find us a cup of coffee. Niclas will be here soon, and he can probably find out something in no time. They're his old colleagues, after all.'

'Do you think so?' said Lilian, clinging to her daughter's arm.

'Certainly,' said Charlotte, carefully loosening Lilian's grip. It actually surprised her how calm and secure she felt. The lost of Sara had dulled her emotions, which made her able to think practically despite her own concern about Stig.

Gratefully she saw Niclas enter the waiting room, and she met him at the door.

'Mamma is hysterical. I'll go and fetch some coffee for all of us. I promised her that you would try to find out more about what's happening with Stig.'

Niclas nodded. He raised his hand and caressed Charlotte's cheek. The unaccustomed gesture made her flinch. She couldn't really remember him ever touching her with such tenderness.

'How are you holding up?' he asked her with genuine concern, and despite the sadness of the situation she felt something like joy blossom in her heart.

'I'm doing all right,' she replied, smiling at him as a sign that she wasn't going to break down.

'Are you sure?'

'I'm sure. Go talk to your colleagues now, so we can get some straight answers.'

He did as she said. A while later, as she and Lilian were sitting together sipping their coffee, he came back and sat down next to them.

'Well? Did you find out anything?' said Charlotte, trying by sheer force of will to make him say something positive. Unfortunately it didn't work.

Niclas's face was grim when he said, 'I'm afraid we have to

407

prepare for the worst. They're doing what they can, but they're not sure that Stig will live out the day. We just have to wait and see.'

Lilian gasped and threw her arms round Niclas's neck. Feeling just as awkward as Charlotte, he tried to console her by patting her back. Charlotte had a sense of déjà vu. Lilian had been in this same state when Charlotte's father died, and the doctors ended up giving her a sedative so she wouldn't totally fall apart. The whole thing was so unfair. Losing one husband was bad enough. Charlotte turned to Niclas.

'Couldn't they tell you anything about what's wrong with him?'

'They doing lots of tests and will probably work out eventually what it is. But right now the most important thing is to keep him alive long enough to be able to find the proper treatment. As things look now, it could be anything from cancer to some viral infection. All they said was that he should have come to the hospital long ago.'

Charlotte saw the guilt flicker like a shadow across his face. She leaned her head against his shoulder.

'You're only human, Niclas. Stig didn't want to go to the hospital, and it didn't seem dangerous when you examined him, did it? He was up now and then and seemed fairly spry, and he said himself that he didn't have much pain.'

'I shouldn't have listened to him. Damn it, I'm a doctor, I should have known better.'

'Don't forget that we've had a few other things on our minds,' Charlotte said in a low voice, but Lilian still heard her.

'Why does all the misfortune in the world have to descend on us? First Sara, and now Stig,' she wailed, blowing her nose in the paper napkin that Charlotte had given her. People in the waiting room who had gone back to reading their magazines now looked at them again. Charlotte felt irritation seize hold of her.

'You have to pull yourself together. The doctors are doing all they can,' she said, trying to make her voice as soothing as possible, without taking the force out of what she said. Lilian gave her an injured look, but obeyed and stopped sniffling.

Charlotte sighed and rolled her eyes at Niclas. She didn't doubt that her mother's distress about Stig was genuine, but her tendency to turn every situation into a drama starring herself was incredibly trying. Lilian had always thrived when she was the centre of attention, and she used every means at her disposal to achieve that position, even in a situation like this. That was just how she was, and Charlotte struggled to accept it and conceal her vexation. This time her mother's suffering was real.

Six hours later they still hadn't got any news. Niclas had gone in to talk with the doctors repeatedly, but they didn't have any more information. The prognosis for Stig was still uncertain.

'Somebody has to drive home and see to Albin,' said Charlotte, talking as much to Lilian as to Niclas. She saw that her mother opened her mouth to protest, unwilling to let either her daughter or son-in-law go, but Niclas anticipated what she was going to say.

'Yes, you're right. He'll be terrified if Veronika tries to put him to bed at her house. I'll go, so you can stay here.'

Lilian looked annoyed, but she knew that they were right and reluctantly gave in.

Niclas kissed Charlotte on the cheek and then patted Lilian on the shoulder. 'Everything will work out, you'll see. Ring if you hear anything.'

Charlotte nodded. She watched him vanish down the corridor and then leaned back in the uncomfortable chair and closed her eyes. It was going to be a long wait.

GÖTEBORG 1958

The disappointment ate at Mary from the inside. Nothing had turned out the way she'd thought. Nothing had changed, except that now she didn't even receive the brief displays of kindness and tenderness her mother had given her when Åke was around. In fact, Mary hardly ever saw her. She was either on her way out to meet Per-Erik, or she had to go to a party somewhere. Her mother also seemed to have abandoned all attempts to control Mary's weight, so she could eat anything in the house. By now she had far surpassed her former top weight. Sometimes when she looked at herself in the mirror she saw only the monster that had been growing inside her for so long. A voracious, fat, loathsome monster, constantly surrounded by a nauseating smell of sweat. Mother didn't even bother to conceal the disgust she felt when she looked at her. Once she had even demonstratively held her nose when she passed by. The humiliation still stung.

This wasn't the way that Mother had promised things would be. Per-Erik was supposed to be a much better father than Åke ever was, Mother would be happy, and they would finally live together like a real family. The monster would disappear, she would never again have to sit in the cellar, and that dry, sickening, dusty smell would never again fill her mouth.

Duped. That was how she felt. Duped. She'd tried to ask her mother when things were going to be as she'd promised, but got only brusque answers in return. When she insisted, she'd been locked in the cellar, after first being fed a little Humility. She had

411

cried bitter tears that contained far more disappointment than she could handle.

Sitting in the dark she felt the monster thriving. It liked the dryness in her mouth. It ate it and rejoiced.

The door closed heavily behind him. Moving slowly, Patrik went into the hall and wriggled out of his jacket. He left it lying on the floor, too exhausted to bother hanging it up.

'What happened?' said Erica in a worried voice from the living room. 'Did you find out something new?'

When he saw her face, Patrik felt a pang of guilt that he hadn't stayed at home with her and Maja. He must look like a wreck. He had rung home from time to time, of course, but the chaos at the station after what happened had made the conversations extremely abrupt and stressful. As soon as he confirmed that everything was all right at home, he had more or less hung up on her.

He plodded into the living room. As usual, Erica was sitting in the dark and watching TV with Maja on her lap.

'I'm sorry I was so curt on the phone,' he said, rubbing his face wearily.

'Did something happen?'

He collapsed onto the sofa and at first couldn't reply.

'Yeah,' he said after a moment. 'Ernst got the idea of bringing in Morgan Wiberg for questioning, completely on his own authority. He managed to stress the poor boy out so badly that he escaped out of a window, ran into the street, and was run over.'

'My God, that's horrible!' said Erica. 'What happened to him?'

'He died.'

Erica gasped. Maja, who was asleep, whimpered but then settled down again.

413

'It was so horrendous, you wouldn't even believe it,' said Patrik, leaning his head back and staring up at the ceiling. 'As he lay there in the street, Monica arrived and caught sight of him. She rushed forward before we could stop her, took his head in her lap, and then sat rocking him and wailing in a way that hardly sounded human. We finally had to tear her away from him. Jesus Christ, it was ghastly.'

'And Ernst?' said Erica. 'What happened to him?'

'For the first time I actually think he's going to be sacked. I've never seen Mellberg so mad. He sent him home on the spot, and after this I don't think he'll be coming back. Which would be a blessing.'

'Does Kaj know?'

'Yeah, and that's a whole other story. Martin and I were questioning him when the accident happened, and we had to run outside. If it had happened a few minutes later, I think we could have got him to talk. Now he's totally clammed up and refuses to say a word. He blames us for Morgan's death, and to some degree he's right. Some colleagues from Göteborg were supposed to arrive this morning to interrogate Kaj, but they had to postpone it indefinitely. Kaj's lawyer put a stop to all questioning for the time being, considering the circumstances.'

'So you still don't know whether he was involved in Sara's murder? And in . . . in what happened yesterday?'

'No,' said Patrik wearily. 'The only thing that's sure is that it couldn't have been Kaj who took Maja out of the pram. We had him in custody at the time. Has Dan been here, by the way?' he said, caressing his daughter and lifting her over to his own lap.

'Yes, he was. He's been like a faithful watchdog.' Erica smiled, but it didn't reach all the way to her eyes. 'I finally had to send him away, more or less. He left half an hour ago. I wouldn't be surprised if he spends the night in our garden in a sleeping bag.'

Patrik laughed. 'Yeah, that sounds plausible. At any rate, I owe him one. It feels good to know that you two weren't alone here today.'

'You know, we were just on our way upstairs to go to bed, Maja and I. But we can sit up a while longer if you'd like company.'

'Don't be offended, but I'd prefer to sit by myself for a while,'

Patrik replied. 'I brought home some work to do, and then maybe I'll watch TV to wind down for a while.'

'Do whatever you feel like doing,' said Erica. She got up and took Maja from Patrik after giving him a kiss on the mouth.

'By the way, how was your day?' he asked when she was halfway up the stairs.

'Fine,' said Erica, and Patrik could hear that there was new energy in her voice. 'Today she didn't need to sleep at my breast at all; she slept in the pram. And now she doesn't cry for more than twenty minutes. In fact, last time it was actually only five.'

'Good,' he said. 'It sounds like you're starting to get control of the situation.'

'Yeah, what a miracle that it actually works,' she said with a laugh. Then she turned serious. 'Although Maja can only sleep indoors now. I don't dare put her outside ever again.'

'I'm sorry I was so . . . dumb last night,' said Patrik hesitantly. He didn't want to risk saying anything stupid again which left him fumbling for every word, even to apologize.

'That's okay,' she said. 'I've been a little oversensitive too. But I think the tide has turned now. The fright I got when she was missing had at least one beneficial effect. It made me realize how thankful I am for every minute with her.'

'Yeah, I know what you mean,' he said with a wave as she continued upstairs.

He shut off the sound on the TV, took out his cassette player and pressed 'rewind' and then 'play'. He had already listened to the tape several times at the station. It was the few minutes that were recorded of Ernst's so-called 'interrogation' of Morgan. Not much was said, but there was still something that bothered him, something he couldn't quite put his finger on.

After listening to the tape three times he gave up, put away the cassette player and went to the kitchen. He pottered about for a couple of minutes and emerged with a cup of hot chocolate and three cheese and caviar sandwiches on delicious Skogaholm bread. He turned up the sound on the TV and switched to 'Crime Night' on the Discovery Channel. Watching re-enactments of real crimes was perhaps an odd way for a cop to relax, but he always found it soothing. The crimes were always solved.

As he watched the programme a thought of a highly private nature began to take shape. A highly pleasurable and invigorating idea, which effectively repressed all images of crime and death. Patrik smiled as he sat there in the dark. He would have to go on a little shopping expedition.

The light was piercing and relentless in the cell. Kaj felt that it was penetrating every part of him, every nook and cranny. He tried to hide from it by burying his head in his arms, but he still felt the light prickling the back of his neck.

In only a few days his whole world had come crashing down. It might seem naïve in hindsight, but he had felt so safe, so untouchable. He had been part of a group that seemed above the ordinary world. They weren't like the others. They were better, more enlightened than everyone else. What the world didn't understand was that it was all about love. Nothing but love. Sex was only a small part of the whole. Sensuality was the closest word he could find to describe it. Young skin was so pure, so unsullied. Children's minds were full of innocence, not befouled by ugly thoughts as the minds of adults were, sooner or later. What they were doing was helping these young people to develop so that they could reach their full potential. They helped them to understand what love was. Sex was the tool, but not the goal in itself. The goal was to achieve an accord, a union of souls. An association between young and old, so beautiful in its purity.

But no one would understand. They had talked about it so much in the chat rooms. How the stupidity of the others and the narrow-mindedness of their thinking made them unable to imagine even trying to understand what was so obvious to the members of the group. Instead, the others were so eager to label what they were doing as dirty, they even then labelled the children in the same way.

Against that background he could understand why Sebastian did what he did. The boy had realized that nobody would understand, that he would be forever after regarded with abhorrence and contempt. But what Kaj couldn't understand was why he'd levelled such accusations against him in his final farewell to the world. Kaj felt hurt. He had really believed that they'd reached a deep mutual understanding during their meetings, and that Sebastian's soul, after the initial reluctance that always had to be overcome, had willingly sought to merge with Kaj's. He had regarded the physical act as something subordinate. It was the feeling of literally drinking from the fountain of youth that had been the real reward. Had Sebastian really not understood that? Had he been pretending the whole time, or was it society's norms that had made him disavow their affinity in his last letter? It pained Kaj to think that he would never know.

He had tried not to dwell on the other matter. Ever since they had brought him the news of Morgan's death, he had tried to push away all thought of his son. It was as if his brain couldn't accept the cruel truth, but the merciless light in his cell forced images upon him that he fought hard to keep at bay. And yet one thought had spitefully caught up with him, the idea that this was perhaps his punishment. But he hastened to fend it off. He hadn't done anything wrong. Over the years he had come to love other boys, and they had loved him. That's how it was, and that's how it had to be. The alternative was too terrible for him even to imagine. It must have been love.

He knew that he had never been much of a father to Morgan. It had been so difficult. Even in the beginning his son had been hard to love, and he had often admired Monica because she was able to show him affection, that intractable, awkward child of theirs. Another thought occurred to him. Maybe they were going to try to make a case that he'd touched Morgan. The very idea made him furious. Morgan was his son, after all, his own flesh and blood. He knew that was what they'd say. But it was only proof of how restricted and narrow-minded they were. It wasn't the same thing at all. The love between father and son was different from the love between him and the others. It was on a completely different level.

And yet he had loved Morgan. He knew that Monica didn't believe it, but it was true. He simply hadn't known how to reach out to Morgan. All his attempts had been rejected, and he some-times wondered if Monica in some subtle way might have been thwarting them. She had wanted him all to herself. Wanted to be the only parent he turned to. Kaj was effectively shut out, and

417

even though she rebuked him and accused him of not engaging with his son, he knew that secretly that was precisely the way she wanted it. And now it was too late to change anything.

As the harsh light of the fluorescent tube flickered at him, he lay on his side on the floor and curled up in the foetal position.

So far the medical examiners on TV had solved three cases in forty-five minutes. They made it seem easy, but Patrik was well aware that it wasn't that simple. He hoped that Pedersen would get back to him tomorrow with news about the ashes on Liam's shirt and Maja's overalls.

Then a new case was presented. Patrik watched the programme listlessly and felt sleep sneaking over him as he reclined on the sofa. But slowly the details of the case began to sink into his consciousness. He sat up and focused his attention on the TV screen. It was a case from the States from many years ago, but the circumstances seemed eerily familiar. He hurried to press the 'record' button on the VCR, hoping he wasn't recording over the last episode of one of Erica's reality shows. If so, the family jewels would be at risk. It was in such situations that his dear life partner usually threatened to get out a rusty pair of scissors.

The M.E. in charge of the analyses spoke at great length and in detail. He showed diagrams and photos to explain the course of events as clearly as possible, and Patrik had no difficulty following along. An idea began to take shape in his mind, and he nervously checked again to see that the 'record' symbol was visible on the VCR's display. He was going to have to watch the show a couple of more times.

After playing the segment three more times, he felt as certain as he could be. But he still needed to get a little help with his memory. Excited and well aware of the urgent nature of his quest, he went upstairs to find Erica in the bedroom. She had Maja next to her, so he assumed that their daughter was getting a little reward for sleeping so well in the pram during the day.

'Erica,' he whispered and shook her shoulder gently. He was terrified of waking Maja, but he had to talk to Erica.

'Unnh,' was the only reply, and she made no attempt to move.

'Erica, you have to wake up.'

This time he got a response. She gave a start, looked around in confusion, and said, 'What? What is it? Is Maja awake? Is she crying? I'd better fetch her.' Erica sat up and was about to get out of bed.

'No, no,' said Patrik, carefully pushing her back down on the bed. 'Shh, Maja is sleeping like a log.' He pointed at the little bundle that now squirmed a bit.

'So why are you waking me up?' said Erica morosely. 'If you wake Maja I'll murder you.'

'Because I have to ask you something. And it can't wait.'

He quickly told her what he'd just learned and then asked the question weighing on his mind. After a moment of astonished silence she gave him his answer. He told her to go back to sleep, kissed her on the cheek and hurried back downstairs. With a grim expression on his face, he punched in a number that he looked up in the phone book. Every minute counted.

GÖTEBORG 1958

Something was wrong. She had let it go on for far too long. A year and a half had passed since Åke died, and Per-Erik had met her demands for action with excuses that kept getting vaguer and vaguer. Recently he had scarcely bothered to answer her at all, and the phone calls summoning her to the Hotel Eggers were now few and far between. She had begun to hate that place. The soft hotel sheets against her skin and the impersonal furniture now filled her with a nauseating revulsion. She wanted something else. She deserved something better. She deserved to move into his big villa, to be allowed to be the hostess at his parties, to be given respect, status, and mention in the society columns. Who did he think she was, anyway?

Agnes trembled with rage as she sat behind the steering wheel. Through the windscreen she saw Per-Erik's big white-brick villa, and behind the curtains she glimpsed a shadow moving through the rooms. His Volvo wasn't parked on the drive. It was Tuesday morning, so he was no doubt at work, and Elisabeth was at home alone, probably devoting herself to being the excellent little house-wife she was. Hemming tablecloths or polishing the silver or doing some other boring task that Agnes would never stoop to do. Surely Elisabeth had no idea that her life was about to be smashed to bits.

Agnes felt not the slightest hesitation. The thought didn't even occur to her that Per-Erik's ever more evasive manner might be due to a fading enthusiasm for her. No, it must be Elisabeth's fault that he still hadn't come to her as a free man. She pretended to be so helpless, so pitiful and dependent, just to bind him to her. But Agnes saw through that act, even though Per-Erik did not. And if he wasn't man enough to confront his wife, Agnes had no such scruples. She got out of the car with determined steps, wrapped her fur coat tighter in the November chill and walked quickly up the path to the front door.

Elisabeth opened it after only two rings and broke into a smile that made Agnes writhe with contempt. She longed to wipe that smile off her face.

'Well, if it isn't Agnes! How lovely of you to come and visit.'

Agnes saw that Elisabeth meant what she said, while at the same time she had a slightly puzzled look. Of course Agnes had been a guest in their home before, but only at dinner parties and celebrations. She had never before dropped by unannounced.

'Come in,' said Elisabeth. 'You'll have to excuse the mess. If I'd known you were coming, I would have picked up.'

Agnes stepped into the hall and looked round for the mess that Elisabeth mentioned. All she could see was that everything was in its proper place, which confirmed her image of Elisabeth as the ultimate, pathetic homemaker.

'Have a seat and I'll fetch some coffee,' said Elisabeth politely, and before Agnes could stop her she was on her way to the kitchen.

Agnes hadn't intended to have a coffee klatsch with Per-Erik's wife. She had planned to get what she'd come for and leave as quickly as possible, but she reluctantly hung up her fur coat and sat down on the sofa in the living room. No sooner had she sat down than Elisabeth appeared with a tray holding cups and thick slices of sponge cake. She set the tray on the dark, highly polished coffee table. The coffee must have been already brewed, because she hadn't been gone more than a couple of minutes.

Elisabeth sat down in the easy chair next to the sofa.

'Please have some sponge cake. I baked it today.'

Agnes looked with distaste at the cake saturated with butter and sugar and said, 'I'll just have coffee, thank you.' She reached for one of the two porcelain cups on the tray. She sipped the coffee, which was strong and good.

'Yes, I can see that you still watch your figure,' Elisabeth said

422

with a laugh, taking a slice of sponge cake. 'I lost that battle after I had kids,' she said, nodding towards a photo of their three children, who were now all grown-up. Agnes pondered for a moment how they would take the news of their parents' divorce and their new stepmother, but felt assured that with a little effort she'd be able to win them over to her side. In time they would probably see how much more she had to offer Per-Erik than Elisabeth did.

She watched the cake vanish into Elisabeth's mouth, and her hostess reached for another slice. The unbridled craving for sweets reminded Agnes of her daughter, and she had to stop herself from leaning over and tearing the sponge cake out of Elisabeth's hand, the same way she used to do with the girl. Instead she smiled courteously and said, 'I realize that you must think it's a bit odd for me to show up like this unannounced, but unfortunately I have something unpleasant to tell you.'

'Something unpleasant? What on earth could that be?' said Elisabeth in a tone that should have alerted Agnes if she hadn't been so intent on what she was about to do.

'Well, it's like this, you see,' said Agnes, carefully setting down her coffee cup. 'Per-Erik and I have come to . . . well, we've developed a great fondness for each other. And we've felt this way for quite a long while.'

'And now you want to build a life together,' Elisabeth filled in. Agnes was relieved that the whole thing was going more smoothly than she thought. Then she looked at Elisabeth and realized that something was wrong. Something was terribly wrong. Per-Erik's wife was regarding her with a sardonic smile, and her gaze had a coldness to it that Agnes had never seen in her before.

'I understand that this may come as a shock . . .' Agnes began, now unsure whether her carefully prepared speech would still hold.

'My dear Agnes, I've known about your little relationship since it started. We have an understanding, Per-Erik and I, and it works admirably for both of us. Surely you didn't think you were the first, did you? Or the last?' said Elisabeth in a nasty tone of voice that made Agnes want to raise her hand and give her a slap.

'I don't know what you're talking about,' said Agnes in desperation, feeling the floor giving way beneath her feet.

'Don't tell me you hadn't noticed that Per-Erik was beginning to lose interest. He doesn't ring you as often, you have a hard time getting hold of him, he seems distracted when you meet. Oh yes, I know my husband well enough after forty years of marriage to know how he would act in such a situation. And I also know that the new object of his desire is a thirty-year-old brunette who works as a secretary at his firm.'

'You're lying,' said Agnes, seeing Elisabeth's plump features as if in a fog.

'You can believe what you like. Just ask Per-Erik yourself. Now I think you should go.'

Elisabeth got up, went out to the hall, and demonstratively held up Agnes's shimmering grey fur coat. Still incapable of taking in what Elisabeth had said, Agnes mutely followed her hostess. In shock she then stood on the front steps and let the wind shove her gently from side to side, feeling the familiar rage rising up inside her. It was even stronger because she felt that she should have known better. She shouldn't have thought that she could trust a man. Now she was being punished by being betrayed once again.

As if wading through water, she headed for the car she had parked a bit down the street and then sat motionless in the driver's seat for a long time. Her thoughts scurried back and forth in her head like ants, digging deep tunnels of hatred and a desire for revenge. All the events of the past that she had long ago stuffed in the far reaches of her memory now came seeping out. Her knuckles holding the wheel turned white. She leaned her head against the headrest and closed her eyes. Images of the horrible years in the stonecutter's house came to her, and she could smell the muck and sweat from the men who came home after a day's work. She remembered the pains that made her slip in and out of consciousness when the boys were born. The smell of smoke when the houses in Fjällbacka burned, the breeze on the ship to New York, the hum of the crowds and the sound of popping champagne corks, the moans of pleasure from the nameless men who had lain with her, Mary's weeping when she was abandoned on the dock, the sound of Åke's breathing as it slowly flagged and then stopped, Per-Erik's voice when he made her one promise after another. The promises he never intended to keep. All that and more flickered past behind her closed eyelids, and nothing she saw quelled her fury, which was rising to a crescendo. She had done everything to gain the life she deserved, recreate the luxury to which she was born. But life, or fate, had kept tripping her up. Everyone had been against her and done his best to take from her what was rightfully hers: first her father, then Anders, the American suitors, Åke and now Per-Erik. A long series of men whose common denominator was that in various ways they had all exploited and betrayed her. As twilight fell, all these actual and imagined offences coalesced into a single burning point in Agnes's brain. With an empty gaze she stared at Per-Erik's driveway, and slowly a great calm descended over her as she sat in the car. Once before in her life she had felt the same sense of calm, and she knew that it came from the certainty that now there was only one course of action left.

By the time the headlights of his car finally cut through the darkness, Agnes had been sitting stock still for nearly three hours, but she was unaware of the time that had passed. Time no longer had any relevance. All her senses were focused on the task that lay before her, and there was not a shred of doubt in her mind. All logic, all knowledge of consequences had been eradicated in favour of instinct and a desire to act.

With eyes narrowed she saw him park the car, take his brief-case which always lay beside him on the passenger seat, and step out. As he conscientiously locked the car she cautiously started her engine and put the car in gear. Then everything happened very fast. She stomped the gas pedal to the floor and the car rushed towards its unsuspecting target. She cut across a patch of lawn and not until the car was only a few metres away did Per-Erik sense that something was happening and turn round. For a fraction of a second their eyes met, and then he was struck directly in the midriff and slammed into the side of his own car. With his arms outstretched he lay collapsed over the bonnet of her car. She saw his eyelids flutter and then slowly close.

Behind the wheel Agnes was smiling. No one betrayed her and got away with it.

Anna awoke with the same feeling of hopelessness she felt every morning. She couldn't remember the last time she'd slept through an entire night. Instead she devoted the dark hours to pondering how she and the kids could escape this situation she had put them in.

Lucas was sleeping calmly next to her. Sometimes he would turn in his sleep and put his arm over her, and she had to grit her teeth not to jump out of bed in disgust. It wasn't worth what would follow.

The past few days everything had seemed to accelerate. His outbursts came more frequently, and she felt as if together they were stuck in a spiral that was spinning ever faster, sending them into the abyss. Only one of them would return from those depths. Which of them it would be, she didn't know. But both of them couldn't exist at the same time. She had read somewhere about a theory claiming there was a parallel universe with a parallel twin of every living organism, and if you ever met your twin, both of you would be instantly annihilated. That was how it was with her and Lucas, but their destruction was slower and more excruciating.

They hadn't been out of the flat in several days now.

When she heard Adrian's voice from the mattress in the corner, she got up cautiously to go and fetch him. It wouldn't do to wake Lucas.

Together they went out to the kitchen and began to make

breakfast. Lucas was eating almost nothing these days and had grown so thin that his clothes hung loose on his body. But he still demanded to have three meals a day set on the table at specified times.

Adrian whined and refused to sit in his highchair. She desperately shushed him, but he was in a rotten mood because he slept poorly at night. He seemed to be plagued by nightmares. Now he got louder and louder, and nothing Anna did seemed to help. With a sinking feeling in her chest she heard Lucas stirring in the bedroom, and at the same moment Emma began to shout. Anna's instinct told her to flee, but she knew that it was hopeless. All she could do was steel herself and in the best case try to protect the children.

'What the fuck is going on here?' Lucas yelled in English. He loomed in the doorway, and the eerie look in his eye was there again. It was an empty, insane, and cold look, and she knew that it would eventually spell their doom.

'Can't you get your children to shut the fuck up?' Now his tone was no longer loud and threatening, but almost gentle. This was the tone she feared most.

'I'm doing the best I can,' she replied in Swedish, and she heard how squeaky her voice sounded.

Sitting in his highchair Adrian had now worked himself up to a fit of hysteria. He shrieked and banged on the table with his spoon. 'No eat. No eat,' he repeated over and over.

Frantically Anna tried again to shush him, but he was so wound up he couldn't stop.

'You don't have to eat. You're excused. You don't have to,' she said soothingly and began to lift him down from the chair.

'He's gonna eat the bloody food,' said Lucas, his voice still calm. Anna felt herself freeze. Adrian was now struggling wildly because she wouldn't put him down as promised, but instead was trying to force him back into the highchair.

'No eat, no eat!' he screamed at the top of his lungs, and it took all Anna's strength to keep him in the chair.

With cold resolve Lucas took one of the bread slices Anna had put out on the table. He put one hand on Adrian's head and held it in an iron grip, and with the other he began to force the bread into

428

his mouth. The little boy began to thrash with his arms, first in anger and then with rising panic, as the big hunk of bread filled his mouth, making it harder and harder to breathe.

Anna stood almost paralysed at first, then all her maternal instincts were aroused, and her fear of Lucas completely vanished. The only thought in her head was that her children were in need of protection, and adrenaline spurted into her bloodstream. With a primitive snarl she tore Lucas's hand away and quickly picked the bread out of Adrian's mouth, who now had tears coursing down his cheeks. Then she turned round to confront Lucas.

Faster and faster the vortex was whirling them into the abyss.

Mellberg too awoke feeling uneasy, but for much more selfish reasons. During the night he had been jolted awake several times from a sweaty dream, and the scene was always the same. He was being given the boot under unceremonious circumstances. It simply mustn't happen. There had to be some way for him to evade responsibility for yesterday's unfortunate event. The first step was to fire Ernst. This time there was no alternative. Mellberg was aware that earlier he might have been a trifle too indulgent with Lundgren, but to some extent he had felt that they were kindred souls. He at least had considerably more in common with him than with the other namby-pambies at the station. But unlike Mellberg, Ernst had now exhibited a devastating lack of judgement, and it had quite rightly been his undoing. It was a cardinal error. He really thought that Lundgren would have known better.

He sighed and swung his legs over the edge of the bed. He always slept in only his underpants, and now he reached down to his crotch under his big paunch to scratch himself and re-arrange his equipment. Mellberg looked at the clock. A few minutes to nine. Almost too late to show up at work, but they hadn't got out of there before eight last night, since they'd had to go over in detail everything that had happened. He'd already begun to polish up his report to his superiors. The important thing was for him to keep the facts straight and not make any blunders. Damage control was the name of the game.

He went to the living room and stood for a moment admiring Simon. He was lying on his back on the sofa, snoring with his mouth open and one leg dangling to the floor. The covers had fallen off, and Mellberg couldn't help reflecting that he had passed on his physique to his son. Simon was no skinny little wimp, but a powerfully built young man who would surely follow in his father's footsteps if he just pulled himself together.

He poked at him with his toe. 'Hey, Simon, time to wake up.'

The boy ignored him and turned over on his side with his face to the back of the sofa.

Mellberg mercilessly kept poking him. Naturally he also appreciated a chance to sleep in, but this wasn't supposed to be some holiday camp.

'Do you hear me? Get up, I said.'

Still no reaction, and Mellberg sighed. Well, he'd have to bring up the heavy artillery.

He went out to the kitchen, let the water run in the tap until it was ice-cold, filled a pitcher full of water and then walked calmly into the living room. With a cheerful smile on his lips he poured the ice-cold water over his son's uncovered body and got precisely the effect he wanted.

'What the fuck!' yelled Simon, and was off the sofa in a flash. He shivered and grabbed a towel from the floor to dry himself off.

'What the bloody hell do you think you're doing?' he said sullenly and pulled on a T-shirt with a skull on it and the name of a heavy metal band.

'Breakfast is served in five minutes,' said Mellberg as he went out to the kitchen whistling. For a brief moment he had forgotten his career-related worries and was instead extremely pleased with the plan he'd worked out for their future father-and-son activities. Lacking porn clubs and casinos, they would have to take what there was, and in Tanumshede that meant the petroglyph museum. Not because he was particularly interested in doodles carved on stone slabs, but it was at least something that they could do together. Because he had decided that would be the new theme of their relationship – togetherness. No more playing video games hour after hour, no more TV-watching until late in the evening since it effectively killed all communication. Instead they would have dinner together with fruitful discussions and afterwards possibly a game of Monopoly to round out the evening.

He enthusiastically presented his plans to Simon over breakfast but had to admit that he was a bit disappointed at the boy's reaction. Here he was taking great pains to do everything so that they could get to know each other. He was renouncing the activities he personally enjoyed and sacrificing himself by going to the museum with the boy. Simon's response was to sit there staring morosely into his bowl of Rice Krispies. Spoiled, that's what he was. His mother had sent him to his father in the nick of time. The boy clearly needed discipline and guidance.

Mellberg sighed as he headed off to work. Being a parent was a heavy responsibility.

Patrik was at work by eight o'clock. He too had slept poorly, more or less simply waiting for it to be morning so he could get going on what had to be done. The first thing was to check whether last night's conversation had made any difference. His finger trembled a little as he dialled the number that he now knew by heart.

'Uddevalla Hospital.'

He gave the name of the doctor he wanted to speak with and waited impatiently as he was paged. After what seemed like an eternity the call was put through.

'Yes, hello, this is Patrik Hedström. We spoke last night. I wonder whether my information has been of any use.'

He listened tensely and then made a gesture of victory with his clenched fist. Yes! He'd been right!

After he hung up he began whistling as he considered the consequences now that his hunch had proved to be right. They would have a lot to do today.

His second call was to the prosecutor. He had rung him with an identical request less than a year ago, and since what he had asked was so unusual, he hoped that the prosecutor wouldn't have a fit.

'Yes, you heard correctly. I need to get permission for an exhumation. Again, yes. No, not the same grave. We've already opened that one, haven't we?' He spoke slowly and clearly and tried not to sound impatient. 'Yes, it's urgent this time as well, and I'd be grateful if the request could be processed immediately. All the required documents are on the way by fax. You've probably received them already. And the documents refer to two requests, both the exhumation order and another search warrant.'

The prosecutor still seemed dubious, and Patrik felt irritation creeping over him. With a hint of sharpness in his voice he said, 'We're investigating the homicide of a child, and another person's life may be at risk. This is not a request that I make lightly. I'm doing so after careful consideration and only because the continued progress of the investigation requires it. So I'm counting on your office to pull out all the stops to process this as fast as humanly possible. I would like a reply before lunch. Regarding both matters.'

Then he hung up and hoped that his little outburst wouldn't have the opposite effect and put the brakes on the whole thing. But that was the chance he had to take.

With the worst task behind him, he made a third call. Pedersen sounded tired when he answered. 'Hello, Hedström,' he said.

'Good morning, good morning. Sounds like you had to work last night.'

'Yes, things really piled up here in the wee hours. But we're about to see the end of it, just some paperwork left and then I'm out of here.'

'Sounds like a rough night,' said Patrik and felt a little guilty because he'd rung the M.E. to nag him after what had obviously been a really tough shift.

'I assume you want the test results from the ashes on the shirt and overalls. I actually got them in late yesterday afternoon, but then things got crazy here.' He gave an exhausted sigh. 'Did I hear right that the overalls belong to your daughter?'

'Yes, that's right,' said Patrik. 'We had a nasty incident at home the other day, but thank goodness she wasn't hurt.'

'That's good to hear,' said Pedersen. 'I can understand why you're on pins and needles waiting for the result.'

'I won't deny it. But I actually didn't think that you'd have the results back already. So, what did you find out?'

Pedersen cleared his throat. 'Let's see . . . Yes, there doesn't seem to be any doubt. The composition of the ashes is identical with those we found in the girl's lungs.'

Patrik exhaled and then realized how tense he had been. 'So that's it, then.'

'That's it,' said Pedersen.

'Were you able to confirm the origin of the ashes? Are they from an animal or a human being?'

'Unfortunately we're not able to determine that. The remains have decayed too much, and the ash is too fine. With a bigger sample we might be able to trace it, but . . .'

'I'll wait for the news from a house search we're doing. Looking for the ashes is at the top of our list. If we find them, I'll send some over at once for analysis. Maybe you can find some larger particles,' Patrik said hopefully.

'Sure, but don't count on it,' said Pedersen.

'I don't count on anything any longer. But I can always hope.'

With the formalities taken care of, Patrik drummed his feet impatiently on the floor. Before the decision arrived from the prosecutor there wasn't much of a practical nature he could accomplish. But he knew that he wouldn't be able to sit in his office for a couple of hours twiddling his thumbs.

He'd heard the others show up at work one by one, so he decided to call a meeting. They all had to be brought up to date, and he realized that more than one of his colleagues would probably raise an eyebrow at what he had set in motion last night and this morning.

He was right. He got a lot of questions. Patrik replied as best he could, but there was still so much he couldn't explain. Way too much.

Charlotte rubbed the sleep out of her eyes. She and Lilian had each been given a bed in a little room near the intensive care unit, but neither of them got much sleep. Since Charlotte hadn't brought anything with her from home, she'd slept in her clothes, and she felt incredibly rumpled and grubby when she sat up and began to stretch.

'Have you got a comb?' she asked her mother, who had also sat up.

'Yes, I think so,' said Lilian, digging in her worn handbag. She found one in the very bottom and handed it to Charlotte.

In the bathroom Charlotte stood in front of the mirror and studied herself critically. The light was mercilessly bright, clearly showing the dark circles under her eyes, and her hair stood on end in an odd, psychedelic hairdo. She carefully combed out the tangles until her hair had more or less regained her normal style. At the same time, everything to do with her appearance seemed so meaningless now. Sara kept hovering in the periphery of her vision, holding her heart in an iron grip.

Her stomach growled, but before she went down to the cafeteria she wanted to get hold of a doctor who could tell her how Stig was doing. Every time she heard footsteps outside the door during the night she had woken up, prepared to see a doctor come in with a serious expression on his face. No one had disturbed them, so she assumed that no news was good news in this case. But she still wanted to hear something, so she went out in the corridor, wondering which way to go. A nurse who passed by showed her the way to the staff lounge.

She pondered whether she should turn on her mobile and ring home to Niclas first, but decided to wait until after she talked to the doctor. He and Albin were probably still asleep, and she didn't want to risk waking them too early. Then Albin would be in a grumpy mood the rest of the day.

She stuck her head in the doorway that the nurse pointed out and cleared her throat quietly. A tall man sat drinking coffee and leafing through a magazine. From what Niclas had said it was unusual for a doctor to be able to sit down even for a moment, and she felt almost embarrassed at bothering him. Then Charlotte reminded herself why she was here and cleared her throat a little louder. This time he heard her and turned with an inquiring glance.

'Yes?'

'Excuse me, but my stepfather, Stig Florin, was admitted yesterday and we haven't heard anything since late last night. Do you know how he's doing?'

Was she imagining things, or did the doctor get a strange look on his face? If so, it vanished as quickly as it had appeared.

'Stig Florin? Oh yes, we stabilized his vital signs during the night and he's awake now.'

'He is?' said Charlotte, beaming with joy. 'Could we go in and see him? My mother's here too.'

Once again that strange expression. Charlotte was starting to get uneasy despite the good news. Was there something he wasn't telling her?'

The reply came hesitantly. 'I . . . I don't think it's a very good idea just yet. He's still weak and needs to rest.'

'Yes, but you could let my mother in for a moment, couldn't you? It couldn't hurt, and it might even help. They're very close.'

'I can imagine,' said the doctor. 'But I'm afraid you'll have to wait. Right now nobody is being let in to see Mr Florin.'

'But why . . .?'

'You'll just have to wait,' the doctor said brusquely, and she began to get really annoyed with him. Didn't they have to undergo some sort of training in medical school about how to handle relatives? He was on the verge of being rude. He could thank his lucky stars that she was the one who had come to talk to him and not Lilian. If he'd treated her mother like this, he would have got such a talking-to that his ears would have fallen off. Charlotte knew that she herself was altogether too compliant in these types of situations, so she merely muttered something and then retreated to the corridor.

She thought about what she was going to say to her mother. Something had felt very odd. Things weren't as they should be, but she couldn't for the life of her understand what was wrong. Maybe Niclas could explain. She decided to take the risk and wake them up at home. She dialled the number on her mobile. Hopefully he'd be able to reassure her. She already sensed that she was probably imagining things.

After the meeting Patrik got into his car and drove to Uddevalla. It had felt impossible just to sit and wait; he had to do something. The whole way there he kept turning over his options in his mind. They were all equally unpleasant.

He'd been given directions to the ICU, but still got lost a couple of times before he found it. Why should it be so damned hard to find his way in a hospital? It must have to do with his unusually lousy sense of direction. Erica was the navigator in the family. Sometimes he thought she had some kind of sixth sense for steering them in the right direction.

He stopped a nurse. 'I'm looking for Rolf Wiesel. Where can I find him?'

She pointed down the corridor. A tall man in a white coat was walking away from him, and he called out, 'Doctor Wiesel?'

The man turned round. 'Yes?'

Patrik hurried up to him and held out his hand. 'Patrik Hedström, Tanumshede Police. We spoke last night.'

'Ah, yes,' said the doctor, pumping Patrik's hand. 'You rang in the nick of time, I have to say. We wouldn't have had any idea what sort of treatment to use otherwise, and without the right treatment we probably would have lost him.'

'I'm so glad I could help,' said Patrik, feeling embarrassed by the man's enthusiasm. But a little proud too. It wasn't every day he saved somebody's life.

'Come with me,' said Dr Wiesel, gesturing towards a door that led to the staff lounge. The doctor went first and Patrik followed.

'Would you like some coffee?'

'Yes, please,' said Patrik, realizing that he'd forgotten to get a cup at the station. There had been so many thoughts buzzing round in his head that he'd even missed such a crucial part of his morning routine.

They sat down at the sticky kitchen table and sipped their coffee, which tasted almost as bad as the coffee at the station.

'Sorry, I think it's been sitting in the pot too long,' said Dr Wiesel, but Patrik raised his hand as a sign that it didn't matter.

'So, how did you reach the conclusion that our patient had arsenic poisoning?' the doctor asked with curiosity. Patrik told him how he'd been watching a programme on the Discovery Channel and then put it together with certain information he'd received earlier.

'Well, it's not the most common toxin, which is why we had a hard time identifying it,' said Dr Wiesel, shaking his head.

'How does the prognosis look now?'

'He'll survive. But he'll suffer the after-effects for the rest of his life. He's probably been ingesting arsenic for a long time, and it seems as though the last dose he got was massive. But we'll be able to determine that later.'

'By analysing his hair and nails?' said Patrik, who had gleaned that much from the programme last night.

'Yes, precisely. Arsenic remains in the body in the hair and nails.

By analysing the quantity and comparing it with the speed at which hair and nails grow, we can see almost exactly when he received the doses of arsenic and even how big they were.'

'And you've seen to it that he has no visitors?'

'Yes, we did that last night when we confirmed that it was indeed arsenic poisoning. No visitors are allowed at all, except the relevant medical personnel. His stepdaughter was just here and asked after him. I told her only that his condition was stable and that they couldn't see him yet.'

'Good,' said Patrik.

'Do you know who did it?' the doctor asked cautiously.

Patrik thought for a moment before he replied. 'We have our suspicions. Hopefully we'll have them confirmed today.'

'I hope so. Anyone capable of something like this shouldn't be on the loose. Arsenic poisoning causes particularly painful symptoms before the onset of death. The victim goes through terrible suffering.'

'So I understand,' said Patrik grimly. 'I hear there's a disease that can be mistaken for arsenic poisoning.'

The doctor nodded. 'Guillain-Barré, yes. The body's own immune system begins to attack the nerves and destroys the myelin sheath. That produces very similar symptoms to arsenic poisoning. If you hadn't phoned us it's not too far-fetched to believe that we might have come up with that diagnosis.'

Patrik smiled. 'Well, it's nice to get lucky sometimes.' Then he turned serious again. 'But as I said, make sure that no one is allowed in his room. Then we'll do our job as best we can this afternoon.'

They shook hands, and Patrik went back out to the corridor. He thought for a moment that he glimpsed Charlotte in the distance. Then the door closed behind him.

GÖTEBORG 1958

It was on a Tuesday when her life reached its absolute nadir. A cold, grey, foggy Tuesday in November that would be eternally imprinted in her memory. Although actually she didn't remember very many details. She mostly recalled that friends of her father came and told her that Mother had done something terrible and that Mary would have to go with the lady from social welfare. She had seen in their faces that they felt qualms of conscience that they couldn't take her home with them at least for a few days. But none of Father's snooty friends probably wanted to have such a disgustingly fat girl like herself in their homes. So in the absence of any relatives, she'd had to pack a bag with the bare necessities and go with the little old lady who came to collect her.

The years that followed she later remembered only in her dreams. Not really nightmares; she actually had no reason to complain about the three foster homes where she ended up until she turned eighteen. But they left her with an all-consuming feeling that she meant nothing to anyone, other than as a curiosity. For that was what a girl became if she was fourteen, obscenely fat, and the daughter of a murderess. Her various foster parents had neither the desire nor the energy to get to know the girl who had been assigned to them by social welfare. On the other hand, they had nothing against gossiping about her mother when their curiosity-seeking friends and acquaintances came to visit to gawk at Mary. She hated every last one of them.

Most of all she hated Mother. Hated her because she had

abandoned her only daughter. Hated her because Mary had meant so little to her compared with a man; she was prepared to sacrifice everything for him, but nothing for her daughter. When she thought about what she'd sacrificed for Mother, the humiliation felt even greater. Mother had merely been using her, she saw that now. During her fourteenth year she also understood what she should have realized long ago. That Mother had never loved her. She had tried to convince herself that what Mother said was true. That she did what she did because she loved Mary. The beatings, the cellar, and the spoonfuls of Humility. But it wasn't true. Mother had enjoyed hurting Mary because she really despised her and laughed at her behind her back.

That's why Mary had chosen to take only one thing with her from home. They had let her go around the flat for an hour to select a few things; the rest would be sold, just like the flat. She had wandered through the rooms as the memories passed through her mind: Father in his easy chair with his glasses on the tip of his nose, deeply engrossed in a newspaper; Mother at her dressing table, busy getting ready for a party; herself, sneaking down to the kitchen to try and find something to stuff in her mouth. All the images came over Mary as if in a crazy kaleidoscope, and she felt her stomach turn over. The next second she rushed to the toilet and vomited up a foul-smelling mess that brought tears to her eyes. Sniffling she wiped off her mouth with the back of her hand, sat down with her back to the wall and cried with her head between her knees.

When she left the flat she only took along a single thing. The blue wooden spoon. Full of Humility.

No one had voiced any objections to Niclas taking a day off. Aina had even muttered something to the effect that it was about time, and then cancelled all his appointments for the day.

Niclas crawled about on the floor chasing Albin, who was running around like mad among all the things scattered on the floor. He was still dressed in pyjamas although it was past noon. But it didn't matter. It was going to be one of those days; even Niclas was still dressed in the same T-shirt and jogging trousers he'd slept in. Albin laughed heartily in a way Niclas had never heard him do before, which made him crawl even faster after him and roughhouse even more.

With a pang in his chest he realized that he had no memory of himself playing with Sara the same way. He had always been so busy. So full of his own importance and everything he wanted to do and achieve. Feeling a little superior, he had left all that playing and fooling around with the kids to Charlotte, who did it so well. But for the first time he wondered whether he wasn't the one who'd drawn the blank lot. Something suddenly occurred to him that made him stop short and take a quick breath. He didn't know what Sara's favourite game had been. Or what kids' show she most liked to watch on TV, or if she liked colouring with a blue or red crayon. Or what was her favourite subject in school, or which book she most liked for Charlotte to read to her at bedtime. He knew nothing of importance about his daughter. Absolutely nothing. She could just as well have been the neighbours' daughter, judging by how little he knew about her. The only thing he thought he'd known was that she was difficult, obstinate and aggressive. That she hurt her little brother, destroyed things in their home, and attacked her schoolmates. But none of those things had been Sara – they were just things she did.

The realization made him curl up on the floor in torment. Now it was too late to get to know her. She was gone.

Albin seemed to feel that something was wrong. He stopped his wild hooting, crept close to Niclas and curled up like a little animal against his body. Then they lay there, next to each other.

Several minutes later the doorbell rang. Niclas gave a start and Albin looked around nervously.

'Don't worry,' said Niclas to him. 'It's probably just some stranger selling something.'

He picked the boy up and went to open the door. Outside stood Patrik with some unfamiliar men behind him.

'What it is now?' said Niclas wearily.

'We have a warrant to search the house,' said Patrik, holding out a document as proof.

'But you've already been here once,' said Niclas, bewildered, as he scanned the document. When he was halfway through his eyes grew wide and he gave Patrik a confused look. 'What the hell is this? Attempted murder of Stig Florin? You've got to be kidding.'

But Patrik wasn't laughing. 'I'm afraid not. He's being treated right now for arsenic poisoning. He barely made it through the night.'

'Arsenic poisoning?' said Niclas in surprise. 'But how . . .?' He still couldn't grasp what was happening, and didn't budge from the doorway.

'That's what we intend to find out. So if you would please let us come in . . .'

Without a word Niclas stepped to one side. The men behind Patrik picked up their cases and equipment and came in with determined looks on their faces.

Patrik stayed behind with Niclas in the hall and seemed to hesitate a moment before he said, 'We also have permission to exhume Lennart's grave. That work has probably already begun.'

Niclas felt his mouth fall open. What was happening was just too unreal for him to grasp.

'But why? What . . . who . . .?' he stammered.

'We can't explain it all right now, but we have good reason to believe that he was poisoned with arsenic as well. Though he wasn't as lucky as Stig,' Patrik added grimly. 'But now I'd appreciate it if you could stay out of the way and let my men do their job.' Patrik didn't wait for his answer, but went into the house.

Unsure of what to do next, Niclas went into the kitchen and sat down at the table, still holding Albin in his arms. He placed him in his highchair and bribed him with a biscuit to keep him quiet. Inside Niclas's mind the questions were tumbling around.

Martin was shivering in the biting wind. His uniform jacket provided little protection from the bitter winds blowing across the churchyard. Just after they arrived it had begun to drizzle as well.

The whole operation turned his stomach. He had only been to a few funerals, and to stand here and watch while a coffin was lifted out of the ground instead of down into it felt as wrong as watching a film running backwards. He understood why Patrik had asked him to take charge this time. Patrik had already been through this experience once, just a few months earlier, and once in a lifetime was surely enough. Confirming this notion, he thought he heard one of the gravediggers muttering, 'You guys must have been placing bets at the station to see how many old coots you could get us to dig up in the shortest possible time.'

Martin didn't reply, thinking that it probably wasn't worth it to make any more requests of the prosecutor for a while.

Torbjörn Ruud came over to stand next to him. He couldn't help making a comment either. 'I suppose they'd better start putting elastic bands on the coffins here in Fjällbacka. Then all you have to do is pull them up when you want them.'

Martin couldn't resist a wry smile despite the unsuitable occasion, and they were both fighting to keep from laughing when Torbjörn's mobile rang.

'Yes, this is Ruud.' He listened, then punched off and said to Martin, 'They're going into the Florins' house now. We've assigned three men there and two out here, so we'll see whether we have to regroup.'

'What exactly do you need to do here, right now I mean?' said Martin curiously.

'There's not much we can do. Right now we're just watching to make sure that everything is removed with as little contamination as possible. Then we'll take some soil samples too. But mostly it's a matter of taking the body to the M.E. so that he can start taking the samples he needs. As soon as the coffin has been sent off we'll go over to the Florins' and help out with the search. You're going too, I assume?'

Martin nodded. 'Yes, I thought I would.' He paused for a moment. 'What a bloody mess this has turned out to be.'

Ruud nodded in turn. 'You can say that again.'

Their topics of conversation run dry, they stood in silence as they waited for the men at the gravesite to finish their work. A little while later the lid of the coffin came into view. Lennart Klinga was above ground again.

His whole body ached. Stig saw blurry shadow figures hovering around him and then vanishing again. He tried to open his mouth to speak, but no part of his body seemed to obey him. It felt as though he'd gone a round with Mike Tyson and lost big-time. For a brief moment he wondered if he was dead. Nobody could feel like this and still be alive.

The thought made him panic, and he used all the energy he had left to try and make his vocal cords work. Somewhere far, far away he thought he heard a croaking sound that might be his own voice.

It was. One of the shadow figures came closer and took on more solid contours. A female face came into view, and he squinted to try and focus.

'Where?' he got out, and he hoped that she'd understand what he meant. She did.

'You're in Uddevalla Hospital, Stig. You've been here since yesterday.'

'Alive?' he croaked.

'Yes, you're alive,' said the nurse with a smile. She had a round, open face. 'It was touch-and-go, I have to tell you, but now you're through the worst of it.'

If he could have laughed he would have. 'Through the worst.' Sure, sure, easy for her to say. She didn't know how every fibre in his body burned and how it hurt all the way down to his bones. But he clearly was alive, at any rate. With an effort he tried to shape more words with his lips.

'Ma'am?' He couldn't manage to get out her name. For a moment he thought that a strange expression passed over the nurse's face, but then it was gone. It was no doubt the pain playing a trick on him.

'Now you have to get some rest,' said the nurse. 'Soon you'll be able to have visitors.'

He let himself be content with that. Exhaustion washed over him and he willingly let it carry him along. He wasn't dead, that was the main thing. He was in hospital, but he wasn't dead.

With great care they went over every inch of the house. They couldn't take a chance on missing anything, but they didn't have all day either. When they were finished it would look like a hurricane had gone through the house, but Patrik knew what they had to find, and he was sure it was here somewhere. He didn't intend to leave until he found it.

'How's it going?' came Martin's voice from the doorway.

Patrik turned round. 'We've got about halfway through the downstairs rooms. Nothing yet. How about you guys?'

'Well, the coffin is on its way. A bloody surreal experience, I might add.'

'You can count on that scene popping up in some nightmare sooner or later. I've had a couple, with skeleton hands coming up through the coffin lid and the like.

'Stop it,' said Martin with a grimace. 'Haven't you found anything yet?' he said, mostly as a way to get rid of the images that Patrik had put into his head.

'No, not a thing,' Patrik replied in frustration. 'But it has to be here, I can feel it.'

'I always thought you had a strong feminine side, so it must be woman's intuition,' said Martin with a smile.

'Go make yourself useful instead of standing here insulting my manhood.'

Martin took him at his word and went off to find his own corner to search.

A smile lingered on Patrik's lips but then vanished. Before him he saw Maja's little body in the hands of a murderer, and the fury he felt was so strong that it made him see red.

Two hours later he began to feel downhearted. The whole main floor and the cellar were done, and they hadn't found a thing. But they were able to confirm that Lilian was an especially assiduous housekeeper. The techs had gathered up a number of containers they found in the cellar, but they would need to be taken to the lab and analysed. Maybe he was wrong after all. But then he remembered the contents of the videotape he'd played over and over last night, and he felt his determination return. He hadn't been wrong. He couldn't have been. It was here. The only question was where.

'Shall we continue upstairs?' said Martin, nodding towards the staircase.

'Yeah, you might as well. I don't think we could have missed anything down here. We've gone over every millimetre.'

The whole team moved upstairs. Niclas had gone out for a walk with Albin, and they could work undisturbed.

'I'll start in Lilian's bedroom,' said Patrik.

He went through the doorway to the right of the stairs and looked around the room. Lilian's bedroom was as well-kept as the rest of the house, and the bed had been made up so tightly that it would have passed inspection at boot camp. Otherwise the room was very feminine. Stig couldn't have felt much at home in there before he had to move to the guest room. The curtains and bedspread had flounces, and there were lace doilies on the night-stands and bureau. Small porcelain knick-knacks were everywhere, and the walls were covered with ceramic angels and pictures featuring angels. The colour scheme was overridingly pink. It was so sugar-sweet it almost made Patrik ill. He thought it resembled a room in a little girl's dollhouse. It was exactly how a five-year-old would decorate her mother's bedroom if given a free hand.

'Yuck,' said Martin as he stuck his head in the doorway. 'Looks like a flamingo puked in here.'

'Yeah, this room would never be featured in *House Beautiful*.'

'If it was, it would be the "before" picture. This place needs a make-over,' said Martin. 'Say, do you need some help in here? Looks like plenty of stuff to look through.'

'Hell, yeah. I don't want to be in here longer than I have to.'

They started at opposite ends of the room. Patrik sat down on the floor to go through the nightstand, and Martin worked on the wardrobes covering one wall.

They worked in silence. Martin's back gave a crack when he reached for some shoeboxes on the top shelf of one wardrobe. He set them down carefully on the bed and then stopped for a moment to massage the small of his back. All that strain from moving was still bothering him, and he realized he should probably pay a visit to the chiropractor.

'What have you got there?' said Patrik, looking up from his spot on the floor.

'Some shoeboxes.' He removed the lid from the first box, carefully inspected the contents, and then set it aside and replaced the lid. 'Just a bunch of old photos.' He lifted the top of the next carton and lifted out a worn blue wooden box. The lid was stuck, so he had to use a little force to open it. When Patrik heard him gasp he looked up at once.

'Bingo,' said Martin.

Patrik smiled. 'Bingo,' he repeated triumphantly.

Charlotte had sauntered past the candy-vending machine a few times but finally gave in. If she couldn't allow herself a piece of chocolate at a moment like this, when could she?

She inserted some coins and pressed the button for a Snickers to drop down into the slot. A 'King Size' just for good measure.

She considered gobbling down the whole thing before she went back, but knew she would just get sick if she ate it too fast. So she restrained herself and went back to the waiting room where Lilian was sitting. Quite right. Her mother's eyes went straight to the candy bar in her hand, and she gave Charlotte an accusing look.

'Do you know how many calories are in one of those? You need to lose weight, not put on more pounds. That thing will go straight to your behind. Now that you've finally managed to lose a few pounds . . .'

Charlotte sighed. She'd heard the same old song her whole life. Lilian had never permitted any sweets in the house, yet she was one of those women who always weighed the same, and she never had one ounce more than necessary on her body. Maybe that was precisely why sweets had been so tempting to Charlotte, who had eaten them in secret. She stole change out of her parents' pockets and then sneaked off to the Central Kiosk to buy chocolate balls and assorted boiled sweets, which she voraciously devoured before she went home. By middle school she was already overweight, and Lilian had been furious. Sometimes she'd made Charlotte take off her clothes and stand in front of the full-length mirror so she could mercilessly pinch her spare tyres.

'Look at yourself. You look like a fat pig! You don't really want to look like a pig, do you?'

Charlotte had hated her mother at those moments. But Lilian had only dared do that when Lennart wasn't at home. He would never have allowed it. Pappa had been Charlotte's salvation. She was grown-up when he died, but without him she felt like a helpless little girl.

She regarded her mother sitting across from her. As usual she was impeccably dressed, a sharp contrast to Charlotte who hadn't brought a change of clothes from home. Lilian, on the other hand, had managed to pack a small overnight case and had changed her clothes and put on fresh make-up this morning.

Charlotte defiantly stuffed the last bit of the large chocolate bar in her mouth, ignoring Lilian's disapproving glance. Imagine that she would bother to worry about Charlotte's eating habits when Stig lay fighting for his life. Her mother never ceased to amaze her. But considering what Grandmother was like, maybe it wasn't so odd.

'When are we going to get to see Stig?' said Lilian in frustration. 'I don't understand it. How can they keep the relatives out like this?'

'I'm sure they have their reasons,' said Charlotte, trying to sound reassuring, but for an instant she pictured the strange look on the doctor's face. 'We'd probably only be in the way.'

Lilian snorted and got up from her chair to pace demonstratively back and forth.

Charlotte sighed. She was really trying to hold on to the sympathy she'd felt for her mother last night, but Lilian was making it damned hard. Charlotte took out her mobile to make sure it was turned on. It was a bit odd that Niclas hadn't rung. The display was dead, and she realized that the battery had run down without her noticing. Damn. She got up to ring from the pay phone out in the corridor, but almost ran into two men. She was surprised to see that it was Patrik Hedström and his red-haired colleague who grimly peered over her shoulder into the waiting room.

'Hello, what are you doing here?' she asked, but then the thought struck her full force. 'Did you find something? Something about Sara? You did, didn't you? What is it? What . . .?' She glanced eagerly and yet with a feeling of dread from Patrik to Martin, but got no reply.

Finally Patrik said, 'At the moment we have nothing concrete to tell you about Sara.'

'But why . . .?' she said in bewilderment without finishing her sentence.

Astonished, Charlotte stepped aside when they signalled that they would like to get by. As if in a fog she saw the other people in the waiting room tensely watching the drama as the police officers went over and took up position before Lilian, who was standing with her arms crossed and looking at them with raised eyebrows.

'We would like you to come with us.'

'I can't do that, as I'm sure you understand,' said Lilian belligerently. 'My husband is fighting for his life and I can't leave him.' She stamped her foot to emphasize her point, but neither of the detectives seemed to take any notice.

'Stig is going to pull through, and unfortunately you have no choice. I'm only going to ask politely one time,' said Patrik.

Charlotte couldn't believe her ears. The whole thing must be a gigantic misunderstanding. If only Niclas were here, she was sure he could calm everybody down and straighten it all out in no time. She herself felt at a loss what to do. The whole situation was so absurd.

'And what is this regarding?' Lilian snapped. She said out loud what Charlotte had just been thinking. 'There must be some kind of misunderstanding.'

'This morning we exhumed your husband Lennart's body. The medical examiners are in the process of taking samples from his remains. Samples from Stig have already been analysed. We have also conducted a search of your house today, and . . .' Patrik glanced at Charlotte but then turned back to Lilian, 'we made a few other discoveries. We can discuss them here if you like, in front of your daughter and everyone else here, or you can come with us to the station.' His voice was devoid of any emotion, but his eyes contained a coldness that she didn't think he was capable of.

Lilian's eyes met Charlotte's for a moment. Charlotte understood nothing Patrik was saying. A brief glimpse at Lilian's eyes increased her confusion and made an icy chill spread down her spine. Something was definitely wrong.

'But Pappa had Guillain-Barré syndrome. He died of a nerve disease,' she said, both as explanation and inquiry, directed at Patrik.

He didn't reply. Soon enough Charlotte would find out more than she ever wanted to know.

Lilian turned her gaze away from her daughter and seemed to make a decision. Then she said calmly to Patrik, 'All right. I'll go with you.'

Stunned, Charlotte stood there, unsure of whether to stay or go with them. At last her indecision settled the matter. She watched as the officers and her mother vanished down the corridor.

HINSEBERG 1962

It was the only visit to Agnes she intended to make. She no longer thought of her as Mother. Only as Agnes.

Mary had just turned eighteen, and she had left her last foster family without looking back. She didn't miss them, and they didn't miss her.

Over the years the letters had arrived frequently. Thick letters that smelled of Agnes. She hadn't opened a single one. But she hadn't thrown them out either. They lay in a trunk waiting to be read one day.

That was also the first thing Agnes asked her. 'Darling, did you read my letters?'

Mary looked at Agnes without answering. She hadn't seen her in four years, and she needed to learn her facial features again before she could say anything.

It surprised her how little the time in prison seemed to have affected Agnes. She couldn't do anything about the clothing, so the elegant dresses and suits were only a memory, but otherwise she seemed to have taken care of herself and her appearance with the same ardour as before. Her hair was newly coiffed, now in a beehive that was the latest style. Her eyeliner was also fashionably thick, and her nails were just as long as Mary remembered them. Now Agnes drummed them impatiently as she waited for an answer.

It took another moment before Mary spoke. 'No, I haven't read them. And don't call me "darling",' she said, then waited with curiosity for the reply. She was no longer afraid of the woman facing her. The monster inside her had gradually devoured that fear as the hatred had grown. With so much hatred there was no room for fear.

Agnes couldn't pass up such a splendid opportunity for a dramatic scene.

'You didn't read them!' she shrieked. 'Here I sit locked up while you're out running loose and having fun and God knows what else, and the only joy I have is to know that my dear daughter is reading the letters I spend so many hours writing. And I never got a single letter from you or a single telephone call in *four* years!' Agnes was now sobbing loudly, but no tears came. They would wreck her perfect eyeliner.

'Why did you do it?' asked Mary quietly.

Agnes abruptly stopped crying. With great composure she took out a cigarette and carefully lit it. After taking a few deep drags she replied with the same ghastly calm, 'Because he betrayed me. He thought he could leave me.'

'Couldn't you simply have let him go?' Mary leaned forward so she wouldn't miss a word. She had gone over this topic so many times in her mind that now she didn't want to risk missing even a syllable.

'No man leaves me,' Agnes said. 'I did what I had to do.' Then she shifted her cold glance to Mary and added, 'You know all about that, don't you?'

Mary averted her eyes. The monster inside her stirred restlessly. She said curtly, 'I want you to sign over the house in Fjällbacka to me. I'm thinking of moving there.'

Agnes looked as though she wanted to protest, but Mary hastened to add, 'If you want to have any contact with me in future, then you'll do as I say. If you sign over the house to me, I promise I'll read your letters and write to you.'

Agnes hesitated, so Mary quickly continued, 'I'm the only person you have left now. That may not be much, but I'm still the only one you have.'

For a few unbearably long seconds Agnes weighed the pros and cons, evaluating what would benefit her most, and finally decided.

'All right, that's the deal then. Not because I can understand why you'd want to live in that hole, but if you want to, then fine . . .' She shrugged, and Mary felt joy rise inside her.

It was a plan that had developed over the past year. She would start over. Become a whole different person. Shake off the past that clung to her like a musty old blanket. Her application to change her name had already been submitted. Gaining access to the house in Fjällbacka was stage two, and she had already begun the work of changing her appearance. Not a single unnecessary calorie had passed her lips in a whole month, and the hour-long walk each morning had also helped. Everything would be different. Everything would be new.

The last thing she heard when she left Agnes sitting in the waiting room was her astonished exclamation, 'Have you lost weight?'

Mary didn't turn round to answer. She was on her way to becoming a new person.

By the next day the storm had subsided, and the autumn was showing its best side. The leaves that had survived the windstorm were red and yellow and fluttered softly in a light breeze. The sunshine gave no warmth, but it still raised the spirits and chased away the raw chill in the air – the kind that crept inside your clothes and made your body feel cold and damp.

Patrik sighed as he sat in the kitchen. Lilian was still refusing to talk, despite all the evidence they had against her. At least it was enough to remand her back into custody, and they still had time to charge her.

'How's it going?' said Annika as she came in to refill her coffee cup.

'Not much happening,' said Patrik with a deep sigh. 'She's as hard as a rock. Doesn't say a word.'

'But do we need a confession if the evidence is sufficient?'

'No, no really,' said Patrik. 'But what we're lacking is a motive. With a little imagination I could come up with a number of plausible motives for killing one husband and attempting to kill the second. But Sara?'

'How did you know that she was the one who murdered Sara?'

'I didn't,' said Patrik. 'Not until now. But all this has made me see that somebody lied about the morning when Sara disappeared, and that somebody had to be Lilian.'

He turned on the tape recorder sitting on the kitchen table. Morgan's voice filled the room. 'I didn't do it. I can't sit in prison for the rest of my life. I didn't kill her. I don't know how the jacket ended up at my place. She was wearing it when she went into her house. Please, don't leave me here.'

'Did you hear that?' said Patrik.

Annika shook her head. 'No, I didn't hear anything special.'

'Listen one more time, very closely.' He rewound the tape and pressed 'play' again.

'I didn't do it. I can't sit in prison for the rest of my life. I didn't kill her. I don't know how the jacket ended up at my place. She was wearing it when she went into her house. Please, don't leave me here.'

'She was wearing it when she went *into her house*,' Annika said quietly.

'Precisely,' said Patrik. 'Lilian claimed that Sara left and then didn't come back, but Morgan saw her go into the house again. And the only person who would have a reason to lie about it was Lilian. Why else wouldn't she have told us that Sara came home again?'

'How the hell can someone drown their own grandchild? And why did she stuff ashes into her mouth?' said Annika, slowly shaking her head.

'Yes, that's exactly what I want to know,' said Patrik in frustration. 'But she just sits there and smiles and refuses to say a thing, either to confess or to defend herself.'

'So what about the little boy?' Annika continued. 'Why did she attack him? And Maja?'

'I think Liam was just a random choice,' Patrik said, rotating his coffee cup in his hands. 'A crime of opportunity. It was a way of deflecting attention from her family – from Niclas most of all, apparently. And attacking Maja was a way of getting back at me for investigating her and her family.'

'I heard that you also had a bit of luck that helped you solve the murder of Lennart and the attempted murder of Stig.'

'Yes I did, and unfortunately I can't claim any personal insight. If I hadn't watched *Crime Night* on the Discovery Channel, we never would have found out about it. But they were featuring that case of a woman in the States who poisoned her husbands, and one of them was first diagnosed with Guillain-Barré. That's when it all fell into place for me. Erica had mentioned that Charlotte's father died of a nerve disease, and when Stig's illness was added to that . . . two husbands with the same rare symptoms; that made me wonder. So I woke up Erica, and she confirmed that Charlotte had said her father had died of Guillain-Barré. But I must tell you I wasn't completely sure until I rang the hospital. It was great when the test results were done and they showed a sky-high arsenic content. But I only wish I could get her to tell me why. She refuses to say anything!' He ran his hand through his hair in frustration.

'Well, you can only do so much,' said Annika, turning to go. Then she turned back to Patrik and said, 'Have you heard the news, by the way?'

'No, what?' said Patrik wearily, showing scant enthusiasm.

'Ernst really has been sacked. And Martin has recruited some woman to work here. He apparently got a little pressure from higher up regarding the lop-sided gender distribution in the station.'

'The poor guy,' Patrik chuckled. 'Let's hope this woman has a thick skin.'

'I don't know anything about her, so we'll see when she shows up. Evidently she'll be here a month from now.'

'I'm sure it'll be fine,' said Patrik. 'Anything will be an improvement compared to Ernst.'

'Yeah, that's for sure,' said Annika. 'And you should cheer up a little. The main thing is that the killer is in custody. The motive may have to remain a matter between her and her creator.'

'I haven't given up yet,' Patrik muttered, and he got up to give it another try.

He went to find Gösta, and together they took Lilian to the interrogation room. She looked a bit rumpled after a couple of days in jail, but she was totally calm. Apart from the annoyance she showed when they took her from the hospital waiting room, she had exhibited an exceedingly well-controlled facade. Nothing they'd said so far had shaken her, and Patrik had begun to doubt that they ever would. But he had to try one last time. Then the prosecutor could take over. But he really wanted to get an answer out of her about Maja. He was proud of himself for managing to keep his rage in check; he'd done it by trying to have a clear goal in mind at all times. The important thing was to get Lilian convicted, and if possible to obtain an explanation. Taking out his personal feelings on her would not advance that goal. He also knew that the slightest outburst on his part would mean that he would be excluded from the hearings. He already had everyone's eyes on him because of his personal connection to the case.

He took a deep breath and began.

'Sara was buried today. Did you know that?'

He and Gösta were sitting on one side of the table with Lilian facing them. She shook her head.

'Would you have wanted to be there?'

She merely shrugged and gave them a strange, sphinx-like smile.

'What do you think Charlotte feels about you now?' He kept changing the subject in the hope of striking a nerve that would make her react. But so far she had been almost inhumanly indifferent.

'I'm her mother,' Lilian replied calmly. 'She can never change that.'

'Do you think she would want to?'

'Maybe. But what she wants won't change anything.'

'Do you think she'd want to know why you did what you did?' Gösta interjected. He was staring at Lilian intently, looking for a crack in what seemed to be impenetrable armour.

Lilian didn't answer, but instead studied her nails impassively.

'We have the evidence, Lilian, you know that. We went over that earlier. We don't doubt for a second that you murdered two people and are guilty of the attempted murder of a third. The arsenic poisoning of Lennart and Stig will bring you many, many years in prison. So it won't cost you a thing to talk about Sara's murder. Killing your husband is nothing new; I could think of a thousand reasons to do it, but why your granddaughter? Why Sara? Did she provoke you? Did you get mad at her and then couldn't stop yourself? Did she have one of her outbursts and you were trying to calm her down with a bath and things got out of hand? Tell us!'

But just as in earlier interrogations they got no answers from Lilian. She simply smiled indulgently.

'We have the evidence!' Patrik repeated, now with increasing irritation. 'The samples from Lennart showed high levels of arsenic, and Stig's likewise. We've even been able to demonstrate that the arsenic poisoning occurred during the past six months, and in ever increasing doses. We found the arsenic in an old container of rat poison that you kept down in the cellar. Sara had traces in her lungs of the ashes that you kept in your bedroom. You smeared a small child with the same ashes to throw us off the track, and you also put Sara's jacket in Morgan's cabin to try to shift the blame on him. The fact that Kaj turned out to be a paedophile was a stroke of luck for you. But we also have Morgan's testimony on tape, saying that he saw Sara go back in the house. And that contradicts what you told us. We know that you were the one who murdered Sara. Help us now, help your daughter to move on. Tell us why! And my daughter, what reason did you have for taking her out of the pram? Was it me you were trying to get at? Talk to me!'

Lilian was drawing little circles on the table with her index finger. She'd heard Patrik's entreaties several times before, and they were just as futile this time.

Patrik felt himself beginning to lose his temper. He realized that it would be best to stop before he did something stupid. He jumped to his feet, reeled off the necessary information to conclude the interrogation, and walked over to the door. In the doorway he turned round.

'What you're doing now is unforgivable. You have the power to give your daughter some meagre peace of mind, but you choose not to do so. It's not only unforgivable, it's inhuman.'

He asked Gösta to take Lilian back to her cell. He couldn't look at her another second. For an instant he'd thought he was gazing directly into the depths of evil.

'Damned women's lib types we keep having shoved down our throats,' Mellberg muttered. 'Now we're going to be encumbered with them at work as well. I don't get the point of that damned quota system. Maybe I was naïve, but I thought I'd be able to choose my own staff. But no, instead they're going to send me a dame who probably hasn't even learned to button her uniform. Am I right?'

Simon didn't answer but kept his eyes fixed on his plate.

It felt odd to be eating lunch at home, but it was another link in the father-and-son project that Mellberg had initiated. He had even made an effort to slice some vegetables, which previously had never even made an appearance in his refrigerator. But he noticed with annoyance that Simon hadn't touched either the cucumber or the tomatoes. Instead he was concentrating on the macaroni and meatballs, which he covered with enormous quantities of ketchup. Oh well, ketchup was tomatoes too, Mellberg supposed, so that would have to do.

He decided to change the subject. It just aggravated his blood pressure to keep thinking about their new colleague. Instead he focused on his son's plans for the future.

'So, have you thought about what sort of job you want? If you don't think that studying at the Gymnasium is for you, I can help you find some sort of work. Not everyone can be the studious type, and if you're half as practically inclined as your father . . .' Mellberg chuckled.

A less experienced parent might have been concerned about his son's lack of initiative regarding his own future, but Mellberg was filled with confidence. Surely Simon was just going through a temporary period of depression; there was nothing to worry about. He pondered whether he wanted the boy to be a lawyer or a doctor. A lawyer, he decided. Doctors no longer made as much money. But until he could get him onto that career track the important thing was to back off and cut the boy some slack. If he got a taste of life's hard knocks he would eventually listen to reason. Of course Simon's mother had informed him that the boy had failed in almost every subject, and it was clear that might place some obstacles in his path. But Mellberg was thinking positive. The whole problem was no doubt due to lack of support at home, because the intelligence must be there; otherwise Mother Nature would have played an especially malicious trick on them.

Simon was chewing listlessly on a meatball and didn't seem particularly inclined to answer his father's question.

'So, what do you say about a job?' Mellberg said again, getting a bit more annoyed. Here he was making an effort to forge a bond between them, and Simon couldn't even take the trouble to reply.

Still chewing, Simon said after a while, 'No, I don't think so.'

'What do you mean, you don't think so?' said Mellberg indignantly. 'Then what *do* you think? That you can live here under my roof and eat my food and just sit and goof off all day long? Is that what you think?'

Simon didn't even blink. 'No, I'll probably go back and live with my mum.'

The announcement hit Mellberg like a kick in the head. Somewhere near his heart he felt a weird, almost stabbing pain.

'Back to your mum?' Mellberg repeated, as if he couldn't believe his ears. It was an option he hadn't even considered.

'But I thought you didn't like living there? You said you hated "that damned bitch," when you arrived.'

'Oh, Mum's all right,' said Simon, looking out of the window.

'And I'm not?' said Mellberg in a grumpy voice. He couldn't hide the disappointment that had crept in. He regretted being so hard on the boy. Maybe it wasn't really necessary for the kid to start working right away. There would be plenty of time for drudgery in his life; taking it easy for a while wasn't going to ruin his chances.

Mellberg hurried to declare his new point of view, but it didn't have the effect he expected.

'Oh, that's not it. Mum will probably make me get a job too. But it's my mates, you know. I have lots of mates back home, and here I don't know a soul and . . .' He let the sentence die out.

'But what about all the great things we've done together,' said Mellberg. 'Father and son, you know. I thought you were enjoying finally being with your old pop. Getting to know me.'

Mellberg was groping for a convincing argument. He couldn't imagine why only two weeks earlier he'd felt such panic, waiting for his son to arrive. Sure, he'd been angry with him occasionally, but still. For the first time, he had actually had a feeling of anticipation when he put the key in the door after work. And now all that was about to disappear.

The boy shrugged. 'You've been great. It has nothing to do with you. But I was never actually supposed to move here. That's just something Mum says when she gets mad. She's sent me to Grandma before, but now that she's sick, Mum didn't know what to do with me. But I talked to her yesterday. She's calmed down now and wants me to come home. So I'm taking the nine o'clock train in the morning,' he said without looking at Mellberg. But then he raised his eyes. 'But it's been really cool. Honest. And you've been bloody great and tried really hard and all that. So I'd like to come and visit sometimes, if that's okay . . .' He paused for a moment but then added, 'Pop?'

Warmth spread through Mellberg's chest. It was the first time the boy had ever called him Pop. Damn it, it was the first time anyone had ever called him Pop.

All at once he found it a bit easier to take the news that the boy was leaving. At least he would be coming back to visit once in a while. Pop.

It was the hardest thing they had ever done. At the same time it gave them a feeling of closure that would enable them to build a foundation for their marriage in the future. The sight of the little white casket sinking into the ground made them hold each other tight. Nothing in the world could be more difficult than this. Saying goodbye to Sara.

Niclas and Charlotte had chosen to be alone. The ceremony in the church had been short and simple. They had wanted it that way. Only the two of them and the pastor. And now they stood alone by the grave. The pastor had spoken the words the occasion demanded and then quietly withdrawn. They had tossed a single rose onto the casket, and it shone bright pink against the white wood. Pink had been her favourite colour. Maybe just because it clashed with her red hair. Sara had never chosen the easy paths.

Their hatred for Lilian was still fresh. Charlotte felt ashamed to be standing in the stillness of the churchyard, with so much hatred gushing out of every pore in her body. Maybe it would be assuaged over time, but out of the corner of her eye she saw the mound of earth on her father's grave, formed when he was laid to rest for the second time. Then she wondered how she would ever be able to feel anything other than rage and sorrow.

Lilian had not only taken Sara from them, but also her father, and she would never forgive her for that. How could she? The pastor had talked about forgiveness as a way to lessen the pain, but how does one forgive a monster? She didn't even understand why her mother had committed these horrendous crimes. The meaningless- ness of the deeds only stoked the fury and pain she felt. Was Lilian completely insane, or had she acted according to some sort of demented logic? The fact that they might never find out made the loss even harder to bear; she wanted to rip the words of explanation out of her mother's mouth.

Besides all the flowers from people in town who wanted to show their sympathy, two small wreaths had also arrived at the church. One was from Sara's paternal grandmother Asta. It was placed next to the casket and had now been carried down to the churchyard to be placed beside the small gravestone. Asta had also contacted them to ask if she could attend, but they had politely refused. They wanted the time to themselves. Instead they asked whether she might consider taking care of Albin while they went to the church. And she had agreed with pleasure.

The second wreath was from Charlotte's maternal grandmother Agnes. Without knowing why, Charlotte had refused to have it anywhere near the casket and had ordered it thrown out. She had always thought that Lilian took after her mother, and in some way she knew instinctively that the evil came from her.

They stood in silence by the grave for a long while, with their arms around each other. Then they walked slowly away. For a second Charlotte stopped at her father's grave. She gave a brief nod of farewell. For the second time in her life.

In the little cell Lilian felt safe for the first time in many years, oddly enough. She lay on her side on the narrow bunk, taking calm, deep breaths. She didn't understand the frustration of the people asking her all those questions. What difference did it make *why* she had done it? The result was all that mattered. That's how

461

it always was. But now they were suddenly interested in the reasoning behind the deeds, in some logic they thought they might find, in explanations and truths.

She could have talked to them about the cellar. About the heavy, sweet scent of Mother's perfume. About the voice that was so seductive when it called her 'darling'. And she could have told them about the rough, dry taste in her mouth, about the monster that lived inside her, still vigilant, still ready to act. Above all she could have told them how her hands, trembling with hatred, not with fear, carefully put the poison in Father's cup and then scrupulously stirred it, watching it dissolve and vanish into the hot tea. It was lucky that he always took his tea with so much sugar.

That had been her first lesson. Not to believe in promises. Mother had promised her that everything was going to be different. Once Father was gone, they would live a completely different life. Together, close. No more cellar, no more fear. Mother would touch her, caress her, call her 'darling', and never let anything come between them again. But promises were broken as easily as they were made. She had learned that back then and would never let herself forget it. Sometimes she had allowed her mind to consider the thought that what Mother had said about Father might not have been true. But she immediately dismissed that idea to the very depths of her soul. She couldn't even think about that possibility.

She had learned another important lesson as well. To never let herself be abandoned again. Father had abandoned her. Mother had abandoned her. Then she was shuttled from one foster family to another like a soulless piece of baggage, and they all had abandoned her too, if only through their lack of interest.

When she visited her mother at the prison in Hinseberg, she had already made up her mind. She would create a new life, a life in which she had the control. The first step had been to change her name. She never again wanted to hear that name that trickled like venom over Mother's lips. 'Mary. Maaaryyy.' When she had sat in the dark of the cellar, that name had echoed between the walls, making her cower and curl up into a ball.

She chose the name Lilian because it sounded so different from Mary. And because it made her think of a flower, frail and ethereal, but at the same time strong and supple.

462

She had also worked hard to change her appearance. With military discipline she had denied herself everything that she previously gorged on, and with astonishing rapidity the pounds vanished from her body until her obesity was only a memory. And she never again permitted herself to get fat. She had watched scrupulously that her weight did not increase by a single ounce, and she showed contempt for those who didn't display the same fortitude, like her daughter. Charlotte's weight disgusted her, bringing back memories of a time she didn't want to think about. Anything flabby, loose, and slack aroused a feeling of rage in her, and sometimes she'd had to fight a desire to tear the flesh from Charlotte's body with her bare hands.

They had scornfully asked her if she felt disappointed that Stig had survived. She hadn't responded. To be honest, she didn't know the answer herself. It wasn't as if she had planned what she did. It had merely happened naturally somehow. And it all started with Lennart. With his talk about how it might be best for both of them if they separated. He'd said something about the fact that after Charlotte moved out, he'd discovered that they no longer had much in common. Lilian wasn't sure whether it was then, with those first words, she'd decided that her husband had to die. She felt that it was something she was destined to do. She had found the can of rat poison back when they'd bought the house. She couldn't explain why she never threw it away. Maybe because she knew it might come in handy one day.

Lennart had never done anything in haste in his whole life, so she knew that it would take time before he got around to moving out. She had started with small doses, small enough that he wouldn't die immediately, but big enough to make him seriously ill. Gradually his health had been broken. She had enjoyed taking care of him. There was no more talk of separating. Instead he had gazed at her with gratitude when she fed him, changed his clothes, and wiped the sweat from his brow.

Sometimes she had felt the monster stirring restlessly again. Losing patience.

It had never occurred to her that she might be found out, oddly enough. Everything happened so naturally, and one course of events succeeded another. When Lennart was given the diagnosis of

Guillain-Barré syndrome, she took it as a sign that everything was as it should be. She was just doing what she was intended to do.

In the long run he left her anyway. But it was on her terms – through death. The promise she had made to herself, that no one would ever be allowed to abandon her, still held.

And then she met Stig. He was so loyal, so confident by nature that she was sure he would never entertain the thought of leaving her. He did everything she said, even accepting staying in the house where she had lived with Lennart. It was important to her, she explained. It was her house. Bought with money from the sale of the house she'd had Mother sign over to her, the house she had lived in until she married Lennart. Then, to her great sorrow, she'd been forced to sell it. There wasn't enough room in the little house. Yet she had always regretted it, and the house in Sälvik had felt like a poor substitute. But at least it was hers. And Stig had understood that.

Eventually, as the years passed, she began to notice signs of discontent in him. It was as if she could never be enough for anyone. They were always chasing after something else, something better. Even Stig. When he began talking about how they were growing apart, about feeling a need to start over on his own, she hadn't made any conscious decision. Her actions had simply followed his words as naturally as Tuesday followed Monday. And just as naturally he, precisely like Lennart, had turned to her in gratitude because she was the one who took care of him, who nursed him, who loved him. This time too she knew that parting would be inevitable, but what did that matter when she controlled the pace and determined the moment.

Lilian turned over on her other side and rested her head on her hands. She stared at the wall, seeing only the past. Not the present. Not the future. The only thing that counted was the time that had passed.

She did notice the loathing in their faces when they asked about the girl. But they would never understand. The child had been so hopeless, so intractable, so disrespectful. Not until Charlotte and Niclas had moved in with her and Stig did she realize how bad the situation was. How evil the girl was. It had shocked her at first. But then she had seen the hand of fate in it. The girl was so much like Agnes. Maybe not in appearance, but Lilian had seen the same evil in her eyes. Because that was what she'd come to realize over the years. That Mother was an evil person. She enjoyed watching as the years gradually broke her down. She had moved her to a place nearby. Not so she could visit her, but for the feeling of control it gave her to deny her mother the visits she desperately yearned for. Nothing made her happier than knowing that Mother was sitting there, so close yet so far away, rotting from the inside.

Mother was evil and the girl was too. Lilian had seen how the girl was slowly splitting the family apart and destroying the fragile mortar that held Niclas and Charlotte's marriage together. Her constant outbursts and demands for attention were wearing them down, and soon they would see no other way out than to go their separate ways. She couldn't let that happen. Without Niclas, Charlotte would be nothing. An uneducated, overweight, single mother of small children, without the respect that came with a successful husband. Some people in Charlotte's generation would probably say that such a view was obsolete, that it was no longer fashionable to win social status through marriage. But Lilian knew better. In the town where she lived, status was still important, and she liked having it that way. She knew that people, when they talked about her, often added, 'Lilian Florin? Oh yes, her son-in-law is a doctor, you know.' That gave her a certain respect. But the girl was going to destroy all that.

So she had done what was demanded of her. She noticed when Sara turned back on her way to Frida's because she'd forgot her cap. Actually Lilian didn't know why she had done it right then. But suddenly the opportunity presented itself. Stig was sleeping soundly from his sleeping pills and wouldn't wake up even if a bomb exploded in the house; Charlotte lay exhausted in the cellar flat, and Lilian knew that not many sounds penetrated down there; Albin was asleep, and Niclas was at work.

It had been easier than she expected. The girl had thought it was a fun game, to be able to take a bath with her clothes on. Naturally she had struggled when Lilian fed her with Humility, but she wasn't strong enough. And holding the girl's head under water had been no trouble at all. The only tricky part had been to get down to the shore without being seen. But Lilian knew that she had destiny on her side and that she couldn't fail. She had covered Sara with a blanket, carried her in her arms, and then tipped her into the water and watched her sink. It took only a few minutes, and just as she'd thought, luck had been on her side. No one had seen a thing.

The second incident had been merely a spur-of-the-moment impulse. When the police began sniffing around Niclas she knew that she was the only one who could save him. She had to create an alibi for him, and she happened to see the sleeping child outside Järnboden hardware store. Terribly irresponsible to leave a child like that. His mother really deserved to be taught a lesson. And Niclas was at work, she'd checked on that, so the police would be forced to eliminate him from the investigation.

Her attack on Erica's daughter had also been meant to serve as a lesson. When Niclas mentioned that Erica told him it was time that he and Charlotte got themselves their own home, the fury Lilian felt had been so strong that she saw red. What right did Erica have to be giving out advice? What right did she have to interfere in their lives? It had been easy to carry the sleeping infant to the other side of the house. The ashes were intended as a warning. She hadn't dared stay to see Erica's face when she opened the front door and discovered the baby was gone. But she'd pictured it in her mind, and the sight made her happy.

Sleep crept up on Lilian as she lay on the bunk, and she willingly shut her eyes. Behind her closed eyelids the faces whirled past in a surreal dance. Father, Lennart, and Sara dancing round in a circle. Close behind them she saw Stig's face, wasted and thin. But in the centre of the circle was Mother. She was dancing with the monster in an intimate embrace, closer, tighter, cheek to cheek. And Mother was whispering: Mary, Mary, Maaaryyy . . .

Then the darkness of sleep rolled in.

Agnes was feeling sincerely sorry for herself as she sat by the window in the old folks' home. Outside the rain was pelting the window, and she almost thought she could feel it whipping against her face.

She didn't understand why Mary didn't come to visit. Where

did she get all that hatred, all that rancour? Hadn't she always done everything she could for her daughter? Hadn't she been the best mother she could be? Not everything that went wrong along the way was her fault, after all. Other people were to blame. If only she'd had luck on her side, then things would have been different. But Mary didn't understand that. She believed that Agnes was to blame for the unfortunate events, and no matter how hard she'd tried to explain, the girl refused to listen. She had written many long letters from prison, explaining in detail why she wasn't at fault, but somehow the girl was unreceptive, as if she'd hardened herself to all other views.

The injustice made Agnes's old eyes well up with tears. She had never received anything from her daughter, even though she herself had given and given and given. Everything that Mary had perceived as nasty and horrid had been done for her own good. It wasn't true that Agnes had taken any joy in punishing her daughter or telling her that she was fat and ugly. On the contrary. No, it had actually pained her to be so harsh, but that was her duty as a mother. And it had produced results. Hadn't Mary finally pulled herself together and got rid of all that flab? Yes, she had. And it was all thanks to her mother, though she'd never received any credit.

A strong gust of wind outside made a branch strike the window-pane. Agnes jumped in her wheelchair, but then laughed at herself. Was she turning into a scaredy-cat at her age? She who had never been afraid of anything. Except of being poor. The years as a stone-cutter's wife had taught her that. The cold, the hunger, the filth, the degradation. All that had made her scared to death of ever being poor again. She had believed that the men in the States would be her ticket out of misery, then Åke, then Per-Erik. But they had all betrayed her. They had all broken their promises to her, just as her father had. And they had all been punished.

In the end she was the one who had the last word. The blue wooden box and its contents had served as a reminder that she alone controlled her own destiny. And that any means were permitted.

She had fetched the ashes in the wooden box the night before the ship left for America. Under cover of darkness she had sneaked to the site of the fire and gathered up ashes from the spot where she knew Anders and the boys had been sleeping. At the time she didn't know why she did it, but as the years passed she began to understand her impulsive action. The wooden box with the ashes reminded her how easy it was to do something in order to achieve her own goals.

The plan had gradually taken shape in her mind as the day of their departure for America approached. She knew that her fate would be sealed if she let herself be shipped off like a milk-cow with her family as a dead weight round her legs. But alone she would have a chance to create a different future for herself. One in which poverty would be only a distant and distasteful memory.

Anders never knew what hit him. The knife sank into his back all the way to the hilt, deep into his heart, and he fell like a dead piece of meat over the kitchen table.

The boys were taking a nap. She stole quietly into their room, eased the pillow out from under Karl's head and put it over his face. Then she pressed it down with her whole weight. It was so easy. He kicked and struggled briefly, but no sound escaped from under the pillow, so Johan kept sleeping peacefully while his twin brother died. Then it was his turn. She repeated the procedure, and this time it was a little harder. Johan had always been stronger and more powerful than Karl, but even he couldn't fight for long. He was soon as lifeless as his brother. With unseeing eyes they lay there staring at the ceiling, and Agnes felt strangely empty of feelings. It was as though she were putting things back in their proper order. They never should have been born, and now they were no more.

But before she could go on with her own life there was one more thing she had to do. In the middle of the floor she gathered a big pile of the boys' clothes and then went out to the kitchen. She pulled the knife out of Anders's back and dragged him to the boys' room. He was so big and heavy that she was totally soaked with sweat when he finally lay in a heap on the floor. She fetched some of the aquavit they had in the house, poured it over the pile of clothes, and then lit a cigarette. With pleasure she took a few drags before she cautiously placed the lit cigarette next to the clothing drenched in alcohol. Hopefully she could get a good distance away before it caught fire properly.

Voices out in the corridor of the nursing home roused Agnes from her reverie. She waited tensely until they passed, hoping they weren't coming for her, and didn't relax until she heard them go by and continue down the hall.

She hadn't needed to pretend she was shocked when she came back from her errands and saw the fire. She never dreamed it would burn so hot or spread so fast. The whole house had burnt to the ground, but at least all had gone according to plan. No one had even for a moment suspected that Anders and the boys might have died in some other way, and not in the fire.

During the days that followed Agnes felt so wonderfully free that she sometimes had to look at her feet to make sure they were touching the ground. Outwardly she had kept up the pretence, played the grieving widow and mother, but inside she had laughed at how easily those stupid, simple people could be fooled. And the biggest idiot of them all was her father. She was itching with the desire to tell him what she'd done, to hold up the crime to him like a bloody scalp and say, 'See what you did? See what you drove me to do when you banished me like a Babylonian harlot that day?' But she thought better of the idea. No matter how much she wanted to share the blame with him, she would be better served by accepting his sympathy.

The whole plan had worked so well. It had turned out exactly as she wanted and hoped, and yet bad luck had hounded her. The first few years in New York had been everything she'd dreamt of when she sat in the stonecutter compound, imagining a different life for herself. But later she had again been denied the life she deserved. And one injustice followed another.

Agnes felt the rage rising in her breast. She wanted to free herself of this old, loathsome skin. Wriggle out of it like a chrysalis and emerge as the lovely butterfly she once had been. She could smell the odour of old age in her nostrils, and it made her want to vomit.

A consoling thought occurred to her: maybe she could ask her daughter to send over the blue box. Mary couldn't have any use for it, and Agnes would like to run its contents through her fingers again, one last time. The thought cheered her up. She would ask her to bring the box over here. If her daughter

469

brought it herself, maybe she would even tell Mary what it actually contained. To her daughter she had always called it Humility when she fed her spoonfuls of it down in the cellar. But really it had been Fortitude that she wanted to impart to the girl. The strength to do whatever was necessary to achieve what she wanted. She believed she'd succeeded when the girl had obeyed her wishes to get rid of Åke. But after that everything had fallen apart.

Now Agnes couldn't wait to get hold of the ashes again. She reached out a trembling, wrinkled hand for the telephone, but froze halfway there. Then her hand dropped to her side, and her head fell forward, with her chin resting on her chest. Her eyes stared unseeing at the wall, and saliva trickled down from the corner of her mouth to her chin.

A week had passed since Patrik and Martin had arrested Lilian at the hospital. It had been a week full of both relief and frustration. Relief that they had found Sara's murderer, but frustration that she still refused to tell them why she had done it.

Patrik put his feet up on the coffee table and leaned back with his hands clasped behind his head. He'd been able to spend more time at home this past week, which eased his guilty conscience a little. Besides, things were beginning to settle down at home. With a smile he watched Erica as she resolutely rocked the pram with Maja in it back and forth over the threshold to the hall. Now he had also learned the technique, and it usually took no more than five minutes for them to get Maja to fall asleep.

Cautiously Erica pushed the pram into the work room and closed the door. That meant that Maja was asleep and they would have at least forty minutes of peace and quiet together.

'There, now she's sleeping,' said Erica, snuggling up next to Patrik on the sofa. Most of her moodiness seemed to have vanished, although he could still catch brief glimpses of it if Maja had an especially fretful day. But they were definitely headed in the right direction as parents, and he intended to do his part to improve the situation even more. The plan he had devised a week earlier had now crystallized, and the last practical detail had fallen into place yesterday, with the kind assistance of Annika.

He was just about to open his mouth when Erica said, 'Oh, I made the mistake of weighing myself this morning.'

She fell silent and Patrik felt panic come over him. Should he say anything? Should he not? Getting into a discussion of a woman's weight was like stepping into an emotional minefield. He would be forced to evaluate carefully each spot where he chose to set his feet.

Erica hadn't said anything more, and he guessed that she was waiting for him to make some comment. He searched feverishly for a suitable reply and felt his mouth go dry when he cautiously said, 'You did?'

He wanted to hit himself in the head. Was that the most intelligent thing he could think of to say? But so far he seemed to have avoided the mines, and Erica went on with a sigh, 'Yeah, I still weigh twenty pounds more than I did before I got pregnant. I really thought losing the extra pounds would go faster.'

With the utmost care he fumbled his way forward in search of safer ground. Finally he said, 'Maja isn't that old yet. You have to be patient. I'm sure those pounds will disappear from the nursing. You'll see, by the time she's six months old it'll all be gone.' Patrik held his breath as he waited to see how she would react.

'Yeah, you're probably right,' said Erica, and he gave a sigh of relief. 'I just feel so damned unsexy. My belly is drooping, my breasts are enormous and leaking milk, I'm always sweating, not to mention these damned zits I've started to get from the hormones . . .'

She laughed as if what she just said was a joke, but he could hear how desperate the underlying tone was. Erica had never been particularly fixated on her looks, but he understood that it must be hard to handle when your body and appearance were altered so much in a relatively short time. He was having a hard time himself coming to terms with the middle-aged paunch that had developed around his waist at the same pace as Erica's belly grew. It hadn't got any smaller, either, after Maja was born.

Out of the corner of his eye he saw Erica wipe away a tear, and all at once he knew that he would never have a better opportunity.

'Sit there, don't move,' he said excitedly, and leapt up from the sofa. Erica gave him a quizzical look but obeyed. He felt

471

her eyes on his back as he rummaged for something in his jacket pocket, which he then concealed neatly before he went back to her.

With a gallant gesture he fell to one knee before her and solemnly took her hand in his. He saw that the penny had already dropped, and he hoped it was joy he saw in her eyes. At least he now had her full attention. He cleared his throat, since his nerves suddenly made him feel unsteady.

'Erica Sofia Magdalena Falck, would you consider doing me the honour of making an honest man out of me and marrying me?'

He didn't wait for an answer before with trembling fingers he plucked out the box he had hidden in his back pocket. With some effort he got the lid of the blue velvet box open, hoping that he and Annika with their combined efforts had succeeded in finding a ring that Erica would like.

The small of his back was starting to ache as he knelt there, and he was beginning to feel alarmed that the silence was lasting such a long time. He realized that he hadn't even imagined that she might say no, but now an anxious feeling crept over him and he wished he hadn't been so cocky.

Then Erica broke out in a big smile and the tears began running down her cheeks. She was laughing and crying at the same time, and she held out her ring finger so that he could place the engagement ring on it.

'Is that a yes?' he said with a smile. She simply nodded.

'And I would never propose to anyone but the most beautiful woman in the world, you know that,' he said, hoping that she would hear the sincerity in his voice and not think that he was laying it on too thick.

'Oh, you . . .' she said, searching for the right epithet. 'You know, sometimes you know exactly what to say. Not always, but sometimes.' She leaned forward and gave him a long, warm kiss, but then leaned back and held her hand out to admire her new ring.

'It's fantastic. You couldn't have picked it out by yourself.'

For an instant he felt a bit insulted that she would mistrust his taste, and he felt like saying 'I did so'. Then he thought better of it and realized that she was actually right.

'Annika came along as my adviser. So, is it all right? Are you sure? You don't want to exchange it? I waited to have it engraved until you saw it, in case you didn't like it.'

'I love it,' said Erica with feeling, and he could hear that she meant it. She leaned forward and gave him another kiss, this time even longer and more intimate.

The shrill ring of the telephone interrupted them, and Patrik felt his irritation rising. Talk about bad timing! He got up and went to answer it, sounding a bit more curt than necessary.

'Yes, this is Patrik.'

Then he listened for a moment before turning slowly to look at Erica. She was still sitting there smiling, admiring her ring-bedecked hand. When she saw him looking at her she gave him a big smile, but it faded when she saw that he didn't reciprocate.

'Who is it?' she said, and an anxious tone had crept into her voice.

Patrik's expression was grave when he said, 'It's the Stockholm police. They want to talk to you.'

Slowly she got up and went to take the phone from his hand.

'Yes, this is Erica Falck.' A thousand misgivings were contained in that simple statement.

Patrik watched her tensely as she listened to what the man on the other end had to say. With an incredulous expression on her face she turned to Patrik and said, 'They say that Anna has killed Lucas.'

Then she dropped the phone. Patrik got there just in time to catch her before she hit the floor.